RAVE REVIEWS FOR SUSAN EDWARDS, NOMINATED FOR A CAREER ACHIEVEMENT AWARD BY *ROMANTIC TIMES*!

WHITE DOVE
"Remarkable. . . . The characters
worm their way into your heart."
—*All About Romance*

WHITE DREAMS
"Susan Edwards has the talent of hooking her readers
in the first paragraph and selfishly holding on to
them until the last page has been turned!
Highly recommended reading!"
—*Huntress Book Reviews*

WHITE NIGHTS
"*White Nights* leaves an afterglow long after the last page."
—*Rendezvous*
"Tender, heartwarming, touching,
White Nights is a story you can savor."
—Connie Mason, bestselling author of *The Outlaws* series

A STEP TOWARD LOVE

"Yes, I want you, Emily. You have a body that only a saint could ignore. And I'm no saint, but that doesn't mean I can't control myself, or that I don't have my own brand of honor." John's gaze hardened on her.

"I gave my body to a savage." She spoke the words harshly, defiantly, standing her ground as if that would make her repulsive to him. As if that would send him running. Well, it was time for her to learn a thing or two.

He cocked a brow at her. "You also said you loved him."

Her eyes turned sad. "It didn't matter to him—to any of them." She drew back. "So what do you want of me?"

Ah, good question, he thought, thinking of his dreams, of his Lady Dawn, of the desire firmly banked, of his need to hold her close and ease her pain. He needed to protect her, and he wanted to see her smile. He wanted everything she could give him. But for now, that wasn't possible.

"How about friendship? I want to be your friend."

SUSAN EDWARDS

WHITE DAWN

LEISURE BOOKS NEW YORK CITY

A LEISURE BOOK®

May 2002

Published by

Dorchester Publishing Co., Inc.
276 Fifth Avenue
New York, NY 10001

ISBN 0-8439-4995-3

The name "Leisure Books" and the stylized "L" with design are trademarks of Dorchester Publishing Co., Inc.

Printed in the United States of America.

Visit us on the web at www.dorchesterpub.com.

*For my agent, Pam Hopkins,
who is there when I need her.
Thanks, Pam.*

*And a special thanks goes to Sue Grant
for the additions to our household known by many names, The
Dynamite Duo, The Terrors, The Terrible Twos, and more
affectionately known as The Purr-Purrs.*

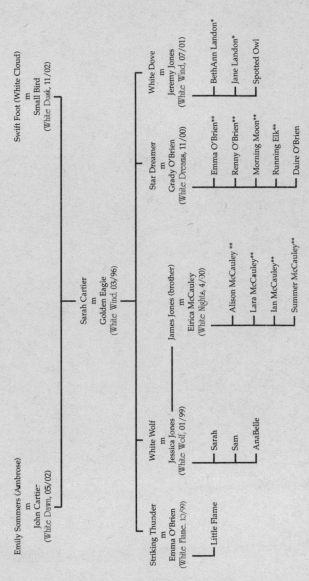

* Indicates adopted child

**Indicates child from previous marriage

WHITE DAWN

Prologue

A chill wind swept across the muddy river, racing over the ground and tearing through treetops. Gleeful as a small child bent on mischief, it sent leaves and other debris spiraling around a man the size of a small mountain.

The trapper wore his long black hair in a single tail, the ends brushing the row of fringe stretched across his broad, muscular back. His arms bulged, his thighs bunched as he lifted a bale of beaver pelts from the ground and smoothly set it in a dugout canoe. The soft beaver furs caressed his fingers. Fox, squirrel, and mink followed. Working quickly, John Cartier lashed

1

and covered the mound of pelts with a square of canvas.

Satisfied that the furs were secure, he strode over to a second canoe and repeated the process. Overhead, the sun rose above the horizon. Excitement danced in him. After he'd endured the harsh winter elements—weeks at a time spent checking traplines, bedding down on the cold ground with only a piece of canvas to shield him from the driving rain and snow—it was time to take the furs to St. Louis, sell his family's cache, and purchase supplies for next year's season.

For the last two years, he, his cousin, and his grandfather, had taken their furs to one of many trading posts along the Missouri. This year his grandfather had business in the city and had decided they should haul their furs there to sell. John grinned. Nothing could dampen his spirts, not even the bitter spring cold seeping through his buckskin shirt and breeches. It seemed like a lifetime since he'd been to St. Louis, not three years.

"What shall we do first?" he asked Fang, his three-legged wolf. The animal lifted its ears and barked, then wagged its tail. John chuckled. Often he went weeks or months without hearing the sound of a human voice, and talking to Fang or the animals he was always nursing back to health was his only relief. Unfortunately, the habit was hard to break—even when his grandfather and cousin were around, as they were now.

He grinned, anticipation of the trip spurring him to work faster. There was so much he wanted to do in the few weeks he'd have in the city: heated baths, a soft feather bed, real food, and the opportunity to be around crowds of people. Trappers from all over would converge on St. Louis, same as him. And if he was lucky, he'd find a woman who'd offer some companionship—and maybe share his bed as well. There would be no shortage of possibilities.

"I'd get me a woman first," a sulky voice intruded. Willy, John's cousin, hunched his shoulders and complained, "Don't see why we can't all go!"

John glanced at him, noting the sullen pull to his cousin's mouth. "There's work to be done here. Traps need repairing, knives sharpening, and someone has to stay with the shack or else we'll lose it." The shack, a crude log building, was their base, a place they returned to with their fur goods.

"How 'bout I pay you half a' my share to stay? I'm sick of this place." John wasn't surprised. Because Willy didn't like to do hand labor, it fell to him to stay at the shack and guard the furs when John and their grandfather went out to lay and check traps. Sometimes John and his grandfather would be gone for weeks at a time, leaving Willy alone here, depending on how far out they had to go.

Shaking his head, John knelt to check the contents of his heavy backpack. "Not a chance, cuz. I won the draw fair 'n' square." He glanced up at his scowling relative. "Besides, you'll spend your share in town before you return."

Willy narrowed his eyes but didn't protest. "Come on, cuz. You're better at takin' care of all this stuff. I ain't got the patience for it. 'Sides, what about that hawk you found yesterday?"

John bit back a nasty retort at his cousin's whining tone. "I'll take the bird with me." Willy acted more like a boy of fourteen than a man of twenty-four. Though only two years separated them, John felt as if it were many more.

When he didn't respond, Willy kicked a rock, not caring that it nearly hit him. "I hate this godforsaken place."

Folding his arms across his chest, John felt the urge to tell Willy it was past time for him to accept his share of responsibility. But he didn't. From past experience, he knew that speaking up wouldn't accomplish anything except to put his cousin in a fouler mood. He gave Willy a hard stare. "You don't have to stay. Gramps would understand if you left to make your own way." Actually, John knew he'd be happy. Willy was often more trouble than help.

The other man narrowed his dark brown eyes, his gaze calculating. "Yeah, bet you'd like that, huh, cuz? Then when the old man goes, you'll git it all."

Disgust filled John. He stood. "Knock it off, Will. You know there's not much. The shack isn't worth anything, and by the time we split the cost of new equipment, supplies, and trade goods for next year, there won't be anything much left. And you know I'll share that with you." He struggled to keep the impatience from his voice. After all their grandfather had done for them, it made him sad to know that Willy stuck around only to be sure he got his share.

His cousin rocked back on his heels. His bushy, unkempt hair was the shade of the muddy river, and the wind tossed it, tangling it beyond hope. "Don't forget the money in the bank from the sale of the house." His tone dared John to deny it.

The two cousins glared at one another. John hadn't forgotten about the house. After the death of Willy's mother, the boy had come to live with John's parents. Their grandfather, who had left to trap in the wilderness, had sold his house, land, and business to John's father. After John's parents died, their grandpa had come back, sold the house, and taken John and Willy off to the woods. Willy assumed that since their grandpa had sold it, he himself was entitled to a share.

John drew in a deep breath. He'd learned the truth only a few years ago—during his last trip to St. Louis. The proceeds of the house and everything from it belonged to him. He was a wealthy man. His grandfather had left it all to him. John had asked his grandfather why he hadn't told him of his wealth before. His grandfather had said he'd wanted to make a man of John before turning him loose with such a sizable inheritance. Remembering how he and Willy had pretty much done as they pleased when they were younger, spent what they'd wanted, John appreciated his grandfather's wisdom. If John had been left to himself, that money wouldn't have lasted. But he was a different man now. He'd grown up.

Willy still hadn't, though. And he didn't know about the house. If he knew about the money, he'd be bitter and angry, and John didn't want to listen to his endless tirades of how unfair life was. Nor did he want to be constantly hounded for money. He had no illusions about that. His cousin wouldn't give him a moment of peace if he knew that money belonged to John, and that John had free access to it. Willy would expect him to feel sorry for him and support him while he did nothing. The only reason Willy was even here now was because he thought their grandfather would cut him out of his will if he left.

More than ready to escape to St. Louis, John faced his cousin. "There's more to life than a bit of coin," he said.

"Only 'cause you've always had some." Willy's voice was bitter. "You always had everything. But not no more. Ain't no one takin' what's mine."

John didn't see a point in arguing. He'd had this discussion before—a thousand times—and the result was always the same: him feeling frustrated, and Willy angry. Troubled by his cousin's bitterness, John picked up his Springfield musket and bag of ammunition, and turned away.

Willy grabbed his arm, forcing him to turn back. "I'll give ya my new hunting knife *and* half my share," he said. He pulled a knife from a leather sheath hanging on his belt and held it up. "Pract'ly brand new."

Staring hard at Willy, John waited until the man released him and stepped back. He was about to refuse when he spotted his grandfather walking toward them. The old man's face bore the leathery lines of too many years in the harsh outdoors. And this year, he looked older. Worn out and tired. The winter had been especially harsh, and Gascon Cartier looked as though he'd aged ten years over the last few months.

Willy eyed his grandfather, then smirked at John. "Come on, cuz." He spoke loudly, deliberately allowing their grandfather to overhear.

John saw his grandfather's mouth tighten. He tried to keep his anger in check, but he knew by the glint of determination in Willy's eyes that his cousin wouldn't let up. He'd keep hounding John until there was another scene like last night's, when John had finally stormed out of the shack, unable anymore to put up with Willy's bitter accusations. It was the last thing John wanted his grandfather to have to endure.

With a sigh of defeat, he gave in. "All right. I'll take the knife *and* half your share." He jabbed his finger at his cousin. "But this is the last time I give in to you. If you don't want to trap, then do us all a favor and stay in St. Louis."

Willy grinned widely and rubbed his hands together. "Can't wait to git outta here." He slapped John on the back. "Gonna gits me a woman when we git to town. Women, some honest-to-God whiskey, and mebbe a few games of cards." Willy started to rush off.

John called his name. When his cousin stopped and looked at him, John held out his hand. "I'll take the knife now."

Willy stared at the gleaming blade still in his hand. "Figured I'd give it to you after I got back. Might need it on the trip."

"Not a chance, *cuz*. You can take my old one with you." John unsheathed and handed his own knife to Willy, knowing his cousin was likely to lose it in the same manner he'd won the other—in a game of cards.

Grudgingly, Willy handed over his blade. Then he hurried off to get ready to go.

Gascon Cartier frowned at John from beneath bushy white eyebrows. "Fell for his line of crap again, did you, son?"

John grimaced. "No. Just figured I'd have to work twice as hard when we returned. A few weeks in St. Louis don't seem worth it." Without anyone around to make him work, Willy would spend his days drinking rotgut and lazing about.

John turned back to the shack.

"Lazy and no good. Just like his pa."

Glancing over his shoulder at his grandfather, John sighed. "Your attitude doesn't help, Gramps."

The old man snorted. "Bah! Only thing Willy's ever cared about is himself. Maybe if your mother had taken him in earlier, he'd have turned out differently. But that bastard he had for a father refused to give him up—used the boy to get money out of me. And I gave it to him—wanted to help support that boy." He sighed in disgust. "No-good drunkard used it to buy drink and women, and let Willy run wild. Forced me to cut him off. By the time the bastard dumped your cousin onto your parents, it was too late—the damage was done." Gascon slung his rifle over his shoulder. "Truth to tell, son, I'll worry a lot less with you here, but I didn't want to deprive you of the trip. God knows you deserve a break."

"There'll be other trips." John swallowed his disappointment. He'd really been looking forward to this. But his grandfather was right: he would be the only one who could get everything accomplished. Aside from equipment repairs, the shack needed major work, and while the abode wasn't much, it was better than a dugout or a lean-to made of canvas, like most trappers used.

Gascon cleared his throat, his voice gruff. "Your father would have been proud had he lived to see you grown into a man." He paused, then said, "Give me one more year. If left to myself, I'd probably stay out here till I die, but you're young and need to settle down." He stretched out an arm, then rubbed his elbow. Then he looked at John. "Hell, I'm getting old. Can't move as well anymore. I need you to help me. I'm not ready to move back just yet."

The last of John's resentment died. He loved his grandfather and would sacrifice whatever was needed to give the man peace of mind. "Go. Sun's up. Don't worry about me. I'll be fine."

"Thank you, boy." And with that, John's grandfather walked away.

Left standing in the dappled sunshine, John watched Gascon and Willy leave, paddling their canoes around a bend where the swift current took them from sight. Staring around, he tried to remind himself that he preferred to be by himself, that he enjoyed the solitude. Once that had been true. Now all he felt was the chill of loneliness. And the dread of many dark nights to come. "Let's go, Fang. We've got work to do," he called.

Striding from the light into the deep shadows of the trees, he felt as though darkness had moved into his heart, stealing away the light and the joy he'd once felt walking this wild land. Returning to the tidy yard

9

in front of the cabin, he whistled softly as he placed a leather hood over the head of the injured hawk he'd found a few days ago. While he checked its broken wing, Fang sat at the base of the tree. John talked to both the wolf and the hawk, trying to recapture the wonder and love of his first years in the wilds.

But by late afternoon, depression had settled around his shoulders. "One more year," he reminded himself while setting a pan of bear fat over the fire. When the fat sizzled, he added kernels of washed and dried corn to it along with some strips of raw rabbit. After eating his supper, John bedded down beneath the trees, bathed in absolute darkness with the sounds of insects buzzing, owls hooting, and Fang, his three-legged friend, snoring at his side. Staring up into the sky, he waited for the arrival of Lady Dawn to bring light into his life to chase away the shadows of the night.

Chapter One

Territory of Michigan, 1810
Late spring

"Satan's spawn!"

The harsh bellow shattered the early afternoon peace, startling Emily Ambrose. Her hands froze in midwring as her gaze flew from the pile of laundry to her father, a tall, rail-thin man with a wild mane of ash-brown hair. The tails of his overcoat flapped angrily behind him as he marched down the bank with a Bible in one hand and a whip-thin switch tucked beneath his arm. He stopped less than a foot away from where she knelt in the shallow water.

"Get up!"

Rushing to her feet, Emily nearly fell when she stepped on the sodden hem of her dress. She gained her balance and stared up at her father with wary eyes. "Father?" Her tongue stuck to the roof of her mouth.

She shivered, not from the cold of the river, but from the icy contempt of the man who'd sired her. Emily cringed and took an involuntary step back at the fury raging in her father's eyes. Since the disaster at the mission, he'd not spoken a word to her, and she'd stayed out of his way. Until now. These horrid words were the first he'd spoken to her in weeks.

She trembled, unable to bear the terse silence and the torturous wait. "Father?" she repeated, her voice a mere whisper. She didn't know what had caused him to break his silence to her, but the fact that his fury had kept him silent for so long boded ill. Her fingers bunched in her skirts, and water lapped at the soaked hem, tugging at the fabric as if trying to pull her out of her father's reach.

The man's eyes narrowed to furious slits, his sharp chin jutting out as he clenched his jaw. His face turned a mottled hue of red and purple. "Devil's daughter!" he exploded, leaning over to deliver a stinging blow to her face with his open palm.

Her cheek stinging, Emily bit back her cry of pain.

"Have you no shame? No decency," he spat, his voice rising, then ending abruptly as he ran out of breath.

Fear kept Emily as still as a deer scenting danger in the air, but unlike that wild animal, she had no place to run. Biting her lower lip to still its trembling, she wondered what had set her father off—not that it took much for her to anger or upset him.

Timothy Ambrose glared down, his gaze raking over her, his hand shaking as he pointed a long, bony finger. "You're no better than the whore who gave birth to me."

Emily glanced down at herself and gasped when she caught sight of the bodice of her mother's old washday dress. To her horror, the swells of her bosom had escaped the too-small confines of both her dress and the long shift she wore beneath it. The shift was low-cut, the dress several sizes too small and far too tight in the bodice. It had inched down without her being aware of it. A frantic glance behind her revealed the shawl she'd worn earlier lying on the bank.

"Please, Father," she begged, "I meant no disrespect. My dress is hanging to dry, and Ma's other dresses don't fit. I-I don't have any others." Her voice shook. Watching her father's mouth tighten, Emily knew it didn't matter. He wouldn't care that she had only one dress. He'd view her lack of decency as another act of rebellion, against not only himself, but against God. In his view; there was no greater sin.

With crazed eyes, he tightly grasped the switch in his right hand. "Whore!" Down came the switch.

Emily ducked to avoid the blow to her face, crying out against the sting of pain burning across the backs of her shoulders.

"No-good—" A second strike seared her back, the thin material of her dress proving no barrier to the slashing force of the switch.

"Sinner!" Another blow followed, and another.

"Father, please," she begged, falling to her knees on the muddy bank, hunching over, using her arms to protect her face.

13

"Daughter of the devil!" He shoved her with his booted foot, then kicked her in the ribs.

Emily whimpered and curled into a tight ball. Her apparent disregard for modesty had destroyed the cold control her father had managed since their family had left the mission. With one innocent action, she'd unleashed the storm. Emily feared her father's wrath as never before.

She cried out with the sting of another lash, this time on her thigh. Sobbing, she cowered on the ground, helpless to stop the indignant rage raining down upon her.

"Timothy!" Emily's mother rushed over, but Emily didn't look to her for help. No one stood against her father when he was in one of his righteous rages.

He speared his wife with mad eyes. "You bore the seed of Satan!" He lifted his arm.

His wife grabbed his arm. "No! Leave her be, Timothy. In the name of Jesus Christ, leave her be," she begged. Beatrice Ambrose was appealing to her husband's religious nature, but it didn't seem to matter.

He tossed her aside. "Look at your daughter. Clad like a whore!"

"Timothy, be reasonable. It's washday. There's no one else around. Tonight I'll sew her a new dress."

The woman's interference earned her a slap. "You're no better, wife, encouraging her sinful behavior. And I won't waste good material on the likes of her. It's her own fault she ruined her last dress."

Emily knew better than to protest. The bodice of her dress had been ripped beyond repair during her struggle with Father Richard.

14

"Please, Timothy. For the love of God—"

"Do not use the name of our Lord when talking about *her!* She led a *Jesuit* into temptation." His voice rose. "A *man of God!* She has no regard for my work. She has destroyed me."

Emily lifted her head and brushed muddy water and strands of wet hair from her face, tired of being blamed. "I didn't do anything wrong, Father," she said with a sob. How many times had she tried to convince him? Yet still he refused to listen to her. "Father Richard tried to rape me. You saw it! You were there!" Her voice broke.

"Spawn of Satan," he continued with unrestrained and unholy fury. He stepped back.

Emily gasped, her father's hate piercing her heart, causing more pain than his beating. And Timothy Ambrose, mired in his own narrow beliefs, stared down at her as if he'd never seen her before, as if she were some condemned heathen instead of his only child. He shot his wife a look of loathing.

"This is *your* fault."

His eyes went blank then. His voice reverted to the cold, flat, unemotional tone he'd adopted since their exile. "No more lies. No more living with the shame. We're leaving. Now." Timothy spun around and stalked off.

Emily shivered. Water lapped at her skirts, but she shook too much to stand. Her father had gone crazy. The eerie light in his eyes frightened her more than had feeling the lash of his anger. Her hair whipped across her face, and she hugged her arms tight around her body.

15

Beatrice Ambrose, white with fear, bent down and stroked her daughter's hair and smoothed the pale strands from her face. "I'm so sorry, Emily." Sorrow edged her words.

"It's not your fault, Ma," Emily tried to comfort her mother. The woman was as much a victim as Emily herself when it came to Timothy Ambrose and his strict religious beliefs.

Her mother laughed bitterly. "It *is* my fault, daughter. And I'm more sorry than you will ever know." She stood, her shoulders bent as if under a great weight. She sent Emily a pleading look. "Stay out of his way this evening, daughter."

Emily stared at her mother, seeing a downtrodden woman who blended with her surroundings, devoted her life to serving God, and tried to be the perfect missionary's wife. She set her jaw, forcing the tears back. Then she asked her mother. "Why won't he listen to me? He was there. He *saw* it. Why won't he admit the truth?"

Emily fought the memory, but it haunted her. Father Richard had shown up at their small one-room house after her parents had left to take food, medicine, and the word of God to a nearby Indian village. The Jesuit had often asked her to help with his correspondence, but that day was different. He'd leaned close, his breath fanning her cheek. Uncomfortable, Emily had tried to shift away. Father Richard had laughed, holding her in place while kissing her on the lips.

She'd told him to stop, but he'd refused. When she struggled, she fell off her chair. He'd pinned her beneath him on the floor and had his hand up her skirts.

That was how it had been when her father returned unexpectedly. He'd found her crying and fighting off the priest.

Emily shuddered. "Father saw me fighting him, saw me trying to get away, but Father Richard said I'd invited him in, that I'd teased him until he gave in to temptation." She stared up into her mother's eyes, needing reassurance. "You believe me, don't you, Ma?"

Beatrice Ambrose closed her eyes. "Yes, Emily. I do."

A loud *thunk* drew their gazes. Emily's father was throwing boxes and equipment haphazardly into the back of the farm wagon he'd purchased years ago, when they'd made their living going from town to town so he could preach. They'd never stayed long in one place, though. They'd stayed at the mission for some time, had been forced to leave because of Timothy's shame, and now they were leaving this small campsite on the edge of nowhere.

Bitterness welled deep inside Emily, seeking release. "He hates me." She waited for her mother to defend her father, to tell her that she was wrong. But the woman didn't. Her mother's silence said it all. Deep inside, Emily hurt. All her life she'd tried to live up to her father's expectations, tried hard to prove herself worthy of his love. But no matter how hard she tried, she'd never gained his affection—or even a kind word. He hated his own flesh and blood.

"I'm so sorry," her mother repeated. "This is my fault. If only . . ."

17

Emily waited for her to finish, but the woman seemed lost in another world. "If only what?" she prompted. But she knew. If only she'd been born a boy. Her father made no secret of his contempt for women.

Shaking her head, her mother looked old, sad, and guilt ridden. "Just stay out of his way, Emily. Millicente said as soon as her husband returns, she'll have him organize a party to come after us. When they do, I'll send you to a friend in Kentucky."

"I hope so," Emily prayed, her gaze following her father's angry movements. Millicente Dufour was their only chance. The woman lived at the mission they'd just left, staying there whenever her trapper husband was away. She helped school some of the native children, and she'd befriended Emily's mother. Sometimes Emily sneaked back to help teach, but it was mostly to be around the cheerful and loving woman.

"Wife!"

Beatrice jumped at the harsh bellow.

Seeing her father watching them, Emily got to her feet. She knew her mother was regretting past choices. After years of traveling from church to mission, going farther and farther away from civilization, her mother had finally tried to put her foot down, here. She'd refused to leave this last mission for the wilds of an unknown and untamed land. She and Emily's father had fought, and Timothy had told Beatrice she could stay but that Emily had to go with him. But Beatrice had given in, and now her father seemed determined to take them even deeper into this wild and untamed land.

Emily tried to smile. It came out a weak grimace. "You had no choice in all this, Ma," she said. "Now go see what Pa wants." She didn't want her father to turn his anger to her mother, for his was a harsh hand. Emily knew better than any. Timothy Ambrose believed women—all women—needed to be sternly governed, for they were the daughters of Eve. It was a man's responsibility to keep them subservient and firmly under control. And if prayer or lectures didn't give him the desired result, a man must resort to physical punishment. He had not spared the rod on his only child.

"Stay here until we're ready to leave," her mother whispered, gathering up the basket of laundry and hurrying toward the wagon.

Emily planned to stay as far from her father as she could. Biting back a moan of unhappiness, she stared out across the flowing river, finding no peace in the sparkle of sunlight on the water or the gentle sway of trees lining the banks. They would soon be leaving here for even more dangerous lands.

Picking up her shawl, she wrung the excess water from it and draped it over her shoulders. She shivered from both the cold and the pain of the water on the welts her father had just given her. Pacing along the bank, she knew she had to find a way for both her and her mother to get away. Her father's fanatical devotion to the Bible, and to all things holy, had gotten out of hand—as had his abuse. More and more, he compared Emily to her grandmother, who'd been forced to use her body in a brothel to survive.

19

Emily thought of her father's mother, a woman she'd never met. Her father had never gone back to see the woman after he'd run away at the age of twelve. A traveling Methodist preacher had taken him in, and later her father had married the man's daughter Beatrice. But Timothy's hatred of his mother ran deep and had affected his ability to deal with women—even those in his own household.

For as long as Emily could remember, her father had been a cold, distant man. The older she'd gotten, the worse he'd become, as if the simple act of her body maturing from child to woman made her evil. And now, at sixteen, she attracted the attention of men wherever she went—which made her father even more unreasonable. Glancing over at her parents, she winced when her father threw a pot of beans at her mother. "He's insane," she whispered. The anger in his voice as he continued to shout at her mother was frightening. Emily had never seen him so out of control.

When he swung his furious gaze in her direction, Emily backed up and quickly averted her eyes. "It's not right," she mumbled, wishing she had the courage to stand up to him. After all, she hadn't asked God for the extra curves and flesh on her short figure. In fact, her looks—her generous bust and her white-blonde hair and blue eyes—had brought her nothing but trouble. It seemed it didn't matter if men were married, young or old. They looked.

A few brave men had even tried to court her, but they had only caused Emily grief. The more persistent a suitor, the more hours her father forced her to spend on her knees in prayer, begging forgiveness. If he caught lust in the eyes of a married man, he'd take a belt or a switch to her, accusing Emily of using her body to entice them into committing adultery. And the final straw had been Father Richard's interest. In Timothy Ambrose's eyes, tempting a man of God had made Emily the daughter of the devil.

It did not take him long to load the wagon and hitch the mules, and when Emily spotted her father heading toward her, holding his well-worn Bible in both hands, she clutched the ends of her shawl tightly around her and swallowed a moan of pain. Her arms and shoulders still burned with her every movement.

"Kneel, daughter of Satan," her father said as he reached her. He closed his eyes and clutched the Bible to his chest, as if drawing strength from it.

Emily bit back a cry of protest at the abominable name he called her. Gingerly she knelt, wincing as she assumed the expected pose: clasped hands, the picture of a sinner begging forgiveness, though she prayed not for forgiveness, but for mercy. She'd done nothing wrong, nothing to be ashamed of. It wasn't her fault that her father refused to part with any of the cloth he reserved for trading with savages so that she could sew a second dress for herself. Sometimes it seemed that her greatest sin lay in being born a female.

Her father lifted his voice in prayer. "Hear me, Father in heaven. I have tried to instill virtue and humility in this child entrusted to my care. But I can do no more. She refuses to act in a manner befitting a humble servant of God. She has forsaken the church; she

21

Susan Edwards

lures men of God down the path to hell."

He paused. Emily risked an upward peek. Her father's eyes were wide open, staring heavenward. His
voice dropped to a whisper, and his eyes closed as if
in pain. "The day I left my mother's life of sin behind,
I promised my life to you to atone for her sins. I can
do no more. Take this child and do with her what you
will."

Timothy Ambrose stepped back and stared down at
his child with eyes that were chillingly empty. "I have
no daughter."

Emily stared up at her father in confusion. Instead
of anger in his eyes, she saw nothing. No emotion. It
was as if she no longer existed. An ache settled in her
chest. This outright rejection left her breathless. "Father?" Her voice choked.

"The Lord has spoken. This is His will." Taking another step away, he said, "You, daughter of Satan, are
at the mercy of our Lord and God. You live or die by
his hand." He called to Beatrice: "Come, wife, we are
leaving. We have His work to do."

Emily's mother rushed forward and put her arms
around her daughter. "Timothy, no! Have you lost your
mind? There are wild animals. And savages. In the
name of Our Lord, be reasonable! Desperation filled
her voice.

Emily clutched her mother's arm. Her father
planned to leave without her; he planned to abandon
her in the wilderness—in the name of God! "You can't
do this," she whispered, numb with disbelief, stunned
to know the depths of his hatred for her.

22

The man walked back and yanked her mother away. "I said, we are leaving." He dragged the woman, sobbing and pleading, toward the wagon without a backward glance. "You, too, will pay for your sins," was all he said.

Shrieking, the woman fought to return to Emily. "No! I won't leave my daughter," she screamed. A hard blow to the side of her face silenced her.

Stunned by the violence of her father, Emily stood rooted to the spot. But when the man tossed her mother's unresisting body up onto the wagon seat, she ran forward. "No!" Fear as she'd never known left her shaking so hard that her teeth chattered. He wouldn't do this. He couldn't. She was his daughter, no matter what he'd said.

"No! You can't leave me. Ma, don't let him do this! Don't leave me! Father! Please!"

Her father whirled around. "You are no daughter of mine. Begone!" He picked up the reins and urged the mules forward. Her mother screamed until another blow silenced her.

Emily ran after the wagon. "How can you do this? This is not the will of God. What about forgiveness? What about love?" She grabbed the back of the wagon as it left the shadows of the tall stand of cottonwood trees where they'd camped, headed into an open meadow.

The wagon stopped. Relieved, Emily tried to still her frantic breathing. Her father would take her back if she begged, if she promised to be good. She'd pray on her knees all day if that was what it took. "Please, Father—"

She froze at the sight of the shotgun in his hands, her heart springing up into her throat. Sitting beside him, her mother sobbed brokenly.

Her father pointed the gun at her. "Get away from the wagon. Didn't you hear me, girl? *I have no daughter.*" The words were cold and devoid of emotion. At his side, Emily's mother had her face buried in her hands, her shoulders shaking with sorrow.

Fearing that he'd actually shoot her, Emily stood in horrified shock as her father snapped the reins and drove on without her. Her breath came in short gasps. Hysteria threatened to choke her. Backing up in disbelief, she felt the hard trunk of a cottonwood stop her retreat.

Numb with fear and shock, she stood there, watching, unable to believe he'd truly meant what he'd said. He'd disowned her. He'd abandoned her. He hated her so much, he wanted her to die.

Surely her mother would stop him. But the wagon rocked and swayed across the uneven meadow and didn't stop. Her mother didn't jump down and run back to her. Instinct urged her to follow, but Emily didn't. She had no doubt her father would kill her if she tried again—and he would justify it because he believed her to be the devil's daughter.

She had to do something, but she couldn't move. She felt like the tree at her back, rooted to the spot. What was she going to do? How could she survive out here alone? She had no food. No blankets. No weapons. No family. She'd die out here, and no one would ever know.

"What am I supposed to do?" she cried to the sky. Panic clawed at her insides. She'd never been so afraid in her life. Each breath came in shorter gasps. "Please tell me what to do." She wasn't sure if she was praying—or if she even believed in God anymore. Closing her eyes, Emily leaned her head against the tree behind her, her fingernails digging into the rough bark as she tried to stop her world from spinning out of control. She had to gain control. Had to think.

But her mind had gone blank, her heart numb. She slid down and wrapped her arms around her knees, unable to accept the fact that she'd just been abandoned. Surely her father would change his mind and turn around. And her mother? Her mother couldn't just ride away and leave her. Emily was their only child. This had to be part of some horrible punishment, but her mother would make sure her father would stop and fetch her. Or if he didn't, *she* would come back. Together Emily and her mother would head back to the mission and let Timothy Ambrose go on his way.

When Emily glanced up and saw the wagon lumbering along without her—halfway across the meadow—reality set in. Her father wouldn't stop. And there wasn't anything her mother could do. Fear overshadowed any lingering thoughts of hope.

"Oh, God, what am I going to do? I don't want to die." Emily sobbed, resting her forehead against her updrawn knees as she fought the nausea welling inside her. Her body trembled and shook so hard, her sides ached. She clasped her hands together, ragged nails digging into her flesh. The trembling increased.

25

It turned to a rumble, as if the earth beneath her was angry at the injustice.

Emily pressed her palm to the ground. It continued to tremble beneath her. She lifted her head and glanced around. Shouts came from her right. Hope rose inside her. Had Millicente's husband gotten help and come after her and her mother?

On the other side of the river, farther upstream, she spotted a large group of riders heading toward her parents. She started to stand, but sudden yells filling the air chilled her soul.

Savages!

This was not help from the neighboring mission. Instinctively, Emily shrank down low, pulling her shawl more tightly around her. Normally Indians didn't frighten her. Those who lived near the mission had been friendly. But from the cries filling the air, and the lances held high overhead, she knew these Indians were not.

They splashed through the water, riding en masse toward her parents. Emily's gaze returned to the stopped wagon and she watched in mounting horror as her father climbed onto the seat and stood tall, his Bible held high for the savages to see.

"No! No!" She tried to warn her father, but the words seized in the back of her throat.

Horrified, she saw a flurry of arrows fly through the air. Stunned and helpless, she watched her father topple from the wagon and heard her mother's screams. The mules bolted, and the savages gave chase. Stunned and helpless, Emily gasped as she saw her mother fall off the wagon and beneath its wheels.

"Dear God, no," Emily sobbed, over and over. She was more scared than she'd ever been, but instinct took over. She slid around the trunk of the cotton-wood tree, farther back under the brush and deeper into the shadows of the grove, making herself as small as possible. She covered her head with her garments, the shades of brown on both dress and shawl blending in with her surroundings.

The Indians' wild yells continued to echo across the meadow. Numb with fear, Emily buried her head beneath her arms, afraid, yet feeling guilty for not having done anything to help her parents. The knowledge that she was helpless to do anything was little consolation.

After what seemed hours, the acrid scent of smoke filled the air, followed by more loud, victorious cries. Peeking through the brush, Emily saw the savages riding away, continuing in the direction her parents had been headed. In their arms, they held the blankets and bolts of material her parents had intended to trade for food and other necessities.

When the earth's trembling and the savages' triumphant yells died away, Emily stumbled to her feet and stared at the burning wagon in the distance. The mules were gone. Cloth from torn clothing was plastered by the wind against a tree nearby.

"Ma," she whispered. A dark shadow passed overhead. Then another. Emily glanced up, then cried out at the sight of the large, dark birds soaring closer, circling overhead, waiting. Running out into the open, Emily prayed as she'd never prayed before. Reaching her mother, she fell to her knees. Blood from an arrow stained the bodice of the woman's dress and dribbled from her mouth. Her legs lay at awkward angles.

"Ma!" Emily grabbed her mother's hand. The skin felt chilled. Her mother couldn't be dead. "No. Please, no," she cried.

"Em—"

Startled by the faint whisper of sound, Emily glanced at her mother. "Ma. Oh, God, you're alive. You're going to be fine. I'll take care of you." The rush of words left her mouth as fear shoved back the impossible truth.

"No. Too late. Take—" Beatrice Ambrose broke off as a spasm of coughing overtook her. Blood bubbled from her mouth.

"Don't talk." Emily glanced around frantically. She had no idea what to do. Should she remove the arrow or wait? "Please," she whispered. "Help me. I don't know what to do." Deep in her heart, Emily knew it was too late, but she couldn't give up without a fight. There had to be something she could do. Pressure on her fingers drew her attention back to her mother.

"Locket. Take it. Yours. Have to tell you . . . before I go—"

"No, Ma. It's yours."

The woman attempted a weak smile. "Father . . . Truth—" Her hand fumbled toward her neckline.

"Wait. I'll do it." Emily didn't want her mother to exert herself. She knew about her mother's locket, how it was worn pinned to the inside of her chemise. Gently she removed the locket and held it in her hands. It felt cold, like her mother's fingers.

"Sorry, child. My—" Another spasm hit.

Emily gently wiped the blood from her mother's lips. "Mother! Mother!"

"—fault. Not his. Father . . . made . . . me . . ."

Alarmed at her mother's growing weakness and the steady trickle of blood seeping down the side of her mouth, Emily begged, "Don't talk, Ma. Please." Tears streamed down her face.

Her mother continued: ". . . always loved you. Go to Kentucky . . . where you . . . born. Matthew Sommers . . . find . . ." Beatrice Ambrose paused, then spoke again, her voice filled with desperate strength. She lifted her head. "Mission—Millicente . . . knows the truth. She was going to take us to him. She knows . . . where to find . . . your father . . . good man. Go to him."

Confused, Emily stared down at her mother as she tried to make sense of the jumble of words. But before she could say anything, ask anything, her mother gave a final gasp.

"Love you—" And with that, her head rolled to the side, all life gone.

Emily stared at her mother's still body in disbelief. "Ma?" She couldn't be dead, couldn't have gone. "Ma, please don't leave me," she said in a sob. Then, leaning over her mother, her locket clutched in one hand, Emily cried.

After what seemed like a long time, she lifted her head. Around her, the dark birds were watching. They inched closer, their long wings outstretched as they squabbled for position.

Jumping to her feet, Emily shouted and chased them away, watched the birds soar up into the air and circle. Turning, she saw her father sprawled nearby. Going to him, she bent over and called his name. She shook his shoulders but got no response.

Returning to her mother's side, she sat, her knees drawn to her chest, unable to comprehend that she was truly alone. Opening her fists, she stared at the locket. Inside, twin ovals with her parents' images stared out at her. Fresh tears welled up as she stared at a much younger image of her mother. On the opposite side a sketch of her father stared back.

Hate rose inside her. How could he have done this to them? Her mother had wanted to return to civilization, to the east, fearing that this untamed land was no place for her or Emily. Her father had refused to listen to her, or to any of the others who'd tried to warn him of the dangers out here.

Furious that Timothy Ambrose's blind faith and religious zeal had ultimately caused her mother's death, Emily scratched at his likeness, unable to bear looking upon it. Finally she tore it out of the locket. To her surprise, she found another portrait hidden beneath. Peering close, she saw immediately that it wasn't her father, but the face of a stranger.

The young man depicted appeared around the same age as her mother in the other picture. He had light hair—much lighter than her mother's. In the portrait, it looked nearly white—like Emily's own. Recalling her mother's jumbled words, and her father's comments, the inconceivable truth dawned. If she'd understood her mother correctly, this man, a stranger named Matthew Sommers, was her blood father.

Timothy Ambrose had not been!

Stunned, Emily stared at the man her mother must have loved tremendously in order to risk her husband's fury by carrying around his likeness all these years. Then, glancing out at the smoking remains of their wagon, Emily tried to accept the inconceivable truth.

So much made sense now: her father's hatred—not just toward her, but toward them both; his obsession with her behavior; his fury whenever she so much as talked to a young man.

She'd thought him overprotective, or obsessed with his hatred over his own mother's lack of morals. Yet it hadn't been just his mother who'd given him reason not to trust women. It had been Emily's own mother's lack of morals as well. And the scene between Emily and Father Richard had sent him over the edge.

Though she should have felt sorrow for her father's pain—sorrow for the man who'd raised her—she couldn't. For sixteen years, he'd blamed her for something she couldn't control. She didn't know if he'd known about her before he'd married her mother, but it was obvious he'd known she wasn't his child. And for all his preaching about forgiveness, Timothy Ambrose hadn't been able to forgive Emily's mother—or accept Emily herself into his life. The irony that it had been his hatred of her that had saved her life wasn't lost on her.

Bowing her head, Emily took a moment to mourn all that had gone wrong in her parents' lives and hers. All the hurt and anger and bitterness. She cried until her throat felt raw and her eyes were hot and dry. Then, standing once more, she pinned the locket to

31

the inside of her shift and rummaged through the debris of the wagon. There she found the shovel, with just a bit of burned handle left.

After spreading her shawl over her mother's body, Emily piled dirt over her, then added rocks and pieces of the wagon to the mound to protect Beatrice Ambrose's body from scavengers.

She did the same for her father, though she had to force herself; her Christian upbringing wouldn't allow her to just leave him. Though she hadn't wanted to feel sorry for him earlier, she did now. Somewhere over the years he'd gone crazy, turning to the Bible to hide his anger. It seemed only fitting to bury that book with him.

When she was finished, she poked through the smoldering ashes for the family's rifle and knives, but the savages had taken everything of value. What was left was useless here in the wilderness.

Emily stood, smoke and ash swirling around her. Above, the dark birds had formed a black cloud. The wind whipped her skirts back, and her long pale hair streamed out behind her as she stood over the scene of the massacre. Shivering, she finally returned to the concealing safety of the grove—and into the woods.

Fear of the return of those savages kept her on the move, following the river back the way her family had come. Anger and her will to survive gave her the courage to attempt the impossible trip back to the mission. It would take her a long time to return, walking, but she had nothing to help in her bid to survive but her own determination. Yet, if she were lucky, she'd come across Millicente's husband, Henry, or some other trappers she knew in the area.

Once she returned to the mission, she planned to go to Kentucky. She'd go to the land of her birth, and there she'd find the man who'd ultimately caused her a lifetime of misery.

Bitterness from a life filled with hate demanded she find the answers. She would let this other man know just what his actions had caused. One thing was clear: if her mother hadn't married Timothy Ambrose, none of this would have happened. And her birth father needed to know that.

Chapter Two

Night shadows stretched across the land. Set against a sky of gleaming onyx, thousands of stars twinkled, welcoming the glow of the moon as it rose high to sit upon its throne and bathe the earth below in silvery splendor. Down below, creatures of the night flew across the sky, ambled through the shadows, and skittered through the underbrush.

Alert to each birdcall, each buzz and chirp of insects, Swift Foot moved lightly, his leather-covered feet making no sound as he followed the glistening river. Around his shoulders, his long black hair danced and flowed, merging into the depths of the night.

A sudden flurry of motion leaping from the bushes startled him, but he didn't stop. Instead, he quickened his steps. It was a mother deer, looking to provide a diversion, so he hoped it would return quickly to guard her babe from more dangerous predators roaming the area.

As he walked, he studied the night sky. The path he took led him farther from his people. He yearned to turn around, to go home, but he couldn't—even if he could abandon the tracks he'd been following since that afternoon. He was seeking answers. The cooling breeze was strong at his back, as if urging him onward. Squatting, he spotted shoe prints and knew the one he followed was tiring—the steps were closer, the toes of the shoes dragging through the soft soil. The trail grew faint and faded near the thick wall of trees lining one side of the river.

Deciding to rest and resume his tracking in the early light, Swift Foot sat with his back to a tree. He didn't want to risk losing the trail in the dark. Leaning his head against the tree's rough bark, he stared out into the night, watching the moonlight glitter over the fast-moving river. The breeze off the water was a welcome relief after the scent of death he'd come upon several hours ago.

Wearily, he thought of the two graves he'd come upon: a couple killed by the Sioux. Killed by his people, but not his tribe. And what concerned him most was the presence of a third white in the area, one who'd survived to mound dirt and bits of wood over the bodies. After a brief search of the area, he'd found small prints following the river, heading east—obviously those of the survivor.

Worried that a child roamed this vast land, he'd followed. Perhaps this was the answer he sought. He'd been led here; perhaps this child held the answer to his troubling dreams. He sighed. Whether or not this youth held any answers, Swift Foot could not leave him or her out here alone. Children were gifts from *Wakan Tanka* and were to be treasured and cared for—whether Sioux or white.

Swift Foot thought of the couple. In the dirt, dug up by wolves, he'd found a thick black tome that he recognized as a white man's holy book. It meant these were the whites who called themselves Missionaries, or Fathers, or men of God—a most contradictory and confusing group. They called his people heathens, savages, and came to teach the Sioux to pray to their god. Yet these men did not seem to understand that man was of the earth. They ignored the spirits of the *maka*. The Sioux did not trust such men who only listened to one spirit, and therefore these men posed little threat. However, his people studied and learned much from them. It was odd that they had been killed.

Overhead, a huge, winged shadow slid across the sky, wings outstretched as if seeking to touch the glittering stars. Then, without warning, the owl folded back its wings and shot silently toward the ground with the speed of a well-made arrow. Swift Foot watched the bird rise once again with a triumphant cry before it soared off with a small creature clutched in its talons.

He silently admired the bird of prey. Strong. Silent. Built for speed and stealth. Qualities he and all other warriors sought to emulate. Once the bird faded from sight, he closed his eyes. The symphony of the night lulled him into a light sleep: the call of birds, the howls and barks of wolves, the rustle of small mice and other rodents scurrying through the undergrowth, the ever-present buzz and cadence of insects. Swift Foot's breathing slowed, each deep breath he inhaled moist from the river and tasting of pine. Images flowed across his mind's eye. His body relaxed as sleep claimed him.

Bursting into the recess of his mind, a sharp and sudden cry startled him awake. His eyes flew open. It was the same cry that had haunted his dreams since winter, and was the reason he'd been sent away from his tribe: his shaman had ordered him to seek answers to this disturbing dream. He was to allow the spirits to lead him until he had his answers. For months he'd searched and found nothing, just this haunting cry that came to him during dreams.

He jumped to his feet, unsure whether the cry had been real or an echo in his thoughts. He listened intently but nothing seemed out of place. Closing his eyes, he stood still and waited. Just when he was convinced it had been only another dream, the cry came again, louder. Shrill. Sharp. Filled with fear. Chills traveled up his arms. With his heart racing, Swift Foot rushed through the trees.

This was no dream.

His fingers tightened around his bow as he slipped from shadow to shadow, following the shrill screams of terror.

Emily stood with her back to the tree, a thick branch in her hands, waving it at two wolves crouched five feet away. "Go away," she shouted, jabbing the limb at the animals. They jumped back, but then crept forward, each coming toward her from a different direction.

Icy chills skittered up and down her spine at the sound of low growling. The beast to her left snarled. She waved the branch at it, then heard the snap of teeth from her right. *Oh, God, I'm going to die.* "Not like this," she prayed, staring in horror at the two animals closing in on her.

Fear made it hard to breathe. Crying wouldn't save her. Maybe nothing would. Yet she wouldn't give up. Moving fast, she swung the branch first left, then right. The wolves sprang back, startled by her move. She tried to back away, tried to find a tree to climb. But the fierce animals didn't give her enough time, and she didn't dare turn her back on them. With heads down, the fur on their neck standing on end, they circled her.

Emily struck out with the branch again and again, but it didn't take long for the animals to anticipate her movements. Hope of making it back to the mission on her own died, and anger at her fate took hold. How could her father have done this to her? How could anyone treat another in so cold a manner?

He'd dragged her and her mother out here, judged her, then had condemned her to death. It mattered not that he had met his own terrible fate; he'd condemned her to die. Bitterness lodged in Emily's throat. She was tired of being a victim. Facing the vicious attack of the wolves, she screamed in frustration, shouting at them, trying to frighten them into leaving her alone. Yet she knew they would not.

Then, with no warning, a dark figure rushed out of the shadows and lunged forward, startling both the growling wolves and Emily. Vaguely aware of rocks being hurled at the animals, she heard the new-comer's voice join hers. He waved and shouted. Her two tannish gray assailants turned toward the new threat.

Emily didn't wait to see if the animals attacked him. The savage posed more of a threat to her than the wolves. She turned and ran. Once out of sight, knowing she couldn't outrun the man, she debated climbing a tree to avoid detection. But the trees were either too tall or too sparse of leaves in the lower branches to hide her.

She found a thick clump of bushes and ducked behind them, drawing her knees up to her chest and burying her head in her arms. She scrunched her eyes closed and waited, praying. Would the savage win over the wolves? In the distance, she heard a howl of pain, followed by high-pitched barks. Nausea made her take several deep breaths. To her relief, silence fell. Abruptly. Completely. Time seemed to stand still.

No insects chirped or buzzed near her head. There was no rustling in the bushes behind her. No owls screeched overhead. The silence unnerved her. The hair on her arms rose, and she broke out in an icy sweat. She shivered, but not from cold. Something was out there. Near her.

The savage.

Her blood hammered in her ears as she slowly lifted her head and opened her eyes. A slight crunch of leaves warned that something was closer than she'd thought.

Please let it be a raccoon. Or a badger. Not a wolf. Not the savage. Please God, not the savage.

Bile burned the back of her throat, the pain so great she couldn't swallow. When two shadowy shapes stopped near her place of hiding, her eyes widened in terror.

Feet. Legs. Two of them. They bent at the knees, and hands parted the bushes. In horror, Emily stared at the shadowy face of the savage. She wasn't sure which would be worse: being raped and killed by him or torn apart by wolves. Both Indian and beast were predators, and either way she was going to die. Tears of helplessness slid from her eyes.

The savage stared at her in wonder. He reached out to touch the wetness on her face, obviously spellbound by the color of her hair and the softness of her skin.

The sound of his harsh, guttural voice and the feel of his fingers skimming over her face released Emily from her frozen stupor. She screamed, scrambled to her feet, and ran for her life. If she was to die out here, she wouldn't do so by giving up. Adrenaline pumped through her as she hurled herself around trees and bushes. The savage shouted. She heard his steps as he ran after her.

"No. No!" She gasped, running as fast as she could in the dark. She hadn't survived today's massacre to be killed or, worse, taken captive.

Heavy steps behind her spurred her on. Harsh, painful sobs tore from her. Even beginning to believe she could not outrun the man chasing her, Emily ran for all she was worth, ignoring the painful slaps of low tree limbs on her face and neck. At any moment, she expected to feel the savage's hands on her, grabbing her. And when something yanked her hair, she screamed. But it wasn't the Indian. A hank of her hair had tangled in a low branch.

Desperately she pulled, but the branch refused to give, and she reeled backward, caught. Using both her hands, she tore at the tangled strands.

The savage reached her. His fingers closed over hers.

"Let me go!" Emily shrieked, flailing her fists, tearing her hands from his. She couldn't turn, couldn't run, so she kicked out with her feet. Her heel made contact with a solid shinbone. The hiss of breath near her ear confirmed she'd done damage. With all her might she aimed another heel at him. But her foot swung free, the force sending her falling forward. She'd have fallen if not for the tree's hold on her hair.

"Please," she said, sobbing, "go away. Leave me alone." Her fingers clawed at his, her skull aching from the pull of her hair. Oh, God, was he going to scalp her? Slice the hair from her head? She'd heard of such out here in this wild land filled with savages who were, according to her father, doomed to an eternity of hell.

"Ayustan!"

The order startled her. When she didn't continue to fight him, he gently pushed her hands aside and tugged her hair free strand by strand. Emily's chest heaved with each breath. When she felt the last bit of her hair come free, she tried to sprint forward, but his hands held her hair wrapped around his fist. His other hand clamped down over her shoulder and forced her to turn and face him.

Ready to lash out, Emily lifted her head, then gasped as the faint moonlight revealed the man's features. It was an impossibly handsome face. She'd seen many savages, young and old, but none with the beauty of this one. It didn't seem odd to use the word *beauty* to describe this man. Shadows hid his eyes, but the moonlight illuminated a long, straight nose, full lips, high cheekbones, and smooth skin pulled across a strong jaw.

A strong, handsome face was her first impression. He seemed young, a few years older than herself, she guessed, her gaze drawn to his dark hair that floated around his face and streamed over his shoulders. The wind blew a few strands of his black hair to lie over hers. Light and dark. Day and night. White and savage.

He took a small step closer, surrounding her with his heat and the scent of pine and man. Her heart, if possible, beat just a bit faster. But when he brought his hand, tangled in her hair, to his face, panic at the thought of being raped took hold. She hadn't survived the fate of her parents just to die at the hands of *this* savage. It surely didn't matter that he was the most handsome man she'd ever seen; he was a savage, and her desire to live gave her courage to shout, "No!"

The savage froze, his hand stilling in midair. He said something, his voice low and soothing. Slowly he released some of her hair, letting it fall slowly so it separated like hundreds of gossamer spiderwebs. He pointed to the moon, then let the rest of her hair fall slowly so the fine ribbons of light shimmered and fluttered around her face. With gentle fingers he traced the slim line of her jaw, running his fingers over her cold, wet cheeks.

All hope of escape fled. Though she feared what he'd do, she didn't bother to run. It was no use. She knew it. He knew it.

Was she about to experience the horror of all the stories of captive women that she'd heard about? Friends of her father had warned Timothy Ambrose against taking his wife and young daughter into the wilderness to do his godly duty. Members of their last congregation had tried to warn him of the dangers. One pastor's wife had even begged him to allow Emily to stay with her and her family, but her father refused. He was heading north and no one could stop him.

She could only hope that the end, when it came, would come quickly. "Don't hurt me," she begged, staring up into the savage's impassive, dark features.

The Indian lifted his hand. Emily ducked instinctively. He gave her a quizzical look, then pointed back the way they'd come. She understood his gesture but her feet refused to move. She felt like a condemned man being asked to walk to his death. He grabbed her arm and pulled.

"U wo!"

Emily knew she had no choice but to go with him. She moved slowly, dragging her feet, lagging a step behind. He stopped in the clearing where he'd found her and let her go. Several pouches and a roll of fur lay on the ground where he'd dropped them.

Noting his bow and a quiver of arrows, she couldn't help but wonder if he'd taken part in the brutal killing of her parents. Did he plan to kill her as well? Biting her lower lip to keep the tears from spilling, Emily glanced away. She grieved for her mother, would always remember the sight of her falling from the wagon and the slow, painful way death had claimed her. She couldn't bring herself to mourn the loss of the man she'd grown up calling Father.

The stroke of fingers down her face brought her back to the present with a jolt. She jumped. The savage watched, the expression in his eyes hidden by the night. Now what? If he grabbed her, she'd fight. If she was going to die, she'd rather it be quick than drawn out. She took a step back, and was relieved when he didn't try to stop her. Survival instinct demanded she run, yet she didn't. There was no way for her to escape. Not in the dark. Not in the day. Not anytime.

The Indian hunkered down and picked up a pouch. He pointed to the ground where a short while before she'd lain curled up trying to sleep. Moving slowly, Emily sat, drew her knees to her chest, and wrapped her arms tightly around herself. She kept her eyes on her companion, watching his every move.

He came to her and sat so close that their knees nearly touched. Emily averted her eyes from the sight of his naked flesh, covered only by a breechclout. The last years spent traveling from one mission to another, she'd seen many nearly naked men—some who even went about with no regard for clothing or those who might see them. Yet it had never been beneath the stars, and she had never been alone.

Smooth, taut skin rippled as the savage leaned forward and held something out to her. He motioned for her to eat it.

Emily took the long strip of dried meat. She and her mother had visited many Indian women in their tipis and had seen them making this jerked beef. Though the meat was bland, hunger demanded that she take it from him. Slowly, the sounds of the night returned. When the savage stood, Emily edged away in fear.

Yet all he did was unroll a large fur and lie down upon it a foot away from her. The fur looked like a buffalo robe. He patted the space beside him. Her heart thudded against her chest. Was this it? Did he plan to rape her now? Wide-eyed, Emily shook her head, making no move to go to him. He shrugged and closed his eyes. Emily held her breath and watched him. Hope rose. Maybe while he slept she could escape.

She waited a long while, her heart hammering. Then she slowly edged away. A sharp command proved he was just as aware of what was going on with his eyes closed. He turned his head and indicated she should sleep.

Hesitating, Emily lay down on the ground and curled up, her eyes fixed on the savage. He was so close, she heard the soft intake of each of his breaths. Realizing he didn't plan to attack her—at least not yet—she let her body, exhausted from the day's events, slowly calm. Its numbness faded and allowed her to feel the cold seeping into her bones. Her teeth chattered, and she clenched her jaw until it ached.

45

She closed her eyes. Though summer was coming, the nights were still cold.

Something warm and soft dropped over her. A muffled gasp escaped as her first thought was that he'd climbed on top of her—but she quickly realized he'd just given her his fur. The weight of the thick pelt, still warm from the Indian's body heat, took the chill from her bones quickly.

Confused at the savage's actions, Emily stared at him as he lay back down. Why had he given her his fur? Why hadn't he forced himself on her? What would he expect of her on the morrow? Too tired at that moment to care, too drained by the day's events, Emily burrowed into the pelt's warmth. She welcomed the oblivion of sleep.

Darkness swirled around Swift Foot. He shifted on the hard, cold ground. He'd put his soft deerskin shirt beneath him, but it offered little protection from the small rocks and twigs poking him. Yet it wasn't discomfort from lying on the ground, or the biting chill in the air, that kept sleep from him.

He turned his head and stared with troubled eyes at the white woman. He had expected a child—not this young woman. And he had certainly not expected a woman of her beauty. In sleep, the girl wore trusting innocence like a newborn fawn. Her hair, woven of moonlight, spilled across the ground, liquid luminescence soaking into the rich earth. Though he had a grandmother, a Frenchwoman, with light hair, he'd never seen locks this pale. He stared at her hands, tucked beneath her chin like a child's. Even her skin was white, as pale as the glittering stars.

Unable to resist, he reached out to touch her hair. It flowed through his fingers. Using two fingers, he rubbed the strands. They were soft, like the fur of his helper, *Mastinca,* the rabbit. Leaving one arm stretched out to caress the woman's hair, he reached his other hand across his body to his upper arm to touch his wide armlet of rabbit fur. *Mastinca* was known for fleetness of foot and endurance on long journeys. Swift Foot had earned his own name at a young age for his ability to run and jump like his helper.

Glancing up at the moon, he thanked *Hanwi* for giving him the answer to the troubling dreams he'd experienced over the long, hard, cold winter. But what did the answer mean? Why had he heard this woman's cries? And more important, now that he'd found the source of his unrest, what was he to do with her? *Wakan Tanka* had spared this woman's life, then led Swift Foot to her. But why? Did she have a message for him?

Save her. The wind whispered the words in his ear.

That thought gave him pause. She was lost and alone. She shifted restlessly, her arm shoving back the fur. He eyed the generous swells of her gleaming white breasts. A stab of desire rolled through his body, startling him as much as did the protective instincts that also rose within him. This woman in no time had touched some hidden soft and vulnerable spot buried deep inside his soul. He wanted to pull her into his arms and hold her forever. She was his. He'd found

47

her. Saved her. She belonged to him. He wanted nothing more than to lie beside her and mate with her.

Unsettled that the attraction was so strong, Swift Foot pulled his hand away, dropping her hair to the ground as if it were evil. He sat, troubled by his thoughts. How could he, soon to be chief of his tribe, feel such need for a white woman?

Leave, his senses ordered. *Let her find her own way back to her people.* But he couldn't leave her here on her own. She'd never survive.

A soft moan from the woman drew his attention. She cried out briefly, then fell silent. He yearned to move closer, to pull her into his arms and comfort her, but her nearness unnerved him. Her presence frightened him. Like that of a rabbit startled by predators on the prairie, instinct told him to run and hide.

Swift Foot glared at the heavens, furious with his weakness. He was Swift Foot, a great warrior, who at twenty winters had fought in many battles and counted coup so many times, he had two coup sticks. He killed his enemy with cold detachment. Soon he'd proudly take his place as leader of his people, an honor his father had not lived to obtain.

Another sharp cry jolted him from his thoughts. The woman thrashed and cried out as bad spirits chased her while she slept. He watched, his gut lurching at the soft, mewling cries choking her. The sound woke her. She scrambled to her knees, her eyes wild with fear and the lingering darkness of her dreams. Seeing him watching her, she tensed. Before she could bolt like *Mastinca,* he reached out, his fingers circling her wrist.

Murmuring softly, he scooted close to her, using the white man's tongue to reassure her that he would not do her harm. His voice seemed to pierce the fog of fear shrouding her. Slowly the tension left her shoulders, yet she made no move to lie back down.

Releasing his hold on her wrist, Swift Foot used his hands to force her to recline again on his fur. "*Istima yo.*" He repeated the words in English. "Go to sleep," he ordered in a voice soft and low, as if speaking to a frightened child.

She watched him through wide eyes. "Who are you? What are you going to do with me?" she asked.

Swift Foot understood her. Like most of his people, he'd learned enough of the white man's tongue to aid him in dealing with trappers and those who came to trade with his tribe. He seldom spoke the words, preferring that whites not know how much he understood.

Listening to her voice, Swift Foot wasn't sure what he was going to do with the woman. He felt strangely vulnerable in her presence. Already he regretted speaking to her in her own tongue; his need to comfort had made him careless. Needing to distance himself from her, he lay down on his side. He turned his back to her, as he was unable to think while looking upon her beauty.

With a few words he could reassure her that he meant her no harm, but if he did, he would remove the one barrier that he sensed was his only protection—and he needed that distance between them. Self-preservation *demanded* he hold his tongue. He could only hope she wouldn't press further. Perhaps she might assume that he knew only a few words of her tongue.

The woman finally fell silent. Relieved, Swift Foot took a deep breath. But the silence didn't last long. Soft sounds of tears battered at his determination to remain impassive. Like a deer tearing through the fragile spiderwebs between trees, this woman's fear and sorrow broke through his resolve.

Again a voice came to him: *Save her. Return her to her people. Prove your worth.*

Then it dawned on him. The Great Spirit sought to test his worth and his devotion to his people before granting him the position of chief of his tribe. And what better way than with a beautiful white woman? His father had taken a white woman for wife and brought dishonor on their tribe, an act that had started a vicious circle of war and death. He knew the Great Spirit was displeased by his tribe. Hadn't the harsh winter and the poor buffalo hunt last summer been proof that the Great One sought to make his people pay for their foolishness?

During his last vision quest, Swift Foot had vowed to make things right when he became chief. And now the spirits demanded proof that he could repair the damage of the past and bring peace to his people. They'd sent him a white woman. They sought to tempt him in the same manner as his own father had been tempted.

Closing his eyes, he thanked the Great Spirit for sending him this woman. He vowed to be strong, to make his people proud of him. Where his father had failed, Swift Foot would not. He would regain the honor his father had squandered.

Save her. The command came once more from *Tate,* whispered in his ear as the wind whirled around him. Swift Foot closed his eyes, drawing strength from the belief that this would be the first step in righting the many wrongs of the past. He'd take her to one of the many trading posts along the big muddy river.

Yet his decision didn't make it easier to ignore the woman's mourning. He realized again that she'd lost her family. Her mother and father. The girl desperately needed comforting. Unable to help himself, he turned to face her. Her eyes were still wide open, filled with grief and fear as she stared into his eyes.

Reaching out, he coaxed her head to rest in the cradle of his shoulder. Speaking, he began to tell her about the pranks and tricks of Coyote and *Iktomi,* a spiderlike spirit who enjoyed causing trouble and took malicious glee in complicating the lives of the Sioux. In his haste, he found himself mixing Lakota and English—a prank of *Iktomi,* he was sure.

The woman's sobs subsided and her breathing slowed. Still, he continued to offer comfort. Her fists relaxed until her fingers rested lightly on his chest. Carefully pulling her body even closer so he could keep her warm, Swift Foot once again found his fingers tangled in her hair.

Yes, he'd save her, take her to safety. Otherwise she'd surely die at the hands of the elements or animals—or worse, end up the captive of either another Sioux tribe or Ojibwa or Mandan, all of whom roamed this land. And in saving her, he'd take the first step to proving himself to the spirits who even now watched and waited. An answering caress of his hair, a brief touch to his shoulders from *Tate*, told him Wind was pleased.

He closed his eyes, giving himself over to the fragile softness of the woman in his arms. Come morning, he'd devise a way to keep distance between them. But for tonight, he'd give in, victim to *Iktomi*—son of *Inyan*, the rock. *Iktomi* had the power to work magic over persons and things, and for tonight, Swift Foot was unable to resist holding the white girl in his arms and murmuring softly to her.

Emily woke to the scent of roasting meat. Her stomach rumbled at the delicious aroma teasing her from her sleep. Heat radiated toward her, making the cocoon she slept in too warm. She held on to the lingering traces of sleep, though, shoving away the horrible nightmares of savages and wolves. It all had been a dream. She'd open her eyes and find her mother cooking. Even a scolding for being lazy sounded like heaven to Emily, for it meant her mother was still alive.

She stretched and opened her eyes, then blinked rapidly. A few feet away, a fire blazed. But it wasn't her mother cooking the morning meal. Instead, an Indian sat before the flames, holding a stick with chunks of meat speared upon it.

With sudden and stark clarity, the night came back to her: sleeping nestled in the savage's arms, his soothing voice in her ears, his hands tunneling through her hair. The events scrolled backward: the wolves, the deaths of her parents, her mother's deathbed confession. None of it had been a dream.

She blanked out all the horror and focused on the here and now—the Indian before her, and the immediate danger he represented. She stared at his body clad in only a breechclout. In the daylight, she saw that her first impression of him had not been wrong. He was young, and had dark, handsome looks, and a body honed to the perfection of a god. The Greek god Apollo came to mind. She'd read about him in a book Millicente had allowed her to read at the mission; her father had refused to allow Emily anything but the Bible.

Frowning, she stared at the warrior. He wasn't what she expected. All during the night, he'd been kind, his voice soft and tender as if reassuring a child. Each time she'd awakened to find the taste of tears on her lips, his touch had been gentle. He'd held her, stroked her head, back, and arms until she fell asleep once more. Despite the circumstances, Emily had felt safer in his arms than she could remember feeling in a long while. Yet this savage, for all his gentle handling, was still an unknown.

Her stomach rumbled again, reminding Emily that aside from that bit of dried meat last night, she hadn't eaten in some time. Wrapping the buffalo robe around her shoulders, she cautiously sat up.

The savage didn't look at her or acknowledge her presence. "Thank you for sharing your fur," she began. Removing it, she laid it a safe distance from the fire. Turning, she discreetly tried to pull up her bodice. The sound of ripping cloth stopped her. It was useless to try to make her dress more modest, so she gave up—before she lost the dress and was down to just her threadbare shift.

Holding her hands out, she warmed them, all the while eyeing the sizzling meat on the fire. Juice dripped into the flames and sizzled. Emily licked her lips, feeling faint with the need for food. "You speak English?" she asked, recalling how he'd talked to her last night. Though she couldn't remember the words, just the soft, reassuring timbre of his voice keeping the nightmares away, she was sure he'd spoken to her in English.

He grunted something in a strange language. Puzzled, Emily shook her head. She could have sworn he'd spoken to her in English. Maybe it had been a dream, she thought. Maybe she'd dreamed that he'd talked to her for most of the night. Leaning forward, she pointed to herself. "My name is Emily." She spoke slowly. When he glanced up at her, she jabbed her chest. "Emily."

Still no response. So she studied him. Last night she hadn't been able to see him in detail. Her gaze slid over his bare shoulders, and she noted that he wore his hair long and loose. One strand fell over his shoulder, drawing her gaze down to his muscled chest. She scanned the rest of him, skimming past the only bit of clothing he wore to note that his thighs, bare to his groin, were enormous. His legs, long for a savage, led to a tapered waist, broad chest, and bulging arms.

He glanced up at her. Embarrassed to be caught staring at his naked flesh, Emily felt heat infuse her body. But he didn't seem to notice, and he held out a stick of meat. With another thank-you, Emily reached out to take the tender morsel. As she sat back, she found his gaze on her breasts, and she found herself wishing she had kept her shawl or suffered the suffocating warmth of the fur robe. As if he sensed her concern, he averted his gaze.

After the morning meal, he walked away, through the trees. Emily waited. He hadn't taken his pouches, so she knew he'd be back. When he reappeared, his hair was wet and she realized he'd gone to the river to bathe. He indicated that she could go. She shook her head. He shrugged as if to say it made no difference to him whether she bathed or not. Truthfully, Emily would have loved to have done so, but there wasn't a chance she was undressing with him so near.

He picked up his pouches, rolled the fur robe, and tied it with a long, thin strip of leather. Emily stood, uncertain. Was he leaving? The thought of being alone again frightened her. Between him and the wolves, she'd learned just how vulnerable she was with no weapon to defend herself. And if she came across another Indian, she wasn't sure she'd be able to save herself.

At least this one had treated her well. Panic hit at the thought of being abandoned to make her way alone. Though she didn't know him, it seemed to her that this gentle savage was her only chance of surviving.

In that moment, Emily realized that she'd rather deal with what she knew than face the unknown. She stepped toward him. "Take me with you. Don't leave me alone," she begged. As she spoke, she couldn't quite keep the fear from her voice.

His gaze impassive, he uttered an order: "*U wo!*" He motioned for her to come to him.

Grateful, yet fearful, Emily did as bidden. The Indian handed her the pouches, rolled up his fur and shirt, and turned to pick up his bow and arrows. Emily shouldered her burden and fell into step behind her unlikely rescuer.

Chapter Three

The gentle warmth and soft greens of spring gave way to the sparkling heat of summer. Sitting atop a ridge, Emily watched the radiant gold-and-crimson sunset spread like clover honey across the horizon. Below her, determined not to be outdone, matching seas of knee-high grass rippled in the breeze like liquid gold racing to meet the setting sun. Meadowlarks added to the beauty with their golden melody.

Never had she seen a land so dominated by one color, yet comprised of so many hues, shades, and textures. Sunflowers, the flower of a cactus, tawny-coated animals, all blended in with the scenery; yet each stood out, offering the observer a beauty not found anywhere else. Even the night seemed to compete, from the dazzle of stars to the cold, green-gold lights that flashed across the dark sky.

Susan Edwards

The richness of this land took her breath away. From where she sat, miles and miles of it lay open to her seeking gaze. Spying a large golden eagle soaring across the sky, she sighed. Oh, to be a bird and soar across this wonderful world she'd adopted as her own! She had no idea exactly how many days she'd wandered the land with her Indian savior, and she didn't care. For the first time in her life she felt truly happy and free.

Breathing deeply, she stretched her arms high overhead, rejoicing in the feel of air caressing her bare skin. Reaching back, she removed the leather thong holding her hair away from her face. Combing her fingers through her heavy braid, she released the confined strands to the playful tugs of the afternoon breeze.

Clad in her thigh-length shift, she closed her eyes and tipped her head back, bringing her hands slowly down, her fingers lightly brushing against her sides. Then she held them out, slightly behind her, as if they were wings and she a bird in flight.

Giggling softly, she opened her eyes and twirled in small circles, well away from the ridge, her hair swirling around her. The grass beneath her bare feet felt so different from the green grass of spring; its long stems, bent over, cushioned her feet like a thick carpet, and its ripening heads caught between her toes.

Sinking down, she rested her chin on one upraised knee. Never in her life could she recall being able to sit and enjoy the afternoon. Not even as a child. If there were no chores to be done, then she'd been expected to read the Bible or pray. According to her father, idle hands and minds led to sinful thoughts and actions.

Soaking up the last rays of the day, she wondered how anyone could believe that time spent enjoying the beauty of God's earth could be considered sinful. For her, it was another aspect of her newfound freedom.

Freedom. The word tasted sweet on Emily's tongue. Never had she realized just how much her life had lacked. She'd been a prisoner to her father's demanding beliefs, a slave to society's rules, and even held hostage by her own body—afraid to do anything for fear of attracting attention and the ire of Timothy Ambrose.

But out here, none of those things mattered. It was just her and the simple world around her.

No pretense.

No falsehoods.

Just the two of them and all this. It was a world she never wanted to leave. A long shadow fell across her. Glancing over her shoulder, she smiled at the warrior watching her. Like everything else around her, he too was golden—from the breadth of his shoulders down to his tapered waist and strong legs. Even the taupe skin below his breechclout and his dark eyes reflected the different earth tones surrounding them.

"You're back," she greeted him happily, jumping to her feet. Seeing the dead rabbit he held by the hind legs, she held out her hand.

Drawing the animal away from her, the warrior sent a silent question with his eyes. Emily grinned, knowing what answer he sought. Over the last week, she'd experienced her second monthly flow, which meant she wasn't allowed to touch anything he touched, including the food they ate.

She recalled her embarrassment when her bleeding had started. Out here there'd been no way to hide it, and he'd quickly made a sign that she was to be secluded while in that condition.

Truth to tell, it had been just fine with her. She'd quickly adjusted to being taken care of. In fact, it had felt good to learn that for that one week, as had happened, nothing was expected of her. No chores. No traveling. Just time to sit and reflect. Going to him, she put her hands on his shoulders.

"It's all right. I'm done."

He smiled back, reached up, and took a strand of her hair, rubbing its softness between his fingers. Emily knew he loved her hair, and of all things, he had probably missed combing, touching, and rubbing it during her time in seclusion.

She reached over to take the rabbit from him. He shook his head, dropped the animal, and swept her up into his arms. Laughing, she circled her arms around his neck and rested her head in the strong curve of his shoulder, relishing the male scent of him, the warmth of his bronzed skin against her cheek, and the strength and security she felt in his arms.

She herself had missed *this*: his touches, the way he made her feel special, wanted, and loved.

The first time he'd kissed her, she'd been scared that he had been about to rape her. But he hadn't forced her. He'd been gentle and patient. And at last, she'd given herself to him freely. At first it was because she felt she owed it to him; repaying his kindness in saving her life with her body had seemed a small price to pay. But now she loved him, heart and soul.

Wanton. Sinner. Whore.

Her father's words echoed in her mind.

Daughter of the devil. Satan's spawn.

The words still hurt. She hadn't been any of those things, but now? She didn't know.

Yet she didn't care. Forcibly, she put thoughts of her father from her mind. This was far too beautiful an afternoon to spoil it with memories of a miserable childhood, and she preferred to just forget about that last day with her parents and pretend it had never happened. It was easier and less painful. But deep down, Emily knew she'd never forget, just as she knew that day had changed her forever.

She stared up at her golden warrior and felt the glow of warmth and happiness. He took her back to the spot where she'd sat waiting for him and gently laid her down on the still-flattened patch of grass.

While he discarded his breechclout, Emily pulled her shift over her head, baring herself to him. It warmed her to see his eyes feasting on her flesh. Lying back, she held out her arms and welcomed his weight over her. Soft, tender murmurs filled her ears, making her feel beautiful. And when he was poised at her entrance, waiting for her to open to him, she felt cherished.

Loved.

Slowly her knees fell apart, and her legs lifted to draw him to her. With a deep sigh, he entered her, then together they flew through the air as one, breathing as one, reaching ecstasy as one. "I love you," she cried when the world around her spun out of control.

A long while later, after she'd dressed, Emily set to cooking their meal. Every so often she glanced at her warrior. He watched her. He touched her. But he didn't speak to her. Yet that was all right. She talked enough for the two of them.

"I missed cooking for you." She grinned and ran an appreciative eye over his body.

"I also missed touching you," she added. His gaze met hers, his eyes darkening as if he understood, but he didn't speak or return the words she wished he could. Yet the heated look in his eyes spoke louder than words.

"You understand by my tone, my voice. I know you do." She went to him, knelt before him, and touched his face, running her fingers across his high cheekbones and lightly over his lips.

"I love you. I don't know what I would have done if you hadn't found me."

Her warrior set his arrow and knife down and pulled her onto his lap, where he rocked with her. "The food," she protested with a laugh.

The food waited.

Swift Foot resumed his arrow making but his attention kept wandering. His gaze strayed to Emily, to her hair. Those white-yellow strands still mesmerized him even after all this time. When she glanced over at him and smiled, heat settled in his groin. From deep within, he vibrated with a need so strong his hands shook. How had this happened? All his efforts to hold her at bay and keep his distance had failed. Even worse, he delayed his return to his people by staying with her.

A sharp pang in the center of his chest grew. He turned his eyes to the ripening land barely discernible in the dimming light. Unrest and worry clouded his mind and filled his heart with dread. He felt as though he stood on an unstable ridge, the earth crumbling beneath his feet.

The peace he'd found with this woman, the relationship they shared was in his mind like that between *Wi* and *Hanwi*. Sun needed Moon to be complete. Without both of them, the world would not be the same. He closed his eyes, trying hard to suppress the emotions raging inside. But he knew deep in his heart that without Emily he would not be the same—just as he knew that soon this nice little world he'd created and shrouded himself in would come to an end.

Trying to keep his mind from his troubling thoughts, Swift Foot attempted to concentrate on making new arrows. He placed the quill of a feather in his teeth, grabbed hold of the top, and pulled one side of the feather out, down, and back, using constant pressure and speed to prevent ripping the vane.

Emily walked past, her hips swaying, her hair swinging, drawing his hungry gaze to her. His attention on her and not the feather, he went too fast and tore the vane. It was the third he'd ruined. Disgusted at his inability to concentrate, he tossed the feathers aside and gave up. Instead, he forced himself to face his future.

The truth could no longer be denied. Or hidden. Or avoided. Already he'd been gone far longer than he'd planned. His people would be worried, for he was to be their next chief as soon as his ailing uncle stepped down. His tribe was small, and many of their strong warriors were gone, killed in battle. They needed a strong leader. They needed him.

The council had recognized the need of their people, yet they also worried that Swift Foot was too young, too filled with the restless abandon of youth despite his many achievements. Fearful that their tribe would soon be wiped out, they'd agreed to his becoming chief—on one condition: he must marry a woman of their choosing. By doing this, they ensured he'd be settled and ready to focus on the demands soon to be placed upon his shoulders.

Too, marriage to a woman belonging to another clan of the Hunkpapa tribe would strengthen his own. Normally the male left his people to join his wife's, but because of their dwindling numbers, the two clans had decided to band together, both under his leadership. The council had made their choice. The arrangements were made. All that remained was his return, and then both clans would be his—and would count on him to find a way to end the war between his tribe and the Miniconjou. The two Teton Sioux tribes had been at war all of Swift Foot's life. It was time for the rift to be mended, and it was Swift Foot's duty to do so.

The trouble was, he didn't want to wed a stranger. Not only had he found the answer to his haunting dreams, he'd found love. Swift Foot loved the white woman named Emily. He wanted to take her back with him.

A test. He tried to block his emotions by remembering that this time with the woman was nothing more than a test. The spirits tested his honor, his worthiness to assume the role of chief.

Gripping his knees with white-knuckled hands, Swift Foot mourned. War and the death of his parents had shaped his life and determined his future. He had to remember who he was, and *what* he was.

Remembering why they'd died gave him some strength to resist the temptation to bring the woman back with him. Yet remembering the nights spent in the woman's arms, the feel of her, the taste of her, the love he felt for her, tore his heart in two.

Tipping his head back, Swift Foot lifted his hands to the deepening sky to pray for strength. His hair brushed the exposed flesh of his buttocks as his upper body swayed in prayer. Love hadn't brought his parents happiness, only death and years of spilled blood.

He thought of the man and woman he'd never known. In order to marry his mother, Swift Foot's father had rejected the woman he'd promised to take for wife—the daughter of a Miniconjou chief. The scorned woman's tribe had declared war on his Hunkpapa clan, and when he had been only a babe, they'd killed his parents. They would have killed him had they known of his existence.

Swift Foot's lips twisted grimly. They now knew he lived, had grown to be a great and feared warrior. That gave him some satisfaction. Yet war between the two tribes continued, a vicious circle of revenge. The selfish act of his father continued to cost the tribe much, and with each new death, the dishonor of his family weighed heavily on his shoulders.

Somehow he had to find a way to restore peace. And honor. If he did not, the two tribes would end up destroying each other.

Swift Foot sighed. He'd accepted with little emotion the arranged marriage his clan demanded. It was his duty to follow the orders of his elders. At the time, he hadn't understood the emotion called love that had made his father risk so much. But now he did. Now, in love with a woman with hair the silvery color of a full moon, he understood. His soul wept for what could not be. His heart cursed *Iktomi* for his cruel joke. To taste love, then to have it ripped away—how could he bear the pain?

Shifting, he watched Emily cook their meal. She'd learned fast and seemed eager to please. And she did please. More than he'd have thought possible.

Again, he was forced to remind himself that love didn't matter. Only honor. He loved this white girl, and wanted to hold on to her as long as he could, but with Hawk Eyes—the new chief of the scorned Miniconjou tribe that sought to kill his people—Swift Foot knew what he had to do. He could no longer delay their parting.

Guilt ate at him. Each day made it worse for them both.

She was not his to claim forever, as his father had once claimed his mother. Even taking her home as a slave for his wife-to-be was out of the question. His people would remember his father's actions, and they would doubt him.

At first he'd thought he could spend the warm months with her, then leave. He'd never expected it to be so painful to do so. He'd never expected to fall in love with her—and it didn't help to see the love in her eyes, taste it in her kisses, or hear it in her voice. He'd never thought he'd yearn to say those words in return. But he couldn't. Not even in Lakota could he say the words, for that would only make it so much harder to let her go.

In her arms alone could he show her the love he felt—but it was a love destined to tear them apart when he finally gathered the strength to leave.

Over the last two weeks, Emily sensed a difference in her warrior. They'd traveled long and fast for a while, and then they'd stopped. Often during the past several days he left her hidden, returning each evening to take her in his arms and love her long into the night, as if he couldn't get his fill of her.

Not that she minded. She grinned, quickening her steps to keep up with him. Today he'd decided they should continue on.

Her gaze lingered on his bare back. She loved to look at him, see the play of muscles ripple beneath his skin. Her eyes skimmed downward. The flap of his breechclout swished from side to side, revealing glimpses of flesh as bronzed as the rest of him. He was her Apollo, bronze, and beautiful. She smiled and stared at her own arms. Her skin had turned a rich shade of honey after hours spent in the warmth of the sun. She was not as deeply tanned as he, still, she no longer looked white.

Her clothing felt heavy on her. At first it had seemed strange to go without. Aside from taking baths, she'd never gone naked. And never outside, in the open. She smiled. Her warrior had convinced her that it was silly to put on clothing each day when he was just as likely to take it off again; so whenever they were camped, she wore only her shift—or if he had his way, nothing at all. But when they traveled, in case they came upon anyone else, she endured the heavy weight of her mother's old dress which she'd salvaged. She had shortened the skirt, enjoying the brush of tall grass against her calves; and the warm air on her bare arms; and the heat had convinced her to tear the sleeves from the shift.

Happy with her life, she laughed. Her warrior turned to see what she found amusing. Reaching forward, Emily stroked her fingers down his back, slid their tips beneath the hide covering his buttocks. His eyes darkened and roamed down her body, making her breasts ache for his touch. With a glint in his eyes, he trailed his finger down across one budded breast, then across and over the other.

She groaned. This time it was his turn to laugh. Then, to her annoyance, he turned and continued on. Again, she wondered about his pace. Perhaps they were returning to his tribe. Beneath her feet the grass crunched, and it surrounded her, along with leaves from trees that had lost their glossy texture. Everything looked dry. Summer would soon give way to fall and winter. Surely he didn't roam on his own during the winter? He must be returning to his tribe. Thinking of that brought a new worry to her.

What would his people be like? Would they accept her? She had no idea.

Dusk was nearly upon them before he stopped and motioned for her to hide. She settled back while he went ahead to scout. They'd gone through this many times, especially when he spotted other Indians in the area. He'd taught her to sit absolutely still, to walk without leaving tracks, and to move through the bushes without breaking leaves or branches.

When he returned and motioned to her, she followed him deep into the lengthening shadows. Without warning, they burst out of the woods into a small, secluded clearing.

There was just enough light to reveal a fallen tree trunk, tall brown grass, and shrubs, all enclosed by a wall of thick tree trunks. Beneath Emily's feet, tiny flowers drooped on fragile stems—another sign that summer would soon be past.

"It's wonderful," she murmured, staring around at this little bit of paradise.

He grunted, then indicated she should make camp. Untying a long leather thong that crisscrossed her back to hold their belongings while they traveled, she quickly unpacked the pouches of food, a blanket of rabbit pelts she'd sewn together, and the buffalo hide that she used to roll everything into. Gathering fistfuls of dry grass and leaves, she piled them together, making a soft bed upon the hard ground. She laid her warrior's buffalo robe on top. Turning, she waited to see if he was going to hunt, or if they'd just eat a meal of dried meat and berries.

The look in his eyes made her smile. Dried meat and berries. When he held out his hand she took it and let him lead her down onto the soft bed she'd just fashioned. Without hesitating, she stepped out of her cumbersome skirt, noting that it was in tatters and would soon be worthless. And when she pulled the shift over her head, she heard it rip. She winced. Soon she'd have nothing to wear—but right now, it didn't seem to matter.

After a bout of leisurely lovemaking, Emily rose and brought the pouch of food to their bed. She also brought the comb she assumed her warrior had gotten from traders. She handed it to him, and as he did each evening, he settled her between his thighs.

"I've never had anyone comb my hair as gently as you do," she commented, leaning back into his hands as he gently untangled her long locks. While he attended to her hair, she sampled from the fresh batch of berries she'd picked yesterday.

"I wish you could talk to me. It's the only thing I really miss, you know." She'd tried to get him to teach her his language, but outside of a few words here and there, it hadn't worked.

So in the evenings, she talked: about what she'd seen during the day, her fears, her childhood. Anything she could think of, just to hear a voice she could understand.

When he tossed the comb aside and slid his hands around to cup her heavy breasts in his palms, she leaned back. Laughing, she tipped her head back and held out a freshly picked berry.

"You really should eat."

He took the food from her, deliberately nipping her pink-tipped fingers with his teeth.

Long into the night, Emily gave herself to her warrior, sensing an edge to his loving. But the touch of his mouth skimming her flesh shoved the worry aside. Her lover wouldn't allow any distraction on her part. When she finally fell asleep, her legs tangled with his, her head tucked beneath his chin, and her fingers twined with his, it was with a smile on her lips.

The howl of a wolf broke the predawn stillness, startling Emily awake. Sitting, leaning on one hand, she blinked against the darkness. The moon had gone behind a cover of gray clouds. Her heart raced. What had awakened her? She no longer feared the beasts of the forest. Not with her warrior at her side. But tonight she sensed something was wrong. Seeking warmth and reassurance, she turned to her companion.

He wasn't there. She reached out and touched the bedding but found only a cold, empty spot where she'd fallen asleep wrapped snugly in his arms. She rose to her knees and peered into the darkness. Where had he gone? She shivered.

Suddenly a small ray of moonlight broke through the blanket of clouds, and Emily spotted a familiar figure moving farther into the gray shadows, away from her. Why the sight of her warrior walking away struck terror into her heart, she didn't know. Yet all of his strange behavior came back to her, and she didn't care if he was going scouting or checking up on a noise he'd heard; she didn't want to be left alone.

Not now.

"Wait!" she cried softly. She jumped to her feet, heedless of the rocks and branches stabbing her bare soles as she stumbled after the departing figure.

Catching up, Emily grabbed his arm, dimly aware of the weapons slung across his shoulders and the animal-skin pouches of personal items hanging from a throng around his waist.

She froze. He never took those with him unless they were moving on. "Where are you going?" Panic edged her voice.

His nostrils flared with emotion; then she was caught close by strong, muscular arms. Emily threw her arms around his neck, clinging fiercely, drinking in his rich scent, a combination of sweat and the woodsy outdoors. It was all right. He wasn't leaving.

He murmured something in her ear. She heard the beat of his heart, and the sharp intake of air as he reached up and pried her hands from his neck, forcing them back to her side. She stared at him, trying to read his expression in the dark of the night.

His arms lifted, his fingers brushing up her bare arms, feathering over her collarbone, and up to frame her small oval face.

"*Kopegla sni yo.*" Leaning down, he gently kissed her.

Emily closed her eyes, comforted by his kiss yet troubled by it. His lips were firm and warm, yet they trembled. When he gently led her back to the fallen log, she sat, staring up at him, catching the glimmer of moisture in his eyes.

He turned and picked up a water pouch made from the stomach lining of a buffalo, and a bulging parfleche filled with meat, berries, and greens. He held them out to her.

Emily took the precious pouches—she'd refilled them just yesterday—and laid them in her lap, wondering why he was preparing to leave so early this day. Then he held out a wooden object that had been sitting among the food pouches. She'd never seen it before. Reaching for it, Emily twisted sideways on the decaying log to find beams of moonlight to illuminate his offering.

A thick piece of bark formed the top of a crudely carved box. Lifting it, she peered inside. Soft brown rabbit fur lined the interior. Curled on the silky fur lay a necklace. Emily lifted it out and held it up. She gasped at the long bear claw strung on a leather thong. It was one he'd worn around his neck, one she hadn't even noticed was gone. Planning to take her mother's locket that she wore around her neck on another length of leather and combine the two, she turned to thank him.

Her cry of pleasure lodged in her throat. She scanned the area but he was nowhere in sight.

Looking at the gifts he'd given her, the necklace dangling from the tips of her fingers, the wooden box resting on her palm, she knew if she stood and ran after him, she wouldn't find him.

He'd said good-bye.

Susan Edwards

Tears slid from her eyes, ran down her cheeks, and dripped down onto her bare breasts. Her head moved slowly from side to side as she refused to believe her protector, friend, and lover had disappeared forever behind nature's wall of greenery.

High overhead, the sky turned gray, the silence of the night broken by birds chirping and fluttering sleepily as they woke to greet the coming light of a new day. Emily heard none of it. She sat perfectly still, too numbed to move. This couldn't be happening!

Hadn't she suffered already? Hadn't losing her family in that gruesome massacre been enough?

A rustling from the bushes behind Emily caused her to jump up from the log. Her precious water pouch fell to the ground, bursting to create a puddle at her feet. Her heart raced. Had he returned? She clutched her warrior's gift to her chest. Rounding the large green bush, she scanned the area, praying that he'd changed his mind and had come back to get her.

Instead, a doe, startled by her sudden appearance, flicked its white tail and bounded into the concealing darkness of the woods. Emily's shoulders slumped in despair. Unsure of what to do or where to go, she staggered back to the bed she'd shared with her warrior and fell to her knees, feeling dead to pain.

She also felt vulnerable sitting there—naked and alone. She grabbed her shift and yanked it over her head, heedless of the sound of more ripping cloth. Garbed, she sat still, trying to reach out with her senses. The feeling of being watched overtook her. He was there somewhere. She felt him. Sensed his presence.

74

"Where are you?" she yelled.

No answer. Why? Why wouldn't he come back to her? What cruel joke was this? Was it a test?

The silence lengthened, unnerved her. What had she done wrong? Had she displeased him? Why had he left? Panic overcame her numbness and disbelief as the sharp pain of the truth hit her: she'd been abandoned. Again.

She covered her trembling mouth with her fingers in an effort to choke back the rage and sorrow that rose from deep within and clawed at the back of her throat for release. This couldn't be happening. He couldn't just have left her out here to die. Not after taking her in. Not after loving her. And he had loved her. She knew he did, just as she loved him. So why? Why? Fear released her voice.

"I love you," she cried out. "Come back. Please come back! I love you. . . ."

Over and over she alternated between screaming for him to come back, begging him not to leave her, and crying desperately for him not to do this.

Finally she cursed him for abandoning her until her voice grew hoarse. Then she was forced to accept the fact that, once again, she was alone in a harsh, untamed land.

Chapter Four

Each piercing scream tore through Swift Foot as painfully as an arrow tearing through his flesh. The despair, the fear, and the agony in her voice nearly drove him back to her. When she paced, staring through the trees, looking for him, seeking him, calling him, he wanted to go to her and end her suffering—and his own. But he couldn't. Not now. Not ever.

The thunk of an object hitting a nearby tree made him peer carefully from his hidden spot between two pines and a thick bush. He watched Emily bend down, grab several rocks, and throw them with all her might into the forest around her. One fell just short of where he knelt.

He listened to her angry shouts, to the names she called him. He didn't understand all that she said, but he knew she cursed him. As he cursed himself. Covering his eyes with his hands, he shuddered. How could he do this to her? To himself. To them. How could he destroy the most precious gift he'd ever been given? Was there anything more important in life than the gift of love?

The weight of his love bowed his shoulders. Added to his own pain, he also felt his father's. The last of his bitterness and resentment toward the man he never knew died. No longer could he blame him for choosing love over pleasing others. Listening to Emily's quiet weeping, he felt his own heart ache. Life without love didn't seem worth living.

So claim her. Take her. She is yours.

Those thoughts rolled through his mind, tempting him. Who would blame him? He suppressed a moan of pain. He himself would. He'd grown up with the results of that love, dealt with the cost of it in lives lost due to warring. From a young age, he'd striven to be strong—all that his father had not been—vowed to restore honor and peace to his people. If he followed in the footsteps of his father, he risked more than just another war. He risked losing all that he was. Without honor, he would not be a man.

Swift Foot watched Emily stumble back to the bed of furs and fall facedown. Her husky sobs brought tears to his eyes. In silence, he cried with her. If he only had himself to worry about, things would have been different. He'd have gladly given up the honor of becoming chief—better a life with love as just a man, than a man of power with no love.

But there were too many others to consider: Emily and any children he and she might conceive, the innocent women and children of his tribe, the old, feeble, and sick among both tribes, all vulnerable to acts of war. Whether he liked it or not, too many people depended upon him to make the right choice. And the choice he had to make lay in putting the needs of the many over his own. And over Emily's.

No, he couldn't give in. Though it hurt unbearably, he had to remain strong.

Time crawled. The faint light of *Wi* stretched across the horizon. Birds swooped overhead, deer ventured into the clearing, only to bound off into the bushes once they spotted Emily. Still Swift Foot watched. And waited. Without taking his eyes off the only woman to claim his heart, he prayed.

From *Okaga,* the spirit of the south, the giver of life, the spirit with a good, kind heart, he pleaded for strength and understanding. And that something good would emerge from the depths of this pain—for all of them.

Standing on the bank of a slow-moving tributary off the Missouri River, John Cartier eyed the new day with hands fisted on his hips. Rich golds surrounding wide ribbons of red-amber shot from the horizon in a wild splash of color.

Giving in to fanciful notions, John pictured the dawn as a woman. The golds became long tresses of silky-soft curls; the reds, her soft, pouting lips; the paler shades of rose, the blush of her cheeks; and the pale sky, her lovely eyes. The greens of the leaves fluttering on the trees became the bodice of her dress, and the wild array of the colors her skirt, swirling around her as she danced across the sky.

This was Dawn at her womanly best, in his opinion. Some days she greeted him with the shy blush of a virgin, and days like today, it was the vibrant beauty of a well-loved woman. Either way, mornings were his favorite time.

Inhaling the sweet morning air, John tipped his head back, taking a moment to enjoy this bit of peace and quiet. "A gift of true beauty." Realizing he'd spoken the words aloud, he sent a rueful grin to Fang, who sat on his haunches, staring up at his master. "Yeah, I know. I'm talking aloud again." The animal shook his head, his great tongue lolling, then bounded off into the brush.

John turned back to the lightening sky, wishing he had someone to share every sunrise with: a woman, not a wolf. He sighed. The image of a perfect woman flashed before him, brought forth from the heavens themselves: sky-blue eyes, hair of the sun, and a richness of spirit to match the earth at his feet. Each night he dreamed of her, and each dawn he waited for her—which was ridiculous, as the only women out here were wives of other trappers. They were mainly squaws or coarse women of indeterminate age who led the lives of their husbands.

Wiggling his bare toes into the muddy bank, John heaved out a long, slow breath, then shrugged off the silly notions that seemed to grow stronger with each day, making him work harder, pushing himself to exhaustion to keep the loneliness at bay. Only in the early mornings did it creep up on him.

"You're a foolish man, John," he scolded himself. "Been alone too long." His grandfather and cousin were long overdue to return. He was starting to worry.

Rolling his shoulders, easing the kinks from a night spent on the hard ground, he set about starting his day. He yanked his buckskin shirt over his head and stepped out of his breeches, leaving them in a heap near his rifle a short distance from the bank. The caress of the gentle morning breeze played over his body, now naked as the day he slid from his mother's womb. Drawing in a deep breath, he stepped farther into the cool river, then dove in head-first.

Surfacing, he shook his mane of dark hair, sending droplets of water whirling around him. He washed quickly, lifting his voice in a bawdy, off-key song. A low whine sounded from the bank. John glanced at his wolf, who'd returned. He called: "Need to hear a voice, Fang, even if it's only my own."

Like the otter and beaver he trapped, he drifted on his back for a while, staring skyward, enjoying the coolness of the morning. By afternoon, temperatures would climb as the sun blazed over this dry land.

His wolf barked and whined. John glanced at the animal. Normally Fang sat quietly or joined him in the water to play. Today he seemed agitated. The beast hopped back and forth from the bank to the path leading away from the shack. John stood, letting water slough off him in sheets. "What is it, boy?" He left the stream, dried off, and quickly dressed, then went to scan the area.

The animal continued to whine and pace. When John picked up his rifle, the wolf took off. John fol-

80

lowed, alert to each sound around him. Between Indians and the other trappers who roamed this land
along the river, he trusted no one save a handful of
friends.

At last the wolf stopped, and John stopped as well.
After a pause Fang continued at a much slower pace,
the fur at his neck standing on end. John lightened his
steps and moved cautiously through the thick band of
trees. He knew where he was, and when he reached
the end of the trees, he hunkered down. Beyond the
tree line lay one of his favorite places—a small, secluded meadow.

He glanced down at the wolf, who was staring intently at something just beyond the trees. An injured
animal? Or a human? John frowned but didn't leave
the concealing foliage. At his side, Fang growled.
"What is it, boy?" he asked softly, his hand on his rifle
tightening as he searched for movement. Then he
heard it: a muffled sound. A cry.

The wolf left the wall of trees and approached the
fallen log on the other side. John followed, sure that
it was another injured animal. Had it been another
trapper or an Indian, Fang would have stayed clear.
The wolf approached the fallen log with his head
down, nose sniffing. Then he sat, cocked his head,
and let out a mournful whine. John stepped around
the log and stopped in shock when his searching gaze
fell on a woman.

She lay sleeping on her side, curled into a tight ball,
her bare arms held close to her body, fingers curled
beneath her chin. She wore a ragged and threadbare
shift that did little to hide her slim waist and rounded

hips; but it was her features, set into a small, perfect oval, that held him spellbound, and made him wonder if he hadn't fallen and knocked himself senseless. He'd never seen such delicate beauty, such perfection.

Shades of browns and yellows dominated her coloring—from pale blond hair the shade of spun silk and sunshine, to eyebrows and lashes a shade darker. Skin the tone of rich honey became the perfect backdrop for freckles as fine as gold dust and evenly distributed across the gentle sweep of her nose. Her lips, he noted with awe, were the rosy kiss of dawn.

His gaze slid down along the gentle line of her jaw and her rounded chin. She mumbled something, her arm lifting, the back of her hand pressing against her mouth in sleep. When she rolled onto her back, the material of her torn shift pulled taut across the generous swells of her breasts. The thin fabric hid little of their size or shape. Even the pale tips were visible. Feeling uncomfortable staring while she slept, John forced his gaze back to her face, and the halo of golden hair spread out beneath her.

"Lady Dawn," he whispered, stunned by the presence of this woman. Just looking upon her fair beauty seemed to ease the darkness creeping through his soul. She couldn't be real. Had to be a dream. Maybe he'd drowned and died and had gone to heaven.

He wanted to reach out and touch her, see if she was real. But if he'd truly gone crazy out here, he didn't want to break the spell. He could look upon her for an eternity and never get enough.

Fang made the decision for him. He bounded forward and sniffed the woman's foot, his cold nose startling her awake. She bolted upright, stared at the wolf, then screamed, startling all of them. John jumped back, Fang ran, and the woman herself watched him warily with eyes as blue as the sky above. She scrambled to her knees, ready to bolt like a frightened doe.

John couldn't have moved if his life depended on it. He fell, long and hard, into the liquid pools of her blue eyes. Fang's muffled bark from behind the log jerked him back to reality. This was real. *She* was real. The fear in her eyes made him snap his jaw closed and remember his manners.

"Easy, miss. Name is John Cartier," he said. His voice was too loud in his own ears. She flinched. He cringed and gentled his tone to a lower, softer timbre. "I won't hurt you." Noticing her gaze straying from him to Fang, he cleared his throat. "That there is Fang. Had him since he was a pup. He won't harm you, either."

For a moment, she looked like she'd bolt like a rabbit. Instead, all emotion drained from her face, leaving her pale, her eyes lifeless, like an empty, unseeing shell. She lay back down without speaking.

Confused and concerned, he moved slowly forward. "Who are you?" Silence met his question. More important, how had she come to be here? He glanced down at the fur she lay upon, then noticed the bear claw around her neck and the leather pouches lying near the log.

She'd been with an Indian. That much was clear. Was she a captive? He glanced around uneasily. If so, where was the warrior who'd claimed her? Bending

83

down, he reached out to touch her on the shoulder. She jumped but didn't look at him.

"Miss? I can help. I have a cabin—not much—but it's shelter. You'll be safe there." With other trappers returning for the coming winter trapping season, and the tribes of Indians who roamed the area, it wasn't safe to leave a woman alone and unprotected.

"Doesn't matter what happens to me." The girl's voice faded and she drew herself tighter into a ball, clutching a wooden box.

Her grief reached out and snared him as surely as his traps snared the prized beavers he hunted. She appeared to be in shock, yet was unharmed—at least physically, from what he could see. "It's not safe for you to stay out here," he added.

Her actions confused him. If she'd been a captive, she should have been happy to see another white man, even one as rough-looking as him. He ran a hand over his ragged beard, and glanced at his filthy clothing. Perhaps not.

She spoke, almost as if talking to herself. "I wanted to live." She laughed, a hollow, humorless sound. "God would have done me a favor had He taken my life and let me die along with my parents." Her voice, hoarse with tears and grief, rose slightly.

Horrified by her talk of dying, John moved closer and reached out. He said, "Come on. I'll take care of you and see that you're returned home." Wherever that was.

Of course, the thought of sending her away left John protesting inside. For the first time he understood how the Indians felt and thought when they found a woman and took her captive. John *wanted* this woman. It didn't matter that he didn't even know her name or her circumstances. Just her presence filled that emptiness inside him, as if she'd been made for him. As crazy as it seemed, he felt a connection to her just from looking at her.

When he tried to scoop her into his arms, she came alive. "No! I have to stay here. He'll be back. I know he'll come back for me!" She fought his hold on her.

He? Trapper or Indian? "Who? Who left you here and why?" John didn't want trouble, but in good conscience, he couldn't just leave her alone without knowing more.

"Please," she beseeched, scooting away. "Leave." She shoved at his hands. "My Indian warrior will return. He won't abandon me." Gut-wrenching sobs shook her. "Not again. Oh, God, not again."

Her words didn't make sense to John except that she'd been left by an Indian. The fact that she seemed to think she'd been abandoned—though John couldn't imagine any man, white or red, doing so— gave him the excuse to effortlessly lift her into his arms. He stood, and she fought, but against his strength she didn't have a chance.

"Calm down, miss. It'll be okay. I promise. We aren't going far. Whoever you're waiting for will find you if they come back." He made his way across the meadow and into the deep shade of the woods.

Most of the tribes knew John and his grandfather, and the two of them were on good terms with those. Still, he worried over any kind of confrontation with savages, especially if the woman had been held against her will. She didn't act like she'd been a captive, but John knew she might have gone crazy in captivity. He'd worry about it later, though. Right now he needed to get her to safety in case there was trouble.

The woman went limp in his arms, as if too exhausted to fight. Cradling her close, John bent low to avoid the stinging slash of a low branch. Once clear, he straightened and glanced down at his burden.

She'd closed her eyes, shutting him out. Up close, he noted the streaks from tears, her swollen eye lids, and her vulnerable beauty. Her hair, nearly white and silky-soft, caressed his arm and hung down in waves to brush against his thigh. A rush of tender protectiveness rose in him toward this woman. Whatever her past—and whatever the future held—it didn't matter. Right now she needed him. And he needed to help her. Fate had sent him Lady Dawn.

For now, that was enough.

Swift Foot watched the white man carry Emily away from him. The trapper he'd observed many times over the last few days had found her, as he'd known would happen. He'd observed the man, seen his gentle and kind way with animals. Though this man hunted and took from the *maka*, he also gave. Emily would be safe with him. Swift Foot could leave. Yet even as he watched the white man carry away the woman he loved, his mind continued to war with his heart. It wasn't too late for him to go to her, to reclaim what was his. But as fast as the thought came, it went. His destiny had been decided long ago.

The spirits had tested him. He'd passed. So why didn't he feel triumphant? Pleased? Because in proving himself, he'd lost. He'd done what had been asked of him, and now it was time for him to return to his people.

When the white man disappeared through the wall of trees, Swift Foot silently bade Emily good-bye. Standing, he shouldered his bow, gathered his belongings, and turned to head off in the opposite direction.

He stopped, staring out into the meadow. Moving quickly, he returned and reclaimed his furs and pouches. Holding to his face the blanket Emily had made for them, he breathed in deeply, inhaling her scent, feeling the wetness of her tears.

Unable to leave this last part of her behind, he slung it over his shoulders, rolled his buffalo robe, and disappeared into the trees. The bleakness in his heart and the ache in his soul warned that for him, life would never be the same.

Chapter Five

Shouldering open the door to his tiny shack, John bent his head and stepped inside its gloomy interior, moving to the center, where he could stand upright. A thin ray of light came through one unshuttered window and fell on the woman in his arms. She lit the room with the sunshine of her beauty. Dropping his rifle onto the table, John went to his bedding and gently laid her down.

She seemed unaware of him as she curled back into a ball, keeping her eyes tightly closed. A single tear leaked from the inside corner of one eye and made him long to brush it away. He backed away, feeling out of his element in the face of her tears and the sadness that cloaked her. "I'll be back with some food and a strong cup of hot coffee."

She didn't reply. John hesitated at the door. The austere cabin, its log walls chinked with mud, didn't usually bother him, for he spent so little time here. But today he surveyed the place with a critical eye. Clothes littered the floor, and a small stack of pelts sat against the far wall along with a dozen traps and other tools. A rough-hewn table with three stools took up most of the center of the room.

He compared this place he'd called home for the last ten years with the grand manor he'd once shared with his parents, and he grimaced. This wasn't just a shack. It was a hovel. The two windows, not much more than square holes in the wall since the shutters had fallen off, were open to let in as much light as possible—which, until the sun rose a bit higher, wasn't much. There was no fireplace. No stove. Nothing.

He walked across the room and kicked his clothes into a pile, then did the same for his grandfather's and cousin's belongings, moving them to the same wall with the furs and traps. He even moved the table over to try to make the single room look bigger. Still it looked cluttered and small—not a place any woman would want to call home.

A wet nose tickled his hand. Glancing down, he stared into Fang's liquid brown eyes. Reality intruded. What was he thinking? There wasn't a chance in hell that she'd stay here with him. Nothing could disguise the fact that this was what it looked to be: a simple shelter constructed of logs and mud and a thatch roof.

89

Yet, with his inheritance and the money he'd saved over the years, he could buy a grand place. Maybe a town house in St. Louis. Or he could go home to Virginia and purchase a house with land. With a wife at his side, he could even pursue his dream of raising horses.

Though he enjoyed what he did, for the most part, and made a decent living at it, the solitude closed in on him. At sixteen, going off to live with his grandfather in the wilderness had been exciting, an adventure. And with grief over his parents' death clawing at his insides, being alone for months at a time had given him the time he'd needed to deal with his loss. But lately, the life he'd embraced as a young man left him restless and yearning for something more.

At twenty-six, he found that the thrill of adventure had long since died. The wilderness that had once been his refuge now felt like a prison. He didn't want to be alone anymore. He wanted a family: a wife to come home to and children to greet and romp with in the evenings. He wanted the love-filled marriage his parents had had.

But first he had to find a willing woman. Again, his gaze swept over the woman lying on his bedding. Hope warred with caution. Right now he didn't have much to offer her—or any woman. Not out here. Again, that vision of a home and family sneaked into his mind, teasing him with what could be.

Fearing that he was truly losing both his sanity and his heart in one fell swoop, John knew he had to get out of there and get a grip on himself. Here he was, planning a future with a woman who was clearly distraught. And her desire to die made him fear that she'd lost her mind.

She couldn't be crazy, though. The thought left him feeling as if someone had slugged him in the gut. Grabbing the rifle he'd set on the table, he left the cabin with Fang at his heels. He didn't trust her with the weapon in her present state of mind.

His pot of coffee sat near the edge of the fire pit, keeping warm. John poured a tin cup of the thick, strong brew and gulped it down. Feeling much clearer in the head, he poured a second cup, which he carried back inside. He dropped to his knees. "This will warm you," he said, setting it down on the hard-packed-dirt floor. When he got no response, he touched her bare shoulder. She flinched. "It's coffee." He made a face. "Don't have any sugar or cream to offer."

She sat up, her eyes filled with pain. "Take me back. I have to stay there. He won't know where to find me."

He. The way she said the word, the desperate yearning in her eyes, told him that she had not been unwilling. At least she wasn't now. He shook his head and ran his fingers through his still-damp hair. "I can't. It's too dangerous. Besides animals, there are savages and other trappers out there. Some would take advantage of you. Or worse." She didn't react. Whatever had happened, she didn't look as though she'd been mistreated.

Her hair fell over her shoulder, drawing his attention to her full figure. With great difficulty, he averted his eyes. He wouldn't frighten her with ogling, but damn, he was drawn to her—and not just her body, though

91

he couldn't ask for more in a woman. No, the haunted pain in her eyes drew him as flames drew moths. He wanted to know what had happened to her. He needed to offer comfort and chase away the shadows. As with many of the animals he found injured and nursed back to health because he was unable to kill them, he wanted to take her pain away.

She lay back down, ignoring his offered cup of coffee, her eyes blank once more. "It doesn't matter. You should have just left me. It doesn't matter what happens to me."

John shook his head in disbelief and scratched at the back of his neck. He searched for words of comfort, but nothing came to him. Only protests that someone so young and beautiful should want to die. "You shouldn't talk like that, miss. Nothing is worth dying over."

She stared at him for a long moment. "Having nothing makes life not worth living."

Shaken and a bit unnerved by the emptiness in her eyes, John stood. "I'll leave you to rest. If you need anything, I'll be outside."

John left the cabin door ajar so he could hear her if she called out. As he paced, he wondered what horrors she'd suffered. His gut clenched. Most certainly she'd been taken captive, but for her not to rejoice in her freedom worried him. Had her mind snapped or did she fear her return to society? Was death better than the stigma of having lived among—survived captivity among—the savages?

Troubled, he picked up his ax and went to a pile of logs. He'd heard that most women who survived captivity were never again right in the head, and those who retained their senses were often driven into committing suicide by the cruelty of their own people. Family and friends and society at large would turn their backs on the poor, innocent women.

It troubled him to think that the woman in the shack might lose all respect over something over which she'd had no control, or that she'd never marry and have children. She might never be invited to parties and never again be accepted into the world of her birth. She'd likely live her life alone, locking herself away behind closed doors.

John vowed there and then that it wouldn't happen. Her situation surely hadn't been this woman's fault, and he refused to accept that her death was better than her alternatives. She would not die if he had any say. He glanced over his shoulder to where an injured hawk he'd found perched on a low pine branch. A leather hood covered its eyes.

Like the hawk, the woman had been wounded— and when John made up his mind to save a life, he seldom failed.

Emily stared up at the steeply sloped ceiling, her eyes blurred with tears. Why had her golden Apollo left her? Over and over, the question swirled within her, demanding an answer. She played and replayed their last days together. There had been no angry words, neither had he acted bored with her. Nothing had changed. She frowned. No, that wasn't exactly true.

Plucking with her fingers at the edge of the wool blanket covering her, small things, things she hadn't thought important, came flooding back—things like finding him staring out at the rolling plains with tears in his eyes, or the faraway look that seemed to overtake him at odd moments. Even the way he'd taken to touching her during the day—as if he couldn't get enough—had made her wonder at the thoughts in his head. Then, at other times, he'd seemed to withdraw from her.

Pulling the material up to her chin, Emily shivered, feeling chilled as she began to see what had been there all along but she'd been too blinded by love to acknowledge—no, she'd been too afraid to see what she saw so clearly now.

During the last few weeks, something had changed in her warrior—something below the surface. She'd sensed a growing sadness in him. He'd been distracted, and had at times seemed so distant. At night, when he'd take her in his arms and love her, she'd put aside her worries; yet even then, she acknowledged, he'd been different—almost reckless in his passion. Only now, as she looked back, did she recognize the desperation in his touches, and in the way he'd held her. It had been especially noticeable last night.

Then, from the time she'd set up their bed, he'd held her. Loved her. Then held her some more. And in the throes of passion, he'd even murmured, "I love you," in English. It was as if the words had been torn from his throat, which had shocked and pleased her beyond measure. She'd assumed he learned them from her, as she said them to him often enough, but her body had been too aroused and on fire for his touch for her to question him.

Closing her eyes against the pain, she felt tears squeeze free and run down the sides of her face. "Why?" she said in a sob. "Why did you leave me? If you love me, why did you leave?" Her voice hitched as tears clogged her throat. Turning, she buried her face in her arms, feeling lost and alone as never before.

She had no idea how long she lay there before she heard footsteps returning. Throughout the day her rescuer had come in to check on her, brought her food and drink. All of which she refused. She felt his presence, and knew he was standing there, trying to decide whether to disturb her or not.

"I brought you more food."

The deep baritone voice sounded so gentle, so concerned, that it was hard to ignore. It wasn't this man's fault that she'd been betrayed yet again, or that she felt like she'd already died inside. He hadn't caused the grief welling inside her . . . yet the thought of eating made her dizzy with nausea.

"Not hungry," she said, her voice sounding scratchy.

"You need to eat." Again that voice drew her, tempted her to accept the help he so willingly offered.

Emily remained silent, hoping the man would just go away. She felt him sit down beside her.

"Miss, can you look at me?"

Shaking her head no, Emily didn't dare look at him. The gentleness she knew she'd find in his eyes drew her like a lifeline thrown to a drowning man. The last thing she wanted was to feel anything—period.

John spoke, drawing her from her ugly thoughts. "Listen, I know captive women are usually scorned, but surely this wasn't your fault. No one knows but me—and I won't tell anyone."

He thought she'd been a captive? Emily laughed, the sound harsh and hollow. She turned her head and looked at him. "I wasn't a captive."

The man cocked his head to the side and looked puzzled. He clearly didn't believe her.

"No?"

"He saved my life." Defiance laced her words.

Her eyes itched and burned with the need to cry, but there were no tears left. At the question in his eyes, she said with a snarl, "He left me. Are you satisfied? He just dumped me there and left me to die."

Anger began to replace her shock at being abandoned. She felt used. Worthless. Her warrior had used her like Father Richard had wanted to use her. Except her golden Apollo had taken the gift of her love along with her body, and he'd tossed them both away as if they held no meaning to him.

"No." She groaned. She refused to accept that he, of all people, had been so cruel. She glanced out the door, surprised to see that it was late afternoon already. What if she was wrong? What if he'd just left her for the day? Maybe he planned to come back, and she'd misread his intentions that morning. Could he have already returned and found her gone? Guilt replaced her anger, and hope rose inside her. The thought spurred her to action.

She jumped to her feet. "Take me back to where you found me. He's coming back. I know he is." He had to. He couldn't have meant good-bye. Emily needed him desperately. He was all she had. She had to believe in him. For without that belief, she truly had nothing to live for.

The man stood, his eyes troubled. "I can't let you go out there alone. There's wolves and bears—not to mention other trappers and Indians."

Recalling the last time she'd been alone in the dark, and the terror of fending off the two wolves, Emily hesitated—but only for a moment. She'd risk it. She'd risk anything to go back, to have him return to her. "I have to go back. I have to be there in case he returns." Picking up her carved wooden box, she walked out the door. Her new protector followed.

"Look, miss . . ."

"Emily." Realizing that for the first time in months she was conversing, carrying on a two-way conversation, Emily faltered. How many times had she longed for someone to talk to, and for someone to talk back? Another spasm of guilt shook her. Outside, she put everything from her mind except returning to the spot where her golden warrior had left her. But as she stared around her, nothing looked familiar. She didn't know where to go. Behind her the man—what had he said his name was? John Cartier?—sighed.

"Fine. I'll take you after I finish my chores." He pointed to a stool. "Why don't you sit and eat? It won't take me long."

Thirsty, she accepted a cup of coffee from him but turned down the food he offered. Her stomach felt tied in knots. Sipping the warm, bitter brew, she felt an unexpected bit of pleasure. It had been a long time since she'd had coffee, and only now did she realize how much she'd missed it.

Cartier pulled on thick, leather gloves, then took several large hunks of raw meat from a tin just outside the door. He strode toward the tree a short distance from the shack. Curious despite herself, Emily followed and watched him stop in front of it. To her surprise, there on the lowest branch sat a hawk with a leather hood covering its eyes.

He murmured something. The bird flapped its wings in response. The man's laugh filled the air. "Smell your supper, do you?" He untied the leather strip that tethered the bird to the perch, then held his gloved hand out to touch the bird gently on the breast. It stepped onto his gloved finger. Using his thumb to hold the hawk's feet in place, John removed the small leather hood. The bird ruffled its feathers, shook its head, then let out a loud screech. As if happy, it threw back its head and flapped its wings.

Cartier laughed and held the bird out from him. "That's it. You're getting stronger. A few more days of rest should do it." After letting the hawk exercise its wings some more, he put the bird back on the branch and tethered one leg, but left the hood off. He impaled several chunks of meat on nailheads driven into the branch, then filled a tin of water that had been fastened to the other end of the perch.

Something in Emily responded to the way this gentle giant of man handled the bird. He wasn't her idea of a coarse, rough trapper. Though looking at him, she certainly didn't get the impression that he even knew the meaning of gentle.

For the first time since he'd brought her here, she really looked at John Cartier. He was as different from her warrior as a hawk from an eagle. He was tall, wide, and packed with solid muscle. But contrary to his size, he moved with a slow, easy grace that rivaled that of her Indian. It intrigued her.

Once the hawk had finished eating, John Cartier placed the hood back over the bird's head and removed his gloves. Emily stared at his hands: ham-sized hands that looked as though they were made for smashing faces. This man could easily crush that bird—or her—with one of those hands, yet he was gentle.

Moving her gaze upward, Emily noted that his hair, nearly black in the shade, looked browner in the sun. To her surprise, the light glittered off it in red highlights. Cartier wore it combed neatly and held in a long tail behind his head. She'd never seen hair comprised of so many different shades. Her warrior's hair had all been a soft black.

A shaft of pain hit when she thought of how his long, flowing hair had caressed her when he made love to her. She'd loved his hair.

Trying to put the painful memories aside, Emily focused on the biggest difference between the two men. John's face was covered with a full, dark beard. She couldn't tell what he looked like beneath it, but it didn't seem to matter. Of all his features, it was his gentle, direct, sherry-colored gaze that told her this man was one she could trust. His eyes mirrored the goodness she sensed within him.

John left the animal to go and grab a blanket from inside the shack, and her leather pouch of food. "You don't mind if we eat while we're waiting do you? Or if we share these berries you picked?"

Emily shrugged. "No."

"Good. 'Cause I love berries." He smiled; then his eyes roamed downward. Apparently overcome by a sudden discomfort, he gulped, then strode back into his cabin.

Emily glanced down and, seeing her nipples jutting out, pressing against her nearly sheer shift, she flushed. So accustomed she'd become to wearing little clothing she'd forgotten how threadbare her shift had become—not to mention all the places it had torn. Embarrassed, she crossed her arms across her chest, wishing she had something else to wear. She wasn't even sure where her skirt was.

Deciding to fetch the blanket she'd used earlier, she hesitated when John returned. He held out a buckskin shirt. "Here," he said, his voice deep and rough. "It's big but clean. You'll swim in it, but it'll keep you warm."

And covered. The words hung between them. Red in the face, Emily turned around and pulled the garment over her head. The sleeves fell past her fingertips, and the hem nearly to her knees. She wanted to say something, to explain why she wore only a thin shift, but nothing came out but a faint "Thank you." She couldn't look at him.

His finger slid beneath her chin and tipped her gaze to his. "You're welcome. And, Emily, you're safe with me."

Staring into his deerlike brown eyes, Emily believed him. Never had she felt so safe—yet so vulnerable.

John turned away and whistled, startling her. To her surprise, she saw a wolf come running—on three legs. The animal went to John, and even from where she stood, she saw the devotion in the wolf's intelligent eyes.

Leading the way, John set off. "I want to be back before dark," he said, his voice gruff.

They reached the glade a short time later, and Emily got some answers—but she wasn't sure what they meant. As soon as she entered the quiet meadow, she'd ran to the spot where she and her Indian lover had spent the night. But, to her dismay, the furs, and the water pouch were gone. Only her skirt and the broken water skin remained to prove that this was the spot where John had found her.

Had her warrior come back? Had he never really left? She'd felt his presence, felt his eyes on her. Had he waited until she'd left to reclaim his possessions? Was he now gone forever? It seemed the only answer. Numb with the pain of rejection, Emily sank down and buried her head in her hands.

John leaned against the log, his rifle lying across his lap and Fang resting beside him. Emily sat a few feet away, unmoving. He'd tried to convince her to return for the night but she'd refused. Short of physically carrying her back, he could do nothing but wait with her.

He knew she was upset. He'd been unnerved to find the furs gone, himself. It meant the man she desperately sought had likely come back. Or someone else had come upon the items—but John would bet all his money it had been the same one who'd left her here. The question was, why? This was one of his favorite places to go, and he usually strolled through here each morning. Had the Indian known that John would find her? Had he wanted to return her to a white man? John didn't know, and he didn't voice his thoughts aloud. Emily was far too upset as it was.

He shifted, uneasy. He didn't like sitting out in the open, exposed and vulnerable. The decaying log, though large, offered little protection in the event of an attack. He grimaced. Any attack from her captor would come silent and swift. His rifle wouldn't offer him much advantage against arrows shot from the shadows of the trees.

Though he didn't believe the savage who'd left her would return for her, John tried to stay aware of his surroundings, yet found himself distracted by Emily. She sat, her back against the log, knees drawn up to her chest, palms resting on her opposite forearms. She looked so lost, so forlorn, he'd have done anything to ease her pain and put a smile on her face.

She hadn't spoken a word, just stared straight ahead. Looking at her, one would almost think she was just soaking up the late-afternoon sun, but for her white-knuckled fingers and the white spots on each arm from gripping herself so tightly. He suspected she'd have bruises on her arms from her own death grip.

He wished he knew what had happened to her. Maybe then he could help put things to rights. First, though, he had to gain her trust. Picking up her bulging leather bag, he drew out a handful of berries.

"Food?" he asked, holding the pouch out to her.

No response. "Emily?"

She shook her head, her body so tense he feared she was near breaking. His gaze took in her profile. Her blue eyes were glassy with suppressed tears, her lips were chapped and bleeding from her constant gnawing on them, and her skin was too pale and drawn. Long strands of blond hair draped over her shoulder, followed the curve of her slender neck, then fell straight down to rest on the inside curve of her breast.

Though he couldn't see them through his shirt, not even the outline, he knew her breasts were there, that the tips were a pale pink, and that they'd more than fill his hands. He tore his gaze away to stare at his hands. Big hands. *Damn.* He shook himself mentally and tried hard to get the seductive image of her standing in the sun, wearing a nearly see-through shift, out of his mind.

It was impossible. Not much had been hidden from him. Only the texture of her skin, the feel of it on his, had been left to his imagination. He tried again not to think of her as an attractive and very desirable woman, then stifled a groan. He was only a man—a man who'd lived far too long in a male-dominated world. He couldn't even remember the last time he'd bedded a woman.

The girl sat close enough that he could see the dusting of freckles on her face, feel the heat radiating from her body, and smell the scent of woman—yet they were separated by a barrier much harder to cross than distance. His body was fraught with frustrated need.

He had to keep telling himself that she wasn't his, over and over.

The fact that she was the woman of his dreams, his fanciful Lady Dawn, the woman he'd created in his mind to give him something to look forward to once he left and returned to civilization, didn't help. How could he ignore her beauty? A single tear slipped down her smooth cheek. A flyaway strand of silvery hair stuck to her face, near the corner of her mouth.

John itched to reach over and gently brush her hair back, but he didn't, fearing she'd shatter like a sheet of glass if he so much as touched her. Her pain tore through him like a gunshot. He rubbed a place on his shin, recalling his first winter out here, when he and his cousin had been learning to shoot.

Willy had been horsing around, not realizing the shotgun was loaded. The gun had gone off and the pellets had passed through the fleshy part of John's leg. Though only a flesh wound, it had hurt like hell.

Minutes ticked by. The shadows lengthened as the sun began its descent in the sky. Keeping his voice low and calm, he spoke. "Emily, we have to return."

"You go. I'm staying here." Her flat, emotionless voice scared him more than her earlier sobs.

"I can't leave you here by yourself." When she didn't respond, he knew he had only one choice, for he didn't want to take her against her will. Clearing a spot close by, he scraped out a fire pit and gathered dried grass and small twigs. Then he collected large pieces of fallen trees and started a fire. Sitting across from her in the dark, he watched orange-red flames begin to dance, their heated color reflected in her eyes.

All through the night, John kept the fire going. It was warm enough that they didn't need more blankets than the one she sat upon—which was good, because he refused to leave her alone even for the time it would take him to go fetch them. Instead, he talked. He told her stories of his time as a trapper. He even tried to sing—anything to get a reaction from her. Fang howled in protest, but the woman continued to stare off into the night.

By the time the moon had risen fully, and the stars popped out across the sky, John couldn't think of anything else to say. He wrapped the blanket around her shoulders. Then he watched. There was nothing else he could do. She refused food. Refused water. Refused even to lie down. At last, giving in to her desire to be alone, he moved over to lean against the log next to her.

Somewhere in those bleak, early hours, she slumped against the log in uneasy slumber. Looking over, he wasn't able to leave her in such an uncomfortable position. He meant to lay her down on her blanket, but as he moved to reposition her, she cuddled close to him. Doing so, she seemed to relax and fall into a deeper, more restful sleep. Unable to resist, he drew her close, brushed the silvery strands of hair from her face, and reveled in her smooth skin.

At last, he finally dozed off himself.

Emily dreamed. Her warrior had returned. She saw herself running through the meadow to greet him. As if she were swimming in a bog, her body movements were slow, a struggle. She had to hurry, had to reach him before he disappeared again. She couldn't let him leave her.

Yet the closer she got, the farther away he appeared. She heard his heart beating, felt each breath he took. Felt his arms encircling her even though he seemed so far away. *Come back*, she called. *Come back!* He faded, yet his heartbeat remained loud, pounding against her ear. Frowning, she wrinkled her brows. Hot breath feathered across her forehead.

A soft snort startled her. Caught in that curious place between waking and dreaming, she wrinkled her brows. The heartbeat was real, she realized—as was the warm breath. She smiled and snuggled closer. He'd come back. He was here, holding her. She slid her arms around him. Something didn't feel right. He seemed so big. So much larger around the chest. He moved. Something rough scraped against the top of her head.

Her eyes snapped open. Fright held her immobile. The man she clung to wasn't her warrior. She tipped her head back and let out a shocked cry when she realized that she lay cuddled next to John Cartier.

The sound woke him. For a moment he looked as confused as she felt. Then he grinned, a silly, sleepy expression.

"Mornin', Lady Dawn," he said, reaching out to brush the hair from her face.

In a stupor, she stared at him. "What . . . How?" She glanced around, then calmed as she realized they'd spent the night in the glade. Then the truth hit. Her Indian warrior hadn't come back. There was no denying the truth now: he'd left her behind. *No!* She refused to accept that. Something had happened to him. He'd left her before but always returned.

He came back and took the furs, she reminded herself.

Why hadn't he come for her? He could have found her. She knew he could have, had he wanted to.

Beside her, John shifted, putting space between them as he stretched, then stood. "I don't know about you, but I could eat a horse. Shall we go back and fix something to break our fast?"

Emily shook her head. She didn't want food. She wanted the man she loved back in her arms.

Impatience lined John's voice. "Emily, he isn't coming back. For whatever reason, he left you here. You have to snap out of it."

The trapper's lack of sympathy angered her. He didn't understand. She glared at him. "Why?" she shot back.

"I can't stay here all day. I have chores to do."

"I'm not stopping you." She resumed her position of the night before. She'd missed her Indian's return yesterday by leaving. Today she'd stay. Maybe he'd been afraid to come and get her while she was in the clutches of this white man.

John raked his fingers through his hair. "Dammit! I'm not leaving you. You're coming back with me."

Emily mentally dug in her heels. "I don't *have* to do anything, John. I know you're just trying to be nice, and I appreciate it, but I'd rather be alone." The unexpected flare of rebellion caught her by surprise. Seldom had she ever argued or refused what was asked of her. She'd always tried to please.

But look where it had gotten her.

"You ask too much, Emily. I won't leave you out here alone."

"Why not? Everyone else has." She hated to sound ungrateful; this man seemed decent and kind. But then, so had her Indian lover. He'd been tender and sweet and . . . then he'd done the worst thing he could do: he'd abandoned her, thrown her love in her face. Like everyone else.

"This is crazy, Emily. Do you want to die? Is that what this is about, and what your refusal to eat is about?" The young trapper's frustrated voice boomed across the glade.

Shrugging, Emily let her gaze dart around her, searching the wall of thick tree trunks, but she knew no one was there. Before, she'd felt her lover's presence. She felt nothing now. Nothing except an overwhelming sorrow. "What's so great about living? There's obviously something wrong with me that makes everyone just leave." She laughed bitterly at the disbelief John wore. "Even my mother was willing to abandon me."

Why had she said that? It had been the first time she'd even allowed that thought to materialize. But it was true: her mother hadn't leaped from the wagon, hadn't tried to stop Timothy Ambrose from riding away to their awful fate. Now that it was out, Emily couldn't stop the flow of bitter words. The anger she'd harbored sought release.

"Oh, yes, she allowed my father to abandon me in the wilderness with no food or weapons. She went with him knowing full well that I'd die out here." Emily tried to keep the rage from her voice, but the anguish of being abandoned by the family she'd loved and given so much of herself to threatened to choke her.

John bent down. His voice was sad but warm. "I don't know what happened to you, Emily, or why, but there's nothing *wrong* with you. They are fools, every last one of them."

Staring up into his intense gaze, Emily felt her heart leap. She wanted to believe him, wanted to let him make her world right again, but she couldn't allow herself to trust him—or anyone else—ever again. There was something about her, in her, that others were unable to love. She suspected that John, like her warrior and Father Richard, wanted only one thing from her: her body. And she'd never allow another man to use her that way again.

When strong arms scooped her up, she started, then shrieked, "Put me down."

"When we get back."

"I'm not going with you."

His arms tightened about her. "Yes, you are."

All the emotions she'd held at bay—the anger, the hatred, the resentment, the misery, and the grief of losing yet another loved one—exploded in Emily. She lashed out with her fists, catching her captor square in the nose.

Startled by her attack, the trapper yelped and loosened his hold on her. She slid out of his arms. "Dammit, woman, what are you trying to do?" he cried.

She whirled on him. "Leave me alone! Do you hear me? I won't go with you!"

John shoved fingers through his hair. "I said you were safe."

"No, I'm not. You're nice now, like *him*. Then I'll get used to it and you'll leave, too."

"What the hell are you talking about?" The trapper approached.

Emily bent and picked up a rock and threw it at him to force him to keep his distance. He ducked as it flew past his shoulder. "You're all the same," she shouted. "My father hated me. He left me to die, and so did the man who told me he loved me. He saved me, took my love, then abandoned me!" Overcome, she sent another rock hurtling through the air. Then another.

The trapper ducked them, and watched warily.

"I hate you. I hate *him*. I hate everyone." Backing up, throwing everything she could lift, Emily ranted and raved, unable to stop the flood of angry words. The dam had burst. She'd had sixteen years of misery that had culminated in her parents' deaths, then she'd been abandoned by a man who'd claimed he loved her. How could she trust anyone ever again?

"Yes. Everyone I've ever loved has left me. Even my mother! *Even my mother*," she screeched, hating the woman who'd betrayed her most of all. She blamed her mother for being weak, for not standing up to her father, for not protecting her child from his hatred, and maybe for marrying him and putting them both through this hell.

The trapper jumped forward and grabbed her. She kicked, scratched, and fought against him, but he easily caught her hands and pulled her into his arms. "I won't leave you, Emily. Not ever. I'm here for you. I'll take care of you. I'll take you back to civilization—wherever you want to go." He ran his hands through her hair, smoothing the wild tangle from her face. "You have to believe me."

Emily laughed, a hollow sound. "Why? *Why* should I believe you when I couldn't count on my own mother? I couldn't even trust a priest." Her voice rose. "He tried to rape me, then told my father it was my fault. That's why my father left me. Then I trusted that Indian. I shouldn't have, but I did. He saved my life. I *loved* him—and I know he loved me. I thought I could trust him. He was gentle and kind, like you're trying to be. But in the end, it didn't matter. He left me out here to die just like everyone else. So tell me, John—why should I trust you?"

The man looked stunned by her hysterical revelations. She pulled out of his arms and tore off the buckskin shirt he'd loaned her, revealing her scantily clad body to him. "Is *this* why I should trust you? Because you want my body? Will you save me and protect me if I give you what I gave to *him?*"

"Emily—" The man's voice was choked.

Glaring at him through her tears, she stuck out her chin, then pulled her shift over her head in one violent motion. "If this is what you want, you don't have to be nice to me. You don't have to pretend to like me or love me." She drew in a deep breath, hating herself.

111

Hating him for making her do this. Hating the way his gaze roamed her naked body.

"If this is what you want, you can have it. Payment for taking care of me. Payment for taking me back to the mission. It doesn't matter. Nothing matters. Just don't pretend to feel things you don't. To feel things you can't."

She was unlovable, and her whole young life had only been an instruction on why.

Speechless, John stared at her. He couldn't help but gaze upon her body. Nor could he stop it from responding to what she offered—no, what she demanded he take. Yes, he wanted her, but not for the reasons she tossed at him with far greater brutality than the rocks. Her accusations hit him square in the heart and angered him. What kind of man did she think he was?

The kind of man who would use her and hurt her and toss her aside like those others did.

But he wasn't that kind of man.

Yet how could she know that? He didn't blame her for her hurtful words. She'd been deeply hurt, and by so many people. Her mother . . .

Gulping past the lump in the back of his throat and stifling the desire hardening between his legs, John even figured she had good reason to believe the worst of him. Staring into her eyes, he saw a hidden hunger deep inside, a child within who desperately wanted to believe—a child who desperately *needed* to believe—that there was still good in the world.

It was that child's yearnings that reached out like thread to bind his soul to hers as if they were joined by the flesh. In that instant, Emily became a part of him.

Drawing on every ounce of willpower he possessed, John picked up his shirt, vowing to teach this young beauty to trust him. Her mouth fell open when he slid his best buckskin shirt back over her head and shoved her arms through the sleeves. As he drew the hem down past her bare buttocks, his fingers skimmed her hips.

Damn!

He struggled to hide his reaction—he didn't want her to know that he wanted her—but staring down into her tear-bright blue eyes, he suddenly realized she needed absolute honesty from him.

He placed his hands on her shoulders, his fingers kneading the taut muscles there. "Yes. I want you, Emily. You have a body that only a saint could ignore. And I'm no saint. But that doesn't mean I can't control myself, or that I don't have my own brand of honor." His gaze hardened. "I won't barter my services for your body."

"I gave my body to a savage." She spoke the words harshly, defiantly, standing her ground as if that would make her repulsive to him. As if that would send him running. Well, it was time for her to learn a thing or two.

He cocked a brow at her. "You also said you loved him." While he was shocked by the truth, it did not repel him. Love was something difficult to ignore. Impossible, maybe.

Her eyes turned sad. "It didn't matter to him—to any of them." She drew back. "So what do you want of me?"

Ah, good question, he thought, thinking of his dream, of his Lady Dawn, of his desire firmly banked, of his need to hold her close and ease her pain. He needed to protect her, and he wanted to see her smile. He wanted everything she could give him. But for now, that wasn't possible. Maybe it never would be.

"How about friendship? I want to be your friend." Gently, he tucked her hair behind her ears.

"For how long?" she scoffed. "Until I let you share my bed? Why pretend? Why not just skip all that stuff and get what you really want?" Despite her challenging words, something in her eyes flickered. A small light. A tiny ray of hope.

Vowing to see it grow into a steady flame, John understood her need to lash out. He needed to calm her. But he also knew he couldn't be dishonest in the slightest. "Most men would take you up on your offer, Emily, but I'm not most men. I'm not saying I don't find you attractive, because I do. I've dreamed of you for a long time." He halted at her snort of disbelief, then shook her gently. "I haven't done anything to hurt you, Emily."

Her face crumpled, all fight draining from her. "Not yet," she whispered weakly, falling to her knees. "Not yet."

With his eyes growing moist with tears at the pain this woman had suffered, John gathered their belongings, then bent down and scooped her unresisting form into his arms. He swore that he'd give her the one thing she needed more than anything—a friend.

114

Chapter Six

Two days later, Emily gave in to the truth once and for all: her warrior wasn't coming back. She'd been deluding herself by pretending that he'd only left for the day and had somehow gotten delayed, but that time was over. She'd been silly too long.

She laughed bitterly. She hadn't fooled anyone, least of all herself. Like everyone else she'd ever loved, her Indian, too, had abandoned her. And no amount of wishing on her part would bring him back or ease the pain of his rejection.

From outside the cabin she heard the rhythmic thuds of an ax slicing through wood. Each blow echoed painfully behind her eyes. Deep inside, her heart felt as though it, too, was being split into thousands of splinters. Rubbing her forehead with her fingers to ease the dull throbbing, Emily tried to stop thinking of her Indian lover. She had to forget him. Forget what they'd shared. It was over. Past. She hadn't even known him. Not truly. But she *had* known his touch, his kindness, his . . .

Staring out the windows, she watched the treetops bend and sway beneath the strong wind. Birds flew and hopped from branch to branch, and dull, dry leaves swirled in circles, carried in through the window by whimsical gusts of wind.

The breezes through the shack relieved some of the stuffiness and cooled her. The day had been unbearably hot and the air felt good. A low whine brought her head around. Fang stood in the doorway, watching. Holding her breath, Emily willed the animal to go away. Though John repeatedly assured her the beast was friendly as a dog, she wasn't so trusting.

The wolf wagged his tail and ran toward her. Emily opened her mouth to call John who, so far, had kept the animal away from her. But when Fang plopped down close by and stared at her with his tongue lolling, she froze, unable to believe that an animal so capable of violence could be so friendly. Surely if she moved wrong, he'd attack. But the wolf's eyes remained a soft, gentle brown, and he bent his head and nuzzled her hand.

Slowly, Emily ran her fingers through his fur, amazed as he allowed her to stroke his thick neck. When he plopped down on his side, exposing his belly for a rubbing, Emily smiled. She'd never had a pet and, because her father hadn't allowed her to go visit friends or girls her age, she'd never been around

116

smaller animals. Only horses. And those were only to care for, never to ride for pleasure.

After a few minutes, Fang snuggled up close, rubbing his cold nose against her neck. He gave her a swift, gentle lick, then rose and walked to the door. He hesitated and looked at her as if urging her to come outside.

When she made no move to get up he left, leaving Emily feeling lost and alone. She'd enjoyed the animal. Somehow his presence had soothed and relaxed her. But he wasn't hers. When she returned to the mission, she'd leave him behind. Along with the past months, the happiest and freest time she'd ever known.

Reminded that her life was in shambles, that she had nothing—not even the comforting presence of a beloved pet to call her own—Emily rolled over and rested her chin on her fisted hands. She was alone. Just her against a world that seemed too frightening to face. So what now? Where did she go from here?

Home.

She laughed, low and bitter. She had no home. No family.

Not true. You have a father.

Right. A father who'd turned his back on her mother.

What if he'd never known?

Frowning, Emily thought about her mother. Had she told the man, Matthew Sommers, her real father, about her? Did the man know he had a daughter? If he hadn't known about her, would he welcome her into his

117

arms? Would she finally find a place where she belonged?

Realizing that her thoughts were taking her onto another path of false hope, Emily squashed the thoughts. More likely her father had taken off when her mother got in the family way. Emily's presence would be an unpleasant reminder, especially if he was married with children of his own—legitimate children who would not be a blight on his reputation.

Fear of another rejection warned her not to find this man. Why should she go to him? Just because he'd sired her didn't make him a father. Hugging herself, Emily didn't know what to do. She had nowhere else to go and had no money to support herself.

She had nothing. A glance at her shift, which she'd put back on because it was cooler than John Cartier's buckskin, made her spirits sink even further. She didn't even own a decent dress. Closing her eyes, she sought relief in numbing sleep. But days of slumbering and lying abed left her wide-awake and her body protesting its inactivity. She felt restless and on edge. Maybe a short walk along the river, or even a bath, would help clear her foggy mind.

She sat up and grabbed John's shirt—to make herself more decent. Staring at the garment, the same one he'd covered her with that day in the meadow, brought forth waves of humiliation, a sudden rush of heat mingled with a buzz of horror that swept through her from the inside out, from her toes to the top of her head. It wasn't just despondency that kept her hidden in the cabin.

Emily fell back onto the bedding with a muffled groan and buried her head in the shirt she clutched as she remembered how she'd revealed herself to him, and how she'd offered him the use of her body. How could she face him again? Why had she acted in such a shameful manner?

Oh, she knew. She'd done it to shock him. She hadn't wanted him to be so nice, believing it better to know the worst he had to offer so she wouldn't get sucked in by his overwhelming kindness. She hadn't believed his gentleness genuine, hadn't believed him to be honorable. She'd fully expected him to have taken her up on her offer and proved her right. And if he had taken her up on it; she'd have let him use her body.

She hadn't cared.

Then.

Surprisingly, she did now. She still had a hard time believing that her shameful behavior hadn't changed John's attitude toward her. He continued to treat her as gently as before. Yet she couldn't keep from being embarrassed—and ashamed.

Fingering the fringe of his shirt, she tried to figure the young man out. He'd wanted her. She'd seen it, recognized the hunger in his eyes; but after the initial moment of shock, he'd dressed her in his shirt as if she'd been a wayward child. Then he'd carried her back to the shack and tucked her in—again with the same tenderness one might show a frightened youth. All while the look in his eyes, the desire he hadn't been able to hide, told her he wanted what she brazenly offered.

119

She laughed, a harsh sound of derision. Her father had been right. She was a wanton. A whore. She'd given herself to one man, a savage. Then, a day later, she'd offered her body to another. She wasn't any better than her grandmother, who gave her body in exchange for money.

But in spite of everything, John's refusal had relieved her—and that relief scared her. She didn't want to like him. Danger lay along this path, like a snake curled up waiting for unsuspecting prey. If she pursued it, it would surely lead her right back down the same road to torment and pain. For that reason she stayed away from him, in the shack. Alone.

As if her thoughts had called him to her, John Cartier appeared in the doorway with a tin of water in his hand. Unable to help herself, she glanced over at him. Sweat soaked his shirt, and his hair was damp with his exertions. He looked tired. His eyes were shadowed, dark with worry. For her? Pangs of guilt seeped through her.

"It's a beautiful day out here. Some sun might make you feel better." He forced cheer into his voice as he brought her the water and set it down beside her.

Their gazes met and held. His dropped briefly to his shirt in her hands; then he glanced away, a dull flush creeping up his neck. Emily flushed as well and turned her head. Normally whenever he came in to check on her or to bring her water or food, they both avoided eye contact, as if trying to pretend that the scene in the glade had never happened. But it had.

Emily couldn't forget the desire that had shot into his eyes—or that one moment when time had stood still and some wicked part of her mind had wanted him to take her into his arms. Had wanted to find comfort with this man in the pleasure two bodies could find in each other.

"What do you say? Won't you come on out for a bit?"

John's deep voice vibrated through her. She shivered and hugged his shirt tightly to her. "I'm fine here," she said. She averted her eyes when his shoulders slumped ever so slightly.

The more she stared at him, the more she wanted to get up and erase the worry from his features. Annoyed with herself for caring, she stared down at the shirt. Was she so weak a woman that she'd just repeat her mistakes? Let herself get drawn in, come to care for another man who would just hurt her? She couldn't risk it.

"Can I get you anything then?"

Without looking at him, she shook her head. "Don't worry, John. I'm not going to die." That much was obvious, especially as John refused to let her. He plied her with food, broth, tiny chunks of meat, water, coffee. That day they'd returned from the glade, he'd told her clearly that he'd force the food and water down her throat if he needed to.

She'd believed him, sensed his determination not to let her waste away. So she ate, but only enough to sustain herself and ease his worry. She closed her eyes, unable to bear the tender regard he gave her. She didn't want him to be gentle or kind. Better for him to be mean and self-centered. That way she wouldn't lose another piece of herself. For she was coming to like this man—it was hard not to like some-one as gentle and kind as he—and she knew how dangerous that was. Like the wolf who adored him, Emily felt the beginnings of trust. And that she had to avoid at all cost.

"Emily." His soft voice drew her gaze once more.

John Cartier hesitated, his expression soft and sad. Then he shook his head. "Never mind."

He turned to leave, but not before Emily saw a long-ing in his eyes he couldn't mask. Yet he hadn't been staring at her body. His searching gaze hadn't been filled with lust. It had been filled with something more. Something different from lust. It was the same emotion that she'd thought she recognized in the eyes of her warrior.

Love?

John was falling in love with her? Or at least he thought he was. She supposed she shouldn't be so surprised; she'd seen the change in his eyes, heard it in his voice, and had felt it in his touch over the last two days. She had tried to convince herself it was just concern on his part, but the truth was now there for her to see. Clearer every day.

Now what? She couldn't allow him to fall in love with her. Or to *think* he had, she reminded herself. He didn't know her. He was just lonely and she was here, available. But that wasn't enough. That would only cause him pain—or her, if she let it. They both needed to realize that love was fickle. It turned on you like a cherished pet, biting the hand that once stroked and fed it.

So what was she going to do? She was stuck out here, in a wild and unpredictable land. She needed him. Was forced to rely on him. Which meant there was only one thing for her to do.

Jumping to her feet, she ran after him. "Wait!"

He turned back to her, his eyes lighting up when he saw that she stood in the doorway, his shirt clutched to her breasts. Emily kept her voice neutral. "You said you'd take me anywhere I wanted to go."

He stared at her for a long moment. "I did." His voice sounded heavy.

She picked at the fringe on the buckskin shirt she held. "Take me back to Lake Superior, to the mission where my family was staying. There's someone there, a friend who can help me find . . . my family."

A chill swept over her. The mission was the last place she ever wanted to see again, but she had to find Millicente, had to talk to her and see if the woman might be willing to travel east with her. The sooner she returned, the sooner she'd get some answers and be free to get on with her life. Whatever life there was for her.

The trapper ran a hand over his suddenly taut jaw. "If that's what you want."

"It is," she said softly. "When can we leave?" Emily didn't want to hurt him, but she knew it would be kinder to leave him sooner rather than later. And now that she'd made up her mind on a plan, she wanted to leave. The earlier the better. Staying would just risk breaking his heart. Or hers, she admitted in a sudden rush of odd sensations. She had a feeling this gentle, kind, and tender man would prove easy to love. She shook herself.

Cartier stared at the wall of trees to his right. "When my grandfather and cousin return." Without another word, he left to return to his pile of split logs.

Emily moved back inside their shack, leaning against the wall, feeling hollow. She'd hurt him. He'd shown her kindness and courtesy. He'd been gentle and patient. It didn't seem fair to repay him this way.

Yet she couldn't give him what he wanted, couldn't be the woman his eyes said he needed. Nor could she just give him her body. She'd made the right decision. So why did she feel sad at the thought of leaving?

Sighing, Emily ran her hands through her tangled hair. First things first. A bath. Then she'd fix their evening meal. It was the least she could do. She returned to the doorway and peered out. John stood with his back to the shack. He'd removed his shirt as he resumed his woodchopping.

The ax swung high and fell repeatedly. Sweat coated the man's skin, his legs were spread apart, and with each movement of lifting the short-handled ax over his head and pulling it down to splinter a log, muscles rippled across his back.

The rhythmic thud of metal crunching into wood resounded through the trees. Over and over the heavy blows echoed. Bits of bark and chunks of wood flew through the air. Stopping for a moment, unaware of his audience, John wiped the sweat from his brow with a red handkerchief. Stuffing the material back into the waistband of his breeches, he swung the ax up.

Go bathe, Emily ordered herself. But her feet refused to move—especially when he resumed his work. His male form held her spellbound. As before, she noted he was much taller and wider than her Indian lover, but every bit as honed. Not a bit of spare flesh graced his immense frame.

His shoulders, toasted to a deep golden brown by the sun, were enormous and tapered to a narrow, gleaming waist. His upper arms bulged with each movement, and though he wore buckskin breeches the shade of a newborn fawn, they were snug enough to reveal the firmness of his buttocks and the power of his thighs.

He was every bit as appealing to look upon as her Apollo had been. Not as smooth in the face, true, but handsome enough to make any woman look twice. And he seemed a true gentleman. A man of honor. The type of man she'd once dreamed of marrying: her handsome prince who would come and take her away.

The wish chilled her. It was too late for that. Yet she could indulge herself and watch for a minute more. . . . One blow aimed at splitting the log down the middle missed. The ax stuck in the wood. After freeing the blade, John straightened, his back still to her.

Emily closed her eyes. Why was she so drawn to this man? It wasn't just his body. His spirit seemed to soothe her and call out to her. She remembered his promise to be her friend. She'd never had a friend—not really—and she longed to be able to call this man that. But she sensed that it would be too dangerous, emotionally, to them both.

Besides, her time spent with the savage should have taught her that men wanted only one thing: a willing body. Once they had that, they lost interest in the woman herself. Hadn't that been why her warrior had left? She leaned against the door frame. The thuds of the ax tearing into wood resumed, a backdrop for her troubled thoughts. She had no doubt that if she accepted the friendship John offered, he'd soon want more. And she might want to give it. And then, when he had all he wanted from her, he too would disappear.

It hurt even to imagine it. Better now than—

A harsh cry tore through the air.

Startled, Emily opened her eyes and her gaze found John. The man stood, doubled over, his hands wrapped around his thigh. Red blood oozed between his fingers. Without stopping to think, Emily dropped the shirt she held and ran toward him.

"John!"

By the time she reached him, the amount of blood dripping through his fingers was already staggering. The sight of all that gore made her dizzy. He staggered as he tried to keep his feet. Instinct took over. Emily eased him down and grabbed a piece of toweling fluttering in the breeze along a nearby clothesline.

"Sit!" she commanded. She and her mother had treated many emergencies at the mission—everything from arrow and gunshot wounds to birthing and illnesses. Folding the toweling, she pressed it tightly over the gash that was midway up his thigh.

Spotting a knife dangling from the belt John wore around his waist, Emily took it from its leather sheath. Her fingers shook as she cut away his pant leg several inches higher than his profusely bleeding wound. Carefully, she pulled the buckskin off his leg. Removing the bandage, she gasped at the deep gash running along the outer edge of his thigh. Its severity took her breath away, and she pressed the cloth back to try to stop the bleeding.

The cloth didn't work. Panicking, she knew she had to work fast. She ripped a wide swath from her shift and folded it into a thick square. Her heart pounded as she removed the bloodied towel and pressed the new pad to the wound. John groaned and fell back. One glance at his white face sent her heart down to her toes. "Don't you die on me, John. You hear me? *Don't you die!*"

He tried to lift his head. "Told you I wouldn't leave you." He groaned.

Terrified that he'd do just that, Emily grabbed the hem of her shift and ripped another wide strip, which she folded into a thick square. She removed the now-soaked pad. The gash was nearly five inches long, and deep, and still bleeding steadily. Pressing the square of her shift to his wound, Emily took John's red handkerchief and bound it around his leg.

Standing, she stared down at him. There was one more way she knew to stop the bleeding. The thought of it left her queasy, but she had no choice. Working quickly, she went to the fire pit and stoked the embers, feeding small chunks of wood into the flames until they grew. Then, taking John's knife, she placed it in the coals to heat. She returned to John and put her weight on his wound to help stem the flow of blood. She called his name while she did so.

He groaned, his head rolling to the side.

"I have to sear the wound. It's going to hurt," she told him. Tears laced her voice. She hoped he would pass out; that would be the best—for both of them.

"Do it," he rasped.

"Oh, God. I don't want to hurt you." She started to leave his side to check on the knife. He called her back.

"Emily—tie me down. Don't . . . don't want to hurt you."

"What?" Then she recalled one time she'd assisted her mother with the same procedure. It had taken four strong men to hold down the injured man while her mother had pressed the hot knife to his skin.

Emily found a length of rope. Moving fast, she bound one end of it to his hands and wrapped it around a tree. Using the bloodied ax, she cut the rope and tied his feet the same way. "Whiskey—do you have any?"

"In the shack. Brown bottle."

Emily returned, then gave him some.

He coughed and lay back down. "Just do it, Emily. No time to get me drunk." He attempted a weak smile but his eyes were dark, nearly black with pain, and his face was white, drained of blood.

"All right." Using more of her shift, uncaring that the length now barely covered her buttocks, she folded it and placed it between John's teeth, then returned to the fire. Grabbing his red-hot blade, she knelt beside him and took a deep breath as she loosened the knot of the bandage and pulled it away.

"Give me strength," she prayed, tears blinding her. She glanced once more at John. In his eyes, mingled with the pain, she saw something that surprised her: faith. Confidence in her.

She hoped it wasn't misplaced. Taking the bottle of spirits, she splashed some of the whiskey over his wound. He hissed in pain, his feet and hands jerking against the ropes. Drawing another deep breath, she murmured, "Forgive me," then placed the flat side of the searing knife against the bleeding wound.

John screamed, though the sound was muffled. He jerked against the rope. His low, harsh moan tore an answering sound from her. This was her fault. He'd been distracted—tired, maybe—because of her. If he died, she'd never forgive herself.

Then he went blessedly still. The acrid scent of burned flesh and hair rose. Nausea welled inside Emily, and bile rose to the back of her throat, but to her relief, John had only passed out. Working quickly, she turned the knife over before it cooled and repeated the process. It took twice more of heating the knife to completely seal the wound and stop the bleeding.

At last she was finished, and she sat back, wiping the sweat from her brow and the tears from her eyes. She studied his wound: puckered, blistered, and raw. But she was thankful the bleeding had ceased, except for a bit of oozing from one end. Running back to the shack on rubbery legs, she searched for decent bandage material and found none. Removing her locket and then her shift, she took her garment and tore the rest of its thin material into strips.

Donning his shirt, she fetched from the nearby stream a pot of water, and put it on to boil over the dancing flames. Using a strip of her shift, she washed the blood from John's leg and his hands after untying him. He still hadn't come to. Sitting back on her heels, feeling exhausted, she glanced around. A poultice next. Then tea to help keep the fever at bay.

Working in a daze of fear, Emily bandaged the trapper's wound, put a rolled blanket beneath his head, then covered him with another. She glanced over her shoulder at the shack, unsure how she was going to move him inside. There was no way she was going to be able to drag him.

Sighing, she stood. She needed herbs.

Fiery pain dragged John through the darkness. His leg throbbed with every beat of his heart. He groaned, fighting the agony. Cool fingers slid across his forehead. He opened his eyes, blinked against the bright rays of the afternoon sun, and gazed into Sunshine herself.

Emily sat beside him, leaning over him, her wide blue eyes filled with worry and fear. It all came back to him in a rush: the ax glancing off the knot, slipping from his fingers, and slicing into his thigh. The rest was hazy—except for Emily. She'd been there, talking to him, telling him not to die. He smiled weakly. "Tol' you I wouldn't die."

Her smile wobbled and she brushed a hank of hair from his eyes. "You're not out of the woods yet, Johnny."

130

He grimaced and licked dry lips. "No one but my ma has called me that since I was a boy." No one had dared, especially as he'd been head and shoulders taller than most boys his age. And his mother had called him Johnny only on rare occasions. From Lady Dawn, it sounded heavenly.

She tried to smile. "Right now you look as helpless as a boy." She sobered, her lips trembling, her eyes dull with worry. "I'm so sorry. This is my fault. If I hadn't been so wrapped up in my own needs—"

He reached up with shaky fingers to still her words. He didn't want to see more pain in those beautiful eyes. He wanted to see them lit with laughter—and love. Yet he knew that was asking for the moon and the stars. Still, somehow he felt as though he'd loved her forever, as if she'd been a part of him that he hadn't known existed.

"Not your fault, Lady Dawn. I was careless." He gasped with pain when he tried to turn toward her.

"Because of me." Using a cool cloth, she patted his face.

"Doesn't matter." He closed his eyes, his lips pinched. He felt her move away. She returned and slid a hand into his hair. "Here, lift your head, John."

He did. She put a cup to his lips.

"Drink."

He did, then gasped at the bitter brew. He tried to pull away but she wouldn't release him.

"More. Please."

"No. What the hell is that?" It tasted as vile as the concoctions his mother had used when he ailed.

"It's for the fever. And the pain. Please, Johnny?"

131

Susan Edwards

He groaned, but not from pain. How could he refuse this woman anything? He took another wary sip,
relieved when she seemed satisfied. "That is the worst
stuff I've ever tasted," he complained.

Seeing her tremulous smile, John knew he'd drink
the whole damn cup just to see it again.

"Can you stand if I help you?" she asked. "We need
to get you inside, and I'm afraid I can't do it alone."

John lifted himself up onto his elbow. The movement made the throbbing in his leg worse, but he gritted his teeth. From his other side, he heard a low
whine. Fang nosed him. Reaching over, he scratched
the wolf behind the ears. "You be good, boy."

Sitting, he stopped to breathe heavily, fighting
waves of pain. He caught sight of his hawk in the tree
and groaned. "The hawk. Have to feed him."

Emily took hold of his arm. "I'll deal with it. Come
on."

He glanced at her, noted the determined set of her
jaw as she prepared to help lift him. "Lady Dawn,
you're a little bitty thing. You're not going to be able
to help get me inside." It amused yet pleased him that
she'd even think she could.

She lifted a brow. "I'm stronger than I look. Now
come on. I want you inside before it gets dark. And
before you pass out on me again."

The fact that she'd just about tossed his own words
back at him made them both smile. To his surprise,
she *was* stronger than she looked, and he knew that
without her to lean on, he'd never have gotten to his
feet.

132

"Careful. Don't put any weight on that leg. Just drag it behind you. I don't want your wound to open back up." She looked him in the eyes. "I don't think I could go through that again."

Smiling weakly, he agreed. "Neither do I."

With her help, he hopped the short distance to the shack. The pain nearly blinded him. Once inside, she left him leaning dizzily against the doorway while she moved his bedding closer. With a groan of relief, he fell onto it.

"Can I get you anything?" She looked anxious as she stared down at him.

"No." His eyes drooped. He fought to keep them open, focused on her. But the pain was consuming him, dragging him into a world of gray. He struggled to hold on to consciousness.

"Okay, I need to make more tea for you." She hesitated, clearly afraid to leave him.

Her image continued to blur. He wanted to tell her that he had all he needed in her presence, but it seemed too hard to talk.

"I'll be right outside." Slowly she went out the door, her gaze lingering on him; then she was gone.

The irony of the situation wasn't lost on John. How had their situation completely reversed itself? But unlike her wanting to die, he wanted to live. This woman had entered his life, chasing away the shadows, bringing sunshine into his world. Sunshine. Emily with her pale hair and warmth. Lady Dawn. "Sunshine." The name tumbled from his lips as darkness descended, dragging him back beneath a blanket of pain.

* * *

133

Susan Edwards

Swift Foot sat in the tribal lodge surrounded by his ailing uncle, the shaman, and the rest of the elders. The rest of the tribe's warriors were seated to one side, watching and listening. He'd just finish telling all of his walk across the *maka,* including his time with the white girl.

Silence weighed heavily as Wind Dancer, their shaman, consulted with the rest of the elders. Everyone waited as Swift Foot's fate was decided. He didn't have long to wonder.

Wind Dancer lifted both hands over his head in a gesture of victory. "Our son has proven his worth. The Great Spirit sent him a difficult test. Our son took up the challenge. He has pleased the spirits this day. He has proven his worth. *Wakan Tanka* was wise when he sent Swift Foot away."

Wind Dancer turned to Swift Foot's uncle. "The council has decided not to make your brother's son wait until his marriage to Small Bird. He will assume his new role of chief starting with this day, and join with Small Bird as soon as her tribe arrives."

His uncle, Charging Bull, beamed, his old, leathery face crinkled with pleasure. "This is good news, for I grow old and weary." His voice ended in a cough.

Talk around Swift Foot turned to the feast that would be held that night to celebrate his return.

He'd passed. Tonight he would officially become chief. It was what he wanted, what he sought. Then why did he feel so sad? He should be celebrating his achievement, but he felt only a cold emptiness inside—as though he'd died, instead of having been given the greatest honor a warrior could achieve.

134

He glanced up into Wind Dancer's knowing gaze. The shaman, though not as old as most of the men present, hunkered down beside him. He spoke low.

"It cost you much to leave this woman, son."

It wasn't a question. Swift Foot could not lie, nor could he prevent himself from touching his sacred medicine bundle, which held a lock of her hair and a piece of her skirt. Two pieces of rabbit fur—from one of the pelts she'd tanned—encircled both arms. "It was the will of *Wakan Tanka* that I return alone. I will find a way to restore peace. I have taken the first step." A very painful one.

The wise shaman nodded. "You will be rewarded." Seeing the lingering, unspoken hope in Swift Foot's eyes, he added, "Not with the white woman. She is not to be your mate. Yet your time with that woman was meant to be. While she is now of your past, she has changed your future."

"What do you mean?" He knew Emily had changed his future: she'd taken away his ability ever to love again.

The wise man smiled. "It is not for me to reveal, my son. I can only offer you hope. Your heart will find love with another, and your spirit will find peace as well. I have seen it."

Swift Foot watched Wind Dancer move away. For once, his heart held doubt. He didn't think he'd ever know true peace, not the kind he'd had for those wonderful weeks with the white woman named Emily.

Chapter Seven

Time lost all meaning for Emily. Her days and nights were filled with caring for John. Despite her efforts with teas and poultices, fever racked his body, chills rattled his teeth, and delirium haunted his sleep. His wound turned red and puffy, the flesh shiny and taut, forcing her to open the skin several times to drain it. She drew on all her knowledge to fight for his life.

Out in the wilderness with her Indian warrior, she'd watched him use a funny plant that looked like a puff-ball to stop the bleeding on a cut to her foot. Hopeful after squeezing out the pus from John's wound, she went in search of that plant, then used it to help stop the bleeding.

From her time at the various missions where there were no doctors, she and her mother had become quite learned in herbs. She found the root of wild four-o'clocks, which she boiled. It aided in reducing his fever. Boiled willow bark made a pain reliever. The inner bark of sweet elder, along with chamomile and sweet clover, was mixed with bear fat and placed over the wound too. And when it seemed that nothing worked, Emily had prayed, begged, and even ordered God to heal him.

Between caring for John, gathering the herbs she needed for his teas, and obtaining greens and berries for food for herself, she also saw to the feeding of his hawk, suffering only one nasty bite from the bird. But when she ran out of raw meat for the hawk's meals, she had to make a decision.

Testing the bird's ability to flap its wings, she finally untethered and released it. To her relief, it had flown high into the tree, then soared off, fully healthy and one less thing for her to worry over.

On the fourth night, John's fever spiked. She'd removed his shirt as soon as the fever had set in, and took up her seat beside him. Wringing out a square of toweling, she ran the damp cloth over his face, down his throat and neck, over broad shoulders, across his chest, and down over the heated flesh of his legs, desperately trying to cool him.

When he thrashed and tried to get up, she used all her weight pressed down on his chest to hold him, and her voice to soothe him. In between such spells, she forced spoonfuls of willow bark tea down his throat and kept his wound clean.

Just before dawn of the fifth day, Emily thought perhaps John's skin felt slightly cooler. A slight sheen of sweat dotted his skin. Drawing a blanket over him, she

137

closed her eyes. She was so tired. Without conscious thought, she slid down beside him, wanting to be near in case his fever returned.

A low moan woke her. Disoriented, she shot upright, her gaze going to John as he fought the blankets twisted around him. "Shh," she cooed, "it's all right, Johnny. It's all right." She used that ridiculous name for him—he was definitely no Johnny with his incredible bulk—but the nickname seemed to please him as much as it did her. He calmed.

The first time she'd uttered the name, she'd almost laughed, close to hysterics as she was. He was the least Johnnyish-looking man she'd ever seen. But somehow the name also fit. It was the tender, gentle side of him. She also remembered his telling her that only his mother had used the name. Hopeful that that was good, she whispered it in his ear whenever he grew restless. It helped calm him, as if his mother truly sat at his side. Yet Emily didn't feel the least bit maternal toward him. Not anymore.

She had tried to put thoughts of his very masculine body from her mind, but it was hard to ignore the firm skin when she ran a cloth over him. Nor could she quite ignore that other part of him. When she'd first undressed him, cutting his breeches carefully down the seams so she could wash and keep him cool, she'd figured that she'd seen *it* before, and *it* wouldn't be a big deal.

She groaned mentally at her naivete. It *had* been a big deal. A very impressive *big deal*, which had prompted her to keep a towel over him to hide that impossibly large part of him. They weren't lovers; she was just the only one around to care for him. It shouldn't affect her. Like being a nurse or doctor, he should have just been a body she tended.

Wrong. His was a very male body, one she couldn't help but appreciate.

Without warning, John tried to get up. Moving quickly, she pressed down on him, leaning all her weight against his shoulders to keep him on his back. She raised her voice when her gentle murmurs had no effect. "John, be still. You'll open the wound." Twice he'd thrashed to the point of causing fresh bleeding, which she'd managed to stop only with pressure.

The man's eyes shot open, his gaze wild one minute, and full of wonder and hope the next. "Lady Dawn. You're here." His voice sounded weak and raspy.

Emily frowned. For some reason, he kept calling her Lady Dawn. Or Sunshine. She didn't know why he called her those names, but she found she liked it. His voice was always soft and so tender, as though the terms were endearments. Now that's silly, she scolded herself. It must be the fever. That thought scared her, as it meant he was still delusional. But rather than correct him or remind him who she was, she smoothed the wet cloth over his face, lingering on his brow. "Yes, Johnny, I'm here," she cooed. He was sweating in earnest now. A very good sign. "Rest, John. Rest." She turned to get a cup of water for him to drink.

"No! Don't go." His arms came around her, pulling her over him. "Stay, Sunshine. Stay. I need to feel you."

Lying chest-to-chest, her knees straddling him, conscious of both his wounded thigh and that other part of him that didn't seem to be covered anymore, she stared into his glazed eyes. "John—"

"Stay," he muttered thickly, his hand sliding beneath the curtain of her hair to caress her neck and pull her closer.

Emily didn't struggle. His mouth brushed hers softly. Then his lips slanted over hers, warm with the end of his fever, yet soft with need. She couldn't resist the tender exploration of his lips upon hers. It was a kiss unlike any she'd ever experienced, as if the fever in him had spread to her. She moaned, and, without warning, the kiss caught fire, leaving her mouth burning with hunger.

She knew she should stop him, had to stop him, but the intimate contact turned the pit of her stomach into a fluttering mass, and that part of her intimately touching him became a wild swirl. Her lips moved with his, willing and eager for all he offered.

Shocked at her wanton response, she was helpless to stop her madness. He was sick with fever. He didn't know what he was doing. But by God, she did. She wanted his kiss.

His arms caressed her back and slid down. The hem of her borrowed shirt had risen, leaving her buttocks bare. Her under clothes had long since disappeared—cast off by her warrior. John's big hands, palms roughened by years of hard labor, cupped and squeezed her gently. She moaned and moved against his hands, wanting him to ease the ache between her legs. When his fingers slid toward her heated core, she held her breath, her body anticipating the release to come, the bright lights, the stars that would seem to burst around her.

She tossed her head back, her open eyes finding a roof over her head instead of an open sky dotted with twinkling lights or the bright glare of the sun. As if doused by icy water, Emily froze. What was she thinking? This wasn't her warrior. She wasn't back out on the plains. She was in a shack with John Cartier—a man who'd been near death and couldn't know what he was doing or with whom. She was about to make love to a stranger, not her warrior. This was not the man she'd given herself to at first because her body seemed the only thing she could offer in return for his kindness, then later because she fell in love with him. This was someone else. Again, she heard her father's scorn: *Satan's daughter. Daughter of the devil. No-good whore.*

She cried out. How could she feel desire for another so quickly? Her father was right. She was no better than the whore he'd accused her of being. She'd enjoyed the pleasures of the flesh and now she couldn't fight that pull. Or could she?

"No, John, stop." She pushed away.

He looked confused at her abrupt end to their kiss. His fingers trailed through her hair and stroked along the line of her jaw. "Sunshine," he murmured, his eyelids growing heavy. "Stay. Don't leave."

Unwilling to upset him while he was still feverish, Emily allowed him to pull her down beside him, his arm around her, her head on his shoulder. His breathing grew slower and deeper, and finally he

141

slept, a much calmer sleep. Against her cheek, his skin felt cool. But her body still felt on fire just as waves of shame chilled her heart.

She buried her head beneath John's chin. She'd thought herself in love before. Now she wasn't sure. How could she have loved her Indian warrior, spent long nights wrapped in his arms, reveling in the way her body sang for his then respond to John like this? Would her body react to every male this way?

Waves of memory swamped her: the first time she'd given her body to her golden Apollo, his patience, his gentleness as he taught her to respond to his caresses, the way he'd shown her how to touch him. Feeling John Cartier's hard, long length pressed to hers, she yearned to run her hands over his body, feel his big, rough hands cupping her and easing the restless ache between her legs. The need coursing through her was frightening. It was wrong. She couldn't feel for John what she'd felt for another, not this soon. She pressed her fingers to her lips to keep from crying out. Maybe the price of her sins was never to know love. Maybe her father had been right.

But no matter how hard she tried to forget the kiss she'd shared with John, or convince herself that it meant nothing, it kept her wide awake. She'd felt something new, different. The summer with her warrior had been filled with lots of touching and loving—more ways than she'd have ever thought possible—but he'd seldom kissed her on the mouth.

And the few times he had, it hadn't been anything like John's kiss. She hadn't thought anything of it, figuring that Indians didn't kiss, or people in general. She knew so little about acts of love; she'd never even been allowed alone with a boy. Now she had to wonder. Why hadn't her warrior kissed her like this? And why had John's kiss evoked such a reaction from her?

Just before she fell asleep, she prayed that John wouldn't remember the kiss, or her own wanton response. More than anything she wanted a friend. The friend he'd promised to be. She had been foolish to risk that on the whim of his body.

The glare of the sun woke John. For a few minutes he lay still, trying to get his bearings. Warm breath on his shoulder made him turn his head. Emily lay in his arms, sleeping. She looked pale, the skin beneath her eyes translucent. Slowly, a memory came back to him: the accident with the ax, and the agony of her burning his flesh. Everything else was hazy except for her voice and her touch. He remembered hearing her voice dragging him back from the darkness. He also remembered pain. Lots of it. He frowned. There was something else. He glanced down at Emily. Her lips were softly parted.

A kiss. Had he dreamed that kiss? It had seemed so real. He shifted, then bit back a groan. The movement brought her awake. She stared up at him with eyes as blue as the early morning sky peeping in through the unshuttered window. "Morning, Sunshine."

She shifted her head to look out the window. "It's late!" She struggled to sit.

He let her go. She wore one of his flannel shirts, which hid her curves, but it didn't matter; the fact that it was his only drew him more, especially with her hair

143

falling over her shoulders in wild disarray. She looked dreamy, as he imagined she'd look after a night of making love.

That thought stirred another part of him, and he glanced down, horrified. He was completely naked, the blanket twisted around his legs. He groaned.

Emily looked over at him with concern. "What's wrong? Do you hurt?" She glanced at his thigh, then turned crimson. "Oh."

Sitting despite the pain, he grabbed the blanket, feeling as embarrassed as she was as he covered himself. Tongue-tied, he didn't know what to say. It was just morning hardness, he tried to tell himself. But he knew it was more than that—not that he'd tell her!

"I, uh, need to get up." He looked pointedly out the door.

"Wait here." Luckily, she seemed to know that he needed breeches.

But when she returned, she had one of his cooking pots. She set it beside him. He shot her a look of disbelief. "I'm not . . . I'll go out—"

Her stern look stopped him. With hands on her hips, Emily stared down her nose at him. "I've seen you naked for four days, John Cartier. Five if you count today. I've bathed your body and taken care of *all* your needs while you fought the fever. Emptying a pot of piss is a lot easier than washing you because you couldn't even use one."

He fell back with a humiliated moan and covered his face with his hands. He was somewhat shocked by her bluntness, but he supposed it was better than her being shy with him. "Four days? I've been out four days?" It seemed like yesterday. No wonder he was buck naked. The thought of her seeing to his bodily needs embarrassed him further. There was only one of his needs he'd wanted her to ease, and it was out of the question.

She gave him another pointed look. "You're not getting up yet. You'll tear that gash open if you do. And John?" She waited until he took his hands from his face and looked at her. "I never want to have to cauterize a wound again." Her voice wobbled. "It was horrible."

Tired just from the short bit of exertion, John gave in. "All right. You win. But I have to get up soon. We need food. And the hawk—" He broke off, horrified at the thought that the bird had been neglected. It'd be almost dead if what she said was true. *Four days!* He'd had enough raw meat left for only one day. "And Fang? Where is Fang?" While the wolf could do some hunting on his own, being on three legs left him at a disadvantage when it came to running down larger game. John always shared his meat with the animal.

Emily tapped her bare foot on the hard dirt floor. "John Cartier! I should smack you with that pan. Do you think I'm completely worthless and lazy? Thanks to my father, I've lived on the edge or beyond with little or no comforts. My mother and I learned to survive on very little, making do with what nature provided."

"But the hunting—"

"I may not have great aim, but I can use a shotgun to defend myself or hunt. And I can set a trap and skin and cook my meal. Lots of trappers came through the

145

mission. I learned to do what it takes to survive." Bitterness edged with anger and resentment turned her voice harsh.

John groaned. "I didn't mean to insult you, Emily." He held up his hands. "Was just worried."

"Well you needn't be. The hawk is fine. I released it. And Fang is fine. He's outside. Now use the pot—think of it as a chamber pot and me as your maid." Turning on her heel, she walked out the door.

John stared after her. Maid? He thought not. She reminded him of the dour housekeeper who'd run his father's household with an iron fist. He grinned. But Emily was not dour. She was beautiful. Sweet. And . . . *bossy.* He laughed. The change in her was nothing short of miraculous. She'd gone from not caring whether she lived or died to taking charge of everything. There was no doubt in his mind that she'd saved his life. When he realized nature was demanding immediate attention, he used the pan, then covered himself and lay back, exhausted, feeling weak as Fang had been when he'd first found the pup barely alive.

All that day and the next, Emily refused to let him up. Truthfully, he wasn't sure he could stand, and was somewhat relieved that he wouldn't have to embarrass himself by falling flat on his face.

Still, he was bored. And hungry. She'd cooked a pot of beans, but he wanted meat—hot, juicy, and tender meat, smoked over the fire. They'd run out of just about everything else.

That thought reminded him that his grandfather and Willy were long overdue. How would the old man react to Emily's presence? And his cousin? John frowned. Willy was notorious for bedding any willing woman. Or even unwilling ones, if he believed some of the stories. He found himself hoping that Willy had remained behind in St. Louis.

Sighing, he lifted himself up onto his elbows and tried to move his leg. Fire shot up his thigh. Still, he tried to move. Sweat broke out on his forehead.

"What do you think you're doing?" Emily said as she stormed in.

"I'm tired of sitting here," he said, wincing at his whining tone. He fell back, fighting the nausea as the throbbing pain in his leg increased.

Her features softened. "You have to give it time, John."

With his hands beneath his head, he stared up at her, trying not to stare at her shapely bare legs. "Stay with me, then. Talk to me."

She flushed. "I'm not sure that's a good idea."

The hazy memory of a kiss came back to him. He wondered if it had been real. Dare he ask? "Tell me, did I dream of that kiss?"

The color across her cheeks darkened. She glanced away. "No."

He lifted a brow. If he recalled right, it had been a very passionate, very satisfying kiss that had left him hungering for more. He grinned. "I'm glad."

"John, we . . . can't." She worried her lower lip.

"Don't worry, Emily. I'm not looking for what you can't give."

She sighed. "That's the problem."

147

Confused, he motioned for her to sit. She did, a respectable distance from him. "Want to explain that?"

"I already gave it to you—in that glade where you found me."

He swallowed. He'd never forget how she'd defiantly bared herself to him, telling him to take what he wanted. Oh, how he remembered. "I didn't accept, though."

"Not yet." She wouldn't look at him. "I gave myself to a man I thought I loved. Then, days later, I'm kissing you, and it felt . . . I felt things I shouldn't. What if I didn't love him, but only thought I did because he saved my life? Now I'm here with you, and . . ."

"And you want me, too?" Secretly it pleased him that she wanted him, but it also bothered him that she might only be reacting to their circumstances. He wanted her, but not out of gratitude.

"You saved my life."

"So you think it's the same. Gratitude." Trying to keep things light between them, John winked. "Well, if that's the way it works, then that means I have to give myself to you. You saved my life, Emily."

Her mouth fell open, then closed. She looked uncomfortable—and nervous. He took pity on her. In truth he felt as though he did belong to her, had since the first moment he'd seen her, but he didn't want to add to her confusion. Emily was special: he wanted her love but knew it was way too early for that. Too much had happened in so short a time.

"Come here, Sunshine." He patted the space next to him.

148

"I don't think that's wise. And why do you call me Sunshine? Or Lady Dawn?"

He smiled. "I found you in the dawn. You took away the darkness and are a bright ray of sunlight in my life." He didn't dare go into more detail, such as how he'd dreamed of her, fantasized over finding his Lady Dawn.

She rolled her eyes.

"I'll stop if you want."

She laughed uncertainly. "No. There's no harm, I guess." She looked embarrassed.

"Ah, you like it. Just a little," he added when she looked as though she'd protest. The thought that it secretly pleased her warmed him.

"Well, maybe. Never had anyone call me by anything but my given name."

John smiled. "Then I'm glad to be the first. Trust me, Emily," he said, holding out his hand.

Slowly she moved over next to him. He took her hand. "Let's start over. I told you that I wanted to be your friend." He held up his hand when she looked as though she was going to question him.

"Yes, I want to be your lover—and more. But for now, let's work on being friends. Where it goes from there, we'll just wait and see." He only hoped he could stick to his own suggestion. It wasn't going to be easy, especially if she continued to nervously lick her lips like that. He grimaced inwardly. Of course, the way he felt right now, she didn't have much to worry about; he was too weak and in too much pain even to think of making love to her.

149

"I guess we could try." She gave him a tentative smile. "I've never had any friends."

He smiled and held out his hand to shake hers. "John Cartier—sort of at your service."

She grinned back. "Emily Ambrose." Her smile faded. "Rather, Sommers, I guess—though I can't really claim the name."

Seeing the light dim in her eyes, he was suddenly wild to know what she meant. "Tell me."

She stared at him. "Tell you what?"

"Why you looked sad and angry at the same time. Tell me who you are."

Emily woke to lengthening shadows. Staring up at the ceiling, noting the cobwebs in the corners and fine particles of dust swimming in a single beam of late-afternoon light, she wondered what it was about John that had made her tell him things she'd never told another soul.

Fingering the locket around her neck, she recalled how she'd opened up to him. In her desire to ease his pain and give him something else to think about, she'd told him everything: her childhood, the hours spent praying on her knees, the beatings that were supposed to make her humble before God. She shared with him her yearnings for a father's love, and her need for roots. How she'd hated the constant moves from city to city, church to church, moving farther and farther away from established cities to missionary outposts.

She'd shared her awe and terror the first time she'd seen a savage, and also what had made her family leave the last mission. How her father had felt too shamed to stay. She explained Father's Richard's actions, and how her father had disbelieved her. She'd told John, and felt his fury on her behalf.

But that had been nothing compared to his rage when he'd learned what her father had done in the wilderness. He'd been incensed that any man could leave a woman alone and unprotected in the wild. He'd pulled her into his arms when she cried, the pain of it still raw in her mind and heart.

He'd grown quiet when she told him how her warrior had saved her from wolves. The rest didn't need much telling. He knew, or could assume, the rest.

She and John had fallen asleep then—him weakened from his bout with fever, and her from the sleepless nights spent worrying about him as she bathed his skin.

Knowing it was time to get up and go find something to eat, Emily eased away from John's body. His arms tightened momentarily, then released her. He yawned as he came awake. "Looks like we slept the day away."

"I'll go—" The sound of Fang's deep growls and loud barking cut her off. The wolf never barked or growled—not like this! Scrambling to her feet, Emily grabbed the rifle from the tabletop. Behind her, John cursed and called her back. She ignored him and went to the doorway to glance out. The wolf was standing near the ring of trees around the shack, tail down, head lowered, fur standing on end.

"Emily, get back here. Give me the rifle!"

She continued to watch, aware that John was trying to stand. When she heard voices, she lifted the rifle, pointing it in the direction the wolf stared. When two figures came into view, she shouted, "Stop! Don't come any closer."

The pair stopped, mouths gaping open at the sight of her. One, a trapper nearly as tall and wide as John, stepped forward, then stopped when Emily trained the rifle on him. "Name is Ben. This here's my wife, Mary. We's lookin' for John."

Behind her, Emily felt large, warm hands settle on her shoulders heavily, as if John needed to lean on her just to remain upright. "It's okay, Emily. Ben's a friend." He reached around her and took the rifle from her shaking hands.

Over her head, John called off his wolf. Ben and Mary joined them. Each of the two newcomers led a mule and wore heavy packs on their backs.

Emily tried to hide her shock. From a distance, she'd never have guessed that the person with Ben was his wife. Mary, though shorter than her husband by a good foot, was still several inches taller than Emily. She wore a cotton shirt, buckskin breeches caked with mud, and moccasins. Her dark hair was cut short, and she wore a floppy hat on her head and a red kerchief around her neck.

Mary and Ben stared at her, too, just as speechless as she. Emily flushed, becoming acutely aware of just how little she wore—and what: John's shirt. And John . . . She glanced back and groaned. He was standing behind her with only a blanket wrapped haphazardly around his waist. To anyone looking at them, it would surely appear as though they'd just . . ." Heat and shame ran through her. "I'm sorry.... This isn't what it seems."

John's fingers tightened. "It's all right, Emily. Ben's a good friend. He'll understand."

"So will his wife, you big oaf," the woman added. She turned to Emily, her face open and friendly. "Pleased to meet you, Emily. It'll be nice to visit with another female out here—one who speaks English, anyway. Most of the women out here come from Indian tribes."

John leaned more weight on Emily. She tipped her chin up and smiled. "I'm pleased to meet you, too, Mary and Ben. But I need to get John back into bed." At the two pairs of startled eyes, Emily realized what she'd said. She threw her head back against John and groaned. His eyes twinkled down at her.

"What she means is, if I don't sit back down fast, I'm going to fall flat on my face."

For the first time, Mary seemed to notice his pallor and the sweat dripping down the sides of his face. "John, what have you done to yourself?"

"He tried to chop his leg off." The thought of John nearly dying still made Emily sick. She turned to lead him back to the bed.

Mary stepped to his other side. "Let me help. If this big oaf falls on you, you'll be squashed like a bug."

"I can get myself back to bed, both of you." John looked to Ben for support, obviously hating the weakness in his body.

His friend shook his head. "Don't think I want to have to pick you up when you collapse." His dark eyes sparkled with laughter as he moved both women out

153

of the way, then started John walking the few feet back to his pallet.

Mary snapped, "Men. Can't stand to appear weak, but that big lug looks like he's gonna pass out any minute."

Emily grinned at her as they watched. Ben, equal in size to John, perhaps a tad taller, wider, and heavier, brooked no argument from John, who was still insisting that he needed no help. He ushered the other man along like a naughty boy being led back to his bed.

As soon as John had stretched back out on his pallet and was decently covered, Mary rushed forward, insisting on seeing the wound. John protested. It did no good; she just shoved aside his hands. Emily earned herself a dark look when she pulled the blanket up past John's ankle, his knee, and over his thigh to reveal the wide bandage. Mary's capable hands unwrapped the cloth, and Emily winced at her sharp intake of breath.

"Holy mother of God, John." Ben's wife gently prodded the reddened flesh, ignoring John's muted groan of pain. "You did a good job, Emily. I've got some ointments and herbs we can use—we just stocked up in St. Louis." She turned her head. "Ben—" Her husband had already anticipated her needs and he handed her a rolled pack.

Emily worked alongside Mary, ignoring John's ill temper. In truth, she felt relieved to know she'd done things right and was grateful for the additional help and advice.

Mary finally stood. "Come with me to the river. I need a bath. We'll leave the men." It was an order.

John met Emily's gaze. They both knew Mary wanted to get her alone to talk. Emily didn't mind, though, and the thought of a bath sounded all too good. She'd been afraid to leave John alone unless absolutely necessary.

In the cool, refreshing water, they bathed in silence. After she dried, Emily put John's buckskin shirt back on. She frowned. As much as she loved the freedom of going about clad in his clothes, she needed to do something about obtaining some of her own.

"Mary, this is going to sound odd, but do you have an extra dress . . . or something?"

Mary's eyes widened. "I don't bother bringing dresses out here—pants and shirts work better to hide the fact that I'm a white woman. Indians usually don't bother us if they think we're just two men, and from a distance no one can tell."

"I see." Emily wrung her hair out.

Mary used her fingers to smooth her own short black hair. Already it was starting to curl around her head. "So . . . would I be considered rude if I were to ask you what a young white girl like you is doing out here, dressed only in John's shirt?"

Emily laughed, nervously. Yet she felt surprisingly fond of this blustery woman. "I have a feeling even if it was rude, you'd ask." Mary didn't respond. Taking a deep breath, Emily gave a brief version of the events that had led to her being here.

When she was finished, Mary stood. Apparently the explanation was enough. She said, "I don't mean to be disrespectful of the dead, Emily, but I can't feel sorry for your father. He sentenced you to death when

155

he left you! If you ask me, and even if you don't, that man got what he deserved."

Emily's eyes swam with tears. "But not my mother," she whispered.

Mary put her arms around her. "No. Not your mother. Wish I could say she should have been stronger, Emily. But she, too, was a victim of your father's fanaticism."

She turned toward the house, suddenly all business. "I've got some material—trade cloth and such for the natives. We'll whip up a dress for you. In the meantime, I can loan you something to wear."

That sounded great to Emily but for one thing. "Mary, I can't pay for the material. I don't have any money!" She ran to catch up with her new friend.

Mary rounded on her, her brownish green eyes fiery her expression indignant. "You saved John's life. That's enough."

Emily stopped the other woman. "Yeah, but it was because of me that he was careless." She still felt guilty about it.

"Nonsense. He's going to be all right now—that's what's important. Sometimes things just happen. There's no telling why."

Emily thought about that. Maybe Mary was right. But doubt still lingered in Emily's mind and heart.

Chapter Eight

Ben didn't waste any time once the women left. "Well? Spit it out. Where did that li'l beauty come from?"

Seeing Ben's bemused expression still trained on the door, and Mary and Emily walking away, John growled low in his throat. "Best remember you're married, *old man*." At the warning tone in his master's voice, Fang lifted his head and glanced from one man to the other. John motioned for the animal to be still and sent his friend a hard glare.

Ben, in his early thirties, had been one of the first trappers John had met when he'd first joined his grandfather out here. John hadn't known the first thing about surviving in the wilderness, he'd been as green and cocky as they came. But Ben had taken him in hand and, as a result, the two had formed a fast friendship. Like most trappers, Ben was single in those early days, and they'd all made the trip downriver together. John and Ben had shared more than one night of drinking and carousing. Two years ago, Ben had surprised them all when he'd returned from St. Louis with a wife.

Grinning, Ben just lifted his brows. "Married don't mean a man can't look or appreciate beauty when he sees it." His smile turned to a grimace. "Course, best if Mary don't know that!"

"Your wife would skin you alive," John agreed, pleased and relieved. Not that Ben actually posed a threat. Of course, it seemed he had given away more of his feelings than he'd planned.

Uncomfortable under his friend's speculative stare, John pulled himself up to sit, shifting his body so he could lean against the wall. "Women! Always fussing and carrying on." Though he had to admit all this moving around had started a painful throbbing in his thigh. Once settled, he turned back to Ben, hoping to distract the man so he wouldn't have to explain Emily's presence. "So what's new in St. Louis?"

"Oh, no, you don't. You're not sidesteppin' this one, pal." Ben settled on a stool and waited.

John sighed, then gave an account of how he'd found Emily. He still remembered his reaction when he'd seen her sleeping on the bed of furs: disbelief followed by wonder. She'd looked so young. So vulnerable. So beautiful.

Then, when she'd opened her eyes, the world had seemed to stand still. One glance into her eyes and he'd felt like a man drowning in those blue pools. In that instant, John knew this woman was something special. Why she was there, who she'd been with— none of that mattered. Only that she was there, a gift to be treasured.

He'd never believed in love at first sight. He'd figured Ben had exaggerated his first meeting with Mary. But he believed now. He could only hope that she'd allow him to court her and prove to her that he would never hurt her.

A shirt landing in his lap jerked John back to reality, and to Ben, who sat staring at him, his eyes wide, his jaw slack. "I don't believe you! You just *found* her? You know how incredible that sounds?"

John nodded. "Couldn't believe it myself." He closed his eyes. "I've dreamed of finding someone like her. Then one day I return home, and there she is. I felt like someone had left me a gift, you know?" His voice softened without his even being aware of it.

His friend let out a long whistle. "Fallen hard, haven't you?"

"Yeah. Guess I have." And he knew he had. How could he bear to take her back to society, knowing he'd never see her again? Yet how could he not? In the days since he'd found her, he'd discovered a hidden core of steel hidden beneath that fragile, lost-girl look Emily wore.

Yes, he was impressed by this woman. Aside from surviving the fate of her parents, having had the presence of mind to keep herself hidden from the attacking Indians, knowing not to run from the wolves, she'd kept her wits about her when he'd injured himself. Though her own life had been in shambles, she'd taken charge of his—and saved it.

159

He admitted, "She's incredible, Ben. I couldn't ask for more in a wife."

Smiling, his own eyes glazed with some fond memory, Ben sighed. "Yep, you got hit hard, pal. Just like me when I first saw Mary storming into that saloon— all piss and vinegar. Lord, was she a handful. And a vision."

John met Ben's amused and besotted glance. His friend's story was unique. Mary had thought Ben responsible for her brother's death, and she'd been prepared to take her revenge. Luckily for them both, Ben had convinced her that she had the wrong man.

John's friend gave him an interested look. "So you're gonna take her back to the mission. Then what?"

Heaving a big sigh, John ran his hands through his hair and grimaced. He needed a bath desperately. He felt grimy, and didn't like feeling that way around Emily. Maybe he would shave, too. "I don't know. Guess it's up to her. I'd like to court her properly. But can't do that unless I gain her trust. She's been hurt badly. And used."

Ben shook his bushy head. Worry shadowed his gray eyes. "She's not one of your many animals to be nursed back to health, you know."

John knew that only too well. True, he'd found her lost and alone, with a broken heart and an injured spirit. But unlike the wild animals he healed, then set free, he didn't want to let Emily go. Deep inside, he'd discovered a very primitive core: a part that urged him just to claim what was his.

And she *was* his. She was meant to be with him. "Can't explain it, Ben. I feel like I've known her all my life, like she's a part of me here." He thumped his chest.

Ben grinned, a silly, lopsided expression. "Same as when I met Mary. Wasn't no one else for me after I saw her. Even when I hauled her out of trouble and got nothing but a slap for my trouble. Had to have her." He rubbed his cheek as if remembering that first meeting.

Deciding now was a good time to change the subject, John asked, "Where are you and Mary off to? Going to your usual place?" He was glad Ben had arrived, and the help was a boon. But he wouldn't presume to ask him to stay any longer than Ben wanted; the man had his own living to see to. He needn't have worried.

The trapper snorted. "You'd like to get rid of me, now, wouldn't you, John? Well, think again, pal. Somehow I think we're gonna be staying right here for a while. Don't think I could drag Mary away. Besides, someone's got to hunt for you. You're not gonna be up and around anytime soon."

Relief washed through John. "Might be nice to have you around for a few days," he admitted. "Do some hunting and such. Then I'll be fine." He winced at Ben's booming bark of laughter.

"Haven't looked at yourself lately, have you? You look like hell, buddy. Mary and I are staying until your grandfather and cousin return. Don't think they're too far behind us."

John nodded. "They'll be home soon, then? I was starting to get worried. They've been gone much longer than usual."

161

"Well, your grandpa isn't lookin' so good, John. Got sick and was laid up in St. Louis, though he was doing better when we left. Between you an' me, John—the doc said he'd make it back but doesn't give him much more time. Mebbe another winter."

Sadness settled in John's heart. He loved the gruff old man. Months after his parents had died, his grandfather had arrived to take both him and Willy back to the wilderness. Gascon Cartier had sworn that the harsh life would make men of them both. There was little argument that it had not. The memory made John smile. His grandfather had no use for soft, pampered cityfolk.

Ben's next words brought him back from his thoughts. "Stubborn old fart." A tinge of sadness edged the trapper's laughter. "Tried to talk him into staying behind for the winter. Said I'd let you know what happened. Hell, even your cousin tried to get him to stay in St. Louis. Still, you know the old man. Says he don't want to die in some fancy boardinghouse. Wants to go out here, to be buried beneath the land he walked."

Silence fell for a few moments as they both thought of the formidable man whom no one dared defy. Gascon Cartier, born into a wealthy family, had left that rich life behind for the adventure of living in the wilderness. A man more fitted to this wild land didn't exist.

Thinking of the savage beauty of the land around the cabin, John understood. He, too, loved it out here. And yet . . . "We'll be leaving next year. I—"

Ben nodded. "It's a lonely life."

He'd hit the nail on the head. Staring over Ben's shoulder out the window at the trees beyond the cabin, John felt torn. Unbidden came the thought that with Emily at his side, he wouldn't be lonely. What would it be like to share all this with her?

"The old man is proud of you. Spoke a lot about you when I saw him."

"Bet Willy loved that."

Ben shrugged, a look of distaste coming over the man's features that said he didn't much care what Willy did or did not love. "Don't much care for your cousin. Shifty. Self-centered. Out drinking and carousing every night, leaving your grandpa alone—and Gascon being sick and all! That boy hasn't earned his grandpa's respect, nor mine. Why should he get it?"

"He's stuck it out here, same as me."

Ben rolled his eyes. His fingers plucked at his beard. "Only 'cause if he left, he'd have to make his own way. Boy's too lazy to get honest work elsewhere and knows Gascon won't just pay his way."

John sighed. "I know." It was the truth, but he still felt guilty for having all his grandpa's respect—and for the fact that Gascon had left everything to him. Yet he knew whatever was given to Willy would quickly be gone in a binge of gambling, drink, and women. Then his cousin would come around looking for more. It seemed a horrible conundrum.

It was time for him to stop feeling sorry for his cousin. Life dealt a lot of men a raw deal. That didn't stop them from going out and supporting themselves. The inheritance was settled. John just wished there weren't such bad feelings between his cousin and his grandfather. Much of it came from his grandfather. Gascon Cartier had never forgiven Willy's father for running off with his daughter, then failing to provide for her. She'd died as a result. Yet as tragic and sad as that was, it hadn't been Willy's fault. Yes, John's grandfather was in part to blame for Willy's bitterness. John wished Gascon, before he died, could find it in his heart to accept his other grandson—but that wasn't any more likely to happen than the Big Muddy suddenly flowing backward.

Ben cleared his throat. "What do you think Willy's gonna do when he sees Emily?"

John frowned. He'd deliberately refused to think of his cousin and Emily. Or at least he'd tried hard not to. But he knew Willy well enough to know his cousin would consider her fair game. Hell, just knowing that John had seen her first, had spent time alone with her, had fallen in love with her, would make his cousin want to take her from him. "I'll deal with that when the time comes." His voice hardened. No way would he allow Willy to use Emily as a pawn in his bitter need to prove himself.

Swiping a hand over his bearded jaw, Ben looked thoughtful. "He's gonna make a play for her. Unless you stake your claim on her."

John cocked a brow at that. "*Even if* I stake my claim on her. But the truth is, I don't have any claim to her. She's free to choose any man she wants." The thought made him feel ill. In his heart and mind, she belonged to him. But he couldn't push her. Wouldn't push her. She'd gone through too much. He needed her to choose him. To love him as much as he loved her.

And for that, he needed her to trust him. To believe in him.

"Reckon you're right. And bettin' man that I am, I reckon she's smart enough to see through that cousin of yours. You're by far the better man."

John laughed without humor as he recalled what she'd gone through with her father, the priest, and the Indian warrior who'd saved her life. "That, my friend, is my biggest problem. I'm a man." Which thought left a dark, depressing cloud over him. Before he could win her, Emily had a lot to overcome.

John felt a wave of exhaustion overtake him. After a few more minutes of talk in which he had to fight to keep from yawning, his friend got up to see about setting up camp, and left John to doze against the cabin's log wall.

Drifting in and out of sleep and occasionally hearing laughter in the background, John dreamed of Emily—with him, the two of them together, hand in hand, running through the meadow. Her blue eyes were filled with love, and her hair streamed out behind them. The scene slowed as they fell down onto the soft cushion of grass, his body beneath hers as he wrapped her in his arms. Her laughter floated on the breeze and her fingers tangled in his hair as her body arched and begged for his.

"Sunshine," he whispered in his sleep.

He woke feeling refreshed. The sun had passed overhead, and, judging from its position, he knew it was late afternoon. The air blowing through the shack teased him with the aroma of cooking meat, confirming that Ben had gone hunting.

With his belly rumbling, John struggled to sit up straight. Outside, he heard three voices: Ben's deep, booming bass, and the soft chatter of the two women. Wanting to join them, he glared at his thigh and his blanket-covered lower body. He needed proper clothing first.

As if she knew he'd woken, Emily stepped inside. John stopped his struggle to scoot across the dirt floor. The laughter in her eyes warmed him. No, it *thrilled* him to see her look so happy. It was the first time he'd seen her so relaxed. Her eyes sparkled, her face glowed, and her mouth curved softly in a smile, making her even more beautiful than before.

"Hand me my breeches," he asked.

Emily tipped her head to the side. "Why?"

He glared at her. "I'm coming out." He wasn't going to stay in here a moment longer—not when they were all outside having fun!

As if she knew she'd lose this battle, Emily went outside and returned with a lopsided pair of breeches. She blushed. "I washed them and mostly sewed them back up. I had to cut them off you."

John ignored his body's reaction to the knowledge that she'd seen him naked, that she'd taken care of his needs. That thought still embarrassed him. He frowned at the missing portion of the pant leg.

"I'll sew that piece back on after you heal and we don't need to change your bandage so often." She hesitated, her cheeks rosy with color. "Do you need . . . I mean, should I send Ben in to help you—"

"I think I can manage, Emily," he interrupted softly. Actually, he wasn't sure how—but somehow he would. It was one thing to know she'd taken care of him like a babe while he'd been unconscious. If she tried to help him now, he wasn't sure he'd be able to stop himself from reacting to her closeness.

Nodding, she left. "I'll ask Ben help you outside, though."

John rolled his eyes. He didn't want Ben to help him walk. Did she think he was still some helpless kitten?

Twenty minutes later, he was thankful for his friend's assistance—though a bit disgusted that he was still so weak. A trip into the trees quashed any idea of taking a bath, too; he was far too tired from this walk. Still, the prospect of a hearty meal with meat cheered him, as it did Fang, who lay happily gnawing on a bone. Over a meal during which they all sat outside on a blanket, John dug in, feeling as though he hadn't eaten in weeks.

After the meal, with the cool night air easing the heat of the day, he, along with Emily, Ben, and Mary, sat talking. John fought waves of exhaustion and struggled to remain awake. At last giving in, he eased onto his back and stared up at the star-studded heavens. Never had a night seemed so beautiful or perfect. He glanced sideways at Emily, his gaze roaming over her silvery hair.

She reclined beside him, laughing at one of Ben's outrageous stories. Tonight she was animated, different from the woman he'd found nearly two weeks ago. Life flowed from her and into him. Listening to the sweet music of her voice and the caress of her laughter, he gave in to his need to sleep. With his Lady Dawn beside him, nights didn't seem so long or dark.

Emily stared up at the stars, finding peace and a sense of rebirth in watching the jewel-bright lights twinkle and dance high above her. One shot across the sky, falling somewhere beyond the horizon. The moon, a silver crescent, hung as if dangling from an invisible wire. The night was balmy, the breeze a soft caress over the land, and she'd opted just to sleep outside.

She'd fashioned two pallets on the blanket. John lay several feet from her at one end of the blanket, and she lay on the other side. He'd fallen asleep shortly after supper and no one had wanted to wake him. Today had been his first day of activity and he'd fallen into a well-deserved exhausted slumber. She studied him, noting his pallor from trying to do so much.

Ben and Mary were bedded down a short distance from her—close enough to be on hand if need be, but far enough that she and John had some privacy. They'd refused the use of the rude cabin, saying they preferred the outdoors to its stale, stuffy inside. She couldn't blame them for that. She herself had found she loved sleeping outdoors beneath the stars. Fully relaxed for the first time in a long while, Emily gave herself over to the night.

As she stared up at the sky, the events of the day crowded in—from the fear of intruders, to the horror of how both she and John must have looked, to the relief that had flooded her to learn that Ben and Mary were staying. Some of the weight had eased from her shoulders.

Maybe now John wouldn't worry so much. *Right*, she thought. She couldn't see John sitting back, allowing Ben to work while he himself healed. Still, he had no choice—not for a while.

With Ben's help, fresh meat wouldn't be a problem. No more boiled beans and bear fat—and in a day or so she'd have something decent to wear. Mary had offered to help her sew a blouse to wear with her skirt, and an extra dress.

John's shirt over her skirt covered her, as well as a pair of heavy wool pants that Mary had loaned her. She rubbed the long sleeve of the buckskin garment between her fingers. She hadn't been able to give up wearing it. She'd miss the comfort the shirt gave her. Like John himself, it was big and reassuring. She felt as safe in his clothing as if he were holding her.

Emily smiled in the darkness. It felt wonderful to be in the company of another woman, too. And to be among people who spoke her language. Over dinner, she'd felt as though she'd stepped into another world—a world of laughter, friendship, and acceptance.

Again she realized just how much she'd missed carrying on a simple conversation—exchanging thoughts and ideas. Tonight's laughter and good-natured arguing in which no one got mad or hurt was new to her. She found she enjoyed it very much.

Laughter had been rare in her family, and arguing nonexistent. There were no other views to be considered—only her father's. She'd thought she found everything she'd ever longed for with her warrior, but now she knew better.

Susan Edwards

There had always been a chasm between her and her godlike warrior, one she couldn't cross—and now she realized it was the ability to talk and be understood. To know what he liked and disliked, how he thought, what he believed in. And they'd been unable to share even laughter over some silly joke.

While she'd shared countless smiles with her Indian lover, it wasn't the same as sharing thoughts and beliefs, wishes and dreams. Emily had loved joining in with Mary in teasing John about some of his and Ben's past exploits. And she'd loved how the men had gotten their own back—at least at Mary—by teasing her in kind.

It truly amazed Emily that in so short a time, she knew so much about John: how he normally hated the name Johnny, yet how it had comforted him when he'd been sick with fever. How he made a lousy patient, because he liked to be in control. How he was stubborn and he'd refused to let her give up on life. Most of all, she knew John Cartier was kind. He had a soft heart when it came to injured animals like the hawk and the wolf . . . and even like her.

She thought hard. What had she known about her warrior? She scrunched her eyes closed, trying to envision her golden Apollo, Sadly, she had to admit to knowing very little. What he ate, how he liked his food cooked, his daily routine, how he liked to be touched and to touch her. How he liked her hair. How kind he'd been to her. And . . . and what else? Surely there had to be more, she knew. She searched her mind, but aside from what she'd said, she couldn't list anything that would tell her who he truly was.

170

She'd known nothing of his thoughts, of the things that made a person who he was. She'd not learned of his family, or who his friends were. She hadn't even learned his name! In a flash, she remembered the first night he'd held her. She'd dreamed he'd spoken to her in English. That night he'd told her some strange story about a coyote and his friend the spider. The next day, and every day after, he'd not spoken one word of English except her name: Emily.

He hadn't even shared his name with her! He had to have known what she was asking, had to have understood that she would have liked to know. She'd just called him her golden Apollo, but had never known anything more.

She called his image to her. It came. She expected to feel pain, to want to weep for him, but she only felt sadness that she hadn't been able to get to know him. Not even his name. If she knew so little of him, how could she have loved him? Yet hadn't her feelings been strong? Overwhelming?

She turned her head to check on John. Truthfully, she just wanted to look at him. A dark lock of hair had fallen across his eyes. Tenderly she reached out and brushed it aside. His head turned toward her, as if seeking her touch. She wanted to give it, but she didn't.

She longed just to close the distance between them, to let him hold her close. But she couldn't. Even if he opened his eyes and held out his arms, she didn't dare. *Because* she wanted him. Because she wanted him as a woman wants a man—and she knew how it felt. Her body tightened with need. But was what she'd

171

known—that intense pleasure her warrior had given her—all there was to a relationship with a man? Wasn't there more?

She hadn't understood before, but now she knew there was. All during the day and evening she'd seen it in Ben and Mary. The pair knew each other so well that oftentimes one would anticipate the needs of the other or even finish the other's sentence. It was something she'd never seen, and to her dismay she wanted to experience it.

Suppressing a moan, she turned away from John and closed her eyes. *Stop thinking of him,* she ordered herself. Her mind and heart were jumbled with need and confusion and doubts. At the bottom of it all, one question demanded an answer: How could she think herself in love with one man, then days later feel an equally strong need for another?

She feared the answer. If it was lust, then she was no better than her father's mother. If love, she feared becoming too close. For surely he'd abandon her as had everyone else . . . eventually.

She didn't think she could survive another hurt like the ones she'd had. And she certainly wasn't ready to try. Not yet. Not for a long time. Maybe never. Too much had happened in so little time; it was hard to accept it all. Yet one truth stood out as clearly as the black sky above her: Survival demanded she protect her heart. As soon as John was well, she'd remind him of his promise to take her back to the mission and her mother's friend. She'd focus on that—on getting back to the mission. She'd pray Millicente was still there. Then she'd seek out her blood father and put the past behind her. Perhaps she could try to secure some sort of post or job wherever he was. Love had no place in her life. She didn't want it. And she didn't need its fickle character to ruin her life.

With her mind made up, sleep should have come easy. Yet the thought of leaving John, of never seeing him again, left Emily feeling hollow inside.

Chapter Nine

In the four weeks since John's accident, he'd recovered amazingly well. Emily was pleased—and relieved. Each day she walked with him to help him regain his strength. Except for still using makeshift crutches that Ben had fashioned from tree branches, he was almost back to normal. And his wound was healing nicely.

Overhead, the sun trickled down between the leaves. The air was hot, still, and stifling. At her side, John kept pace with her deliberately slower rhythm. She enjoyed their morning and afternoon strolls—and they had nothing else they needed to do. With Ben's and Mary's help, there was lots of free time to be had for all.

The quiet and easy companionship she and John had formed over the last month soothed and healed her battered heart and calmed her fraught mind. For the most part, she managed to keep fear and worry over the future at bay. It was easy to do out here, she supposed. Drawing in a deep breath, she released it slowly. Of course, sooner or later she'd have to leave this quiet, beautiful land and return to the real world. And that meant saying good-bye to John. Some of the pleasure in this outing dimmed. How could she, in so short a time, have come to rely so much on another person? Hadn't she learned better?

He'd promised to be a friend. And he'd kept that promise. She'd never felt so close to another person in her life. Even with her mother there'd been a barrier. Timothy.

When John's wolf raced ahead of them, Emily put the depressing thoughts from her mind and gave herself over to the moment. There would be time enough later to worry over the future and examine her feelings for John.

Fang ran into the shallows and rolled on his back, then leaped to his feet and loped back to them, dripping water. Emily yelped when the beast shook himself off with a delighted bark.

John waved the wolf away. "Outta here, mutt," he said in a growl. But Emily heard the laughter in his voice.

"I notice he didn't spray *you* with water," she grumbled, though not really put out. In fact, she felt slightly cooler and wished she could just strip down and swim. But those days of going about as she pleased were over. In truth, if given the choice again between a silent lover who would show her a new freedom

175

she'd never even dreamed of, or the friendship and pleasant companionship John offered, she'd choose John. Having someone to talk to, someone with whom to share ideas was more valuable than being able to spend afternoons swimming lazily in the water with a man who looked like a god.

Fang barked again, as if urging them to hurry. Emily's laughter rang out. "Patience, wolf. Your master cannot run about."

The animal, frustrated that no one would play with him, cocked his furry head to the side, then lunged toward one of John's crutches. John whipped the crutch out of reach and easily blocked the jumping animal. The wolf fell back and sprawled on the ground, but not for long. In a flash of gray, his jaws locked onto the other crutch before John could lift it out of his reach. With one sharp tug of his strong neck and with his hind legs planted, the animal yanked his master off balance.

Emily rolled her eyes, knowing what was to come. She stopped and waited and watched with undisguised amusement as John launched himself at the wolf with a fierce roar. Fang barked and growled, but kept a firm grip on the crutch. Emily shook her head, watching man and beast finally fall to the ground, ignoring the crutch to wrestle beneath the shade of the tall cottonwoods.

At last, John pinned the squirming animal and yelled in victory. He released his pet, earning himself a few swipes of the beast's tongue on his face. Fang jumped up and rested his one front paw on his master's chest.

It still amazed Emily to see a wild animal—one that she knew from experience to be capable of ruthlessly stalking and killing even human prey—behaving more like a spoiled dog.

"I never knew a wolf could be tamed so easily," she said, more to herself.

John glanced over. "Loving he might be, but make no mistake. He's still a wild animal. The nature of the wolf runs in his blood." John grabbed a hunk of the beast's ruff and gave a tug.

Emily frowned. "Are you saying he could turn?"

John paused. "Don't think he'd ever turn on me or you. Since I found him as a young pup barely able to scamper about, he's bonded with humans. At least ones he knows. But don't forget the call of the wild runs deep. There might come a day when he gives in to it—decides to leave and go live with his own kind."

"I hope not." She knew John would miss Fang. When he and the wolf started back in on a game of tug-a-war-with the crutch, Emily stepped between them.

"This is not taking it easy, Mr. Cartier," she scolded between giggles. "Not to mention that you're getting that bandage dirty." As it still needed to be changed twice a day, he had continued to wear his one-legged buckskins. Using her foot, Emily scooted the wolf out of her way.

John glanced up at her, his eyes sparkling with merriment. The corners of his eyes crinkled. "Yes, Miss Emily," he said, trying to sound like a properly chastised schoolboy.

Susan Edwards

"Don't try that look with me. It won't work. You're no little boy."

"No?" He grinned. "What am I, Sunshine?" The world seemed to stop as they stared at one another.

"A handsome man," she said softly, unable to stop herself.

The golden sunlight slid over the slightly paler skin of his freshly shaved jaw—he'd taken off the beard this morning—and his strong white teeth flashed. The wicked humor in his eyes, and the wide grin, made him all the more appealing. And heart-stoppingly, breathtakingly handsome, not in a pretty, polished sort of way, or with the molded perfection of her golden warrior, but something grander.

Without his beard, the rugged strength was even more apparent in his strong jawline, and his firm chin had a deep cleft that fit the rest of his face. Also, to her surprise and pleasure, she'd discovered that he had one dimple in his left cheek that remained hidden until he grinned. Then that small little indent softened his features and gave him a boyish look. Like now. Still, she refused to let him know just how weak it made her when he grinned up at her like that.

Fang barked, breaking the spell as he hopped between them, his tail wagging furiously and his tongue lolling happily. Without warning, John reached forward and tried to grab one of the wolf's legs with his hand. The beast nimbly hopped back, balancing on his two back legs.

It amazed Emily that the wolf didn't seem the least bit hampered by his missing limb. Before they could start their silly game over, Emily chased Fang off and

178

shook her finger at John. "Enough. You'll just rile him even more."

And wasn't that the truth? Their play would get rougher as both man and beast sought to be the victor in their wrestling matches. The first time she'd seen John pull one of the wolf's feet out from beneath him, she'd been incensed on the animal's behalf. Then she realized it was a game.

Her lips twitched. Fang didn't need her sympathy. She'd never seen an animal so nimble. And now the wolf assumed that the pair of crutches John used was there for his own entertainment—he'd proved equally adept at tripping John up.

John grinned at her. "It's good for him—keeps him alert. Besides, he likes it."

Her lips twitched as she fought a smile. "You are incorrigible."

"Yeah, I know." He held up his hand. "Join me, Emily. Let's sit a bit."

His boyish look faded, and John became all man again. All desirable man with a love of life glowing from deep within—joy, and an inner peace she envied. One that could be hers if she reached out and took what he offered.

I can't. Over and over she had to warn herself not to get involved. *Too risky.* She just couldn't take the chance. Yet she couldn't resist taking his hand and allowing him to ease her down beside him. He gazed out across the water, and she found she couldn't take her eyes off him.

Without the beard, John Cartier looked younger, more carefree. And yet, at the same time, the strong

179

lines of his face warned that this was a man who lived on the edge. A man who knew what he was about. A man who was strong and who had enough strength to share. As Emily had learned firsthand.

Staring at his face, she realized that his mouth gave insight into his character. The fullness of his lips and his easy smiles spoke of the humor and compassion that were part of him. Yet, of all his features, John's eyes were her favorite. Like his dimple, when he laughed or smiled his eyes softened his face and revealed his true personality. When he was worried or in pain, those eyes showed his vulnerability. And when he was determined—as he'd been when she'd wanted to die—his eyes were hard. This was not a man to be crossed.

As she'd quickly discovered, everything he felt was mirrored in his face. All she had to do was look into his eyes to know what he was feeling. That made him human. Approachable. Safe.

"It's so beautiful out here," she said. Nature and man. The combination was powerful—something she feared she'd have a hard time resisting. John glanced down at her. The humor in his eyes had been replaced by an appreciation for the world around them. Their whiskey-colored depths darkened as they roamed over her features.

"Sure is," he agreed, his voice husky.

Ducking her head as heat crept up her cheeks, Emily felt her heart thud in response. It didn't take much for him to cause that; even his nicknames pleased her. Lady Dawn. Or Sunshine. Each evoked powerful images, and to be compared to either was flattering. It made it difficult as she tried hard to not let her heart become involved.

As they sat, soaking up the quiet peace of the afternoon, Emily didn't feel the need to chatter. With John it didn't feel awkward just to sit without having to talk. She felt a soothing companionship in just being with him.

He was so different, had so many facets to his personality, and he shared them all with her. His humor lifted her spirits, and gave her a taste of what it was like to live each day with joy in one's heart. His ability to take every moment and make the most of it while still looking to tomorrow gave her the determination to survive and find happiness someday—or at least peace. His quiet strength gave her hope that she'd be able to put the past behind her and make her own way in the world.

With her parents, she'd spent all of her time trying to stay in the background, afraid to draw attention to herself. There'd been no joy, no excitement, nothing to look forward to. No dreams. Those, she'd learned early on, led to disappointment and a crushing of the spirit. It was better not to hope for or to expect things that would not happen.

With her Indian warrior, she'd found joy in living each day as it came, blindly trusting and following wherever he led, content with what he gave her. But those days had been filled with mixed feelings she hadn't recognized. Something had still been missing

Now, being around John, she knew what it was: balance. The freedom to be herself, accepted for who and what she was. And the growing hope and dream of a better future. A future where she could venture out of her shell and explore a new and exciting world.

For the first time in her life, she was free to form her own opinions without fear of being struck. John listened. He didn't laugh at her thoughts. He asked questions. Made her think. Made her believe in herself and gave her hope that she could find the strength to go on and take her place in the world without allowing anything to suffocate her.

Yet as much as she dreamed of this life she'd once thought out of reach, the thought of leaving here now left her scared. She wanted the freedom to follow her heart, but she didn't know where life's boundaries lay. She feared failure. Here, she was cocooned. She couldn't fail. John was her safety net.

"What are you thinking about, Emily?" He tossed a stone into the river.

Emily watched the sunlight dance off the water, heard the gentle splash of the rock, and thought that there was no place on this earth so peaceful. "Before I lost my parents, I'd never just sat and did nothing but enjoy the day. Idleness was a sin to my father." Her voice hitched. Sometimes the past angered her to the point of tears; she'd been denied so much. Reaching up, she felt the locket lying between her breasts, the only thing she had from a life that now seemed so far away.

John turned his head to look at her. "When I was a boy, my pa used to take me fishing. Said it was a man's job to think more than he talked." His eyes softened with past memories. "I used to think he used that as an excuse not to work or hang around and listen to my mother nag him."

Frowning, Emily laced her fingers together. "Did your parents love each other?"

He gave her pointed look. "Yep. They died together, and I know that's how they would have wanted it." His voice was rough.

"But you said he went fishing because your mother nagged him." Her mother would never have dared to nag her father. Like Emily, Beatrice had done what Timothy ordered without hesitation or question.

"It was just their way. She nagged him, he barked orders, and they both did as they pleased. They wouldn't have had it any other way. They loved and trusted each other not to take undue advantage."

"That seems so hard to imagine," Emily said. But she *could* imagine two people living just like that. Hadn't she acted in the same manner with John? She'd taken charge, stopped him from playing with the wolf because she worried about his wound. And he did the same with her: refused to let her leave the vicinity of the cabin alone, insisting on going with her, standing guard when she bathed—just in case of unexpected trouble. And as she accepted the boundaries he imposed, he accepted hers.

They fell silent again. Emily glanced up. A few fluffy clouds drifted slowly overhead. To the right, she spotted a soaring hawk. The bird dipped a wing and flew lower, right over their heads, then down along the water.

"I wonder if that's your hawk," she mused.

John shaded his eyes. "Might be." A thread of sadness tinged his voice.

"I hope you hadn't wanted him for a pet." She worried her lower lip. She hadn't given thought to his plans for the bird when she released it.

He sighed. "You can't cage one of nature's wild creatures. You were right to free him."

"What about Fang?" It still amazed her that he had a pet wolf.

He shifted then stretched his leg out, massaging his thigh. "Found Fang when he was just a pup. Couldn't save the leg and couldn't destroy him. He survived. It's his choice to stay. He's free to go anytime he wants."

Emily heard the affection in his voice. "You'd miss him, though," she said. The wolf had become John's friend; she recognized that.

He met her gaze. "Yeah. I'd miss him. Sometimes it gets lonely out here, but I never feel alone when he's with me."

Emily thought about the loneliness she'd sensed in him when John had first found her. "Why do you do this? Why stay here? I'm not sure I could stand to live out here alone and go months with no one to talk to— and that's aside from the fact that there's no town close by to get fresh supplies. What *is* out there?" Emily shivered. "Besides Indians." Sometimes she couldn't wait to leave, to return to civilization and safety. The sheer vastness of the land intimidated her as much as it fascinated her.

John chuckled and pulled lightly on the single braid hanging down her back. He held out his hand, encompassing everything before them. "This is the ultimate challenge: living alongside Mother Nature. And surviving to tell of it."

"I should have known," Emily retorted wryly. "Man's need to rule."

"Yes and no. We think we've conquered her with our large cities, but one storm or fire can destroy those. Out here there's no question—*she's* in charge. It's not about trying to rule. If I'm to survive, I have to learn to live *with* Mother Nature, not rule her or live in spite of her." He leaned back on his elbow. "A man learns real fast that he has to respect everything: the seasons, the wildlife, and the ground he walks on— else he bears the consequences."

Emily wrapped her arms around her drawn-up knees. "You mean he'll die." She still recalled her fright and fear of dying when she'd been cornered by the wolves. Nature had nearly won that night.

"Exactly. And death isn't always clean and fast. The worst hell I can imagine is to die slowly, alone." He rolled a pebble between his thumb and forefinger. "But that comes from being careless. A fire not properly doused will destroy and chase away the animals I trap. No furs. No pay. Storms can destroy our supplies. Some men come out here thinking to get rich. They don't have any idea what it takes to survive. Those not prepared get sick. Most don't make it back to get treated. And misjudging animals—I've seen men who went up against bears and come away minus arms. Or worse."

He paused. "Carelessness with an ax can cause a man to bleed to death."

185

Emily shivered. John had come so close to dying. But he hadn't been alone—this time. She shook off the memory of the attack. "If it's so bad, why stay?"

"Well, Sunshine, this is a life of contradictions. Life and death. Joy and sorrow. Hatred and love. The beauty of spring, the harshness of winter. It's real out here. Everything is. Raw. And there's no greater thrill than to survive and live as one with a force greater than yourself."

He paused and lifted his fingers to her braid, rubbing the soft bit at the end. "The rewards make it all worthwhile. Sometimes a man finds rare beauty when he's given up all hope." He glanced up into her eyes.

The breath left her lungs as John's gaze captured hers. Some emotion she feared to name crackled between them. She tried to ignore it, told herself that nothing could come of it. This man lived here, in the very wilderness that had claimed her parents. Yet she, too, had begun to see the beauty of life out here— despite the hardships. Contradictions. She mused over that. She craved freedom, yet wanted safety. She desired peace, yet had to disturb the past, find the answers surrounding her birth. She had to know if her father had known of her, had to know if he had wanted her—despite the pain the knowledge might bring.

Sitting here, safe and protected, she felt it was impossible to have it all. In order to get the answers she needed, she had to leave—which meant leaving John. Yet he had become such a crucial part of her happiness.

Suddenly nothing else mattered. For one moment, she wanted to pretend that there was only her and him. Them. She felt drawn into John Cartier's warm protection. Like an unsuspecting insect trapped by molasses, she'd been snared.

John reached up and caressed her cheek. The pad of his thumb grazed the corner of her mouth, his touch light as a cloud of dandelions.

"Emily—"

"John—"

They both spoke at once. John lifted himself up, his hand sliding around to cup the back of her neck. He drew her to him. Emily dipped her head. Their lips met in a tentative kiss.

Drawing Emily close, John savored the sweet taste of her. He hadn't kissed her since he'd been delirious, but recently it was all he thought about, dreamed about.

Her breath mingled with his and sent hot waves of desire coursing through his veins. Blood pounded in his brain, his heart, and his loins when her lips moved with his in a union as sweet and light as a summer breeze. *Go slow. Just one sweet, little kiss.* That was all. But he couldn't stop. One taste made him crave more. He needed Emily as much as he needed the sun. Maybe more. His lips slanted over hers, still gentle in their explorations.

She twined her arms around his neck and slid her fingers through his hair, pulling off the leather tie, freeing the long, dark strands. Twisting his body, he reversed their positions, lowering her to the soft bank.

187

He broke off their kiss and stared down at her.

Her eyes mirrored the intense need he felt. Her lips parted, her eyes silently begging for him to resume the kiss. Her fingers trailed up the sides of his face, stroking, touching, learning him.

With the speed of a summer storm, passion erupted. He crushed his mouth to hers. Their tongues met, his plunging into her mouth, tasting and stroking. He groaned. *Heaven*. This was heaven. Emily's kiss was bliss. Sweetness. Nectar from the rarest plant. His fingers tangled in her hair.

Beneath him, her breasts rose and fell with each deeply drawn breath, a soft pillow for his hard chest. Then she took control of the kiss. He retreated, meeting her questing tongue with tiny licks as she tasted him. The tips of their tongues met and twined—first slowly, then in a frenzy of need.

Reeling from the taste and feel of her, John broke away, his body on fire. His mouth blazed a path along Emily's jaw and down her throat, feeling the jump of her pulse. His own leaped in response. Beneath him she shifted, allowing him to fall into the cradle of her hips. His manhood, hard and throbbing with need, pressed against her. Dots of color danced behind his eyes as he closed them.

He wanted her. He *needed* her. His palm slid down her throat to one round breast. He cupped her through the material of her dress, felt the hard pebble of her nipple, and used his palm to stroke it to an even tighter bud. She moaned, pushing closer. Her hips arched, the juncture of her thighs pressing up against him. John felt as though he'd burst into flames.

Beneath him, Emily moaned, her eyes closed, her lips parted. Memories of when he'd found her—her naked body, so made for loving—nearly made him explode. But then he remembered the emptiness in her eyes when she'd offered herself to him. He hadn't been able to take what she'd been willing to give then—and he couldn't now.

Passion. They had that between them. But he wanted more—much more. He wanted her trust and love. He wanted all of her, and he knew this moment of bliss didn't mean she was ready to give it to him.

The thought of stopping made him shiver: his body protesting what his mind had decided. But then he said, "We have to stop, Emily."

His mouth claimed hers in a final kiss meant to soothe, but it left him aching with need.

Stop? Emily, her thoughts muddled by passion's storm, blinked her eyes open. John's gaze, heavy with desire, met hers. Her gaze shifted to his mouth, his wonderful, full, sensuous lips that left her hungry for more. "No," she protested, trying to draw him back.

His forehead dropped to rest on hers, his breath feathering across her lips. "I can't do it, Emily. I can't use you like this."

His words chilled her desire. She shoved at his shoulders. "Use me?" Furious and horrified, she stared up at him. "I thought it was more than that! I thought you lo—"

She broke off, humiliated and hurt. Turning her head, she tried to scoot from beneath him. He refused to budge. His strong fingers forced her to meet his

189

gaze. She had to blink rapidly to keep tears from forming.

"That's the problem, my sweet, desirable Lady Dawn. I *do* love you."

Confused, she stared into eyes that showed the truth of his words. "You're not making sense, John." Confusion replaced some of her hurt.

"I love you, Emily, with all my heart. You are the light of my life. My Lady Dawn. Without you, I'm not whole." His large hands cupped her face, his fingers trailing into her hair to gently massage her scalp.

"I don't understand," she whispered. "I want this."

John smiled weakly. "I know, sweetheart. But do you love me, too?" His voice was low, husky with emotion.

"I . . . I—" Troubled, she lifted her fingers to his rough cheek, scraping their backs against his shadow of stubble. "I don't know," she answered, unable to tear her gaze from his.

"*That* is the problem, Sunshine: I want you to be sure. And until you are, I won't have you thinking that I'm using you. Nor will I allow you to give yourself to me out of gratitude." John smiled tenderly, and sadly. "There's more to making love than the mating of bodies. When I join my flesh to yours, I want our minds, hearts, and souls to join as well."

"Do you think I kissed you because I'm grateful?" It troubled her that he might be right. Yet she felt something else. Something that frightened her.

"You're vulnerable out here. Choices are few. But it won't necessarily always be that way. I want you to know what you want and why." He ran a hand over his jaw and around to the back of his neck. "A short time ago you were devastated, ready to die when the man you loved left you. I don't want to go through that same thing if you leave."

He sat and drew her up beside him, then pulled her across his lap, his chin resting on the top of her head. Her back was flush with his chest. She felt the wild thumping of his heart. It matched hers.

"Can a person love another without really knowing them, John?" She thought of her Indian savior and how much she'd loved him—how much she'd *thought* she loved him. But compared to what she was beginning to feel for John, she didn't know what it was she'd felt. Had she truly loved the Indian, or had she just loved the way they'd lived? Or maybe she'd loved him out of simple gratitude.

With John, everything was different. There were no secrets. No walls. He was as open to her as a book. She'd accepted him willingly, but he was right: This was his world—much the same as roaming the wilds had been the life suited to her golden Apollo. This wasn't her. She wasn't here by choice. Only circumstances.

John's breath teased the tip of her ear as he rubbed her head with his cheek. "I believe there are many kinds of love, Sunshine. Some deeper, more lasting than others. Yet when things aren't meant to be— when loves don't work out—that doesn't mean what you felt wasn't real. And the pain of it ending is still there."

Knitting her brows together, Emily took John's other hand into hers. "I did love him and the freedom he

191

gave me. But I didn't know him. And he didn't really know me. We were lovers but not friends." She tipped her head back, resting it in the cradle of his neck, her temple brushing his jaw. "But I feel like I've known you all my life."

John bent his head and brushed his lips across hers. "I've waited for you for a long time, Sunshine. I won't lie and say I don't want to become your lover right now. But more than anything, I want you to be sure of your heart. When the time is right—if it's right— you'll know. For now, we'll stick to being friends."

Some part of her felt relieved. She realized he was right: she wasn't ready to commit herself into John's hands. Before she allowed the urges of her body to rule, she needed to know and understand her heart and mind. It was only fair to him—and to herself.

Yet there was something about John that made her want to toss caution to the wind and take what his eyes, his touch, and his kiss promised. Reason, caution, and desire all warred with each other, and finally she ran the tip of her finger across his lips. "Good friends?"

"The very best." He nipped the tip of her finger.

Her voice dropped to a husky whisper. "Can friends kiss?"

"Absolutely." John lowered his head and kissed her. After the brief touch of their lips, his finger stroked the moist fullness her mouth. Though the kiss had been gentle, the smoldering heat in his eyes was anything but.

John undid her braid and ran his fingers through her hair. Then he wrapped his arms around her. Emily relaxed. "What's your happiest childhood memory, John?"

"Happiest? Well, that's kinda hard. But Sundays were fun."

Emily's breath caught. Sundays had been pure hell for her. She found herself desperately wanting to hear that, for some, the Sabbath had some sort of meaning. "Tell me."

"Well, we had to attend church. Ma insisted. But after that, Pa and I would go fishing. We knew this one spot." He laughed softly. "Unfortunately, everyone else knew about it so we didn't always catch anything. But it never seemed to matter. I ran and played with my friends while my Pa talked with the other men or napped in the shade."

"That sounds fun," Emily said wistfully. Though she regretted much of her childhood, she loved listening to stories of his. Loved the way his deep baritone vibrated through her as he spoke.

"Yeah. It *was* fun. After, we'd trudge home and Ma would have a big fancy Sunday supper ready. Or sometimes she'd surprise us by bringing a picnic supper to the pond.

"What about you, Sunshine? Surely there's a happy memory for you as well?"

Emily felt tears well. "I can't think of anything," she whispered. While there had been good times, fun moments with her mother or others, each was overshadowed by her father in some way.

"Then we'll just have to make some fun memories for you," John whispered, his hands tenderly rubbing her arms.

Leaning back in his embrace, remembering their first kiss, the warm acceptance of his friends Mary and Ben, the laughter they shared each day, and John and Fang and their roughhousing play, Emily smiled. "I think we're already doing that."

They spent the afternoon talking with the gurgle of the stream and the song of birds lending a soft backdrop of noise. The sun was slowly sinking when they stood and leisurely made their way back to the shack. As they walked hand in hand, Emily thought that if what she felt growing in her heart was really love, then the seed planted earlier had sprouted today—when he'd put her needs ahead of his. Content now to wait and see if it grew and blossomed, she gave herself over to the pleasure of walking shoulder-to-shoulder with a friend. A very good friend who knew how to kiss her senseless.

They were nearing the shack when, without warning, John went flying. One minute he stood beside her; the next he lay flat on his back. Emily stared down into his stunned gaze. The bark of Fang, who was now sitting a short distance in front of them with John's crutch lying on the ground in front of him, drew her attention.

Realization dawned. The wolf had sneaked up from behind and grabbed one of John's crutches. That was what had sent John tumbling to the ground.

Laughter welled in her at the crippled animal's victory over his huge, healthy master. *What a sneaky beast!* "Oh, that was good—I mean, are you okay?" She tried to clamp down on her humor.

Before John could sit or react, Emily felt the swipe of the crutch across the back of her knees as the wolf rose and ran past, taunting his master with his prize. Emily's legs buckled, and she fell.

John reached up and caught her as she fell on top of him. This time it was her turn to be shocked by the suddenness of losing her balance.

"You were saying, Sunshine?"

Sprawled atop him, Emily felt the rumble of his laughter roll through his chest into hers. The tips of her breasts tightened. The sheer absurdity of it all released her own mirth. Their laughter rang out, mingling with the smug barking of John's wolf.

Chapter Ten

Clear skies paled against the heat of the blazing sun. Bereft of water, the grasses darkened to a honey brown, became dry and brittle. Leaves lost their luster and the summer flowers drooped. Nothing moved. Even the river seemed sluggish.

Riding in the afternoon heat, Willy wished he were back in St. Louis. He hated it out here. Hated the summer heat; the cold, rainy, and snowy days of winter; and the wind, which often blew viciously across the land. He hated the openness. He hated the thick stands of trees. He hated the deep ravines that came out of nowhere and the rolling plains. In short, he hated this godforsaken land.

Most of all, he hated the work necessary to scratch out a meager living here. He scowled. What was the point in slaving long hours during the winter, trudging all over hell and back in conditions that sane folk refused to go out in, just to get a small, piddling amount of money that flowed through one's fingers like a swollen river raged over the land in the spring? His share of the winter's trapping hadn't even lasted him a month in St. Louis.

He glared at his grandfather, who rode ahead of him leading one pack mule. Willy led two behind him. Due to the old man's health, they'd traded their canoes for the mules and bought horses. More money lost to him.

It was also the old man's fault Willy had lost his money so fast. His grandfather had given him only half his share, keeping what Willy had promised John for the right to go to St. Louis. He tightened his hold on the reins, making his mount shy nervously.

What right did his grandfather have to interfere? Willy knew if he'd had more cash, he could've won back what he'd lost—doubled it even. And now the whole damned cycle would start over.

Swatting at an annoying bee, he narrowed his gaze on his grandfather. Too bad the old man hadn't done the decent thing and died while they were in town. Then he could've gone to fetch John so they could go to the bank to claim their inheritance. He'd be free, then. Free to do as he pleased.

His grandfather was rich. Hadn't his father complained bitterly enough about the old man's tight fist? Aside from money in the bank—lots of it from the sale of the land and business—there was a cache of money and gold buried somewhere out in this godawful land.

Susan Edwards

The thought of being rich, being able to do what he wanted, was the only thing that kept him at his grandfather's side. He had no use for Gascon Cartier, who did nothing but nag and order him about. But Gascon wouldn't live much longer, he mused. Then he'd be rich. With the money the old man hoarded, burying it like a dog buried its meatiest bones, Willy would be able to live the way he wanted. A nice house. Women. The best whiskey. Whatever he wanted.

"Yeah, not much longer." He didn't realize he'd spoken until his grandfather glanced back at him.

"You could've stayed, you know. Didn't have to come back."

Startled, Willy shifted his gaze. He stared into his grandfather's eyes—his mother's eyes. "Don't have much choice," he groused.

The old man lifted a stern brow. "You could have found work—or saved your earnings instead of gambling and drinking and whoring them away."

Willy stared to one side of his grandfather so he wouldn't have to see the disgust written across the man's face. "A man's got to have some fun now and then."

Gascon spat on the ground. "Boy, that's all you care about. Fun. Women. Drinking. When are you going to start looking to your future?"

Willy shrugged. "I'm young. Only twenty-four. Plenty of time," he said, hating to be put on the defensive. The old man just didn't understand.

His grandfather shook his wild mane of white hair and snorted. "Boy, time's running out for you. You'll be old before you know it, and you won't have any-

198

thing to show. Not like your cousin. He saves his money—has me bank it for him. When he leaves this, he'll have enough to do whatever he wants."

Willy fisted his hands and glared at them. John had always been able to do whatever he wanted. He didn't *have* to work out here. He had money. After the death of John's parents, he'd been set. He could have just stayed in the house and lived a life of luxury. And Willy could have stayed, too. Then their grandfather had shown up and ruined everything. He'd sold the house, land, and business. Said they were too young to manage it, then dragged them off to the wilds.

Willy slid his grandfather another assessing look. How long could the old man live?

"Stop looking at me like I was on my deathbed. I'm not gone yet, boy."

Willy flushed. He hated the way the old man made him feel—like he was no good. He remained silent.

Gascon cackled. "I know you better than you think, boy. Always looking for someone else to give you what you want. Your pa was no good—had a good farm after his parents died, but he lost it because he was too lazy to work it. He only married my daughter because he'd figured he'd get rich off her."

Unable to look his grandfather in the eye, Willy knew it was the truth—and he hated knowing the old man was right. His grandfather dropped back and met his resentful gaze with a hard, piercing stare.

"Your pa was wrong. I don't give nothing to anyone for doing nothing. Didn't matter to my father that we had money—I had to earn my way, and I made my son earn his. Your pa could've had a job in our family business. Could've worked his way up. But he refused. Took your mother away just to spite me, then let her die."

Willy protested. "It's not his fault he didn't have money for a doctor. You hated him because my mother loved him more than you." He closed his mind to all the fights, the sounds of his mother weeping that she wanted to go home, the furious shouts of his father telling her it'd be a cold day in hell before he let her go, and the sounds of his father's palm against her face.

"Boy, your father never even tried to get her to a doctor. He knew I'd pay for the best money could buy, but he just let her die—out of spite. For that, I won't forgive him. Not ever."

Willy felt sick with hatred. He still remembered how afraid he'd been as he watched his mother waste away. She'd been the only one who'd loved him. His father hadn't wanted him, had made it clear he was a burden, not a cherished child to be loved and doted on. Not like his cousin's parents who'd given John everything he himself had lacked.

"It wasn't my fault she died," he said. "I tried to take care of her." For the first time, he voiced his bitterness.

"I've never blamed you for her death," Gascon said, his voice gruff. He drew a deep breath. His eyes, set below thick, bushy brows, watered at the painful memories. Then his jaw tightened, and his voice took on an edge.

"I've judged you by your own actions, and from the time you went to live with my son and his family, all you cared about was making sure you got your share.

Maybe you weren't to blame then—you were an angry, hurt child. But you're a man now, and a man has to stand on his own two feet and make his own way. All you've done is hold on to the past and use it as an excuse for your failings."

He kicked his horse in the side and sped up. "I've given you more chances than you deserve, boy. And you've disappointed me every time. This is my last year out here; then I'm retiring and you'll be on your own. You'll get what you earn this winter and no more. Let's go. We're nearly home."

Willy glared at the old man's back. His grandfather might not give him money, but his cousin would. John had always felt sorry for him. He'd always been able to get what he needed.

Tired of dealing with the old man, Willy actually looked forward to arriving home—if one could call their rude shack a home. Very soon he'd be able to go back to spending his days doing pretty much whatever he wanted. He'd take off with his third of the traps and rendezvous with his pals. All he had to do was kill a few animals, win some more furs from his buddies in card games, or trade for them from the natives, and wait for spring to come. Only one more year of this hell; then he could get his money from John.

As they entered the thick wooded area surrounding their shack, a strange sound reached Willy's ears. He paused and glanced around. It sounded like laughter. He listened. There it was again. It sounded like . . . like a woman's voice: sweet and lovely. Like the wind itself.

Spurring his mount faster, Willy hurried through the trees toward the shack where it was hidden from Indians and trappers just passing through the area. At the edge of the clearing he came to a startled stop, sure he was seeing things. His cousin was walking toward the shack with a woman who looked like an angel.

Willy blinked. Then rubbed his eyes. Angels weren't real. But when he looked again, the angel with long silvery-blond hair floating around her face was still there, walking toward the shack with his cousin.

Her beauty and sweet laughter held him immobile. Her dark blue skirts swirled around her, making it look as if she walked on air. Spellbound, he let his mouth gape open as he stared at the vision. Next to John, she looked small and fragile, yet her figure was every man's dream: large breasts, tiny waist. Willy's breathing quickened.

"Well, I'll be," Gascon said.

Together the two men stared, mesmerized. When John's wolf sent both its master and the woman to the ground, the pair laughed—and the sound beckoned. Willy followed his grandfather out of the cover of trees. He kept his attention focused solely on the woman, afraid to even blink, in case she might disappear.

"What have we here?"

A shadow fell across Emily. Startled by the gruff voice of a stranger, Emily glanced up . . . into the twinkling gaze of an older man. She scrambled off John and stared up at the two men towering over her. One glance into the speaker's bright eyes was all she needed to identify him as John's grandfather. They had the same sherry-brown eyes. Like John's, this man's love of life shone down on her. Literally down: John's grandfather was a giant of man. She assumed the person standing with his mouth open must be John's cousin. John had told her a lot about his family. She sent him a friendly smile.

John shoved himself up to sit beside her. "Gramps, Willy, you're back," he called. Ignoring his crutch, he got to his feet.

Emily handed it to him and walked over to where Fang lay with the other. She snatched it from the disgruntled animal and gave it back to John.

He smiled in thanks, then held out his hand to her. Emily placed her fingers on his palm. His gentle grasp swallowed her hand completely. Together they faced the visitors.

Emily felt dwarfed by the three men, like a child in the presence of grown-ups.

"Emily Ambrose, this is my grandfather, Gascon Cartier—and my cousin, Willy Tucker."

"A pleasure, Miss Ambrose." Gascon's gaze slid from her to John's thigh, his brows drawn together. "What the hell did you do to yourself, son?"

John explained his injury, glossing over the severity of it. Before his grandfather could comment, Willy snapped his mouth closed and stepped in front of his grandfather, cutting him off. "She's an angel," he whispered, staring at her. "A real angel." He gaped at Emily with wide-eyed wonder.

203

The term brought painful memories for Emily. All her life, while her family moved from church to church, members had told her father she looked like a tiny angel with her pale blond hair and blue eyes. She'd grown to hate being compared to the heavenly spirits. For reasons she had never understood, it had always angered her father and made him even stricter with her. Now she understood: the circumstances of her birth had made it impossible for him to accept her—not only as his daughter, but as an innocent child. Comparison to an angel would only be heretical to him.

To one side, John answered more of his grandfather's questions. Willy continued to stare at her with the intensity of a man who'd gone hungry and was now salivating over a plate overflowing with food—a look she recognized all too well.

She laughed self-consciously. "I'm no angel—" She broke off with a slight choke when she realized she was implying the opposite—especially considering she'd been lying atop John when this pair arrived. "I mean, I'm just me—Emily Am-Ambrose, stranded here until I can get back to civilization."

Willy stepped forward and grabbed her other hand and carried it to his lips. "I'll take you," he volunteered in a rush.

Emily pulled her hand back, but he held fast. She tugged her fingers free. Embarrassed, she wasn't sure what to say. For all of John's obvious attraction to her, he'd never made her feel self-conscious or uneasy. Willy's glazed adoration unnerved her. It reminded her of Father Richard.

John turned from his grandfather and put an arm around her shoulders to draw her close. "I already said I'd take her back," he explained.

Willy blinked, the dreamlike softness fading from his brown eyes. The corners of his mouth turned slightly downward. "Why don't we let the little angel decide who gets to take her?" His grin widened as his gaze roamed over her figure. "Ya see, I'm a lot more fun than my boring cuz." He moved closer.

Startled at his boldness and the hunger in his eyes, Emily stepped back. She stared at John's cousin, but the man's beard made it impossible to make out his features—except his eyes, and what she saw there made her uncomfortable: no humor, no genuine friendliness.

Willy seemed the opposite of John. Willy's reaction upon meeting her was typical of most men. Only John had taken the time to look beyond her angelic looks to the woman beneath.

John's hand rose to her waist, reassuring her, giving her the courage to address his cousin. "Thank you, Willy, but I've already accepted John's generous offer."

Unfazed, the trapper never let his gaze leave her face. "Don't look like my cousin's going to be able to take you anywhere for a while." He looked downright pleased about John's injury, and he gave John a triumphant grin. "Might have to let *me* take the little lady back to civilization."

Emily narrowed her eyes. She hated the man's condescending tone, and the way he ignored her, thinking she had no say in the matter. She wasn't a parcel to be delivered. "I said I'd wait until spring. He'll be fine by then."

"Now, don't be in a hurry to say no. Gotta get ta know me first. I gots lots of time ta change yer mind." He looked supremely confident.

Emily stifled a retort. She had no desire to get to know him any better. Aside from not seeming to care what she wanted, John's cousin hadn't shown any concern over his cousin's injury. At her side, she felt John stiffen. Again, he told his cousin that the decision had been made.

She glanced down at her toes to avoid looking at Willy, who was still arguing. No way would she go off alone with this man. Just a few minutes of conversation were enough to warn her that Willy was as different from John as could be. And not just in speech— though that surprised her. John spoke well, and so did his grandfather. Cultured. Refined. The speech of gentlemen or men of money.

But Willy's speech was as rough as his looks. It was also clear that Mary was right. She'd told Emily that Willy was a self-centered, boring braggart.

From the front of the shack, she heard Mary's and Ben's shouted greetings. Seeing her new friends running to join them, Emily was thankful they'd decided to winter with John and his family. Emily now appreciated how awkward things could have been without them.

Gascon waved his hand at Willy to silence him. "Time enough to discuss this later." His grave voice brooked no argument. When Ben extended his hand, the older man shook it, then returned Mary's hug. Then Gascon turned back to John and Emily. "So, how about some answers? What's going on here?"

John explained that Emily's parents had been killed by Indians, and that Emily had hidden herself. He said only that he'd found her and had promised to take her back to civilization.

Gascon fingered his bushy white beard, his dark eyes staring at her intently. Emily suspected he knew that there were things being left out, but he didn't challenge the story.

Emily felt guilty for leading everyone to believe her parents had been killed near here, to omit the wandering days with her Indian, but she knew enough to know that the fewer people who knew the entire truth, the better.

Once more, the air grew thick with tension as Willy sought to continue to protest over John taking her back. To ease her unhappiness, Gascon patted Emily's shoulder in a fatherly manner. "Glad you'll be with us for a bit, Emily. Tell you what. Come spring, if it's all right with Miss Ambrose, we'll all go. I'm gettin' too old for this kind of life. Might be nice to settle down again." His eyes flashed with mischief. "Especially if there's a chance at John settling down and giving me great-grandbabies." His gaze danced between her and John.

Emily blushed, thankful for Ben and Mary as they protested and said Gascon would be missed out here. They couldn't believe he'd actually give up the trapping life.

Across from her, Willy scowled. Then, after a few

moments, they all moved back toward the shack. Emily walked with John on one side and Willy on the other. Mary and Ben assisted Gascon with the horses and pack mules.

Emily missed the comforting warmth of holding John's hand, but she didn't want to escalate things between the two cousins. Instead, she let the news from St. Louis surround her. John glanced down at her and winked. "Looks like a full house, Sunshine," he admitted. His voice was low.

Her lips curved into a grin. She loved it when he called her Lady Dawn or Sunshine. Sunshine was life. Growth. Warmth. And the husky drawl of his voice was a caress. And when he looked at her with that soft, loving look, she saw into the garden of his soul and found herself longing to be the sunshine he needed to thrive.

Afraid to trust herself, or her mushrooming feelings, she put them aside. "A happy house," she agreed, loving the feeling of being accepted by a group of boisterous people who knew how to laugh.

The men unloaded the horses and brought the supplies into the neat and tidy shack, and while they did, Emily decided to bring in the laundry that had been hung out to dry. With no pins, some of the garments had blown to the ground. Luckily, they were not muddy. She brushed and shook the dust from each, then folded the clothing and set it into one of Mary's supply baskets.

As she worked, the low rumble of male voices punctuated by roars of laughter surrounded her. She grinned. Except for Willy, all the men had such deep voices. It felt like thunder on a summer day—all booming noise, no rain.

She sneaked a glance at the men and spotted Willy standing off to one side, not working. He still looked disgruntled and put out. Folding one of John's shirts, she stared at it, worried. Would her presence cause problems between John and his cousin? She didn't want that. Straightening, she contemplated the patch of bright blue sky dotted with fluffy bits of white cloud.

What did she want?

John. His kisses. The friendship he'd promised.

And a lifetime of being his Lady Dawn. Her birth had put a cloud over her mother's head, and anger in the heart of the man who'd raised her. To find that she brought someone joy was something she'd never experienced.

In such a short time, she'd found what had been missing from her life: laughter, joy, contentment. But could it last? She frowned. Once she returned to civilization, would these feelings remain and continue to grow, or would they fade?

She knew how fast things changed. Just a short time ago, she thought she'd found love and happiness. She'd been wrong. So how could she trust herself to believe her growing feelings toward John were any more real or lasting than anything that had come before?

Sighing, she moved down the line. She was better off sticking to her plan to go to Kentucky to find her father.

"Angels ain't supposed to frown."

209

Emily whipped her head to the side to see Willy watching her, a friendly smile on his face. But his gaze, focused on her breasts, gave his thoughts away. Averting her own gaze, she moved past Willy, careful not to brush against him.

He picked up the wicker basket Mary used to load supplies onto the mules when they traveled—she had two of them, one for each side of the mule—then followed.

Taking a pair of Ben's long johns down, Emily folded them and set them in the basket. "I'm sure John is glad that you and your grandfather are back." She knew from spending long hours talking with John in the evenings that he was close to his grandfather. He hadn't said much about his cousin—just that Willy had come to live with him and his parents at the age of ten when his father dumped him and left.

Her heart had sympathized then with the boy Willy must have been. To have been abandoned at that tender age must have been horrible. To be abandoned at any age was horrible, she amended. But at least John's cousin had had a loving family to take him in. She herself didn't. She was alone. Except for a father she couldn't count on wanting her.

Willy followed again, moving when she did, giving her little room. "I'm glad I'm back, too," he agreed, licking his lips as he grinned down at her. "Weren't lookin' forward to another long, borin' winter out here, but things sure is lookin' up. Never thought I'd git to spend the winter courtin' me an angel."

Emily bit back a frustrated sigh. It was one thing to have John courting her. Even though she wasn't sure

White Dawn

how she felt, or what would happen once she left here, it made her feel special. But it was different between her and John. To be fair to Willy, she had to make her position clear. "Willy, I'm only here until spring. Then I'm returning home." Wherever home was. She smiled gently to take the sting from her words. She didn't want to hurt or antagonize him.

"Never planned to live here all my life, neither. Nope. Just long 'nough to make me some money. Got dreams of buildin' a nice big ol' house on a plot of land somewhere. Gonna settle, marry, and raise some young'uns." He inched closer so his arm brushed hers.

Emily ducked beneath the clothesline to put distance between them. She avoided his eyes. His boldness unnerved her. Keeping silent, she took down the last item, a towel with rust-colored stains on it—stains from John's leg wound. Memories of that day still made her shiver. Tossing the towel into the basket, she took it from Willy before he could protest and headed back to the safety of the house. Willy stopped her by grabbing her wrist. "How 'bout a walk? I'll show you some of my favorite places."

Pulling away, Emily shook her head, forcing a polite smile to her lips. "No. I have to start supper."

"Come on," Willy cajoled, using his hands to attempt to smooth his oily, tangled hair that hadn't seen water or soap for weeks. "Mary's here. You can leave for a little while. We won't be gone long."

Arching her brow, Emily shook her head. "Willy, that wouldn't be fair to Mary, especially with two more men to feed." Emily glanced over to where the three men were still unloading supplies—even John strug-

211

Susan Edwards

gled to help by using just one crutch so he had a free hand. From a distance, his limp was pronounced. He'd been standing too long, but she knew he wasn't going to just sit back and watch the others work.

"I think they could use your help," she said to Willy. She allowed a bit of censure into her voice. Not only was Willy shirking his own duties, he thought nothing of asking her to do the same.

The dirty trapper moved in front of her, blocking her path, ignoring her strong hint that he should be working as well. "Tomorrow, then?" His voice rose a fraction, and sounded just the tiniest bit hurt. The laughter fled his eyes, replaced by hardness.

Emily resented Willy's bullying. She stepped around him, feeling out of her element. She'd never had to deal with suitors before—her father had forbidden it.

What about John? a voice in her head asked. *Isn't he a suitor?* She and John walked together each day, and she didn't think anything of it. She wouldn't have hesitated had he come to her and asked the same thing. Of course, she wouldn't have left Mary with her chores, but neither would John have chosen that time to try to go off with her.

She didn't want to hurt or antagonize John's cousin; however, he was acting oddly and making her uncomfortable. She quickened her steps. Behind her, Willy dogged her heels like a besotted puppy. She joined Mary, who knelt over a cooking pot of stew, slowly adding meat and beans to the mixture.

Willy's shadow fell over her. "I'll help with supper; then you'll have time to go for a walk."

212

Emily set her basket of clothing down. "I'll make myself clear. I am not interested in being courted, nor would it be acceptable for me to go off with a man I've just met. That you expect me to do so is insulting!" She glanced at Mary when Willy continued to stand there and stare down at her.

Mary winked. "But we'd love some help, Willy."

Emily stared at the other woman in horror. Here she was trying to get rid of Willy, and Mary was encouraging him to stay?

Her friend held out to Willy an empty pot. "Would you fetch some water?"

John's cousin stuck his hands in his pockets and backed away. "Said I'd help Emily. I'll finish cuttin' the meat while you go for the water."

Mary shrugged. "I'm nearly done." She held out the pot for Emily. "No sense in two of us getting our hands all bloody. Here, if you grab the water, I'll finish cutting the deer meat into chunks for the stew."

Emily stood, uncertain. The last thing she wanted was for Willy to follow her down to the stream. She needn't have worried.

Willy jumped forward and grabbed the pot by the handle. "I'll carry it for you, angel. The stream is a bit far and the pot will be heavy."

Emily bit back a grin as she caught on to Mary's plan. "Thank you, Willy," she said. Then she paused as if coming up with an idea. "You know, you and your grandfather must be starved from traveling all day. If you'd be so kind as to fetch the water, then I can start on the pan bread. We'll have supper ready in no time."

213

Susan Edwards

Willy, obviously realizing he'd been outsmarted, glared at Mary, but he knew if he refused now, he'd look bad in Emily's eyes. "For you, my little angel, I'll do it. Then we'll take that walk." He stalked off, not looking too happy.

Relieved, Emily shuddered. "Ugh, I hate being called angel." She grabbed the ingredients she needed. "Thanks, Mary."

Mary hacked at a large chunk of meat. "Don't have any use for Willy. As you can see, he don't do much around here. Only reason he wanted to get water with you was to get you alone."

"That's pretty obvious," Emily agreed dryly.

The humor vanished from Mary's eyes. "Don't go off with him, Emily. He'll get you flat on your back before you know it."

Sitting back on her heels, Emily stared off into the distance. Bitterness crept into her voice. "Isn't that what most men want?" *Even men of God,* she added to herself.

Humor laced Mary's voice. "Yeah, but some men—like John and Ben—are nice, decent folk despite the fact that they are ruled by what hangs between their legs."

Feeling her depression lift, Emily giggled. "You're shameful." But Mary was right. She trusted John with her life, even though she knew he wanted her.

And the thing was, she wanted him just as much.

Glancing around, she spotted the man who was taking up far too much of her thoughts sitting on a stool, his injured leg stretched out as he repaired a coil of

214

rope on the small table. Overhead, the late-afternoon sun filtered through the trees, casting shadows over him. Bits of sunlight danced over his head and shoulders, emphasizing his size. At his feet, his wolf lay on its side, tongue lolling. Nearby, on a low branch, a hawk sat and watched.

Ben worked near John, and Gascon was nowhere to be seen. The scene, one of quiet friendship from beast to bird to human, felt perfectly right. Perfectly normal. And Emily felt as though she belonged.

The next morning, John sat on a stool with a length of rope coiled between his feet. Across from him, Ben also worked on making repairs, and across the way, Emily and Mary sat on a blanket doing the mending. Willy sat next to Emily. A coil of rope sat untouched beside him. John watched Emily—or more honestly, his cousin.

Willy was smitten. Not only had he gotten up early— something Willy seldom did—but he'd bathed and shaved his beard off. From the looks of it, he'd also trimmed his hair. John didn't blame his cousin for wanting to look his best. Each morning, John also went to the extra trouble to remove the overnight stubble, and if he worked hard during the day, he often went down to the stream a second time so as not to offend Emily.

But what irritated him was the way Willy had risen early to go pick flowers for her. When Emily had left the shack, he'd presented her with a small bunch of sunflowers, goldenrod and poppies.

John frowned and pulled hard on the strands of rope he was joining. Not once had he thought to give Emily flowers. His fingers tightened on the frayed ends of the rope he was repairing.

Flowers. Sweet talk. He wasn't good at that stuff, but his cousin knew how to impress a woman. When he chose, Willy could be charming. Trouble was, it was all show. To his cousin, women were conquests. He used them to prove his own worth. He took but seldom gave.

In their youth, John had envied his cousin, who was as bold, outgoing, and outrageous as John was quiet, shy, and even uncertain around the opposite sex. Back then, it had all been a game to Willy, and the boy had taken great pleasure in boasting to John of each of his latest conquests.

John had never cared. He'd never met any woman he'd wanted bad enough to fight his cousin for. Until now. Until Emily. Things were different with her. Everything was.

Their whole relationship had been unconventional. There had been no uncomfortable introductions, no moment of awkwardness while he tripped over his tongue trying to make conversation, no awkward first meeting. They'd been dropped into each other's lives with the suddenness of a summer tornado. From the first, the threat of death had brought them together— and kept them together, stripping away all pretense. Emotionally, they were twined as one. And yet he recognized how fragile those threads were. So much could happen to tear them apart.

John's hands stilled in their twisting of the rope as he watched Emily talking with his cousin. She was everything he'd ever dreamed of and more. From the first time he'd seen her, his soul had recognized his other half. Given the choice he'd pledge his heart to her today, right now. He'd rescind his wise words of yesterday and make her his.

From the passionate kiss they'd shared, John knew it wouldn't take much on his part to do so. If he asked her to stay, she probably would. But he couldn't bring himself to try. He didn't want her to stay unless it was her choice, and the only way for her to make that choice was to have the option to leave.

When Emily rose to go into the shack several minutes later, Willy followed. She reappeared with her repaired skirt and a green blouse over her arm, then rejoined Mary, who held two towels and a bar of soap. The two women headed down to the stream behind the shack. John narrowed his eyes when Willy continued to follow. It'd be a cold day in hell before he allowed his womanizing cousin to watch them bathe!

"Willy! Don't think they want us men down there right now," he called.

Willy stopped and glared at him. "Someone should stay near to guard them. Could be some Injuns hangin' 'round."

Ben snorted and stood, grabbing up his rifle. "If there were some *Arikara* around, you'd have a hard time defending anyone against them with no weapon. I'll go, and make sure *no one* disturbs them."

John grinned with satisfaction. Willy wouldn't argue with Ben. The big trapper had a few pounds and a lot

217

more brawn over Willy. No one went up against Ben.

"Thanks," he murmured to his friend as the big man passed by. "I owe you." It frustrated him that he wasn't mobile enough to walk around for long. As it was, his leg ached something fierce from doing just his share of the work. Yet he refused to lie about and let everyone else do it all. That would be something Willy would do.

Ben lifted a brow. "Think I trust your cousin near my wife? He stays." The big man stalked off and joined the women, putting a massive arm around each of their shoulders.

Willy glared after him, then turned his sulking gaze to John. His eyes cleared. He swaggered over, looking confident. "Jealous that the li'l angel might prefer me to you, cuz?"

John struggled to his feet, ignoring his crutches. Though his thigh pained him from being on it too much, he wasn't about to allow Willy to tower over him in an attempt at intimidation.

"Back off, Will."

Willy rocked back on his heels and folded his arms across his chest. "She's fair game."

John narrowed his eyes. His cousin wore the same look he had the time John had received two wooden boats for his birthday. He'd given Willy one of them, but Willy hadn't been grateful. The boy had sulked and thrown a fit because he'd wanted the one John had kept for himself. Well, they weren't kids now, and Emily wasn't a possession to be fought over.

"Emily isn't a toy, Willy, nor is she some serving wench or whore for you to bed for sport. She's a woman who's lost her parents in a brutal massacre. She's been through a lot." He kept the part about her Indian lover to himself. That was for Emily to divulge. Or not.

Willy thrust out his chest. "We'll just let the little lady choose which one of us she wants." He smirked, his eyes glittering with malice.

John drew himself up to his full height, which made him just a hair taller. "I mean it, Willy. Leave her alone. I promised to take her home, and that's what I'm going to do." And if she decided that she didn't want or need him any longer? John put the depressing thought from him. Spring was a long way off.

"Mebbe it's time for me to think of settling. Emily will make a fine wife, don't ya think? Yep, think I'll talk the old man into givin' me my share of the money from the house now. He ain't got no use for it." Willy grinned. "Hell, mebbe he'd give it to me for a weddin' gift."

When Willy spotted his grandfather heading toward them, he winked, then left.

John struggled to hold his temper. He had a better understanding now of what drove men into fisticuffs over women. But he refused to let his cousin bait him into losing control. Especially with his grandfather still looking worn and tired. And yet it was so hard to sit back and watch Willy trying to woo Emily. His only consolation lay in the fact that Emily didn't seem even close to being swept off her feet. She was polite, but nothing more. He shouldn't feel so pleased, but he was.

Susan Edwards

Willy stomped away, and Gascon frowned at his re-
treating back. He leveled a piercing stare at John.
"You'd be wise to keep an eye on him, and watch out
for your young woman."

John sighed. "Emily isn't my woman." *Yet.* He
wished with all his heart she were, though. He thought
of her as his. His Lady Dawn. The sunshine in his life.
Since she'd come, each day seemed brighter, fuller.
He couldn't imagine not seeing her face first thing
each morning or whispering good-night to her at the
end of each day. "She's free to choose either of us, or
neither of us. Come spring, she may just want to go
home—without either." Once home, she could make
her own way or find a place to hide and lick her
wounds. Alone, if that was what she wanted.

Like a cloud sliding over the sun, the joy faded. The
fear that she'd leave him made him heavy-hearted. If
she disappeared, she'd take the sun from his life.

The bright glare of sunlight woke Emily. She swallowed a frustrated sigh, wishing for another few hours
of sleep. She tried to open her eyes, but they felt gritty
and heavy. Familiar sounds drifted in from the open
window: Mary's humming as she started on the morning meal, Ben's booming voice, and John's deep
laughter. She waited. No sound of Willy.

Sighing, she rose up on one elbow and brushed her
hair from her face. The first thing she saw made
her fall back, flat on her back with her arm across her
eyes. She groaned with frustration. Turning her head
to the side, she peeked again. Flowers.

Again.

Sitting, she glared at the posy of orange flowers lying next to her pallet. Wild geranium, Mary had called them. Every day for the last two weeks, she'd found some sort of offering from him awaiting her: flowers, feathers tied in a bundle, an unusual rock. At first she'd thought it sweet. Now, combined with his attentions during the day, it was becoming too much. He wasn't just courting her; he was bullying her. She'd tried several times to discourage him, but to no avail.

Emily ran her hands through her hair, loosening its braid. It was clear she was going to have to speak more firmly. Having never had a man court her or even ask her to a dance, she felt lacking in knowledge of how to handle the situation.

She thought about talking to John, but they never had time alone anymore. If Willy saw them talking, he came over to join them, inserting himself into their conversation.

"Conversation, bah!" Emily muttered. Willy didn't talk. He boasted, he bragged, and he preened. And he was lazy to boot. Whenever he was ordered to go and attend to some chore, he sulked.

She smoothed the strands of her hair with her fingers and deftly rebraided them into one long tail down her back. Then she sat and wished for the days when it had just been her and John. She missed those. Missed him. Missed their long walks and afternoons spent sitting along the stream, talking.

Heat crept into her cheeks. And the kissing. She couldn't forget that last afternoon together. She definitely missed John's kisses.

Emily tightened her lips in determination. This was crazy. They were friends. Maybe more. How were they to get to know each other better unless they continued to spend time together?

"Hey, Sunshine—you going to stay abed all day?"

The object of her thoughts poked his head through the door. She smiled at him, feeling as though he were the bright ray of light chasing away her dark thoughts. She stood. "I'm coming."

Seeing John's gaze lingering on the flowers lying on the corner of her blanket, she wrinkled her nose. "I don't suppose those are from you?" A thread of wistfulness crept into her voice.

John looked startled as he met her gaze. He looked uncertain as he entered. Taking her hands in his, he asked, "Are those what you want, Emily? Do you want me to give you flowers and sweet words?"

Emily considered the question. In many ways she supposed that she did want the physical proof of John's love. Each time she woke to find some offering beside her bed, her heart thumped in the hope it had been from John. But one glance at Willy's expectant gaze was always enough to tell her it was he who had left it.

Yet, staring up into John's serious amber-brown eyes, Emily realized that such wasn't really what she wanted from John. She wanted what he'd given to her before his family had returned: himself. His laughter. The sparkle of life in his eyes. His friendship.

She shook her head and smiled. "No. Words spoken with falseness and gifts given to impress are not what I want." She lowered her gaze and smoothed her skirts to hide the need in her eyes. Ever since that kiss, she'd dreamed of being held in his arms.

"What *do* you want, Emily?" John's voice was rough.

Startled by the question, she glanced over, captivated by the passion lurking deep in his eyes. Feeling as though she stood on the edge of a cliff, she couldn't tear her gaze away. She was drowning in those liquid depths. "A walk." Her voice fell, husky with longing.

"A walk. Is that all you want?" John reached out, his fingers closing gently around her upper arm. He ran his palm up and down from her shoulder to her elbow. His voice lured her closer. Her fingers touched his chest and spread out. She felt the beat of his heart beneath her palm. Then he pulled her close and drew in a deep breath, the wall of his chest lifting up her breasts. Her nipples tightened at the contact. His gaze darkened, letting her know he felt the reaction.

Her face flamed. "Some conversation. Real conversation with a friend." The words came out breathy, as though her lungs were on the brink of failing.

His head dipped. "Just a friend?" he asked.

"A very, *very* good friend," she whispered, aching deep inside with the need to be kissed by him. She'd never felt a desire so powerful.

His breath caressed her face. "And?"

"And—" She licked her lips. The air between them thickened as desire flowed forth, cocooning them in their own little world. She bit her lower lip, suddenly shy. "A kiss would be nice. Or two." The words came out a mere whisper.

John's lips brushed lightly over hers. "Now, that's a request I can't refuse."

The sound of steps behind John made him drop his arms and step away from her. Willy stomped in behind him.

"Hey, angel. The old man and I are gonna go set some traps today. Why don'tcha come?" Willy stopped and stared at the two of them.

John's gaze kept hold of hers. "Emily has plans for today," he said, putting her hand on his arm. He led the way outside.

Emily walked past Willy without realizing she'd stepped on the flowers he'd left her.

Chapter Eleven

Willy glared at John and Emily, then kicked at the flowers he'd risen early to pick for her. He'd hoped that her first waking thought would be of him. He was disappointed.

He followed them out, refusing to leave them alone. Damned if he would let John take her from him. She was his. His angel.

He remembered the day his ma died. She'd promised him that an angel would come and watch over him, and care for him, and love and protect him when she was gone. He hadn't believed her. No angel had come. No one had protected him from his drunk old man. He'd given up. Forgotten about his ma's promise. But now he believed. Emily was his angel and he'd waited a long time for her. Recalling her sweet smiles, he knew that she'd be his. She was just blinded by his cousin—hell, maybe she felt she owed John something. But the only person owed around here was him, and he'd just have to prove it to her. She was his. Not John's.

When Emily left his cousin's side to join Mary, Willy hesitated. Ben sat beside his wife. The big man stood, then walked the two women down to the stream. It had fallen to Ben to take the women down there each day.

Willy narrowed his eyes. That wife of Ben's guarded Emily like a bear her cub. But soon they'd leave. Then John and his grandfather would start leaving each day to begin trapping. And Willy usually stayed behind them.

He grinned. Finally he'd be alone with his angel. Without John around, he'd be able to convince Emily that she belonged to him.

Gascon strode up and addressed him. "After we break our fast, we'll go check the streams, see what the beaver population is and where their dams are. Pack enough for two nights."

"You didn't say nothin' 'bout bein' gone for two days." Earlier, he'd agreed to go because he'd thought Emily might go with them. Now he didn't want to leave. No way was he gonna leave her alone with his cousin. "What about John? *He* can go with you." Which would leave Emily with him.

His grandfather lifted a bushy brow. "John's not up to a long trek."

Before Willy could protest, his grandfather drew himself up and gave him his no-arguing look. "Boy, if you don't want to carry your weight this last year, then

I suggest you take yourself back to St. Louis today. I don't have time to argue with you. Either you come with me or you're out."

Spinning around angrily, Willy stormed back to the shack to gather his stuff. He hated this place. Hated the old man. If it weren't for the money he'd get when the old bastard died, he'd leave. He paused. The old man would love him to leave. That would allow John to court Emily.

"Not a chance in hell," he said with a sneer. He'd claimed his angel and no one was going to take her from him.

Outside, he tossed his pack down. The women had returned. They worked side by side while John and Ben sat a few feet away, getting the traps ready. The men's conversation, carried out in low tones but for an occasional bark of laughter, complimented the soft voices of the women. Willy's resentment built. No one noticed that he stood alone. No one invited him to join in.

He sat on a stool and leaned back, resting against the side of the shack, ignoring the rough slivers of the logs. His gaze returned to Emily. Soon he wouldn't need his cousin or his grandfather. He'd have her. She'd be his wife. He'd have his angel all to himself. All he needed was a chance to prove himself to her. If he were in the city, he'd buy her the biggest and the most expensive gifts: fine dresses, jewels, hair ribbons. It didn't matter that he had no money. There were ways to get it. Easy ways. Then she'd have it all, and when she married him, he'd be the envy of every man in St. Louis.

Susan Edwards

Dreams of his future made him smile. He didn't need his cousin or his grandfather. All he needed was this angel. Staring at her, he imagined her naked and writhing beneath him. Maybe he was going about this courting business all wrong. Maybe it was time to show her the kind of man he was.

His hand covered his swollen penis. Women understood dominance, and their cries of pleasure when he bedded them proved they liked it. He would simply show Emily what she was missing.

The skin between her shoulder blades twitched. Emily glanced up at Mary, who sat in front of her. "He's staring at me again, isn't he?" She didn't need Mary's answer; she felt Willy's gaze upon her.

Mary added pork fat to the hot cast-iron skillet. "Yep."

Emily scowled and added the leftover cold meat from supper last night. The air crackled as the fat bubbled around the meat.

Mary sent a dark look over Emily's shoulder. "I'll speak to Ben—have him talk to John or Gascon. That boy is obsessed."

"No. That'll just make things worse. I don't want to cause trouble. I'll deal with him." Emily bit her lower lip. His daily gifts, the way Willy managed to corner her, and his attempts to get her to go off with him alone were putting her on edge. There was no place where she could go to get away from him—even just out of eyesight. Even when she tried to sleep at night, she felt him watching her. It had forced her to sleep with the blanket covering her face.

228

She chewed her lower lip as she stirred the frying meat. She hated strife and confrontation, but she knew she was going to have to lay it all on the line with Willy—though she'd have thought he'd have gotten the message long before now. Obviously not. At least she'd have a couple of days without having to deal with him while he went with his grandpa.

When he returned, she was going to have to be brutally honest with him. No more gifts and no more letting him try to court her. His staring at her she would probably have to live with. She sighed. It was going to be a long six months.

Using more force than necessary, Emily scraped the meat from the pan to keep it from burning. A chunk flew into the dirt. She picked it up and, when it cooled, tossed it to Fang.

She considered why she was so repulsed by John's cousin. Sharing himself was not Willy's problem. All he did was talk of himself. No one mattered to Willy except Willy. How strange life was, flip-flopping as it had. Living with her Apollo, she'd often felt as though she'd shared all of herself while the man inside him remained an enigma to her. She'd relied on him. He'd taken care of her, and it had seemed natural to fall into his arms and share what he wanted without realizing how much more there was to be had.

She recognized now that her own sense of loneliness and gratitude had made her heart vulnerable to him. He'd been the first to care for her—it had been natural for her to fall in love and not question the wisdom of her actions. Hadn't it?

Then she'd met John, who'd shown her what true friendship was: two people getting to know each other, sharing with one another and listening and learning about the other. It was something Willy didn't understand. Not once had he asked about Emily's parents, or what had brought them out here. Not once had he considered how his attentions were affecting her. From watching him, Emily had learned enough of him to know he just hoped to wear her down enough to get what he wanted.

She sat back and stared out through the dense ring of trees that hid the path to the glade where she'd been found. She hadn't gone back since that last time with John . . . when she'd offered herself to him. Heat, but not from the fire, made her scoot away from the flames. The thought of acting so wanton still embarrassed her. But John had given her a gift: friendship. He'd accepted Emily for the person she was and hadn't judged her. He'd even refused to let her give up when all she'd wanted was to throw away her life.

Just as you gave him back the gift of his life she thought, recalling the terror of his accident and the harrowing days when she'd feared John would die. It all came down to that: life. Both men had in some way shown her the value of that. Both men loved her. And she loved them. One past. One present. But was John her future, too? How would she know?

Her gaze sought and found John talking to his grandfather. As always, his sheer size awed her, as did the easy way he moved. She watched him lift his head to the wind and sniff. The aroma of frying pork filled the air. John turned toward her and gave her a wide

230

smile, then followed his grandfather into the shack.

Mary returned wearing a satisfied grin. "Ben just told me that Gascon *and* Willy are leaving for a couple of days. I am glad of that," she said. Leaning forward, she whispered, "I'll take Ben off, too. We have some things to do as well. You and John will have time to be alone."

Startled out of her thoughts, Emily glanced behind her to see John and his grandfather talking and using sticks to draw in the dirt. Ben walked over and joined them. Willy hung back, hands in his pockets, shoulders hunched. It was his sulking pose, and one she knew well. "Mary, how do you know the difference between love and lust?"

Mary's brows lifted. She took the pan off the fire and set the coffeepot over the flames. Adding beans she'd roasted and ground earlier, she said, "When you love someone, you can't live without them. You can't bear to be apart. You need to touch them, or at least know they are close enough to touch." She winked. "And you can't keep your eyes off them, either."

"That sounds like lust to me." Emily sighed. "All I feel is confused." She frowned, troubled by her thoughts. She didn't want to hurt John or lead him on, yet there was something between them. Something definitely other than lust. Of that she was sure. But what was it? How did one define the spark of true love?

"It's that too, Emily." Her friend paused. "It's the falling in love part of love that's so hard. But when you know you're in love, and you know the man loves you in return, nothing seems impossible." Mary slid a loving look toward her husband. "Even living out in the wilds of nowhere."

"It seems so easy watching you and Ben."

"But it wasn't." The woman chuckled. "Damn near killed the man the first time I met him. Good thing he convinced me he hadn't been responsible for Robert's death."

How Mary had thought Ben responsible for her brother's death, Emily didn't know. Or how she had set out to kill him in revenge. But it was a good thing it all had been straightened out. Emily sighed. It was such a sweet, romantic story. "But you didn't."

"Nope," Mary agreed, her voice softening.

"Do you miss your family?" Emily knew from her conversations with Mary that the woman had six brothers and three sisters, and that they were close.

"Yes, but my life is with Ben now."

Emily wondered if she would ever feel that way: completed by someone else, made whole by him. It came to her that she felt safe with John. Safe to spread her wings without fear that he'd take advantage of her or pressure her before she was ready. He'd taken the time to listen to her, and he respected her—even when she'd have given in to the desires clouding her mind. But safety wasn't love. Or, at least, she didn't think it was.

The men came and got the food they were cooking. When Willy sat beside her, Emily got up and moved next to John. She didn't want to deal with his cousin. All she knew was that the thought of being alone with John, without fear of interruption, made her smile.

And the anticipation of his kisses made her heart thump a whole lot harder.

Lying on his side on a blanket spread beneath the shade of a tree, John glanced over at Emily. She was putting away the leftover food they'd brought along for their picnic. "Do you still miss him? Your Indian?" The minute the words spilled from his mouth he mentally kicked himself for bringing up her past. Ben and Mary had left shortly after Gascon and Willy, and he and Emily were at last alone. The last thing he wanted was another man—the Indian, especially—to intrude. He watched her closely, gauging her reaction.

She surprised him by smiling as if she understood, then moved to sit beside him. "I'm glad you don't try to pretend that it never happened, John. Sometimes I want to talk about it." She fiddled with a long blade of dried grass.

He waited, but she didn't say anything else. He glanced at her. "Well? Do you?"

"Do I miss him, or do I want to talk about him?" For long moments, they stared at one another.

"Both." His voice came out gruff.

Sliding down onto her side, she faced him. "Yes and no."

"Well, that answers that." He tried to instill humor into his voice.

Emily reached out and touched his arm with her fingers. "I don't really miss him anymore, John. But sometimes I miss the freedom I felt when I was with him."

233

John's pulse raced beneath the touch of her finger-tips. His gaze traveled over her features, noting the sparkle of life in her eyes, and the sweet curve of happiness to her lips. This was a far cry from the melancholy woman who'd wanted to die just over a month ago.

"Freedom to do what?" Intrigued, he watched the color creep up her neck and settle in her cheeks.

She cleared her throat and stared down at her hand on his arm. "You'll think me shameful, but I loved not having to wear clothes. I never knew how wonderful it felt to run around in just my shift or—" She broke off.

"Or nothing at all?" John grinned widely. "Don't let me stop you, Sunshine. Hell, I might even join you," he teased.

She giggled and lay back to stare up at the cloudy sky. His body reacted to the thought of Emily dancing around with nothing but sunshine warming her body. He grew aroused just thinking of it. Clearing his throat, he asked, "What else?"

She turned her head to look at him. "I loved just wandering. Seeing something new every day. Or spending a few days so high above the land that I could see beyond forever. I felt like I owned the world."

John reached out and slid his finger down her nose. "You know I'd take you anywhere. I'll buy you a mountain and build you a grand house if you want." All trace of humor fled, replaced by a raging need to touch and hold her. Her eyes darkened to a midnight blue. Rosy color crept back into her cheeks.

John lifted the backs of his fingers to her face. "What are you thinking about, Emily?" he prompted.

"N-nothing." She turned her eyes back to the sky.

John moved next to her and gripped her silky-smooth chin gently between his fingers. He forced her to look at him. "Liar. You're remembering our last kiss." His voice dropped to a husky whisper. "Know how I know?"

"How?" she asked, licking her lips.

In her gaze, he felt like a man drowning in three feet of water helpless to save himself because he'd lost his wits. He ran the pad of his thumb across her cheek, over the bridge of her nose to sweep the curve of her face to the corner of her mouth. Then he traced the line of her lips, feeling them part beneath his touch. "Because you look like you want me to kiss you again."

"Do you want to?" The question came in a breathy whisper.

John groaned, his hand sliding into her hair above her ear. "Look at me, Emily. Tell me what I want. What am I thinking?"

Emily stared deep into his gaze. She reached out to rest her palm against the side of his face. Then, as if coming to a decision, she said; "I think you want what *I* want."

Groaning, John moved over her, his lips inches from hers. "You'll never know how much." And yet he was hesitant. "I don't want to rush you, Emily."

She wrapped her arms around his neck and pulled him to her. "You're talking too much," she teased.

John didn't need a second invitation. Using all of his strength, he meant to be gentle, to go slow and stop before things exploded. But the minute his mouth touched hers, his control snapped. His mouth claimed hers with an intensity that left him aching. He demanded and he needed. His tongue plunged inside and took. Passion clouded his mind and urged him on.

He had to stop, but she tasted so sweet, felt so good. So right. His mouth merged with hers. Where he ended and she started he couldn't tell. All he knew was that he had to have her and wouldn't survive without her. A sharp nip to his tongue broke his daze. Fearing he'd been too rough, he tried to pull away and apologize. It took him a moment to realize she'd captured his tongue between her teeth. She sucked and caressed it with the tip of her own. Flames of desire shot from his mouth to his groin.

Emily became the aggressor, then, kissing him in a way that left him breathless. She forced her way into his mouth with her tongue. Plunging and withdrawing, she drove him wild with the rhythm his body yearned to imitate. They pulled apart reluctantly, breathlessly, each gulping with lungs starved for air. The sound of their harsh breathing drowned out all else. Her breasts rose and fell, grinding against his chest.

Keeping his weight from crushing her by resting on his forearms, John dropped his head to the softness of her breasts and heard the frantic beating of her heart. Her fingers slid over his shoulders, curved around his arms and down to his hips. He had to move off her, put distance between them. Yet the words died in his throat.

Nothing short of an act of God could have stopped him from lowering his mouth to hers. This time he went slowly, his tongue stroking gently over her swollen lips before trailing the line of her jaw. He nipped her earlobe. His hand slid between them and cupped her breast, his fingers feathering lightly over its taut peak through the fabric of her dress.

"You're teasing me." Emily moaned, trying to bring his mouth back to hers. She needed his kiss, had to have his mouth on hers, wanted to feel his hand cupping her breasts, skin to skin.

Instead of answering her plea, John continued to tease her with his tongue. From her ear, he blazed a heated path down her neck, back along her collarbone, and up to the hollow of her throat, where his hot breath sent shivers dancing down her spine. The ache lodged between her legs. She arched her back, forcing her breast harder against his palm.

She felt on fire. She ached. She needed this man—now. Throwing caution to the wind, Emily rolled him over, slipped out of her skirt, and straddled him. Without thought, she pulled off her blouse and tossed it aside.

She watched John's eyes widen. She stared down at herself, seeing the bold jutting of her heavy breasts, their pink nipples tight, their tips large peaks. She felt self-conscious sitting there with him staring at her. She'd hated her size, hated having men stare at her, until her Indian Apollo had made her feel beautiful. And now, again, watching John's eyes widen with first

237

appreciation, then desire, she no longer hated the shape of her body.

"You're beautiful," he said in a croak, taking a breast in each hand. "Perfect," he said under his breath, squeezing gently.

Seeing his hands cupping her, Emily thought so too. It was as though she had been made for him. Another claim of her father's fell by the wayside. He'd told her that her size was a sign of the devil, and only a man with evil in his heart would want her. With married men so often bold in their advances, she'd believed him.

John raised up, his lips closing tenderly around one breast's proud tip. As he suckled first one, then the other, Emily threw her head back and moaned. With each sharp tug, blood throbbed in her groin. She shifted, finding the bulge of his arousal beneath her. She rocked upon it, slid over him. His hands moved around her buttocks and pulled her tight against him. His fingers followed the curve of her spine, then returned to her buttocks. He held her poised over him. Her wet heat locked against his swollen length. She moaned and he groaned as they kissed.

He rolled her over, settling his hips into the cradle of hers. "I want you, Emily."

She sobbed his name then, for he had slid the length of his covered erection ever so slowly over the damp mound of her sex. Her legs parted farther. She wanted to feel him against her. In her. She tore at his shirt. "Yes," she cried, jerking her hips upward.

Another slow slide of his buckskin-covered shaft over her sensitive flesh brought a sheen of sweat to

John's brow. It sent waves of need coursing through her. "Don't make me wait, John," she begged. "I need you. Now."

John yanked off his shirt and unbuttoned his breeches, rising up onto his knees. "Be sure, Sunshine. Be sure. I couldn't live with your unhappiness."

"I'm sure, John. Please!" And she was. She needed him. She wasn't sure this was love, but she needed him in a way that left her scared and vulnerable as she'd never felt before. She could no longer control herself.

Standing, John kicked off his buckskins. Emily drew in a breath at the sight of him. When he knelt over her, his manhood large and erect, her mouth fell open. His hands weren't the only part of John that was huge. Awed, she reached out and took him in her hand, her fingers barely able to close around him. He shuddered.

Her heart pounded when he moved over her, but her legs parted and her knees lifted and fell to the side.

"I love you, Emily." He stroked the moist folds of flesh of her sex with the tip of his.

"I—"

John's lips silenced her. "Don't. Don't say it just because I did. When you're ready, the words will come. And if they don't, then give me—us—this. Just tell me that you want this as much as I do and that you won't regret it."

Emily's breath hitched, waiting desperately as she was for him to enter her. She felt him throbbing at her entrance, pulsing lightly against her flesh like the beat of a butterfly's wings. "I want you, John. More than

239

I've ever wanted anything. I don't know if that's love. All I know is that if you left me today, I'd turn to dust and blow away."

With a cry of some tightly held emotion, John gathered her close and kissed her. Emily wrapped her legs around his waist and cried out when he pressed into her, slowly merging them into one. For a long moment, it was enough. The feel of him stretching her, filling her. Her hands stroked his back, his sides, then tangled in his hair.

His head lifted, then ducked down to find her breasts. His tongue lapped and laved and circled her aching nipples. One of his hands traveled down her belly to the place where they were joined. He touched her, igniting a new fire as he stroked the most sensitive spot on her body. The pleasure, pure and explosive, burst from her. Her hips rose, her cries turning to whimpers of need as she tried to force him to move inside her.

John whispered words of love while teasing and taunting her breasts. His tongue flicked their hard peaks while his fingers stroked the swollen bud between her legs. Her hips fought against the heavy weight of him pinning her to the ground. She wanted him. Needed to feel harder strokes. But she couldn't move. She squeezed her buttocks, feeling him throbbing inside her.

The tension built. She arched her back, thrusting her breast into his mouth. He suckled at it, the tip of his tongue stroking across its peak in time to the pulsing deep within her. "Please, John. Now." The world spun.

White Dawn

John lifted his head and stared down into her eyes. "Yes, Sunshine. Now. Let me feel you explode around me." His finger circled harder, faster. His throbbing manhood shifted as he moved up to claim her mouth with his.

His words and his touch and his kiss sent her over the edge. Her fingers clutched his shoulders as she burst into flames that erupted through the heavens in millions of glowing sparks.

Chapter Twelve

John gritted his teeth against the spasms of Emily's sex convulsing around him, urging him to begin the hard and furious strokes that would take him over the edge. But he held back. Held himself rigid until he felt Emily go limp.

Reaching down, he slid his hands beneath her buttocks and lifted, bringing her hard against him. He withdrew, then slid back into her, burying himself to the hilt, stretching her, feeling himself fill her completely.

She gasped. Lifting her legs, she planted the soles of her feet against his shoulders as he pulled out, then pushed in with slow, even strokes. She arched her back off the ground. Faster and faster he thrust, and louder and more frantic came her cries. Her hips jerked, her feet pushing against him in her frantic

need. With each thrust, he clenched his fingers over
the cheeks of her buttocks to grind her quivering body
tightly against him. His control slipped, the pinnacle
loomed, and he pounded against her. Each breath he
released was a harsh moan.

"Now, my sweet Lady Dawn. Now."

"Yes, yes," she cried, throwing her arms over her
head, her head rolling back and forth with each of his
wild thrusts. She gasped his name then. He felt her
stiffen, felt her body tighten around him, squeezing
and squeezing until John himself went rigid. His cry
of release mingled with hers.

The sensation of flying overtook him. John tried to
hang on to it, wanted it to last forever, but his body
collapsed atop Emily's. Her legs relaxed and fell from
his sides, and his and Emily's chests rose and fell with
shallow breaths.

Lifting his head John stared down at Emily, en-
chanted by her full, parted lips, the wild disarray of
her hair spread out around her head like a halo, and
the sound of her breathing. Her eyes, heavy with passion, opened. She flushed, stains of embarrassment
creeping up her neck.

"You're beautiful, Emily. That was beautiful. A gift
I'll treasure always."

Her fingers slid through his hair, long, dark strands
of which fell to frame his face like a dark curtain, se-
creting the two of them from the world. "I never . . I
mean, not like that—"

John silenced her with a gentle kiss and whispered,
"I understand. I've never felt this way with any other
woman. Never wanted to watch, needed to make it

last as long for her as I could." He lifted his head. "This is different. You are different, and you make me feel different—as if this were the first time." And it was, in a sense, because it was the first time he'd ever been in love. He rolled to one side, taking Emily with him, refusing to part them. His hand lifted to brush the hair from her face.

She traced the tip of her finger over his lips. "I was so afraid you'd be disappointed."

Startled, he lifted his head. "Why would I be disappointed?"

She ran her finger over his chest, refusing to look at him. "I'm used."

John forced her to look at him. "Would you be disappointed if I told you that you aren't my first? Or second? Or third?"

Emily wrinkled her nose. "No one expects a man to wait."

"I don't hold to double standards. I love you, and that's all that matters. The past is past. For you. And me."

Emily smiled up at him, relieved that he didn't hold her past against him. For it *was* the past. Now there was only John and the incredible way he made her feel. Right now, she was very much afraid it was love she felt—a deeper and truer love than she'd known before. "You're wonderful, John. Sometimes I'm afraid to believe that you are real. I don't deserve someone like you."

He brushed her lips with his. "That's where you're wrong, Sunshine. You've lived your hell; you deserve a bit of heaven. Maybe I won't be the one to give it to you for eternity, but I want that for you. And I'd try to give it to you if you let me."

And he would. She knew he'd try to move the earth and the heavens if she asked. "You do make me happy, John."

Pulling her on top of him, he gave her a wicked grin. "We have the rest of today and all of tomorrow before my family returns. I'd like to make you a lot happier." He moved inside her, showing her what he intended—and that he was capable.

Settling herself over him, Emily smiled, satisfied at the feel of him hard and throbbing inside her. Taking a deep breath, she lifted up, then lowered herself all the way down his newly swollen length. He filled her and, to her delight, her body responded as if they had not even paused. "Well, are you going to talk or finish what you started?" She squeezed the inner walls of her body and felt his hips jerk in response.

John reached up and grabbed her. "Damn, woman, you'll finish me off before I'm ready." He groaned.

Emily fell forward, her palms cushioned by the soft mat of hair on his chest. "But I'm ready, John," she said, panting. And with that she gave in to the renewed passion flooding through her.

John and Emily spent the rest of that day and the next walking, talking, and kissing. They spent the night together alone in the cabin, simply making love.

Emily woke before the sun and sat up. She ran her fingers through her hopelessly tangled hair. John's grandfather and cousin were due back today. She hated to see her time alone with John come to an end.

He pulled her back to him. "We'll find a way to be alone again." He kissed her long and hard.

"Not while your cousin is here. I don't want to cause trouble." Emily rested her head on his shoulder, her fingers absently trailing a path through the thick mat of hair on his chest.

"My cousin will have to accept what is." John's voice was hard.

Emily lifted her head. "I hope so. But out of respect for your grandfather, we can't flaunt it." She sighed. "I'll miss our walks, though."

John's fingers slid down to cup one breast. "Just our walks?"

"Well . . ."

At his shocked glare, she laughed. "I might miss kissing you."

John growled and rolled her onto her back. "Just kissing?" He was hard, already aroused. His swollen manhood pressed into her, probing the entrance to her rapidly moistening sex.

Biting her lip to keep from begging him to make love to her, Emily tried to keep the laughter from her voice. "What else is—" Her voice caught when he slid into her. He penetrated her fully.

"This. Will you miss *this?*" His mouth latched onto the engorged tip of her breast. "And this?" He moaned then, as he nipped her. Withdrawing, he left just the tip of himself pulsing within her throbbing heat. "Tell me, Emily. What will you miss?"

"This." Her fingers slid down his chest and found his flat male nipples. She lightly pinched them, felt the rumble in his chest as he caught his breath. He thrust back inside of her. "And that." She gasped. Then her fingers trailed lower, to where they were joined. She looked down to where her pale curls nestled against his midnight-black ones.

Lifting her arms, she pressed her nails into his buttocks—then she whimpered, bringing his mouth to hers. "And this. All of it. You. You're right. We'll just have to find a way to be alone."

The sun had fully risen before Emily woke again. This time she dressed. John woke and dressed as well. Before they left the cabin, they placed their bedding back in the usual spots, and opened the shutters and door to air the scent of lovemaking from the tiny shack.

Outside in the warm fall day, John pulled her into his arms and held her tightly. "Marry me, Emily."

She closed her eyes tight. She wanted to marry him. Thought what she felt was love. But she had to be sure. And as long as she lived here, where she was dependent on him, she'd never know for sure. "John—"

Holding her from him, he smiled sadly. "I know. Just know that I've asked you. I'll take you back to the mission, then to Kentucky to find your father. I won't rush you. And I won't pressure you. You don't have to give me an answer right away. But I want you to know that my intentions are honorable. I don't want you for just a few days or a few months. I want you at my side forever. I want to laugh with you. Cry with you. Even fight with you so we can make up. I want to spend my life with you and grow old with you. I want to share the dawns and sunsets of every day with you. I *love* you."

"That's the nicest thing anyone has ever said to me." Tears spilled from Emily's eyes, and a funny feeling in her stomach made her rub at the spot. Hand in hand, they left the shack.

Emily started the morning meal. It was odd, cooking alone, but since Mary and Ben had taken off after Gascon and Willy had left, she'd gotten used to it. She grinned. Mary had understood all too well Emily's desires. And Emily appreciated her friend's disappearance. This time alone with John had been heavenly. But now other things were intruding on her happiness. Though they still had the day ahead of them, Emily dreaded the return of Willy.

As it had for the last few mornings, her stomach seemed to knot up, making her nauseated. Figuring it was the combination of being tired and fearing Willy, she ate a biscuit and drank some tea that Mary had left behind. As she was sipping the tea, she saw Ben and Mary returning.

Sitting very still, Emily was shocked to find the sick feeling didn't go away. This morning, the aroma of frying fat made her stomach turn. Finally, when she could stand it no longer, she crashed past the incoming Ben and Mary and ran down to the stream, fighting overpowering waves of nausea. She lost.

A few minutes later, she knelt at the water's edge and splashed the cold liquid on her face.

"Are you all right, Emily?" she heard.

She glanced over her shoulder to find Mary. She didn't want the older woman to worry. "I'm fine.

Haven't felt well for the last few days. It'll pass."

Mary frowned. "What's wrong? Besides being sick to your stomach."

Shrugging, not wanting to make a big deal out of it, Emily started to stand. When another wave of sickness hit, she sat back down. "Mostly I'm just tired," she explained. But, in truth, she was starting to get a bit worried. There were no doctors out here if she was gravely ill.

Mary sat down. "Emily, did you and John sleep together?"

Emily stared at her friend. There was no censure, no hint of condemnation in her voice or eyes. Just curiosity. "Yes," she admitted.

"Well, I've got three older sisters. When they each got with child, they were all sick. And tired. Could you be with child?"

"John and I only made love for the first time a couple of days ago," Emily said, feeling her face heat with embarrassment at such frank talk.

Mary looked relieved. "Oh. Then it's way too early."

A sudden chill went through Emily. For John, yes. But not if she was with child from her Indian lover. Frantically she tried to recall her last monthly. Surely she'd had one since John found her. With horror she realized her last flow had been during her time with her Indian warrior—right before he'd abandoned her.

"Oh, Mary," she cried, panicking. "I've missed two flows."

Puzzled, Mary stared at her. "I thought you said you hadn't slept with John until recently."

Tears welled in Emily's eyes. "That's true. But—"

"But what? Tell me what's wrong, Emily."

Needing the advice of her friend, Emily told her the full truth of what had happened to her. When she finished, Mary's mouth was open. For once, the outspoken woman was speechless.

"Well?" Emily demanded. Had her confession cost Mary's friendship?

"Oh, my! That's a fine pickle," the woman said. Her eyes were wide. She leaned forward and hugged Emily. "I hate to say this, but it's my guess you're with child." Her face, when she sat back, was full of sympathy and understanding.

"What am I going to do?" Emily felt as though the world had crashed at her feet. Strangely, it had taken until this moment, but she had finally realized that she loved John. Loved him so deeply and naturally that she hadn't even felt the change. But she did. For days she'd felt giddy with happiness just believing they were going to marry. She wanted it. She wanted him. She wanted all that they had together. But now . . .

"You're going to tell John," Mary said firmly. "Trust him, Emily. He'll understand."

Emily stared out across the stream, unseeing. Yes, she'd tell John. Because now she couldn't marry him. Like her mother, she'd gotten in the family way with someone other than a husband. But unlike her mother, she would never marry. The consequences of that—the possibility love turning to hate—were too great.

Mary tapped her shoulder. "The food is still on the fire. Are you coming?"

Emily shook her head. "Not yet. I think I need to be alone."

Mary stood. "All right." Then, before she left, she bent down and gave Emily a hug.

Emily waited until she was alone before she let herself cry. Her heart felt like it had just broken in two. That she could never marry the man she finally realized she loved was almost more than she could bear. But she couldn't now. And she had to tell him the truth.

Willy wasn't happy. In fact, he was downright furious. Across the way, John sat on a log with Emily in front of him. His cousin's arms were draped over her shoulders as he helped her tie a complicated knot. Emily leaned back in his arms, John's head dropping so his mouth grazed her temple. And this hadn't been the first time he'd seen them sitting so close. Or looking like they shared something special.

He and his grandfather had been back for more than a week, and it was clear that something had happened between Emily and John while they were gone. The two often went off alone now, returning with freshly gathered berries or greens. They acted like nothing serious had happened between them, but Emily's flushed cheeks and the sparkle in her eyes gave her away.

Also, Willy's cousin had changed. He had grown more possessive of Emily. He would touch her now, sometimes just a brush of his shoulder or hand, or sometimes a lingering look. Other times he'd sit close to her—as he did right now.

251

Suddenly Ben yelled out for John's help. As his cousin got up and left Emily to practice tying the knot, Willy grinned. Hurrying over, he took John's seat. "How 'bout I teach you another knot. I know lots," he boasted, moving behind her.

Emily got to her feet, dropping her rope. "No. I've had enough for today."

Willy stood and stepped in front of her. He reached out and grabbed her arm. "Then we'll go gather some of those plants ye're always lookin' fer." He wasn't going to take no for an answer this time. She never refused John.

Emily tipped her chin at him. "No—"

Willy interrupted her. "You go off with John all the time. You have to be fair. You have to give me a chance. Women like me. Let me prove it to you." He winked. "And don't go telling me you ain't kissin' John when you two are alone. I got eyes. I see what's goin' on." He forced his smile to remain in place and his tone to be joking, but he was serious. No one took what belonged to him. If his cousin hadn't been around and just happened to have saved his angel, Emily would have chosen him. Willy knew it. Felt it in his heart. How could she belong to anyone else but him when her smile sent his heart soaring, and her beauty eased the bitterness in his soul? She was the angel his ma had promised! The woman he'd spent his adult life searching for. They were meant to be together. He just had to convince her.

Emily yanked her arm from his grasp and stared at him, her blue eyes sparkling with fury. "Then pay at-

252

tention to what you are seeing." Anger burned in her voice.

"I've tried to be patient with you, Willy. I don't want to hurt you, but you won't listen—so that leaves me no choice but to make myself perfectly clear." She jabbed him with her finger. "Leave. Me. Alone. Period. I am not interested in you. I don't want you to court me. I don't want you to teach me to tie knots or anything else. I don't want to go off with you. I want *nothing to do with you*. I want you to leave me alone. Is that clear enough for you?" And with that, Emily stormed away.

Stunned at the vehemence in her voice, Willy stared after her, his jaw hanging open. No! She couldn't be serious. How could she not feel what he felt? Hurt welled from his heart to his throat, leaving him unable to speak. She never talked to John that way. Or anyone else. The old bitterness and resentment built. When she slipped into the shack, he glanced around. No one had witnessed their exchange. John and Ben were busy carrying a large fallen log to the chopping area. Off among the trees, Mary was hanging the wash, and Willy's grandfather was out traipsing around somewhere.

Moving fast, he followed Emily inside the shack. She jumped when he did.

"Willy," she warned, glancing out the window. She tried to edge past him, back out the door. He blocked her way. He was tired of coming in second to his cousin, getting the leftovers. He'd had women, sure, but no good ones. Those apparently all liked John more than him. From his childhood came snatches of rebukes.

Why can't you sit still? Be good, like John.

Why can't you study harder? Be smarter, like John.

Willy was tired of everyone comparing him to John and finding him lacking. He stepped forward, forcing Emily back farther inside the building. Grabbing her by the arms, he yanked her close and kissed her. He'd show her he was as good as his boring cousin! His hand closed over her breast and his mouth forced hers to open.

She struggled, but he held her tight. As soon as her lips parted to scream, he thrust his tongue inside. She would be his. No one would take this prize from him. She just needed convincing.

But the sharp bite of her teeth on his lip made him pull back with a howl. Her elbow slammed into his stomach, and her knee kicked up, smashing into his groin. He yelled, then bent over, the air gushing from his lungs as pain replaced all desire. He fell to his knees.

Emily wiped her mouth and glared at him. Bending down, she picked up a pouch of blue glass trade beads and threw them at him. "How dare you?" The bag slammed into his head. A second one landed a blow to the side of his face.

"Hey! Stop!" Willy fell back, trying to dodge the flying missiles. The throbbing in his groin made it hard to stand, and her shrieks made him cringe.

"What's going on in here?"

Willy whirled to see John looming in the doorway. He tried to stand.

One look at Emily's bruised lips, and fury brought John's brows together. His fist shot out and into Willy's face.

A moment later, Willy felt himself picked up and thrown across the room. He slammed into the log wall. His nose throbbed and his mouth filled with the coppery taste of blood. Using the back of his hand, he wiped the blood away and got to his feet. He hurt all over but he was ready to battle for the right to claim Emily. "Ye're not takin' her away from me, cuz. She's mine."

John pulled her to his side. "Emily isn't a prize to be won in a fight." His voice held contained fury. "And I've asked her to marry me," he announced quietly.

Shocked, Willy wiped his bleeding nose on his shirt. He shook his head. "I don't believe you." He gasped past the pain.

"It's true," Emily said, tilting her chin, staring down at him as if he were beneath her contempt.

Willy glared at John. "I didn't hear the angel say she accepted," he challenged. "I can still court her."

Emily narrowed her eyes and took John's hand in hers. "I have accepted."

"So don't ever go near her again," John warned. And with that, he turned to usher Emily outside.

Willy got to his feet and stood in his grandfather's shack, shocked and still bent over in pain. He watched John hold Emily close; then they were gone from view. He staggered to the doorway to see them heading into the shelter of the trees.

Pain, worse than his throbbing nose or groin or head, struck. The angel, like everyone else, had rejected him.

John led Emily into the trees, then stopped when they were out of earshot of the others. "I'm sorry, Sunshine. I won't hold you to that. But maybe if Willy thinks we're going to be married, he'll leave you alone."

Seemingly exhausted, Emily rested her head on his shoulder. "Do you really believe that?"

John hesitated. "Maybe." Probably not. He knew his cousin well. Willy would keep at Emily, refusing to believe she'd turned him down. He was kind of slow that way, and he would despise that she'd agreed to marry John, instead. It would hurt his pride, and that was something Willy did not take well.

John rubbed his bruised knuckles with some satisfaction, then was surprised when Emily said. "Maybe I should leave, John. I've caused enough trouble."

He shook his head. "No more than I've always lived with. Worse, I used to give in to Willy's tantrums. It was easier than to listen to him complain. And easier on my parents, who tried their best to give him what he needed. But he didn't want their love. He just wanted everything that I had." He fell silent. "But you may be right. It might be best if we leave."

"We?" She looked at him with sad eyes. "I can't ask you to leave your grandfather, John."

"You're not asking. And he'll understand. I'll ask Mary and Ben to remain for the winter. He said he only wants to stay one more."

"John?"

Pulling the woman he loved into his arms, he held her close. "Yes, Sunshine?"

"I can't marry you." The words ended on a choked sob, but John barely heard. Blood was pounding in his ears.

"Because of my cousin?" His stomach clenched. If Willy had messed this up for him, he'd beat his cousin to a bloody pulp.

She shook her head no and wouldn't meet his eyes.

He tipped her chin up and fingered the tiny indentation there. "Then why?" He'd felt so sure that she loved him, that once they left here, she'd have all her fears put to rest.

Emily pulled out of John's arms and hugged herself. Her blue eyes swam with tears, reminding him of the sky during a summer storm when there were still patches of blue peering through the pouring rain.

"I'm with child."

It took a moment for the words to sink in. His first reaction was joy. Then he realized it was way too soon for her to know she was pregnant with *his* child. Understanding dawned. She'd gotten with child during her time with the savage. The air left his lungs. He wasn't sure what to think. What to feel. Did it matter? No. At least he didn't think so. He wouldn't let it. He *couldn't* let it.

"It doesn't matter," he said. But to his own ears, the words lacked conviction.

Emily smiled sadly. "I can't accept that, John. You haven't even had time to think about it, let alone know your feelings." She pulled her heart-shaped locket from its place between her breasts and opened it, then

257

pointed to one of the portraits. "That's my father, Matthew Sommers. I've never met him. And I don't even know if he knows I exist. My mother married Timothy Ambrose, the man I grew up *believing* to be my father. She was pregnant with me, yet married someone else—who ended up hating both my mother and me. He made her life hell. And mine."

She snapped her locket closed, then said, "I can't do that to you, or my child." Tears flowed down her face, and she paused. "The funny thing is, I discovered that I *do* love you. But I can't have you." Having said those words, she turned and fled.

John stood there in shock, wanting to run after her; yet she was right. He needed time to sort things out.

"You going to let that girl go? Going to let something in her past pull you two apart?" Gascon Cartier stepped out from behind a tree.

John glanced at his grandfather.

The old man shrugged. "I couldn't help but overhear. I was coming back to camp, but . . . Didn't want to crash in on the pair of you."

John gave his grandfather a hurt look. "Well, then, as you said. You heard her: I can't force her. It's got to be her choice."

"And yours as well." Gascon lit a pipe. Blue-gray smoke curled up over his head. "If you truly love her, the babe won't matter."

John did love Emily. Deep down, he knew the babe didn't matter. The father was long gone, out of Emily's reach. Especially if John took her away from—That thought made him realize he did harbor some insecurities. Even some resentment that the child she'd give birth to wasn't his. Though he'd meant what he'd said when he reassured her that the past was past, that it didn't matter that he hadn't been her first or only lover, a child was a different matter. It brought the past, the present and the future together. A child would forever be a reminder of the man she'd once loved.

John sighed. Until today, her past hadn't mattered. What if she married him and lived to regret it? He welcomed his grandfather's interruption to his depressing thoughts.

"Take her back to the mission she came from, son. There's no question she has to leave before that fool cousin of yours does something stupid." Gascon gave John a hard stare. "And you don't want to be the one who punishes him for it."

Left alone once more as his grandfather wandered back to camp, John knew the old man was right. If Willy tried to force himself on Emily again, John would kill him, family or not. In that, Willy had gone too far and things would only continue to get worse between them—unless John left. He had to take Emily away. But what lay ahead? He wished he knew.

Chapter Thirteen

Emily sat on the bank, staring blankly out over the water. She'd run here, needing solace and comfort from what had just happened. She tossed a rock into the shallows. It splashed and created ripples, those circles widening just like the consequences of her carefree summer. The pain and problems just kept growing.

Tears threatened to spill, and the lump in the back of her throat made breathing difficult. She should have told John sooner, as soon as she'd learned she was with child. But she'd been afraid. And ashamed. And in love.

She'd never given thought to becoming with child. And since so much had happened since the baby's father had left her, she hadn't paid attention to her monthlies. She thought of her Indian Apollo. What would he have done had he known about the child? Would it have made any difference? Would he still have abandoned her?

For a brief moment she tried to imagine how it could have been; then she realized it didn't matter. It was too late. There was no way to find him and tell him of the child their love had created. There was no way to go back to what had been—even if she could make it seem as if he'd never left.

Frowning, Emily realized she wasn't sure she'd even want that. Yes, they'd shared an idyllic time. Yes, she'd been happy. But hadn't she been happier since? Even if it was now tearing her apart, the love she had for John had made her feel complete.

In his own way, she now knew her golden warrior had loved her—his obvious anguish when he'd left her in the meadow had told her that much. Or at least she chose to believe it.

Why he'd left, she'd never know; but he'd given her so many gifts that she no longer hated him for going. Aside from the necklace and wooden box that she'd hidden among her things—reminders of that first love—her Indian had given her something much more precious: the beginnings of a new life for herself. Freedom. He'd briefly shown her what it was like to be without fear and worry. He'd taught her to live each day to its fullest, appreciating the very land that both supported and threatened her. No matter where she went in life, she'd always be grateful to him for that. And now, as she considered her future, she also realized that he'd given her another gift: the new life growing inside her.

No matter the circumstances of her baby's conception, she'd already formed an unbreakable bond with this child. She'd guard this innocent life with her own. But the joy and the anticipation of being pregnant were dimmed by the hurt that came from knowing that because of it she could no longer marry John. She didn't dare.

Opening her clenched fist, she stared down at her mother's locket. In her palm, Emily held the proof of a past sin. Her mother had gotten with child and married another man. She'd paid for it with her happiness and—ultimately—with her life. Emily, too, had paid for that sin. Such a cycle would not be repeated.

Still, it hurt. Emily knew now that she truly loved John, and a future without him seemed bleak. She rested her head on her drawn-up knees. "What am I going to do?" she asked herself.

"You're going to talk to your friend, that's what you're going to do." Mary appeared out of nowhere and plopped down beside her. "What did Willy do back there?"

Emily turned her head. She'd forgotten about Willy. His actions paled in comparison to her pain at having to turn down John's desires for their future. "He just had some trouble understanding what 'no' meant."

"So I heard." Mary looked amused when she added, "Guess you took care of him, though." She sobered. "Not that it will stop him from trying again."

Shrugging, Emily sighed. "He won't be a problem for long. John's taking me back to the mission."

Mary's eyes turned sad. "I'll miss you. I was looking forward to spending the winter in the company of another woman. But I understand. John's smart to leave with you. It'll just get uglier if you stay." She looked uncomfortable. "You know what I mean."

"I do." Emily touched Mary's arm. "I'll miss you too. Maybe I'll come to St. Louis someday and see you there."

"That'd be nice. So, what will happen between you and John?"

Emily scooped up another handful of rocks and tossed them one by one at the river. Some hit the water. Some fell short. "I told him about the baby."

Mary lifted a brow. "And?"

"He wants me to marry him."

"That's wonderful, Emily. You two belong together."

Emily thought so, too. If only circumstances were different. She stared at her friend. "I said no."

"What?" Mary's eyes clouded. "Emily, why?"

Staring down at the portraits of her parents—her true parents—Emily let her tears fall. "If I marry him pregnant with another man's child, I'll be no better than my ma."

Her friend drew herself up. "What nonsense is that? Now, you listen to me, Emily. You don't know your parents' story. You can't judge them. For all you know, they were in love and something happened to prevent them from marrying."

Her lips trembling, Emily snapped her locket shut. "Doesn't really matter, does it? I only brought shame and anger into my mother's life." It hurt to remember how her mother had been so unhappy. That she'd never laughed. That she'd aged and died long before her time. That she'd never been free to have friends and experience the joy of living. Likely because of her daughter.

Shaking her head, Mary reached out and took one of Emily's hands in her own. She squeezed gently. "That doesn't mean your life will be like hers. For whatever reason, she chose her life's path."

"Did she? I'll never know. Not unless I can find my father and learn what happened." Emily tossed the rest of her pebbles into the water and pulled away from Mary, afraid the other woman's kindness would break the fragile hold she had over her emotions. Crying wouldn't solve anything.

Another unpleasant thought occurred to her. Her future was truly uncertain, for she couldn't bear to find her father now. How could she face him with the evidence of her shameful behavior? She didn't say anything to Mary, for she knew her friend would try to make her see things differently. But she knew her own guilt.

Mary leaned back on her hands. "Did John ask you before or after he knew of the babe?"

"Before."

"And he's still willing to marry you?"

Emily sighed. "He thinks he is. But I know he'll resent this child. And he'll grow to hate me. I don't think I could bear that, Mary. I can't do to him what my mother did to Timothy Ambrose. What if he was once like John—a nice man who wanted to do right by my mother. Maybe he knew about me before they married. What if he loved my mother? Thought it didn't matter that she was pregnant with another man's child?" She used her skirt to wipe the tears from her face. "I'd die before I saw that happen to John. Or my child."

Mary sighed. Then again. The breeze ruffled her short curls. "I'm not sure what to say, Emily." She looked her in the eyes. "Except John is a good man. He'd never hate you or the child. It's not in him."

"I wish I could believe that, Mary. But from my experience, I can't. Who's to say what it is that makes a man angry? And bitterness and resentment turn to hate sooner or later."

They sat in silence. The crunch of footsteps made them both glance over their shoulders. John stood there, hands hanging at his side, his eyes shadowed. "Mind if I talk to Emily alone?" he asked.

Mary jumped to her feet and, with a reassuring smile, she left. Emily turned back to stare at the water. She felt John move behind her, then take up the spot Mary had vacated. He, too, put his arms around his drawn-up knees.

"I'm sorry, Sunshine."

Emily bit her trembling lip. "For what? That I'm with child? Or that you asked me to marry you?" She hurried on before he could answer. She didn't think she could bear to hear him take back all the wonderful things he'd said. "Don't worry, I've already released you." She couldn't help the hurt and bitterness that edged her voice.

He reached over and gently turned her to face him. "I don't regret asking you to marry me. I love you. That hasn't changed."

"But the baby changes everything. It's proof that I'm a fallen woman. That I made love with a savage."

John's eyes flashed. "I've never held your past against you. You did what you had to do to survive. Maybe you weren't forced, but you were living a life where the rules were different. I don't blame you for that, or view your actions as sinful. You were in love, and the child you carry was conceived in love."

"But—"

His fingers cut off her protest. "Listen. My offer to marry you stands." He paused as he gathered his thoughts. "You're right. I'm not sure what to think of the babe, but not for the reasons you fear. I'm sure I could accept your child as mine and give him or her the same love I'd give a child of my own flesh and blood."

His thumb lifted to wipe away the tears falling from her eyes. "I'd never blame an innocent babe for something it had no control over. Nor apparently is there any threat of the father coming to claim a child I'd grow to love or the woman I love more than life itself—I do admit that relieves me. And while, if I'm honest, there is a part of me that is disappointed that this child isn't mine, that doesn't mean I will love it less."

He looked down, taking both her hands in his. "Part of my hesitation came from the fear of how you'd react. Will you always doubt me? Hold to your past so tightly that you smother our future? That's what I'm afraid of, Emily. I can't live with such fear and doubt. I wouldn't survive seeing our love turn bad."

Emily tried to stop the flow of her tears. How she loved this man, and her heart was breaking. "The answer is simple. We can't marry." No matter that she knew she did right—the words hurt.

"No. We must marry. We'll give the child a name so that he or she doesn't live with the stigma of being a bastard. You don't want that, do you? Then, whether we hold each other to our marriage is something that can be decided later. Once the babe is born, we can decide what will be best for all of us." John gave her a small smile. "How about it?"

Emily wanted to marry him. Wanted his name. Wanted him and all he was for her child's father. But . . . "I'm so afraid of losing your friendship, John. This will change everything." She let him pull her into his arms. His chin rested on top of her head.

"No, it doesn't, Sunshine. It just makes everything a bit more complicated." He smiled again, gently.

Glancing up, she looked into his eyes. It thrilled and astounded her to see love shining there. The thought of one day seeing hatred in its place was terrifying.

He lowered his head and kissed her. The touch of his lips was soft and sweet. "You don't have to decide right away. Let's take it one day at a time. All right?"

Not knowing what else she could do, Emily nodded. "All right."

They sat there for a while, each lost in their own thoughts. When John finally rose, Emily allowed him to escort her back to the others. Soon she'd be back at the mission, where it all had started. Then she'd have to make some decisions regarding her future. And that of her child.

* * *

John left Emily with Mary and went in search of Ben. He and Emily had agreed that the trapper should be told the truth so that they could leave as quickly as possible for the mission without any unnecessary difficulties. He told his friend what he needed to, then went in search of his grandfather. Gascon would be understanding, John knew. He would approve of John's plan. The only person who wouldn't be told what was going on was Willy, and John's cousin was too busy licking his wounds and wallowing in self-pity to notice anything amiss.

Which was fine with John. Willy could only cause problems if he knew they were leaving. John planned to be long gone before Willy discovered that they'd left. Then Ben would simply tell him that they'd run off to get married. Even if Willy tried to follow, they were counting on him to head south, back to St. Louis. He wouldn't go east. As far as John knew, Willy didn't know about the mission.

Supper that night was a strained affair. Willy glared at John then eyed Emily as if she'd betrayed him. He ignored everyone else. Only Ben and Mary's chatter kept the others' silence from turning awkward. Yet all too soon, the married couple decided to go to bed.

When Mary rose, Emily stood too. "I'll turn in as well." She went inside the shack and motioned for Mary to follow.

John got out his knife and starting chipping at a hunk of wood. He needed something to keep his hands busy or he'd be tempted to smash his fist into his cousin's face again. All through the meal, he'd watched Willy stare at Emily. He knew his cousin, knew the man was plotting how to take Emily away.

For the first time, he allowed that perhaps his grand-father was right in his assessment of Willy. His cousin cared only for himself, no matter how much those around him gave. It was never enough—would never be enough. And he was ready to wash his hands of the man once and for all.

"Ben said there's some new dams two days' ride from here. Think I'll go check on them, tomorrow, see how big the beaver colony is." He let his announcement sink in.

Willy's head shot up. "Ye're leavin'?" He couldn't hide his glee.

John gave him a sharp look. "Yes. But leave Emily alone, Willy. She's agreed to be my wife."

"She ain't married to you yet, cousin."

It took all John had inside him not to jump up and wipe the grin off his cousin's face with his fist. Only the knowledge that Ben would be around to keep an eye on Willy, to keep him from harming Emily, al-lowed him to continue on with the plan. Between Ben and John's grandfather, Willy would find even less chance to talk to her than when John was around. And at night, as arranged earlier, Mary slept with Emily in-side the cabin. She'd never let anything happen to the girl.

Still, John slept fitfully. In the early dawn, he fas-tened his pack to one of the horses his grandfather had brought back from St. Louis. The pack was filled with rocks to look laden with traps and other equip-ment. In front of everyone, John bade Emily good-bye. "I'll be back in three days—four at most." He didn't kiss her, not wanting to rub salt in his cousin's wound. Emily nodded, knowing she'd be joining him soon.

John's grandfather followed him into the trees. When they were out of sight of the others, Gascon stopped. For an awkward moment, the two men stared at one another.

"Hell," Gascon said. Then he stepped forward and hugged his grandson. "You be careful."

"I will, Gramps. I'll see you in St. Louis—next year."

"Yeah, well. That lovely lady of yours might have something to say about that."

Pretending that there wasn't any strained feeling between him and Emily, or that his grandfather didn't know about it, John forced a smile. "Maybe. But I'll find you. wherever."

Gascon stared around at the forest. "Might stay here. Was only going to leave so you could find a life. You need a woman and young'uns." He leveled a hard stare at John. "Figure you got lots of time to work things through now. Don't waste it. I want to hold great-grandbabies before I die."

John sobered. "I hope to give them to you, Gramps."

Taking a leather pouch from inside his shirt, the old man tossed it to him.

John caught it and frowned at its weight. He opened it and glanced inside. "This is more than what I had," he said. His grandfather had agreed to go and dig up John's hidden cache of money.

"Don't argue. Use it for whatever you need." Gascon backed away. "If I don't see you in St. Louis next year, I'll be here."

John nodded. He hated to take the money. He had more than enough of his own. Trouble was, most of it was in a bank in St. Louis—and he didn't know how much he'd need to take Emily to her mission. Or after that. He nodded to his grandfather and vowed to pay him back next year.

Gascon walked away as Ben emerged from the trees.

"You know what to do?" John asked the big trapper.

Grinning, his friend helped him unload the rocks in his pack, leaving enough food for two days. "We'll be there. You sure you don't want me to make the trip to the post instead?"

"Nah. My thigh doesn't give me too much of a problem anymore."

"Liar."

John shrugged. After nearly two months, it had healed. Still, if he did too much the muscles tended to ache, and he still had a bit of a limp—especially when tired. With his grandfather's horse, though, he should be able to make the trip to the nearest trading post, get what he needed, and return to the rendezvous point in plenty of time. He patted his friend on the shoulder and shook his head.

Mounting, he rode off. He set himself a fast, punishing pace.

Two days later, in their usual morning bathing ritual, Emily and Mary went down to the river. "I hope this works," Emily said. She kept her voice low though she knew Willy wouldn't dare follow, not with Ben stand-

271

ing guard and his grandfather keeping him busy chopping wood.

"It'll work," Mary replied. "Tomorrow you'll be with John and on your way. By the time Ben and I return, you two will be long gone." She grinned with satisfaction.

Emily looked worried. "What if Willy is so angry he takes it out on you or Ben?"

Mary burst into peals of laughter. "Not to worry. William won't try anything. Ben scares him. And so does his grandfather. 'Sides, all he really wants is the old man's money. He'll be angry about losing you, but there won't be anything he can do about it."

The woman wiped her eyes, then got down to business. "Now, 'bout you and John."

Groaning, Emily gave her friend a look. "Not again, Mary. I told you, it won't work."

"Why are you so set against this?"

Feeling the warmth of her mother's locket against her heart, Emily stared up into the treetops. "Such an arrangement didn't work for my mother. How can I ask John to sacrifice himself for me or the baby? There's too much at stake. It's too great a risk."

Mary leaned forward and grabbed Emily's hand. "Listen to me. You are not your mother. John is not your father. Don't judge yourselves by the actions of weaker people. I know John. If he says he loves you, he does. And if he says he'll accept your babe as his, then he'll love him or her like his own." She waved up into the trees, where a hawk perched staring down at them. "Does a man who takes the time to care for wounded birds or wolves seem like a man who'd treat a child the way Timothy Ambrose treated you?"

"No. But how can I be sure?" Emily whispered. She wanted so much to believe John could accept her child and love it. But experience told her it wasn't likely.

In response, Mary smiled. "It's called trust, Emily. There are no guarantees in life. You of all people should know that. But you're going to have to find it in yourself to trust John—and yourself. And to trust the love you share. Those are worth the risk. Trust and love are your answers, Emily. If you have both, then you have a future."

Emily thought about that while they finished bathing. At last she rose, and they headed back. As soon as they returned and were safely under Gascon's eagle eye, Ben went about his duties. Emily knew he had a lot of work to do before morning and her escape.

For the rest of the day, Emily had to fight to hide her nervousness from Willy. Tomorrow she'd be gone. She didn't want him to be suspicious. Sitting on a log, she stitched the seam of a new dress she was making herself. Already she missed John: food had no taste; she couldn't sleep from worrying about him out there alone.

What if something happened to him? What if he didn't make it back? She shoved the thoughts away, realizing her silliness. She couldn't allow the fear of losing another loved one to paralyze her. Noticing her sloppy work, she ripped out her stitches and admitted that she couldn't concentrate. Even thoughts of the baby couldn't keep her mind from straying to John. Where was he? Was he all right? Would he succeed?

A shadow fell over her. She glanced up . . . and saw Willy standing over her. "Want to—"

"No," she interrupted. She refused to be bullied.

"Hey, you don't even know what I was gonna ask," he complained.

Emily resumed her sewing. "Doesn't matter. The answer is no."

"What if I just want to sit here beside ya and keep ya company?"

Emily stood. "Feel free to sit if you want." She turned to leave but John's cousin grabbed her arm.

"Be a shame if something happened to John. Then ya might have to be nicer to me." Willy's features held a cold fury.

From the corner of her eye, Emily saw Gascon rise from where he was cleaning his rifles. "Unhand me, Willy," she said. She wanted to handle this herself.

He made no move to do so. Furious, Emily jabbed him in the arm with her sewing needle. Willy yelped and jumped back, allowing her to stalk away. She didn't bother to tell him that if he was the last man on earth, she'd have nothing to do with him.

She waved Gascon off, then joined him at the table. Neither spoke, but they both heard Willy crashing off through the trees.

"You got spunk, girl," John's grandfather said. There was admiration in his voice.

Startled, Emily glanced up at him. She'd never thought of herself as strong or spunky. "I guess I do," she agreed, realizing she was becoming spunkier each day.

274

"Good. That keeps a man on his toes." His eyes softened and filled with unshed tears. "Like my dear wife. Kept me in line, she did."

Emily reached out to cover his hand with hers. "You still miss her?"

Gascon smiled. "Yep. Someday soon, I'll join her." He shot her a stern glare. "But not before I see my grandson settled."

Flushing, Emily took up her sewing and applied herself to her needle, making tiny stitches to make the seams of her dress stronger. She didn't know what to say, so she said nothing.

"Don't be stubborn, girl," Gascon said. "Listen to your heart. You love my grandson." It wasn't a question.

"Yes," she agreed.

"Then keep an open mind and heart. Things'll work out between you."

Staring at the kind old man, Emily tried to smile. He meant well, but he likely didn't know all the facts. "I wish I had your faith," was all she said.

He replied, "Before you can have faith in someone else, you have to have faith in yourself." He resumed cleaning the gun. "Think about that."

Emily did. And, as she went back to her sewing, the rest of the afternoon passed peacefully. Willy returned shortly before they sat down to eat. Over supper, Emily put the second part of her and John's plan into action.

She addressed Gascon. "I want to go and visit the graves of my parents." She didn't have to fake the tears of grief that welled in her eyes for her mother. "I need

275

to go and see them once before winter comes. Ben and Mary said they'd take me."

Gascon played his part. "Noticed you've been looking a mite peaked lately. Do you good to get away for a day."

"That's a great idea. We can all go. Have a picnic. That'll cheer you up," Willy said, daring anyone to protest.

His grandfather just lifted a bushy brow. "Thought you said you'd go with me to check the traps we laid this morning? Business isn't going to wait, boy."

"You don't need me to go," Willy complained. He narrowed his eyes, his gaze coming to rest on Emily.

She responded, "I don't think I'll be in the mood for a picnic or a lot of conversation. This is something I need to do, and I'd rather do it alone."

"*They's* goin' with you."

Emily set her nearly untouched plate of food down. Nearby, Fang waited eagerly. John had left him. "I'm not sure I could find the spot by myself, but Ben thinks he knows the area."

"Seems that as we's almost family, I should take ya." He glared at Ben and Mary.

Gascon shook his head. "Our traps won't wait."

Willy sat back, looking disgruntled, but he knew there wasn't anything he could do to change the old man's mind.

Relieved to have the fight over with, and seemingly without too much argument, Emily escaped with Mary to go wash the dishes. Fang followed, knowing he'd get to eat the leftovers.

* * *

Some mornings dawn raced across the sky, flooding the world with color. Other times it bloomed slowly, like a rose unfurling its petals one by one in the dewy air. Today it crept across the horizon, a shy maiden teasing her lover.

Normally John loved each incarnation of Lady Dawn—slow or fast. Today he impatiently awaited daylight. He paced, a dark shape in the gray morning as he waited for the hour that would bring Emily to him. Each sound of the awakening land made him spin around to peer through the trees.

Going to the log in the glade where he'd found Emily, he sat and rubbed his thigh. After three days of hard travel, his body was letting him know he'd overdone it.

This plan was worth it, he reminded himself. He knew his cousin well, and if he didn't take Emily away, Willy's advances would continue. The fact that she was "engaged" to him wouldn't matter. Only if they were married—maybe—would Willy give up. Still, John had never seen his cousin so set on one particular woman before.

Of course, John couldn't blame him. Emily was special. She was everything he'd ever dreamed of in a woman. Though she'd been listless and full of anguish when he'd first found her, she'd quickly recovered to reveal her true nature. Beneath her soft, angelic looks lay a core of steel. He rubbed his thigh, feeling the ridge of scar tissue. It'd taken courage on her part to save his life, to cause him pain to ensure his survival. And in the days following, she'd shown dogged determination in her care of him, refusing to let him die.

More than anything, it had taken courage to overcome her broken heart and allow herself to love again. John frowned. Had she really done that? With love came trust, and he realized she hadn't learned to trust again. The pain of her father's hatred, of being abandoned by her parents, had left her afraid to trust. Combined with the circumstances of her conception and birth, those facts made John suddenly fear she might never find it in her to trust him.

Somehow he had to convince her that he could love her child as his own. For three days he'd thought of her, the baby, and himself. Over and over he'd searched his heart, mind, and soul, asking himself if he could truly accept another man's child as his own. For her sake—and his own—he wanted to be sure. He never wanted to hurt her or hurt an innocent child.

The answer was yes. Yes, he could love this child. Yes, he would love Emily forever. What convinced him was the fact that he'd never felt resentment for her past—for the man who'd been her first love. The past mattered nothing to him. Only the present—and the future.

Standing to resume pacing, John stared up at the rose-gold sky wondering how could he prove his love and devotion. Words alone couldn't convince her, yet what else was there? It all came down to one word: *trust*.

He was back at the start. It was a vicious circle. Without Emily's trust there was nothing, and sadly that was the one thing he had no control over. Either she believed in him and trusted him with her heart, her soul, her life, and her child, or she didn't. And if she didn't, then there was nothing more he could do. His happiness lay in her ability to overcome her past and learn to love and believe in their future.

The realization left him despondent.

A swish of wings overhead drew his attention. He saw a hawk sitting on a branch. It was the one he'd healed. In the weeks since its release, the bird had often returned to sit near the humans who had helped him recover. The hawk had learned to overcome its fears. During its time of captivity while it healed, the hawk had learned to trust John. All it had taken was lots of patience and time. Time to soothe the bird. Patience to prove he only wanted to help. Pushing his shoulders back, John decided he just needed time. And he had that aplenty.

A low whistle from deep among the mist-enshrouded trees around the glade broke the morning stillness. Fang broke from the underbrush, running toward John, barking happily. The hawk rose up into the sky, then dipped one wing as if bidding John good-bye forever.

John waited, his breath held, his body still. On the wolf's heels, Ben stepped into the clearing, followed by Mary. Then came Lady Dawn, the sunshine of his life. She stepped into the midst of the small glade. The nut browns, tawny yellows, and russet reds of falling leaves rained down on her. Like tarnished jewels, several formed a crown of color on her head and shoulders. Absently she brushed the leaves from her and slowly glanced around. John went to her.

Though he was afraid he'd see longing and regret for her Indian lover, sparked by her return to this place, when Emily glanced up at him, his heart eased. Except for a lingering sadness, there was no regret in her eyes. And he could live with that. The Indian had touched Emily deeply, but as long as John had most of her heart, he'd not begrudge a small corner of it for the past.

"Are you ready?" John took her hands in his, needing to touch her and reassure himself that she was there—and that in a few minutes they'd be on their way.

Emily smiled, the ghosts of her past fading from eyes that rivaled the sky for blueness. "I'm ready." She turned to hug Mary.

The older woman had tears running down her face. "I'll miss you, Emily. You take care now." She dabbed at her eyes with the sleeve of her plaid shirt.

Ben set his pack on the ground and withdrew two small parfleches—the ones that belonged to Emily. She took them. The big trapper then pulled his wife into his arms and addressed John. "Don't worry about your grandfather. We'll stay and help him out."

John shook Ben's hand. "Thanks, friend."

"Take care. And let us know what happens to you." He cleared his throat, and for once it didn't boom through the treetops. "Mary and I'll return to the camp in the morning as planned. That gives the two of you a full day to get out of here without Willy trying to follow."

John nodded. After a moment, he went into the trees and came back leading two chestnut geldings, each with saddlebags and supplies tied to its back. A third horse was hitched nearby. "Figured I should just get two more horses so you could take back the one I borrowed. Old Charlie still had these two—ones I'd broken and sold to him three years ago."

Originally, John had just been planning on purchasing one horse, but in case his cousin tried to come after him, he didn't want to leave his grandfather without any. And he knew Willy would not think twice about taking Gascon's only mount.

Leaving his grandfather now, knowing the old man's health was failing, was the hardest thing John had ever done. But Emily needed him more. As well as the danger from his cousin, John wasn't sure he wanted her giving birth out here in the wilds. He wanted her near a doctor, or at least a midwife.

Holding out his hand to Emily, he gave her an embarrassed look. "I couldn't get you a sidesaddle, Sunshine. I was lucky to get these two beat-up ones." *Lucky hell.* He grimaced. They'd cost him plenty.

Emily's eyes glinted with mischief as she stood back and held out the skirts of her dress: they were full. She pulled the hem up through her legs and over the skirt's waist. "I was prepared in case you couldn't. Mary helped me sew a new dress with fuller skirts."

John grinned. "A practical woman. I like that." His smile faded. "Emily—"

"What is it?" she asked. Her blue eyes clouded with worry.

"If you want to find your baby's father, we can try." The words came out in a rush, his voice raspy. He'd thought a lot about it and knew he had to at least offer her the choice. With the carved box and necklace that she'd said she wanted to keep to give to her child, along with knowing the location of the attack on her parents and the spot where John had first found her, John knew a good scout would probably be able to locate her child's father's tribe. They could find the babe's father: the man who'd saved Emily, the man who'd made love to her.

Holding his breath, he waited for her response.

"Why are you offering to do this?" she asked. "Have you stopped wanting to marry me?"

John reached up to cup her face between his hands. "Hell no, Sunshine. But I don't want you to have any regrets. If you still love the father and want me to try to find him, I will. I can take you to him, can return here . . ."

Emily smiled but her eyes grew moist. "I thank you for the offer, John. It's one of the nicest things anyone has ever done for me." She reached down to stroke the hard line of his jaw. "But the answer is no. I did love him, and he'll always have a special place in my heart. But it wasn't a love that was meant to be. Maybe it was to show me something. To teach me. Just as loving you has shown me things."

"Yet you can't take all that I offer?" His confusion and sadness filled his voice.

Emily looked uncomfortable, glanced down at the wolf hopping between the horses. "What about Fang?" she asked, changing the subject.

John felt even sadder. "He'll have to stay here. Gramps will bring him to St. Louis in the spring." He stared down at the wolf. "You stay, fella. I'll see you again." He gave Ben and Mary a long look, wishing they hadn't heard any of the earlier exchange. "You two make sure Gramps takes good care of Fang. And make sure Willy stays away from him."

Then, mounting, he waved farewell. With sadness in his heart, he and Emily rode away.

Chapter Fourteen

Over the next few weeks, John and Emily made steady progress east over flat plains broken only by river valleys. They rode around heaps of earth and stone and spent the night atop a *coteau,* a high rolling area with lower land on each side. Short grass gave way to medium-high grass, burned brown by the summer heat. Trees losing their leaves gave way to woodlands of evergreens and large bodies of water.

Emily remembered much of it—though it was not the same path, this was the same land she'd traveled during her months with her Indian lover. She drew in deep breaths and let her gaze wander, soaking up the vastness of this country. It still frightened her even as its sheer beauty took her breath away. Late summer had given way to fall. The wind whipped around them and the nights grew cooler, warning that winter was once again on its way.

Emily deliberately rode a few paces behind John. While the land they traveled over held its own fascination, she loved even more to watch him. She loved the way he sat a horse; tall and proud, at one with the majestic animal, as if he'd been born to ride and be one with an untamed land. He was as much a part of this world as her Apollo had been, even though each was different in how he walked, lived, and worked it.

She couldn't picture John in a city or on a farm. Yet he was willing to leave here for good, to settle with her elsewhere. He'd give everything up for her. But would he be happy back in the confines of society?

Catching the direction of her thoughts, she tried to banish them. Whether or not John might be content in a city or on a farm didn't matter—because she would make him return to his grandfather. She wouldn't cage him or tie him down with responsibilities that weren't his.

The baby was hers alone. The consequences, too.

Not true, a small voice reminded her. The child would bear the brunt of her actions. Thinking of that, Emily better understood why her mother married. John had been right; to bear a child out of wedlock meant a lifetime of contempt. Emily didn't want her child to be called a bastard.

Yet the only solution—pretty as it might seem at first—wasn't fair to John. Emily's only choice was marriage—letting John give her child his name, and in doing so, giving them both protection. But how, could she tie him down with her mistakes?

Of course, many women were left behind while their husbands explored new lands or trapped. If she married John, she could set him free to get on with his life. But was that fair either?

She knew she couldn't get on with her life if they married. In fact, the thought of living among society and all its restrictions no longer appealed to her. For years she'd hated traveling from one mission to another, hated going farther and farther away from civilization, had dreamed of returning to put down roots. She'd wanted a home. Friends. A place where she belonged. Yet could anything make her happy ever again?

As she stared around her, Emily felt a wave of sadness roll through her. Her time here with John had seemed like home. They'd built their own world. And it was a world she knew she'd never find back in the East.

John turned, waiting for her to catch up. "We'll stop over there." He pointed to a sheltered area near the river they'd been following for the last four days.

Grateful for an end to her depressing thoughts, she attempted a smile. "Good. I'm tired."

John's gaze roamed over her face. "Just hang in there, Sunshine." As soon as John found a likely spot, he dismounted, hitched his horse, then came to help her down. His hands, large enough to span her still-trim waist, lifted her off the horse. She slid down, brushing against him, her palms resting on his shoulders. Their gazes locked, each filled with hunger for the other.

But, as he had for the last two weeks, John released her. He began unloading their supplies and Emily watched. Because of the threat of Indians being attracted to their fire, they didn't cook their meals but ate dried meat, that and the pan bread she and Mary had made while John had gone to the trading post. He had also returned with enough hard, thin biscuits to last for some time.

"Maybe we should stay here a day or two," John said, studying her. "We've been riding pretty hard."

Glancing up, Emily shook her head. "I'm fine. Just tired. But that seems to be the way of it nowadays."

He nodded. "The sooner we get to the mission, the better. Winter's coming early this year."

Biting into a hard, dry biscuit, Emily wrinkled her nose. She longed for a hot meal. Still, she made the best of the situation. Attracting hostile Indians was the last thing she wanted. The memory of her parents' deaths still haunted her dreams.

Dusk fell and John laid out their pallets—a few feet from each other. Staring down at them, Emily wondered how she'd get through another night without crawling over and begging him to make love to her. She loved him. Needed him. And wanted him badly. The look of love in his eyes told her that all she had to do was ask.

But no matter how much she needed him, she wouldn't ask. She had to be fair to him, because in the end the love she felt wouldn't matter. She might not be able to stop herself from loving him, but she could prevent a catastrophe. She could avoid a marriage that would sour. She could prevent his love from turning to hate. This pain seemed a small price to pay.

Wandering downstream a bit, keeping John in sight, she stared out into the inky water of the river. Little daylight remained. The air had cooled, and the wind was brisk as it pulled at her hair. Suddenly she felt hemmed in, needed to feel the air on her skin as she'd grown used to—but she felt too shy.

Instead, she unbound her hair and let the long strands fly free through the air. Using her fingers, she separated her locks until they were threads of gossamer in the wind. She twirled in small circles with her arms stretched overhead and her eyes closed, letting the cool air stream through the cloth of her dress to caress her body . . . the way that John could not.

Standing a few feet away, John watched—and yearned to catch Emily's whirling body in his arms. Swaying in tune to her own inner music, she reminded him of an elusive fairy. Or an angel. He didn't dare blink for fear that she'd disappear. She tipped her head back, her hair floating around her.

His body reacted and hardened with the painful intensity of his desire. How could she not see that they were meant to be together? Couldn't she feel it? She was his other half.

The light to his darkness.

The laughter that made his tears fade.

The half that made him feel alive. Whole.

For weeks he'd kept his distance. He couldn't force her to accept what he so freely offered. She had to want it, and want his love. She had to trust and believe in him. A relationship without those things would destroy itself. So he waited and kept his distance. And he prayed she'd overcome her fears of the future.

But as he watched, his heart near to bursting with unspoken love, he took a step toward her. His rational thoughts were scattered. His patience had fled. He couldn't bear to waste another day. They had each other and today. The problems of their future could be dealt with later.

As if she'd placed a spell on him, he took another step. Then four. Then eight. And when she twirled close, he reached out and pulled her to him, all the reasons why he shouldn't take her in his arms gone.

Emily felt John's presence, knew he was there. Then he reached out and grabbed her. Her arms slid down over his head and encircled his neck. She stared up at him with eyes full of hunger.

"Emily—"

She placed a finger over his mouth. "Don't talk. Just love me."

She lifted her mouth to his in an explosive kiss. It consumed her. Their hands touched, caressed, demanded; they spoke louder than words, conveying love, overriding the voice of reason.

John's fingers fisted in the full folds of the skirt, then her dress was gone in one smooth movement. In the soft, dreamy twilight, he stared at her gleaming body, ran his hands down the gentle indent of Emily's sides and over her smoothly rounded hips. The fingers of his right hand slid down to grip her left thigh. He

289

pulled her leg up and over his raised right knee. His other hand slid around her back and pulled her close. His breath hitched when he felt the soft mounds of her breasts press against his chest.

God help her, but she loved this man. He spoke to her, returning her feelings: "I love you, Emily." The words came out harsh, for raging need was consuming them both. With his mouth he forced her head back and took her lips in a kiss that was wild, hot.

Emily's fingers closed over his shoulders, her mouth opening under his assault. She gave. And gave. Then, when she couldn't stand it, she became the aggressor, taking from him. Needing what he so willingly offered. She moaned at the feel of his smooth, buckskin-covered thigh beneath her.

She ached and throbbed. When his hands cupped her buttocks and pressed her hard against him, she tore her mouth free and let her head fall back. Tiny eruptions deep inside had each of her breaths coming faster. She moved, pressed down; he pressed up, rubbing insistently against her. Shivers shook her body as desire took hold, driving all from her mind except him. Everything but the storm of fire he'd released within her.

John's fingers dug into her buttocks, squeezing and clenching, pulling Emily forward, releasing her, then pulling her forward, faster and harder. She shook and clung to him as her body responded to the demands of his every touch. If not for his grip on her, the leg she balanced on would have given way; she trembled and shook with raw need.

Her hips jerked, and her insides clenched and released as he rocked her against him. Her tension built. It was not a slow, leisurely rise in passion, but it came with the suddenness of a prairie storm. This was no sprinkling of desire but a downpour of passion.

How could she respond so fast? So hard? So completely that nothing else mattered? She tried to hold back, to retain some control, but the moans tore from her lips and her body moved with the desperate need of the release he promised.

"God, don't stop, Emily. Don't stop." He held one hand to her back, keeping her pressed hard against him.

"Like this? We can't," she said in a gasp, not certain she could give herself over in such an uncivilized, almost savage fashion. Standing, with him still clothed, and her so shamefully falling apart, made her feel sinfully wanton.

"Exactly like this," he rasped, covering her breasts with his other hand. Slowly that hand moved down over her belly, then slid between her and his knee. Suddenly she was sliding back and forth against the ridge of one long finger.

His head bent, his mouth nipping at the tender underside of her throat.

Emily bit back a scream. Her body lost control, jerking wildly while brightly colored stars of reds, blues, and greens exploded behind her closed eyes. The breath left her body, and she felt herself flying away, soaring as one with the wind, as spasms racked her body.

The sound of a soft cry brought her back. It was her own, she realized, feeling hot tears sliding down the sides of her face.

John drew her back against him, lifting her high so she had to look down at him. They kissed as he twirled them around. Supporting her, he yanked at the buttons on his buckskin breeches. When he had freed himself, he lowered her until they merged as one. Emily wrapped her legs tightly around his waist and let him carry her to that special place where the world could not intrude. There were no problems for now. No doubts. Only him. And her.

Willy paced along the bank of the Missouri. Darkness had forced a stop for the night. Balling his hands into fists, he stared out into the inky blackness impatiently. It didn't matter that his cousin would have to stop for the night, too; all Willy could think of was finding him. And Emily. His angel.

He couldn't believe that she was gone. Pain tore through him, increased the pounding in his head. His eyes blurred with the force of it. How could John do this to him? His lips hardened. His cousin had always taken more than his share, been given more, stuck Willy with the leftovers.

For the last days, he'd ridden hard during the day, trying to catch up with the pair. He'd been stunned when Mary and Ben had returned without Emily. He'd been furious when they'd told him they had run into John, who'd volunteered to take her to the grave site. Fury had turned to gut-burning rage when they didn't return that night. Just thinking of them spending the night out together, alone, had made Willy see red.

And when they hadn't returned by the following night, he knew they'd left. No one had to tell him so. It was clear that they all had known that John was going to take Emily away. When he'd told them he was going after them, his grandfather had tried to stop him. But no one was going to stop Willy—not from reclaiming what was his.

It worried him that they'd had two days' head start. He'd ridden hard to catch up and still there was no sign of them. Panic clawed deep inside him. He had to find them before they reached St. Louis. Before they married.

"I'll find her. She's mine," he whispered. Never had he wanted anything so badly. The blond angel was special. With her at his side, Willy could do anything. Be anything. He had to have her. He just had to have her.

Sinking down with his back to a tree, he buried his head in his hands. Without her he was nothing. No one special. He needed his angel. His beautiful angel.

Rocking back and forth, Willy waited for the dawn.

Far away, beneath the rising sun, Emily and John woke and made slow, tender love. No words of feelings or the future were spoken. They knew only the here and now. It was a time of joy. But it had to end.

After a quick bath in the river, John went to saddle the horses. Emily packed their belongings. Kneeling on the damp ground, she watched him work. He moved stiffly—not from soreness of body but from a broken heart.

Despite the fact that they had spent last night in each other's arms, nothing had been resolved. Emily felt more lost and alone than either time she'd been abandoned.

When John had their horses loaded, she went to him. All this way she'd ridden her mount. What she truly wanted was to be cradled in his arms. Amazingly, he seemed to know. As he mounted, he held out a hand. She breathed a sigh of joy. It was selfish of her, but she wanted as much time with John—close to him—as she could get.

He cuddled her close, and she realized he needed the same thing. They set off.

They didn't talk while they rode—or if they did it was about the land. Impersonal things that wouldn't destroy the fragile bond of love between them. Later, the words would have to be spoken that would break that bond. Not now.

She dozed on and off, tired from lack of sleep. When John came to a sudden halt, she woke with a start. "Are we stopping?"

Behind her she felt the hard wall of his chest tense, warning that something was wrong. Her heart hammered when she saw two rough-looking men leaving the concealing stand of trees near the river. One held a shotgun pointed at them, the other a pistol. They looked like trappers, but were obviously on the wrong side of the law.

"Well, lookee here. Mighty fine woman you have there." The speaker urged his horse closer.

John remained silent, his hold on Emily tight. He didn't dare go for his own gun, though Emily was able to reach down and unsnap the scabbard. "What do you want?" his voice at last boomed out.

The two men didn't seem the least bit intimidated. "Well, now. Interestin' question." The speaker, obviously the leader, chuckled. His friend looked shifty.

"Looks like someone beat us to tha reward, Slick."

Slick laughed. "He ain't delivered her yet, Nat," he said to his friend. Then, "We'll jest take the woman," he called out to John.

"The woman's mine," John called back. His arms tightened around her.

"Don't think so, pal. We's gonna get the reward fer findin' the girl."

"What reward, and from who?" Emily asked.

The two men eyed each other. Slick looked pleased. "Seems some folk at the mission near here posted a nice, fat reward fer yer return."

"You can have the money," John proposed.

Slick rode up closer and leered at Emily. "Mebbe I wants somethin' else more than the money. This here's one fine-lookin' lady." His gaze roamed down over her. "Real fine-lookin'."

Slick's pal rode up next to him. "Hey, Slick. What about *him?*"

Lifting his rifle, Slick grinned. "Dead men don't tell no tales."

"Yeah, but if we wants the money . . . If she says anything, then we won't get nothin'."

Slick gave an evil smile. "Don't you worry none. The reward is for information—whether the girl is dead or alive." He licked his lips and looked at Emily. "Seems yer father jest wants to know what happened ta ya.

Now, how 'bout it, lady. You get on down."

Emily cringed. Behind her, John nuzzled her hair, hiding his mouth so he could reassure her. "Stay calm." He slid off the horse and pulled her down behind him.

"Ah, come on, pal. Don't think to hog the lady all to yourself." Slick had also dismounted. He motioned for John to move away.

Before John could do so, Emily reached down and grabbed his knife from the sheath dangling on his belt. He started when he felt the movement, and turned slightly to hide her actions. She wrapped it in the folds of her dress, using her hand to bunch her skirts enough to hide it.

Not having seen, Slick motioned for her to move toward him. She did. He reached out and grabbed her free arm. His lips brushed the tip of her ear. "Now, that's better."

Staring at John, she saw fury in his eyes. *Oh, God, don't let him do something stupid like trying to save me,* she prayed, glancing around wildly. What could she do with one knife against two armed men.

Slick nodded at John. "Kill him, Nat."

"Me? You want me ta do it?" Nat narrowed his eyes. "How 'bout you let me hold the girlie, and you do the killin'?"

"I'm in charge," Slick ground out. "Now quit arguin' and kill him."

Nat lifted his pistol.

"No!" Emily shrieked, horrified that they planned to kill John, then use and kill her, too. Fear for John and her unborn babe fueled her fury. She spun around and slashed at Slick.

Startled by her movements, the outlaw dropped his shotgun in order to grab at her left hand. He tried to wrestle the knife from her.

While Emily was fighting with Slick, she saw John reach down into his boot for the knife he kept there. In one fluid motion, he threw it at Nat. The blade sank into the man's chest. Then John lunged at Slick, tackling him around the middle. The force knocked Emily clear. Gaining her feet, she grabbed up the man's shotgun. She aimed it at him. Trouble was, she couldn't get a clear shot, as John and Slick were wrestling for control of the knife.

The two men rolled, both their hands on the knife. At last, when Slick managed to roll John over and sat straddling him, forcing the knife blade downward, Emily aimed. Her heart hammered. She'd never had to shoot a person before. What if she missed?

She hesitated. In that moment, John flipped Slick over his head. The outlaw landed hard and John leaped atop him. Beneath, Slick moaned. John stood. When he rolled the outlaw over, Emily saw the knife was embedded in his gut. Slick twitched once, then was still.

John glanced at Nat, to be sure he was dead, then came to Emily. "You all right?"

"Yes." She looked him over, searching for any wounds.

"I'm fine." He took several deep breaths. "I'm not sure if I want to swing you around and praise you for

297

being so brave, or curse you for scaring the life out of me."

Emily released her own shaky breath. "Praise sounds a whole lot nicer," she said, trying to smile in spite of her trembling lips.

"You could have been killed! No way could you have kept him from gaining that knife and using it on you."

"Good thing I only needed to distract him, then, wasn't it?" Emily narrowed her eyes and wiped her sweaty hands on her skirt. "Did you truly think I'd just stand there and let them kill you, then me?"

"Didn't think you could do much to stop it, Sunshine." He ran his fingers through his hair.

Emily noticed his hands were trembling. "You underestimated me," she said.

He sighed. "Sure did. Now, if only you could stop underestimating yourself." Shaking his head, he ran a hand down the side of her face. He looked astonished.

"What are you talking about?"

"Well, you obviously know how to take care of yourself. I don't know where you got that strength, but it's real. I can't imagine anyone being able to hurt that babe of yours. I just wish you would have trusted me."

Emily looked at him in surprise, but he just turned away.

It was midmorning before they were finished burying the two outlaw trappers. They did so in silence. Then Emily went down to the water to wash her hands. As she sat there, she remembered what the trappers had said about a reward offered by her father.

But how could that be? She didn't know where he was. And he had no idea where she was. She frowned. Had Millicente somehow gotten word to him? According to her mother, the woman had known where to find him. Wasn't that the reason Emily had wanted to return to the mission?

She went back to John. "Do you suppose it's true, that my father's there?"

John wiped sweat from his brow. "I don't know. Someone offered a reward for your return. If it's your father, I guess you won't need me so much." His voice was bleak.

The thought churned Emily's stomach. "You won't have to—"

John laughed without humor, cutting her off. "We should still marry. Your child still needs a name. And, Sunshine, in case you hadn't thought of it, chances are your child will look like a breed. At least if we marry, you can let people believe what they want about me. If folks know you spent the summer with a savage, you and your child will *never* be accepted. Won't matter who your father is."

"Oh, John. I wish—"

"Don't wish, Sunshine. Find the courage in yourself to see the truth." With that enigmatic comment, John walked away and fetched the two horses belonging to the trappers. The men had also left two loaded pack mules tied to a tree nearby.

Taking the loaded beasts of burden with them, they resumed their journey. A new tension had sprung up between them. Each covered mile brought them that much closer to the mission and the decision that would await them there. For him, good-bye; for her, hello to a new life.

Emily closed her eyes and let her horse follow John's as she tried to blot out the confusion raging inside her. There was so much to think about, to worry about—including the prospect of facing her father, the man who'd sired her. Now that the decision as to whether to seek him out had been taken away, she wasn't sure she was ready to meet him and learn the truth behind her conception. What would it mean to her future?

And uppermost in her mind was John. True to his promise, he'd become her friend—friend, lover, and, soon, he could become her husband. And the choice as to whether it would be in name only or forever lay with her. *Do it. And make it for forever,* her heart cried out. Her hand slid down to cup the soft swell of her stomach where new life grew.

The thought of taking his name as her own made her want to burst into tears. She wanted more than his name. She wanted him forever, but was too afraid to take the chance. He'd told her she was strong. Gascon had told her she had spunk. But in this matter, she had none. She had only uncertainty and fear. For the baby, she supposed she'd marry. For her own heart, she'd take his name—so she'd have some part of him with her forever.

But for John's own good, she'd set him free. She'd not burden him with her and the baby. Better for her and John to hurt now than be destroyed by love gone wrong at a later date.

They reached the edge of Lake Superior late that afternoon. John stopped and dismounted. He led her horse, his, and the other four beasts who were tied behind their mounts into the deep cover of forest. "We'll stay here tonight."

Emily knew they had several more days of travel ahead of them before they reached the mission. Tired and heartsore, she allowed John to help her down. For a brief moment, they stared at one another, the air fraught with emotion. Then they both pulled back, each trying to put distance between them.

They ate supper in silence. Afterward, Emily went straight to her pallet. Staring down at the bedding, she couldn't help but think of the night before, when they'd made love long into the night.

Snuggling beneath a blanket, Emily missed having John beside her—badly. She wanted to be lulled to sleep by the soft pulse of John's heart and the warmth of his breath fanning her skin. She longed for the comforting feel of his arms around her, and she missed his deep, rumbling voice in her ear as they talked in between making love.

Staring up at the star-laden sky, Emily felt absolutely alone. She wasn't sure she'd be able to live with it. Life without John didn't seem like life. It was just . . . existence.

" 'Night, Emily." John's voice sound hoarse.

Her own throat clogged. " 'Night, John."

She heard him shift. "It doesn't have to end like this," he whispered at last into the darkness.

She turned to her side so that she could see him in the glowing embers of the fire. "Better like this than in hate."

"I could never hate the other half of my heart." He spoke softly, as if speaking to himself.

Emily squeezed her eyes shut to try to stem her silent tears, but they fell anyway. She wished she dared believe him. She wanted to trust her heart—and that of her child—to him.

But how could she? She better than anyone knew the power of bitterness—and how it could turn love sour. Hearing John roll over, she turned onto her back.

Above, a star fell from the inky heavens. Emily gave in to a childish urge and wished with all her heart that he'd love her forever. But as quickly as the hope grew, it died, fizzling out like the star. Like everyone else in her life, he would abandon her eventually.

Chapter Fifteen

For the next four days they followed the shore of the lake, keeping to the cover of the wood on their right to avoid Indians and trappers. John didn't want a repeat of what had happened before. As an added precaution, he made Emily wear her hair beneath his fur cap and his bulky coat. As the days turned cold, Emily was grateful for the extra warmth.

The roar of waterfalls tempted him to ask her to dally and spend time examining new sights, but he didn't. They both feared the mounting tension that gathered between them, a force to rival the darkening clouds overhead. The closer to their destination they came, the slower their pace and the stronger the storm of their emotions.

John glanced at Emily, and saw the whiteness of her knuckles and the set of her features. Just by watch-

Susan Edwards

ing her, he knew they were close. His own control felt close to shattering. He wanted to jump down, pull her to him, and make love to her until she agreed to be his—not for a few days, but forever.

She met his gaze. Before he could demand she give him a chance, thunder crashed overhead. It was followed by the bursting of the clouds. In seconds, they were drenched. Emily wore his heavy coat, but he was cold.

The ground shook, and the horses shied and tried to bolt. John grabbed the reins to Emily's horse and rode for a rocky outcropping ahead, forcing their other animals to also follow. Nearing, he saw that the outcropping was actually a waterfall.

Hitching all the horses and mules beneath a nearby cluster of trees, he shouted, "We've got to find some shelter." Grabbing Emily's hand, he ran toward the rocks. Upon reaching them, John steadied her, keeping her from slipping on the slick ground as he searched for a ledge or cave. A flash of lightning brightened the sky.

"Look!" Emily pointed to the waterfall.

John looked in the direction she indicated. All he saw was water until another flash lit the sky. Then, behind the slow-falling water, he saw rocky walls with a deep recess: a cave for shelter. Autumn had shrunk the falls to a gentle flow. He found a way behind the water, pulling her after him.

"Wait here." He left and returned a few moments later with their packs. "We'll keep reasonably dry here," he said, using his arm to wipe the water from his eyes. "Of course, it might be hard to keep dry when

304

we're already soaked." A thread of humor entered his voice. Emily smiled in return, warming him. With the wind whipping around, she'd removed his hat before it could blow away.

"Although I know plenty of ways to keep warm," he said, his voice husky.

Her hair, plastered to her head, gleamed with every flash. Her eyes, staring up at him, snapped with blue fire. They eyed each other, neither able to move or speak. The ground above them shook as bolts of lightning slammed into the trees outside—but the soft music of the water curtaining them created a magic he couldn't resist. He reached out and tenderly brushed the hair off her forehead.

The air between them sparked with fire and crackled with pent-up emotion and physical need. "Emily—" He broke off, searching for the words that would bring them back together and give them this day and many more.

"John."

Suddenly John didn't want words. He didn't want to hear her say she had to leave, that no matter what, she couldn't risk his unhappiness. For him, there was nothing at risk anymore. He'd lost. When they arrived at the mission, he'd lose her forever. He knew it. Felt it.

He pulled her roughly to him. Their lips met in a dazzling kiss that rivaled the forces of nature erupting outside. He tried to gentle his touch, his kiss, but his need overwhelmed him. His love left no room for thought or worries. There was only this. Her. Now.

*   *   *

Emily held on tight as the onslaught of emotions swept her away. Tears trailed down her cheeks as she met John kiss for kiss. As savage as the storm, her needs rose. Heat filled her. She pressed her body to his, urging him closer.

Her head fell back to allow John's lips and tongue to blaze a trail along her jaw and down her throat. One leg lifted as he tipped her back, giving him full access to the depths of her. Sorrow and pain mixed with her soul-shattering need. How could she let him go? She needed him. Now. Today. Forever. Sobs tore past her lips.

"Tonight, Emily. Give us tonight," John begged. His lips burned hers.

"Yes," she said, sobbing. "Yes."

John's hands were everywhere: around her, smoothing along her curves, caressing the swells of her breasts. Then she felt cool air on her skin as he lifted her dress away, pulling it up past her knees. He stepped back, his eyes as dark as the sky outside. They glittered with an inner storm of his own as he tortured her with his fingers on her thighs, his hands bunching her dress as they went.

Inch by inch, the material lifted and air caressed her flesh. "Please, John," she begged at last, wanting to take the dress and yank it over her head.

"Watch me, Emily," he whispered. His gaze held hers as the dress slid up, leaving her exposed from the waist down. He stopped. Glancing down, he groaned.

Dropping to his knees, he wrapped his hands holding the folds of her skirts behind her, pulling her close to lave the skin of her belly with his tongue.

306

Something inside her sparked, then caught fire as he inched downward slowly, so slowly that Emily tensed in anticipation and need. Her hands fell to his shoulders as her legs trembled. He stopped at the beginning of the hair over her womanhood. She dug her fingers into his shoulders.

"Please, John." She was tortured by his closeness, his breath on her.

He glanced up. "Tell me what you want, Emily." He pushed her against the rocky wall and slid his hands down over her hips.

"You," she cried, rotating her hips in invitation.

"Tell me," he repeated, his fingers sliding up the inside of her thighs.

"Touch me. There. Now." She rolled her head back and forth against the wall, waiting for the magic only he could make.

He touched her: one finger, then two, opened her to him. Cool air brushed against her heated core. She gasped, waited. Then he kissed her with his lips and tongue. Flames licked her sensitive flesh. Her legs shook, and her fingers dug into the wall behind her.

"John!" she screamed, the touch of his slowly stroking tongue a mixture of pleasure and pain.

His touch grew demanding. Suddenly he was insistent, all tenderness gone as need governed both of them. Still he laved her most sensitive places. Passion claimed her not once, but twice before he released her. She sank to the ground, kissing him. Tasting herself, she found that still the fires of need raged within her. While he pulled his shirt over his head, she shoved his breeches down, freeing his manhood.

307

It stood before her, ready, throbbing.

Begging.

He dragged her down onto the pile of their clothing.

Emily took him in hand, and shoved his chest so that he fell down onto his back. Her tongue glided up the hard length of his swollen shaft, lingering at its soft, moist tip. Beneath her, John bucked and moaned, trying to pull her atop him.

She ignored him, took him into her mouth, and loved him the way he'd given her pleasure—with hands and mouth and tongue.

She loved him with all her heart, every inch of him. And she wanted to show him with actions what she didn't dare say with words ever again. For if she said the words aloud one more time, she'd give in and take what he offered: forever.

"Emily. Enough!" John groaned, pulling her over him. She slowly reclined, easing him into her. As she watched, he stared up at her breasts, the pale globes jutting out proudly before her. His palms each cupped one. Lifting his head, he took one's tip into his mouth and suckled.

She shivered, felt her body clench tightly around him. She began to rock until he couldn't stand it. Then, like the storm raging outside, he exploded. Need burst from him. Sitting, he rolled her beneath him, grabbed her hips, and lifted her to meet his thrusts. Fast and furious, he pounded into her until at last her cry rose to join his. Their joining was hard, but it was beautiful.

For the rest of that day and night, they stayed in each other's arms. Made love. Touched. It was as if they were committing to memory the feel of each other.

At last they rested. Emily tried to hold back her despair. Outside, the rain stopped but the dark clouds remained. The sun had already gone from their lives. She felt that John was still awake, holding her, but she drifted into quiet oblivion.

They arrived at the mission around noon of the next day. Neither spoke of the night of passion, for once again, reality had intruded. In the courtyard, Emily stopped to stare at the crude, white-washed building with the cross outside. Her eyes scanned the area, finding the small house she'd shared with her parents. The place where her world had been turned upside down and her faith in the world shattered.

Her pulse raced, and it was all she could do not to turn and ride away, as fast as she could, from a place that held bitter memories instead of the peace and oneness with God it should have provided.

"Are you all right?" John asked.

No, she wasn't. But she nodded anyway. Still, her body refused to urge her horse any closer. She wasn't ready to face Father Richard. Yet he was the one who would know where Millicente was. Or if her father was here. She glanced at John.

"I didn't think it would be this hard," she whispered, feeling frozen in her saddle.

His large hand reached out and covered her shaking ones. "Emily, he can't hurt you. Not with me around."

Emily met John's gaze and saw the fury there. He'd discerned her fears. Knowing that John would like nothing more than to show Father Richard his knuckles—close up—eased some of her tension. He was right. With John here, she had nothing to fear from the priest.

Before she could urge her horse forward, she noticed a man in long robes coming toward them. Unlike Father Richard, this man was short and round and had a bald head that gleamed from the sun. His skin had the look of old leather.

"Welcome," the man greeted, stopping a few feet away.

"Where is Father Richard?" Emily asked. She breathed a sigh of relief at not having to face the man just yet. Her emotions were too frayed to handle a confrontation as well as the memories of the past that were now bombarding her.

The man of God looked uncomfortable. "He's no longer here. I'm Father Jacob. Can I be of assistance?"

Emily felt a wave of relief slide through her. The sun had come out from behind the clouds, warming the day. Tendrils of steam rose from the rocks, trees, and waterlogged earth.

Removing her hat, she shrugged out of John's heavy coat. "I'm Emily Ambrose. And this is John Cartier," she announced.

The priest gasped and stepped closer. His brows drew together as he stared at her, seeing the pale strands of her hair. "Emily . . ." His eyes filled with tears. "Can it be? Is it really you?" He grabbed the large cross dangling from his neck.

The warm welcome and tears of relief surprised Emily. "Yes, it's really me. I've come back to—"

The priest interrupted her. "Praise be! Child, everyone thinks you dead."

Closing her eyes briefly, Emily willed her voice to remain strong. "My parents were killed. I survived." The words came out stark as she struggled to control her emotions. She feared that if she broke down now, she'd start crying and never stop.

"We know, child. Trappers found where you buried them. They were brought here for a proper burial."

Emily sagged in her saddle. Her parents—her mother!—were here. She glanced from the priest to John. "I want to go see them. Please." Talking was growing hard. Beside her, John dismounted, then lifted her down. Her knees shook and she nearly fell in her haste to go to her mother's grave.

"Easy, Sunshine." His hands remained around her, supporting her.

The priest clapped, and a boy with skin as dark as the earth came running out of nowhere. "Samuel, see to these animals," he called. The boy, who'd been standing in the background, nodded. "Yes, Father Jacob." The boy took the horses and mules, but not before staring in awe at Emily, as if she were a ghost.

Emily smiled at him. "Hello, Samuel," she greeted. The boy's eyes brightened. He left with their animals, shouting for everyone to come see.

Father Jacob gave Emily a sympathetic look. "Are you sure you wouldn't rather sit and have a cup of coffee or some food before—"

311

"No. I need to see where my mother is buried." No one commented on the fact that she didn't mention her stepfather. Did that mean her real father was here?

Emily followed the priest. When John reached down to take her hand, it seemed natural. Right now she needed his strength. At the mission's small cemetery, she found her mother's grave. John laid his coat down for her.

Kneeling, Emily stared at the wooden cross, at her mother's name and the word *beloved* carved in large letters across it. She traced each letter. Tears streamed down her face. At the base of the cross, she spotted a bunch of wilted wildflowers.

Next to her mother's grave, a cross bore the name of the man who'd raised her as his own but had never come to accept her. The man who, in the end, had hated her so much he'd left her to die.

Emily's hand went to her belly, to the soft place where her babe grew. Love warred with hate inside her. She turned back to where her mother was buried. She loved her mother, missed her terribly. But beneath the grief was the knowledge that her mother had chosen her husband over her daughter. She'd left Emily to die as well.

How could one live with that? Her hands fisted, and her lips trembled. Emily bowed her head, ashamed to feel such resentment—and even a bit of fury—mixed in with her love toward her mother. She felt guilty, yet she'd been betrayed by the one person whose love she should have most been able to count on.

At her side, John knelt and took her hand. He eased her fingers from her palm and leaned close, his breath fanning the side of her face. "Don't torture yourself, Sunshine. Don't blame her for not being strong. Just know that you are a strong woman. You are different."

Emily glanced at him. He knew her so well, it seemed as though he'd read what was in her mind—and heart. He did so often. Recalling her wish after seeing Mary and Ben sharing this same bond, recalling her own desire for it, Emily realized she had it. Had that bond—but she couldn't keep it.

She bit back the cry of protest. "I'm *not* strong. If I were, I wouldn't be so afraid." She stared up at him. If she were strong, she'd take the chance, she'd risk everything for John's love. She'd dare the future. But she was weak. She was too afraid to trust him—not with her heart, but with her child. He had her heart. For better or worse, she'd never love another. But her child . . .

Unable to deal with all the conflicting emotions boiling inside her, she rose. She turned to the priest, who stood a short distance from her, giving her the privacy she needed. "Thank you," she whispered.

The priest smiled kindly, then stepped aside. He motioned toward a man running toward them with Samuel and another woman. "I think your father will be anxious to see you, too."

Emily recognized the woman as Millicente. Realizing that the time had come to meet Matthew Sommers, Emily felt her nerves make her head spin and her stomach heave. She pressed a hand to her stomach. "Oh, God, I'm not ready for this." She held her breath.

John put his arm around her. "Just breathe, Emily."

313

Emily blinked, stared, then blinked again. The stranger had nearly white hair with traces of pale yellow still in evidence. His eyes were blue—as blue as the sky after a storm. As blue as her own. He smiled. She recognized that smile. This was the same man, though older, from her locket. This man was her *father*. The world spun.

He stopped in front of her. "Is it? Can it be?" His voice was choked with tears. "You don't know me but—"

"Father?" she interrupted. She choked on her tears.

The man called Matthew Sommers stepped closer, his hand held out. "Yes. Emily. My daughter," he whispered, his gaze roaming over her as if he couldn't believe she was real.

It was all too much. She'd come here to marry John, then had planned on finding somewhere to settle where she could raise her child. She hadn't settled on seeking this man out. Even though she knew he'd found out about her, had posted a reward for information about her, she hadn't determined to search him out. She might have let him know she was alive. But not once had she believed he'd still be here. Waiting. She hadn't planned on having to face him so soon. Ever, perhaps.

Now, here he was. She couldn't take it in. His features swam in and out of focus. "John . . ."

John caught her and gently lowered Emily to the ground. He stroked her face. "Easy, Sunshine. Just relax and breathe."

"I can't." Emily closed her eyes and tried to blot out everything but the feel of John, the sound of his heart beating beneath her ear, the feel of his fingers brushing her hair off her temple.

"Better?"

Emily opened her eyes. The dizziness seemed to have passed. "I think so." Feeling foolish, she sat and glanced up at the crowd of people now hovering around her and John. Her searching gaze collided with her father's.

The white-haired gentleman knelt beside her. His soft accent surrounded her with love. "It's true," he whispered. "I have a daughter." Tears filled his eyes—those eyes that were so much the same blue as her own.

Listening to her father's soft drawl, Emily stared up at him. She wasn't sure what she'd expected. Yet after months of men with booming voices, Matthew's soft-spoken, gentlemanly voice came as a pleasant surprise. As did the sight of the tears shimmering in his eyes.

"How . . . Why . . . I don't understand—" She broke off, confused. "You're supposed to be in Kentucky."

Millicente leaned over Matthew, balancing with one hand on his shoulder. In her haste to reach Emily, to see if Emily had truly returned, her hair, always neatly confined in a bun, had come loose. It spilled down her shoulder.

"I sent for him, child. Your mother was afraid for you—and for herself. She couldn't stop Timothy from leaving, going off into that savage country and taking the pair of you with him. She knew he was crazy—especially not to believe you over that lecherous old priest—"

She hesitated and sent the new priest an apologetic look. "She was going to leave him. We'd made plans to take you and return to the States, but Timothy refused to let you go." The woman's voice hitched on a sob. "She had no choice but to go with him. But before they left, she begged me to send for help. She told me the truth and asked me to try to find your father and see if he'd come for you."

Matthew reached out and took Emily's hand in his. "Which I did. I was still living on my family's farm. I had no idea, my daughter. No idea." He smiled sadly. "By the time I got here, Millicente had contacted several other missions in the area, and already had a search organized." He fell silent. "They'd already found Beatrice and Timothy."

He ran a hand over his face. "Of you, there was no sign. Everyone thought you'd been captured by the savage who killed your parents. I sent word out by way of every trapper who came through the area and offered a reward for your recovery. I'd just about given up hope."

"Seems we met up with two of them," John said, explaining what had happened with the two outlaw trappers.

As John and her father talked, Emily tried to take everything in. All her hopes of finding this man had died once she'd learned she was with child. What if the love in his eyes turned to contempt once he knew the truth? That she'd loved and been loved by a savage? And then by John.

With John's help, she got to her feet. Father and daughter stared at one another for an awkward moment. When he held his arms out, she hesitated. There were so many unanswered questions. So many answers she needed, and she wasn't sure she could trust him. Not yet.

Yet one look into his eyes told her that no matter what lay in the past he shared with her mother, her father wanted her now. Emily's throat clogged with emotion, and her legs shook.

She wanted to go to him almost as much as she feared his rejection. At last, she gave in to her need to be held by him. She'd have her answers, and soon, but right now it was enough to know that he'd come for her. When he'd learned of her, learned that she needed him, he'd come. And even when hope for her recovery seemed lost, he'd stayed. That faith, the love she saw brimming in his eyes, welcomed her home.

"Father," she said with a sob, stumbling into his loving embrace. She clung to him, rejoiced in the strong arms holding her so tight she could barely breathe. But such discomforts didn't matter. Anymore; all she could do was sob, her face pressed against his chest.

This was the first fatherly embrace she could ever recall, and the soft, broken murmurs in her ears reassured the child within that her father truly loved her.

Chapter Sixteen

Matthew stared down at the young woman in his arms. His daughter. His beloved Beatrice's child, conceived in a night of the most tender, soul-shattering loving he'd ever known.

Noticing the pallor, the dusting of freckles that stood out across her cheeks and nose, he saw his one true love as she'd looked all those many, many years ago. Only Emily's hair and her eyes belonged to him. And maybe the faint cleft in her chin. The rest of her delicate features belonged to her mother.

Scooping the girl up, he cradled her close. He had a daughter! Until this moment, he hadn't really believed it. It seemed unreal. He'd gone seventeen years believing he was alone. No family. Just his farm and a few close friends.

He followed Millicente to her cabin and stood back while the woman fussed over Emily. Content to just watch her and study this child of his, Matthew let the unfamiliar feelings in him simmer. As if he'd held her from the moment she'd entered this world, a bond was already developing and forming.

He was a father! The knowledge was incredible, heady. Already he loved Emily. In his mind, he began to make plans to take her home—home to his farm, where they could get to know each other.

For so many years he'd lived his life content. His only regret lay in not having his love at his side. He'd searched for her for years. Then, at last, he'd given up. He'd never married. He'd never found another woman to love. In truth, he'd always hoped to find Beatrice again.

He hadn't found his love, but he'd found their daughter—a miraculous gift.

Shoving his hand in his jacket, he caressed his pocket watch, the only bit of Beatrice he'd had left. Now, looking upon their daughter, Matthew felt joy fill him. He had the best part of Beatrice. He had her daughter. She was a part of them both, a living testimony to the love they'd shared.

"I have a daughter," he whispered to himself, feeling the warm glow of love in his heart and a fatherly bit of possessiveness as well.

Emily sat in Millicente's small one-room cabin in a crude rocking chair. The motion soothed her as she used it. A quilt lay over her lap and a cup of strong, sweetened tea sat to her side. "I'm fine, truly," she told the woman who'd befriended her mother. The woman who'd done so much toward making Emily happy again.

"You look peaked." Millicente bustled around, then sat in a similar chair. Both pieces had stuffed cushions.

"I'll be fine," Emily said. She reached out. "I'm sorry about your husband, Mrs. Dufour." She'd just learned that the woman's husband had died in his sleep a few months before.

"Thank you, child. Henry was a good man. I'll miss him."

"Are you going to stay here?"

Millicente shook her head. "No. I stayed to wait for news of you. I couldn't leave until we found you."

Emily's eyes swam with tears to think that she had another friend—that her mother had a friend—who'd done so much for her.

A fire burned in the fireplace to Emily's right. Beside her, John sat on a hard-backed chair, his legs stretched out, his arms folded across his chest. He'd been quiet since he'd brought her things in. She was staying here, while he'd accepted the hospitality of the priest.

Emily glanced at him. His eyes were dark. No spark of humor resided there. She knew it was her fault. She'd ended up hurting this person who'd brought laughter into her life. He was her friend. The only true friend she'd ever had, and she'd dimmed the light in his eyes.

Glancing down at her hands, she wished she could ask her father or the priest for advice. Yet deep down, she knew the decision had to come from within her.

If only she had more time! The presence of her father meant that John no longer had to journey to Kentucky with her to find him. He was free to return to his grandfather. Now that such was the case, Emily wasn't sure she could bear to see him go.

Across from her, her new found sire sipped his tea. He finally broke the silence. "So what happened to you, daughter? Where have you been? You seem healthy." He glanced from Emily to John.

Emily stared at him, wary and uncertain as to how much to tell. Would he turn his back on her if she told him the truth? Would he reject her and her baby? Tipping her chin, she decided she had to tell him everything. If he truly loved and accepted her, nothing would get in the way. If he didn't, it was better to know now.

Slowly she gave her account. Millicente gasped when she told them how her father had abandoned her. She left out her mother's part in it, sparing Matthew unnecessary pain. In truth, she wasn't sure she could speak of it without bursting into tears. The agony of the betrayal still ate at her. It probably always would.

Then she told them how the golden warrior saved her life, and how he'd taken her with him. She spoke of the freedom she'd gained, and though she didn't spell it out, her listeners knew from her voice that they'd shared their nights as well as their days They said nothing.

Then she had to tell them how he'd left her, and how John had found her, and how she'd saved his life. At that point, John spoke up. Between them they

321

finished the tale, leaving Willy out of it. But there was one last thing she had to confess. As if he knew, John reached over and took her hand in his.

Emily took a deep breath and looked her father in the eye. "I'm with child," she blurted, bracing herself for his contempt.

Matthew's eyes grew wide. "With—" He rose and came to her. "I'm to be a grandfather? A father *and* a grandfather all in so short a time!" He sounded delighted. He turned to John.

"I assume you plan to marry my daughter." Matthew Sommers sounded like a stern man now.

John nodded. "I love Emily." He glanced at her. "I've asked her."

Curls of warmth wrapped around Emily. In all this mess, that was the one thing she didn't doubt. She just didn't know if it would be enough. She knew John would claim her child. He'd marry her and allow everyone to believe him to be the father. But she would have to tell her father the truth. And when her child was old enough, she'd tell the child the truth as well. Such secrets had a way of causing hurt and pain to all involved. Better the truth be out in the open— at least among those to whom it mattered most. And who knew how that truth would change someone?

She gripped John's hand but stared at Matthew. "John's not the baby's father." She held her breath, praying that it wouldn't matter that his grandchild would be a breed.

For just a moment, Matthew was stunned. Then he smiled. It was an oddly wise smile, and Emily found herself loving the man for it. "A baby is something to be thankful for."

"You aren't angry?" she asked, still wary and afraid to believe.

"Emily, I'm so glad to see you alive and healthy that the last thing I'm going to do is judge you. You survived, and you've come back. That's all that matters. The rest can be dealt with."

John sat up straight, drawing his legs under his chair. "I still plan to marry her. Her child won't be a bastard."

"John!" As much as Emily wanted his name, she felt guilty taking it. If she couldn't give him what he truly deserved—her devotion and trust—she had no right to take his name.

"The matter has been settled, Sunshine," he said.

Matthew glanced from Emily to John. "I sense there's something going on here. But we shall deal with it later. Or perhaps just the two of you will. I'm sure you have lots of questions for me as well." He glanced at Millicente.

"Millie has already told me that you didn't know about me, that Beatrice—your mother—was afraid to tell you."

Emily glanced at him. She'd accepted him as her father and had even allowed herself to envision a normal, loving relationship. "I never knew. Why didn't she tell me? Did she think I'd have judged her?"

Millicente shook her head. "No, she was afraid you would try to run away and find your father—and she knew Timothy wouldn't have let you go. It would have made things worse between you. If she could have found a way to send you safely to Matthew, she would have. But she had no idea if his family still owned that farm, and Kentucky was a place Timothy refused to return to." The woman took a deep breath and released it, then wiped the tears from her faded blue eyes and addressed the men.

"Beatrice and I had a plan to leave. My Henry had agreed in a letter to take us. If Timothy refused to let them go, Henry would have seen to it that he didn't cause anymore trouble or stop them from leaving. But Timothy decided to leave before Henry returned."

"Because of me," Emily whispered, crying deep inside at the timing of things. They'd been so close to escaping. Her mother might have been alive today. She wasn't. Again, it was all because of her.

"No. The blame lies with Father Richard. He'd been bedding some of the young Indian girls. But none of us ever thought he'd try it on you, dear. If I ever see him again . . ." Millicente's voice rose with anger.

Matthew's hand covered Millicente's. "If he shows his face here, I will have a few words to say to him myself."

"Take your turn," John said, flexing his fingers and rubbing his knuckles. "I'll leave his ears to you, but I have first claim on his hide."

Silent understanding passed between the two men. Millicente and Emily rolled their eyes. "What's done is done," Emily said. Now that the time had come, she was afraid to ask her father about the past. As she'd said, it was gone. Nothing could bring her mother back or change her childhood. Yet she had to know.

She addressed her father. "I need to know. You and my mother—what happened?"

Matthew stared into the fire. "Beatrice's father was a preacher. The hell-and-damnation, fire-and-brimstone sort. He came and held a revival just outside town. He'd sent Timothy and Beatrice into town to buy supplies. She was sixteen, and Timothy a few years older. At first, I thought they were brother and sister.

"Our church invited them to stay, as our own preacher only came once a month." He laughed softly. "Only time I ever went to church was when I knew your mother would be there. She played the piano, and sang like an angel." He fell silent.

"I never heard her sing," Emily said, remembering all the church ceremonies. Her mother's lips had moved, but Emily couldn't recall the sound of her voice.

Matthew looked sad at that. "We fell in love, but when my father found out I was courting the daughter of a minister, he forbade me to see her again. He wanted me to marry the daughter of the man who owned the farm next to ours. Had greater ambitions for me. We had a huge fight. I told him I was going to marry Beatrice no matter what he said."

Emily held her breath as her father stopped once more to become lost in memories. When he looked back at her, she saw tears in his eyes.

"The next week, when I rode into town for church, Beatrice and her father were gone. I tried to find them, rode out to the nearest towns, but no one knew of their whereabouts. I returned home, told my father I was leaving, and packed my things."

"You left?"

"For ten years. Just rode around. Took odd jobs; then I received word that my mother was ill. I returned. She died a few months after. I made my peace with my father. I've been there ever since."

"You never married?" Tears swam in Emily's eyes. Her father had loved her mother, had wanted only to marry her.

Matthew pulled out a pocket watch. He flipped one side open to reveal the time. Then he flipped open the other side to reveal the same portrait of her mother inside her own locket. "We had our portraits done secretly. I bought her a locket, and she did odd jobs around town to earn the money to purchase this. She gave it to me the last time I saw her—the night you were conceived."

Emily pulled her ma's locket from beneath her dress and slid the leather thong over her head. She held it out to her father.

With trembling hands, Matthew opened the two halves and stared at both portraits. "She kept it all these years." His voice choked.

Emily didn't tell him that she'd hidden his image behind Timothy Ambrose's. The fact that her mother had kept Matthew's likeness confirmed that her mother had loved him.

Yet, if Beatrice had loved this man, why hadn't she found a way to return to him? "I still don't understand why she married Timothy."

Matthew handed her back the locket and looked to Millicente. The older woman took up the story. "Your mother was scared when she found out she was with child. She wanted to return, but her father wouldn't let her. He made her marry Timothy. Timothy hadn't wanted to marry. He'd wanted to devote his life to God, but he owed Beatrice's father for so much, he agreed. He never forgave her for destroying his dreams." Millicente sat back and wiped the tears from her eyes.

Emily sighed. "And lived to regret it." She kept to herself the depth of Timothy's resentment and hatred. For the first time, she allowed that perhaps Timothy had been a victim in this as well. It didn't make things better, though. Only sadder.

The next morning, Emily walked beside her father. The wedding between her and John would take place later that day. Between her father, John, Millicente, and even the priest, they'd all told her this was best. Even if John wasn't around, she needed a husband if she was going to return to society—for her own sake and the baby's.

"I can't wait to take you home, Emily." Her father stared down at her. "Call me selfish, but I want you with me. Of course, I'm hoping John will come as well."

Emily knew neither John nor her father wanted her to have the baby out here in the wild. Matthew wanted them to return with him to his home. *Home,* she thought again. A place where she belonged.

327

The thought should have pleased her. Made her ecstatic, even. But when she thought of *home*, she thought of a tiny shack in the middle of nowhere. Bending down, she picked up a small twig and broke it into tiny pieces. Like those of destroyed lives. "Love didn't bring any of you happiness. It caused problems."

Her father stopped. He tipped her chin up so he could look into her eyes. "Do you love him, Emily?" he asked.

The air smelled of rain. The wind was growing cooler, warning of another approaching storm. She couldn't help remembering the last storm and the fierce lovemaking, she and John had shared. The feeling of being one. Without him, she knew she'd never be complete again.

"Yes. I love him." With all her heart—what was left of it.

Her father looked confused. "Well, what else is there? Why are you so sure this can't be a real marriage?"

Concern lined his features. He'd been shocked when Emily had told him that John would be leaving to return to his grandfather.

"Look at what happened to my mother! It's a risk I can't take," she whispered, dropping the remaining sliver of stick that she'd broken.

Matthew Sommers's eyes clouded. "Daughter, love *is* a risk. Perhaps the greatest a man or woman can ever take." He paused, his gaze sharp. "Tell me, what would you do if you weren't with child? Would you marry him? Would you risk your heart for him?"

With trembling lips, Emily nodded. "It's *not* just me, though. I can't put my child through what I've gone through." At her father's raised brows, Emily was forced to confess what her childhood had been like. "It's not fair to the baby or to John." Her voice dropped. "I don't think I could bear watching it happen."

Matthew stopped and turned Emily's face to his. "Is it fair to deprive this child of a father's love?"

"John's not the father."

Matthew smiled sadly. "There's more to being a father than planting the seed, child. I'm your father, yet Timothy Ambrose was your father in many ways that counted."

Emily yanked away, angry and disgusted. Her voice trembled with bitterness. "Exactly! And he failed. He never loved me. He didn't want me. He hated me."

"Well, there was never any love to begin with. He married your mother to please someone else. To save her reputation. Not because he loved her and wanted to claim you. He never wanted to marry. His hatred of his mother had destroyed any feeling he had toward women. He wanted nothing to do with them."

At Emily's surprised look, Matthew smiled sadly. "I was around him enough to know of his contempt. Plus, Beatrice eventually told me how he'd come to be traveling with her and her father. Timothy Ambrose had no room in his life for a woman. Especially one who'd sinned."

"We were reminders of his own mother," Emily whispered. That much she'd known. Timothy had never let her or her mother forget that women were creatures of sin. So why had Timothy never told her the truth? Why had he pretended? Pride? He'd have done anything to protect his reputation. Having others know that Emily wasn't his child would have been the last thing he'd have wanted.

Emily stared at her hands. She didn't want to feel sorry for Timothy.

Matthew took her by the shoulders. "That's no excuse, I know. But if you can understand the pieces of the past, then maybe you won't fear the future so much."

Emily felt her father's fingers press into her flesh. She glanced up.

"Love is the key, Emily. Had Timothy loved your mother, it wouldn't have mattered. Had I known, I'd have married her, and your life would have been much different. I'm so sorry things happened this way, but don't deny yourself, or this child, the gift of love. Trust me. You'll regret it all your days."

Emily wanted to believe her father. Badly. She wanted to marry John and be his wife, form a family— a true family with love and laughter.

"Do you trust this man with your life?" her father asked.

Startled and confused by the abrupt change of topic, Emily nodded. "Of course."

"Then give yourself and your child to him. Part of loving someone is trusting them with your heart as well as your life. The gift of love is rare and should be guarded and cherished. It can be taken away in the blink of an eye. Think about that. I'll see you in the church." And with that, he left.

Emily watched her father walk away, then turned her attention to the rough water of the lake. Trust. She did trust John, didn't she? In times of trouble she knew he would protect and take care of her.

And love? She loved him. Knew he loved her. She'd known it for a long time now. And she'd shared herself with him, made love with him, because she loved him back. But, she realized with sadness, she'd held back, hadn't given herself completely over to him. She hadn't been able to bring herself to trust him with her heart. Even before she realized she was with child, she'd held some part of herself away.

Putting her hand over her abdomen, she recalled John's gentle handling of the hawk, the humorous by-play and devotion between him and Fang.

She thought of how he'd treated her; kindness when she'd been most vulnerable. He could have treated her with contempt, considered her ruined and not worthy except to bed. She knew when she returned to civilization, she'd never be able to tell anyone else of her time with her Indian lover. And if her child bore the dark looks of the father, she and that child would forever be spurned.

But John had never seemed to care that she'd spent the summer living with an Indian. And even after she told him of the baby, he'd professed his love, and his desire to become the baby's father.

He loved her.

The words made her heart swell. Suddenly a life without love didn't seem worth living. No matter that she'd found her father. If she returned to his farm with him—without John—she'd always feel empty inside.

Susan Edwards

And what would she tell her child? That she, out of fear, had denied them a father's love?

Remembering her own desperate need for that exact thing, Emily knew she couldn't deny it to her child. She couldn't deny herself love. Or John. She needed him to feel whole. Alive. Like the grass and flowers needed fresh water to grow and renew, she needed John's love and friendship. Without him, she'd become a stale pond.

Her smile faded. Love *was* the answer for her and John. But there was one other thing she needed to do before she went to him. When she did, it would be with a clear mind, and an open heart.

Hurrying, she ran to do what was necessary.

From the stable door, John watched Emily enter the church. Would she go through with the wedding? He glanced at the position of the sun. If she did, soon they'd be married. Man and wife.

He turned and found the stall where his horse waited. The animal nickered softly. "Eat your fill, now. We'll be riding out soon." Picking up his saddlebags, he finished packing them. After the wedding, he'd head back home—to a shack that would be unbearably empty without Emily.

He thought of his cousin. Willy would gloat. And his grandfather? John's heart grew heavier. He'd wanted to make the old man happy.

John led the animal from the stall and started saddling it. He wanted to be able to leave immediately after the ceremony. Any prolonged good-byes would be too painful. She'd made her decision. He'd promised not to push.

Push, hell. He wanted to shout at her and shake some sense into her. He rested his forehead on the saddle. He'd told himself he could let her go, had accepted it, felt the pain of it—but in truth, he'd only deluded himself. The pain he felt now was far worse than he could have imagined. And it would get worse.

His heart felt numb. It had broken beyond the point of pain. His eyes burned. He couldn't deny the truth any longer: she didn't need him anymore. She had her father now, and from what he saw, the man loved her. Staring out the open door, seeing only a gray cast to the sky, John realized the sun was truly gone from his life.

John spotted Matthew heading his way. He turned and resumed his travel preparations.

"You planning on just giving up?"

John didn't turn. "It's better this way. She has you now. That's all she needs." His lungs couldn't expand enough to draw in a deep breath, so his sigh wasn't as big as it might have been.

"There's a reward for her return."

Those words brought him around. His eyes blazed as he stared at Emily's father. "It wasn't for the money. Was never for the money." He tightened the girth strap. When his horse protested, John loosened it and gave the animal a rub behind the ears by way of apology.

"I know, son. I was just checking. So, I repeat: You just going to give up? You're not going to fight for her?"

John glanced over the horse at Emily's father. He looked like a man set upon righting things. "Would

333

have thought you'd want her to yourself a bit."

Matthew grinned. "I do. But I want her happy more than that. And I don't think either of you will be happy apart. Think about it. Her mother and I were denied a life together. Don't want my daughter to have the same difficulty. You might not get a second chance." He turned and left John to his thoughts.

Staring at the big, trusting eyes of his horse, John grimaced. He wanted to fight for her. But how? *What can I do to convince her to stay? I've said the words. What else is there?*

There had to be some way to convince her. He paced. He looked around. The horse just bent its head to greedily snatch up bits of hay strewn on the ground for dinner.

Chapter Seventeen

Emily entered the small, whitewashed church. She found Father Jacob at the altar, getting ready for her wedding.

"Child, you should be getting ready," he scolded lightly. But his eyes were kind and questioning.

"I need to talk to you, Father."

The cleric led her to a bench and motioned for her to sit. She couldn't. She paced, then faced him. "I'm angry at my mother." She stopped herself. "No, it's more than that. Sometimes I hate her. And I shouldn't. She's gone. But it doesn't seem to matter." She clenched her hands.

The hurt and anger she felt for her mother felt like a hard, cold ball in her stomach. Seeing her mother's grave had made it grow until Emily felt as though she'd choke on it. She knew enough of what hate could do to a person, and she was afraid of what it might do to her if she didn't get rid of it.

"Sit, Emily," the priest said.

Ready to be healed, she obeyed.

"Tell me why you feel this way."

Emily gripped her fingers tight. "She knew why my stepfather hated me and treated me so badly. She knew and never stopped him. Then she left me to die." The words were torn from her. "She abandoned me. She was the only person I could count on, and, in the end, it didn't matter. *I* didn't matter."

Father Jacob took her hands in his. "Could she have stopped him?"

"No. But she didn't have to go with him. She could have stayed with me. And lived," she cried, tears streaming down her face. If her mother had refused to go with Timothy Ambrose, had stayed hidden in the woods, she'd be alive today. And that was another reason, Emily realized, why she couldn't forgive her.

"There are no easy answers, child, and you know that. Sometimes things happen for reasons we cannot understand."

Emily wiped at her tears. "You mean, if Timothy hadn't left me behind, if we'd just continued on, I'd have been killed, too?" That thought also haunted her dreams. If her stepfather hadn't left when he had, the savages would have spotted their little campsite and killed them all.

The kindly priest smiled grimly. "Perhaps. Or you would have been taken captive." He stood. "Let the past go, Emily. Forgive your mother. And—"

"Timothy wasn't my father," she said, cutting him off, unable to mask her defiance.

The priest took her hands in his. "He was in some ways. A poor father, but he had that role for sixteen years. And he did provide for you. Forgive him. Forgive both of them. Don't judge too harshly, child. You have a choice to make. You can either choose to dwell on the past, or seek a future free of bitterness. You know what resentment and bitterness lead to. Don't let them destroy your heart. Think about that. And pray." Then the priest walked away, leaving Emily alone with her thoughts.

Emily closed her eyes and made herself relive that day. She saw how her mother had tried to fight for her, saw her grief when her stepfather rode off. Then had come the attack.

Emily also recalled how her mother and Millicente had tried to find a way to leave. The tension eased from her when she remembered that Millicente had said she'd rounded up help to go after them but had arrived too late. Though the help came too late for her mother, Emily knew the woman had been trying to get Emily to safety. To happiness.

Perhaps her mother had left her behind in the hope that Millicente and her husband would find her, that any fate was better than one with the vengeful Timothy Ambrose. Emily didn't know for sure, but suddenly, she believed it.

Her mother had loved her. And even with her dying breath she had tried to confess the truth to her. Maybe her mother had been weak, unable to stand up to her husband. But in the end, she'd set the wheels in motion to make things right. Perhaps that was enough for Emily to make peace with it.

She closed her eyes and drew an old, a happy memory of her mother reading to her. Emily sat in her lap, secure in her mother's arms. Even after reading the book, her mother had continued to hold her until Emily fell asleep. It had been a rare day when Timothy had been gone. Emily still recalled the soft, gentle voice that had sounded like sweet music in her ears as sleep claimed her.

With a start, Emily realized her mother hadn't been talking. She'd been singing! The words were lost, but not the voice. She'd thought it angels singing to her while she slept.

Tears slid down her cheeks. The tiny memory was so much. It was a sign that the woman had cared; she had just hidden it from her husband so that he would have no more reason to hate Emily. Her mother had loved her.

Leaving the church, Emily ran to find John. She had to talk to him before the ceremony, wanted them to marry for real—forever. Seeing her father coming toward her, she asked, "Have you seen John?"

"In the stable," he said.

Emily flung her arms around him. "Thank you, Father. I'm going to marry him."

Running through the door, she crashed into someone. Strong hands reached out to steady her. "Easy, Sunshine."

"John! We're getting married." Through her tears, she stared up at him. Tall, handsome, he was the most precious sight she'd ever seen.

John narrowed his eyes at her, his fingers still gripping her shoulders. "Damn straight we're getting married. I was just coming to tell you. And not just for today. I'm not letting you go. We marry. We *stay* married. And we stay together."

Emily grinned. "Precisely. For better or worse. No matter what. You're mine. You're my friend, my lover, and soon you'll be my husband and the father of this child. So you'd better be sure, because I won't let you go."

John froze, his gaze searching hers. "Do you mean it, Sunshine?"

"Yes. Oh, yes." She reached up and touched his face, skimming the tips of her fingers up the hard planes of his cheekbones. "I was so wrong. I love you, and if you're still willing, if you still love me, I'd like to be your wife. Forever."

"Because of the baby." His eyes were guarded even though his arms wrapped her in his embrace. The sudden change was obviously too much for him to hope. She had to convince him!

"Because I love you!" The words glided over her tongue. She hadn't said them in a long time, and they sounded so right. More than right: they sounded heavenly.

"Love wasn't enough before. You were afraid to trust me. Why now?"

Emily couldn't look away from the happiness shining in his eyes, from the clear path she saw into his very soul. "I didn't trust *myself*, John. I was so afraid of making the same mistake as my mother, I let my own doubts stop me from listening to my heart. *I* was

339

angry. But you're not Timothy; I'm not my mother. We are two different people. We'll make mistakes, but they won't be their mistakes."

"No, I'm not him, and you are not your mother. And what's more, you'll fight me or anyone else who tries to hurt your child." He smiled proudly at her.

Laughing softly, Emily reached behind him and ran her fingers through his hair. "Our child. And I'll fight anyone who tries to hurt you as well." Lifting herself up onto her toes, she brought his mouth to hers and kissed him.

The kiss was warm and sweet. John groaned and kissed her back gently, tenderly, fighting to keep the passion at bay. She was his—forever. His Lady Dawn had returned, bringing the brightness of a sunny day.

"Do you know how much I love you, Emily?"

She pulled back. Her lips curved into an impish grin. "I think so. You might have to show me often, though. And tell me over and over to make sure I don't forget."

John chuckled. "Every day, Sunshine. Every day." He lowered his mouth back to hers.

"In case the two of you have forgotten, there is a wedding in a few minutes and neither of you is dressed."

John broke off the kiss. They turned to face Emily's father, who was looking mightily pleased. "I think she's beautiful just as she is." He smoothed the hair from her face. It tumbled down her back in ripples.

"Ready to get married, Sunshine?" he asked her. "For real? Forever?"

"I'm ready," Emily said, staring at him.

They followed Matthew out, back to the church, and inside took their places. John kept his eyes on Emily as she walked down the aisle on her father's arm. He couldn't stop himself from meeting them, from taking her arm so he could walk her the rest of the way. Matthew joined a sobbing Millicente. The older woman seemed so happy.

John repeated his vow when asked, his gaze on Emily. He let her see that he meant each word he spoke. He held her hands while she spoke her vows with tears in her eyes.

Then, when Father Jacob asked if he took her for his wife, he brought her hands to his lips and kissed the backs of her fingers. "I do."

Emily reached up to caress his cheek as she repeated the same. "I do." And she did. Forever. She waited for the priest to declare them man and wife. To her surprise, Father Jacob then asked John, "Do you, John Cartier, claim this child that Emily carries as your own child, to love the babe in sickness and in health? No matter what, so long as you shall live?"

John lowered his hand, the one that still gripped Emily's to her abdomen. His fingers lay over hers. Beneath the warmth of their hands, Emily felt a slight fluttering. He replied, "I do. Whether this child is a boy or a girl, I'll love it with all my heart."

"Then I pro—"

Emily stopped the priest with her hand. John's touching addition to their vows was the sweetest, most beautiful thing he'd ever done for her. He couldn't

341

have found a better way to prove his intentions. And she wanted to repay him in kind.

"I, Emily Ambrose Sommers, give this child into the loving hands of John Cartier, the man I love more than life itself. He shall be this child's father forever." She brought his other hand down to rest over their child.

John blinked rapidly, but the tears of joy and love he shed were there for all to see.

Father Jacob set his Bible down with a wide grin. "Then I pronounce you man and wife. You are now a family."

Emily lifted her face to her husband's. "I love you, John," she whispered.

"I love you, Mrs. Cartier." His kiss didn't disappoint her, and no one protested when he scooped her into his arms and carried her out of the church. He set her upon his horse and together they rode off to find a private glade where they could start their forever.

Epilogue

Emily sat with her back against a tree in her favorite spot: her glade. The sky was still gray, the air cold. She glanced around. Finding the log that was still there, though decayed and rotting into the soil, she sighed. So much had begun here. Pain. And joy. Everything.

Across the way, her husband and Ben chased little Sarah in the early dawn. The sun hadn't risen completely yet, but as this was their favorite time of day, and the three-year-old was often up before dawn they often came here to start their day.

Yawning, Emily wondered how her daughter could wake with so much energy. The child was a bundle of energy from the moment she opened her eyes until she fell into an exhausted sleep each night. So curious and eager to explore, the girl hated to sleep. It was as

343

if she was afraid she'd miss something new and exciting.

Childish giggles floated on the breeze. Emily shook her head at the sight of the two men giving her their undivided attention. Sarah loved the attention and was hopelessly spoiled; John and Ben didn't care. Barking when Sarah ran toward the woods, Fang ran after and blocked her. The wolf protected and watched the child. Sarah pouted and protested, looking like a tiny angel with her white-blond curls and bright blue eyes. Ben managed to distract her by pointing out bugs in the rotting log.

John ran over to his wife. "Whew. I swear she's going to wear me out."

Emily grinned. "You love it, and you know it."

Scooting next to her, he put his arms around her and drew her to him. "Yeah. I sure do." His eyes followed his daughter's movements.

"You happy, Sunshine?"

"Very," she said without hesitation. Not once had she regretted coming back here to live.

She and John had gone to Kentucky, where Sarah had been born. To her surprise, Millicente had offered to go with them, and then had married Matthew. She and Emily's father were now very happy together on his farm, and Emily was glad. Her father deserved a second chance at love.

When Sarah had been three months old, Emily, Sarah, and John had traveled to St. Louis to meet up with John's grandfather. From other trappers returning to the city, they'd learned that Gascon hadn't been well enough to travel downriver. They'd returned to the shack immediately. John had been afraid his grandfather would be gone, but he'd still been alive. And the minute he'd seen them—and his great-granddaughter—he'd gotten a new lease on life. He'd only passed away this year.

John, as usual, seemed to know what she was thinking. "You know, we can leave and return to the city. With Gramps gone, there's no reason why we have to live out here."

Emily leaned her head against her husband. "After all the work you and Ben did to build our new home?"

"Sunshine, it's not much. I can buy you a much grander place in St. Louis—or anywhere."

"But it wouldn't be the same. I *love* our home." She glanced up at him. "I have what I need out here." And she did. She'd found living back in civilization confining. She wanted freedom for herself, and for her daughter. She wanted Sarah to grow up without the strictures of society. She wanted her child to experience all that life had to offer. Between their yearly trips back to city life, and the schooling Emily provided, Sarah, when she became an adult, would be able to choose her own path.

"Have you heard anything from your cousin?" she asked. John had sent word downriver about his grandfather's passing that winter.

"Not yet. I expect that we'll see him in St. Louis. Now that Gramps is gone, he'll want his inheritance." Sadness laced John's voice.

Emily put her palm on his jaw. "You can't change him. At least he seems to be doing reasonably well." And he was.

345

Susan Edwards

To John's surprise, after that initial confrontation when they first saw Willy in St. Louis, he'd seemed to have come around. He'd accepted the fact that John and Emily were married.

To protect the truth of Sarah's parentage from Willy—whom they couldn't trust to keep it a secret— they had let him believe John was the father. With the baby's pale hair and blue eyes, Willy hadn't had any reason to doubt it.

At first he'd been furious, but John had been prepared. Peace in his family was more important than what belonged to whom. He'd given Willy what he wanted most: money. He'd withdrawn a large portion of his funds from the bank—enough to placate the man.

John had no need for all of it. He'd kept enough to purchase a home for his family, and to have enough left over to live on until he found work or started his own business. Now things seemed to have calmed between the two cousins. Emily still didn't trust Willy, but at least there was peace between him and John.

Sarah's cry had them both turning their heads. Ben held the little girl, who was rubbing her eyes. Then the child made a hungry face.

Emily went to stand but Ben waved her away. "I'll take her back. No need for you two to come. Enjoy the sunrise. Mary'll have the morning meal ready. We'll feed the little tyke and watch her for a bit."

As soon as they were gone, John pulled Emily onto his lap so she faced him. "Alone at last. Be a shame to waste it just sitting here doing nothing."

346

"A real shame," Emily said, feeling him growing hard beneath her. "But shouldn't we watch the sunrise first? That *is* why you dragged me out of bed so early on the one day Sarah didn't."

John slid his fingers into her hair. He lifted the strands and let them drift over them. "I'm watching my Lady Dawn right now. No one is more beautiful than you." With practiced ease, he undid his breeches, lifted her skirts from beneath her, and slid her down onto him.

For a long moment they sat there staring at each other, their bodies joined as well as their hearts and souls. "I love you, Sunshine," he said.

"I love you, too, John. Now, can we stop talking and start kissing?" After all those years, she still yearned for his kisses.

"Whatever you want, Sunshine." John slid the top of her dress down her arms and palmed her breasts.

"I want," Emily said, her lips meeting his.

The sun rose and gentle light bathed them, but neither noticed.

AUTHOR'S NOTE

I hope you enjoyed Emily and John's story. Going back in time to discover the events that shaped and gave birth to my first book, *White Wind*, was an adventure and a lot of fun.

I love to write stories of hope, where no matter how bleak the present looks, there is a grand future just around the corner if one is courageous enough to move forward and overcome setbacks. For Emily, this was certainly true. But what about Swift Foot? He traded love and happiness for duty and honor.

In *White Dusk*, the next book in my White series, we return to the Sioux village where Swift Foot battles the past. Can he restore peace, not only for his people but within his own heart? Find out in November 2002.

praying he wouldn't be too late to catch it before it drifted forever out of his reach.

It might have been any peaceful spring night at Cameron Manor.

Brian and Alex played chess before the drawing room fire. Pugsley dozed on the hearth. Elizabeth tucked a slender needle through the ivory linen of an embroidered fire screen, her sewing basket open at her feet. Dougal sat behind a walnut desk, surrounded by the leather-bound registers of the spring planting. Pugsley's snores counted off the unfolding minutes.

They all started baldly as a thunderous banging sounded on the door. Pugsley lifted his head. His curly tail began to wag.

Dougal flipped a page, his eyes still riveted on the ledger. Elizabeth tied off a knot and snapped the excess thread away with her teeth. Alex captured Brian's rook and removed it from the board, his face grim.

The massive wooden door trembled in its frame beneath the force of the blows being rained upon it. A manservant rushed in from the kitchen, but Dougal stayed him with a warning glance. Pugsley leapt up with more enthusiasm than he'd shown in weeks and began to caper back and forth in front of the door.

Dougal stroked his beard, weariness etched in every cranny of his brow. He wasn't sure his family could survive another MacDonnell siege. He knew his daughter wouldn't.

The ancient wood of the door splintered beneath one mighty blow. Pugsley scampered out of the way, then began to bark in short, excited yips as the chieftain of the MacDonnells stepped through the debris. Morgan quieted him with a single look. Chastened, the dog slunk to his belly and buried his nose beneath his paws.

"I've come to see my wife." Morgan's voice rang in the taut silence.

Dougal stood. Elizabeth continued to sew, her needle flying through the linen with flawless rhythm.

Brian scrutinized the chessboard as if his entire future hinged on his next move.

"Sabrina is no longer your wife," Dougal said.

A spasm of pain crossed Morgan's impassive countenance to be replaced by dark fury. "Perhaps not in the eyes of your English laws. But in the eyes of God, I'm still her husband."

Alex lumbered to his feet to stand at his father's side. "Now, friend, there's no cause to be unreasonable—"

"I'm not your friend," Morgan snarled. "Nor am I interested in reason. Not when the Camerons twist it to suit their purposes. The only thing I'm interested in is Sabrina."

Dougal's shoulders slumped. "Very well. Brian, fetch your sister."

"No!"

Morgan's sharp command made them all flinch. But it was the pistol in the MacDonnell's hand that stilled Brian half out of his chair and made Elizabeth gasp.

"No," Morgan repeated. "I'll stomach no interference from any of you this time. Especially not you, Dougal. I've had enough of your meddlin' to last me a lifetime."

Dougal stepped in front of his wife. "Don't do something you're going to regret, lad."

The lamplight gleamed off the sleek barrel of the weapon as Morgan leveled it at the laird's chest. "I already have. I trusted a Cameron."

Morgan thundered up the stairs, clearing three of them with each stride. He marched around the gallery, his steps echoing eerily off the wooden floor as if the manor had never known the ripple of human laughter or the joyous strains of song. A darkened corridor unfurled before him.

He plunged down it without hesitation, seeking the door he remembered from boyhood, the door he had so often endeavored to pass, lured by the tinkling music of girlish laughter.

He threw open that door now to find that time had stopped for all but him. The chamber was deserted, the bed's coverlet as smooth and undisturbed as the faceless visage of the rag doll perched on the pillow. A miniature tea set still sat on a rosewood table. Morgan picked up one of the tiny cups, his fingers grown suddenly too big for his hand.

Then the little chairs were no longer empty, but filled with the ghosts of his regrets: Sabrina, eyes sparkling, spiral curls dancing; the faceless doll slumped over her cup; a paint-spattered kitten licking cream from a saucer and looking absolutely ridiculous with a doll's feathered hat tied beneath his furry chin.

A little girl's pleading voice bled through the silence. *Come have chocolate with me, Morgan. Isabella, Doll, and I are having gingerbread today.*

The cup slipped from his graceless fingers, shattering on the floor.

Morgan eased the chamber door gently shut as if to preserve its memories intact. He flew through the darkened corridors of the manor, throwing open door after door to find only more ghosts, more regrets. He burst back onto the gallery, fists clenched and chest heaving with frustration.

At the top of the stairs, a single door remained undisturbed. Morgan's breathing slowed as he approached it, measuring each silent step as if it would be his last.

The polished oak of the solar door felt cool beneath his palm. It swung open without a sound.

He should have known she'd wait for him there, bathed in moonlight as she'd been that autumn night a lifetime ago. She reclined upon the settee by the widow, her white nightdress glowing beneath the kiss of the moon. Gazing at the luminous orb as if held rapt by its spell, she dragged a hairbrush through her unbound hair, the motion dreamy, her profile pensive.

Morgan hesitated in the doorway. He felt as if he were profaning holy ground. Disturbing a shrine to the

life she had chosen over the one he could give her. A
life of empty peace instead of bittersweet joy and tra-
vail. No risks. No pain. No loss because there was
nothing to lose. He knew what he must do now. His
own sense of loss threatened to overwhelm him.

The finches chirped a welcome from their cage,
but Sabrina didn't even turn her head.

She stroked the brush through a dusky curl. "It
wasn't very sporting of you to lock my family in the
kirk. You gave the servants a terrible fright."

"You know damn well I don't fight fair. If they
want out badly enough, they can break the bloody windows."

She cast him a chiding glance over her shoulder.
"Mama would never permit it. Those windows are over
a hundred years old. They were shipped all the way
from Heidelberg."

Morgan moved to stand behind her, his own gaze
not on the candlelit kirk across the ancient bailey, but
on the shimmering waves of silk spread over Sabrina's
shoulders. She eased the window open an inch, as if
polite curiosity were all that motivated her.

She tilted her head, utterly aloof and farther out
of his reach than the distant moon. "They're very
quiet, aren't they? Perhaps they're praying for your
soul."

"They ought to be prayin' for yours. If you still
have one, that is."

She pushed the window shut, cutting off the night
breeze and smothering them in a peace Morgan now
found to be more oppressive than his clan's querulous
demands had ever been.

"If you've come to rob us," she said, laying the
brush aside, "Mama's jewels are in the coffer beneath
the loose floorboard in the corner. You'll find the snuff-
box on the table inlaid with genuine gold. Oh, the
Cameron claymore is right over there above the hearth.
It belongs to you rightfully anyway."

"Just as you do?"

A delicate bloom stained her cheeks. It was gone

as quickly as it had come, leaving her face both blood-less and expressionless.

Morgan destroyed the serenity with vicious satis-faction, his voice ringing harshly in the perfumed air. "I didn't come to take anythin', lass. I came to return somethin' that belongs to you." He reached into his plaid and drew out the spray of dried gorse, tossing it carelessly into her lap.

Her hands betrayed her, scrambling to gather the scattered blooms. Then as if realizing what they'd done, they collapsed like broken wings into her lap. Her lower lip began to tremble.

Morgan moved to block her line of vision. "What did you tell yourself, lass? That you were bein' noble? Makin' a grand gesture of sacrifice by settin' me free?"

"You deserved more," she whispered, a tear cling-ing to her lashes before falling to water one of the shriv-eled blooms.

He dropped to one knee beside the settee. "You're damned right I did," he choked out between clenched teeth. His vehemence shocked her into meeting his gaze. "You lied, lass! You lied to me and you lied to yourself. You're not noble or brave. You're nothin' but a petty coward, Sabrina Cameron, and even if your legs were sound, I doubt your spine would support you!"

Tears were running freely down her pale cheeks, but Morgan ignored them as well as the betraying sting behind his own eyes. "You were right about one thing though. You're not worthy of me. I want a woman of courage who'll stand beside me through good times and bad, whether it be on her feet or on her knees. I've no use for some feckless lass who runs away at the first sign of trouble. Aye, Sabrina, I deserve far more than the likes of you for a wife."

He climbed to his feet, forcing a note of dispas-sion into his voice even as agony flayed him. "So god-speed to you, lass. I wish you no ill. I wish—"

But Morgan couldn't finish. A lifetime of lost wishes and broken dreams clogged his throat. Reaching down, he gently wiped beneath her eye, catching a trembling teardrop, more precious than any gem, on the callused pad of his fingertip.

Sabrina's eyes were beseeching, and he knew that if she had uttered one plea, one word in her defense, he would have stayed. But she held her silence, the very silence that had been their undoing. Morgan's fist clenched, destroying the tear in the same motion that sought to preserve it.

He turned on his heel and left her without another word.

Sabrina sat in numb misery, listening to Morgan's footsteps recede. The terrible truth of his words excoriated her. All of her noble intentions had been a sham, a pathetic travesty of self-sacrifice. Rather than risk his rejection or the mockery of his clan, she had struck the first blow, rejecting them first. She hadn't been able to walk, but that hadn't stopped her from running away.

She reached for one of the precious gorse blooms only to have it crumble to dust at her touch. It wasn't Morgan's pride that had finished them, but her own. The same pride that had kept her from falling to her knees at his feet one last time, the same pride that now clamped her hand over her mouth to keep from calling him back.

The serenity of the moon seemed to mock her. A haunting wisp, white against the darkened sky, floated past the window. Sabrina blinked away her tears as another ghostly plume drifted upward to disappear against the ivory backdrop of the moon.

She tugged the window open. The acrid stench of smoldering wood stung her eyes. She traced the wisps of smoke downward to discover a single stained-glass window at the back of the kirk writhing with flame. In a moment of sheer madness she thought Morgan had set the blaze to punish her for her cowardice. Her heart rejected the notion in the same beat.

"Morgan!" His beloved name tore from her

lips, the longing of a lifetime written in the single word.

But Sabrina was deafened to her own scream by an unearthly keening that swelled and rolled, cresting on a wave of pure unbroken majesty.

Chapter Thirty-two

The sound was both beautiful and terrible. It was a sound never meant to be confined to manor walls, and Sabrina's first instinct was to clamp her hands over her ears.

She could not bear it. Her fingertips flew to her temples, but still it swirled around her, penetrating every pore, flowing with unerring instinct into the gaping wound in her heart. It wailed of love and loss and a lifetime of missed opportunities. It wept bitterly of betrayal and regret, dropping shimmering notes like tears into a bottomless well of grief.

It was the voice of every woman, Cameron or MacDonnell, who had lost a father, brother, husband, or son to the senseless hatred that festered between their clans. It was the broken lament of all women throughout time who were forced to sacrifice love for pride.

It was Penelope weeping by the sea for Odysseus's return. Dinah crying over the broken body of Shechem, the man who had both raped and adored her. Eve cast out of the garden, bewailing the serpent's treachery.

Eve.

Sabrina sat straight up, fighting to shake off the spell of the dark lament. Its melodious tendrils wove a web of destruction, a web her family was already caught in, a web Morgan was walking straight into. She struggled against it, knowing she had to find something strong and enduring enough to cut through its cloying fibers.

Her frantic gaze searched the shadowy solar, finding nothing but her mother's treasures, fragile luxuries costing an embarrassment of riches, but utterly worthless at that moment.

The back of the kirk coughed out smoke in thickening billows. If the fire spread to the front, where her family was held captive, they would no longer be silent, but screaming. Each wailing note of the pipes pounded at Sabrina's brain, drowning out their imagined cries. At least she was to be spared that much, she thought despairingly, her head falling against the back of the settee.

Moonlight rippled along the massive blade of the claymore hanging above the hearth. Sabrina's breath caught at the sight. The ancient weapon, scarred and nicked from countless battles, had no place in this elegant solar, yet there it hung, sparkling in the ethereal light like fresh hope.

She didn't know whether to laugh or cry. The blade would have been no more unattainable had it dangled from the moon by a gossamer thread. But winning Morgan's affections had once seemed equally impossible, she reminded herself. And if her papa's tenacity had taught her anything, it was that nothing was impossible if you wanted it badly enough.

She hadn't the time or the patience to wrestle with her feeble legs. Supporting her weight with her palms, she dragged herself to the edge of the settee and heaved herself over. She thumped hard to the floor, biting her tongue.

Using her arms and hips to maneuver, she

crawled toward the hearth. The skirts of her nightdress
hindered her, twining around the dead weight of her
calves. The ceaseless wail of the bagpipes muffled her
struggle.

She arrived at her destination grunting with exertion. Before she could see the Cameron claymore, she
had to tilt her head so far back that her hair brushed
the floor. The sword wavered before her bleary eyes,
swaying like a grim pendulum between doom and
hope.

She dug her fingers into the hearth and inched
herself up, stone by stone, until her polished fingernails
were cracked and bleeding. After minutes that seemed
like an eternity, she dragged herself to a standing position. Her legs quivered at the unaccustomed strain. She
teetered on the uneven stones.

The solar started to shrink, and she knew she was
falling. There was no time to neatly disengage the claymore's hilt from its pegs. With a last desperate lunge
she grabbed the blade itself, feeling it slice deeply into
her fingers as she crashed backward to the floor.

For an agonized moment Sabrina's only concern
was where her next breath would come from. She finally managed to suck a tortured gasp into her lungs.
The stench of smoke drifted through the open window.
She could feel blood from her wounded fingers seeping
into her nightdress. She lifted one hand and wiggled
them, more pleased than she could say to find them all
intact.

Dragging the sword behind her, she scrambled
for the door on hands and knees. The blade gouged an
ugly trail in the polished oak of her mother's floor.
Sabrina thought with a grim flare of humor that she'd
have to sneak back in and throw a rug over it if any of
them survived the night.

She crawled out the open door onto the gallery.
The steep edge beckoned her.

The wail of the pipes ceased. In a silence more
shrill than the music, Sabrina flattened herself against
the floor much as she had done the night Morgan had
wandered into her mother's solar to steal her heart. She

would have to choose her moment with care, or she stood to lose both Morgan and her family.

From the hall below came slow, mocking applause and the ring of Morgan's voice. Sabrina had never heard anything so welcome. Its deep, familiar cadences made Eve's song seem shallow by comparison.

"Bravo, Eve," he said. "A command performance for a captive audience. How very impressive."

Sabrina peeped over the edge of the gallery. Eve and Morgan faced each other in the hall below, their profiles to Sabrina. Eve set aside the pipes.

"What the hell are you doin' here anyway?" Morgan asked, folding his arms over his chest.

"Watchin' ye make a bloody fool out o' yerself just as ye did in London," Eve replied, crossing her own arms over her chest in like manner.

Morgan's composure slipped a notch. "*You* were in London?"

"Aye." She pulled something out of her plaid and tossed it at him. As it thumped against his chest, Sabrina saw it was a fat purse similar to the one she had seen her father give Morgan. "But I canna be bought by Cameron gold as easily as ye."

Morgan stared at the purse, his expression stunned. "The beggar?"

"I'd rather beg than sell me soul to Dougal Cameron."

The purse slipped from his hands to clank on the stone floor. "Why did you come back here, Eve? I forgave you for teachin' Ranald to play the pipes. I might have eventually forgiven you for mistakenly killin' my da. But I'll never forgive you for cripplin' my wife."

My wife. Sabrina pressed her eyes shut against a rush of moisture. Those words again. Precious. Beloved. Not even a magistrate's seal had the power to wipe them away. But Eve's next words made her eyes fly open with shock.

" 'Twas no mistake, lad. Me aim was true when I struck down yer da."

If there had been a chair behind him, Sabrina

sensed Morgan would have sat. His brow clouded with confusion. "But why?"

Sabrina ducked as Eve swung around to pace the drawing room in lurching strides, her braid swishing over her shoulder at each turn. Passion trembled in her voice. "Because I couldna bear it anymore! When he lifted his goblet to his precious Beth, I just wanted to shut him up. *Beth!*" she spat out. "It was always Beth! He wanted her to be yer mother, ye know. He used to tell me her bloodline was fit for a king, worthy of a mighty chieftain o' the MacDonnells such as *his son* would become."

"I don't understand. I thought you loved him."

Eve swung around to face him, almost beautiful in her fury. Sabrina was so compelled by her transformation that she forgot to duck. But Eve had eyes only for Morgan.

"I loathed the wee miserable rooster! The only reason I didna kill him sooner was that I wanted to watch him die slowly, chokin' on his own pickled blood!"

"But he kept them from stonin' you," Morgan whispered. "He saved your life."

Eve's words rang out, harsh and irrevocable. "He saved *your* life!"

Morgan looked wary now, fearful of another trick, another twist of her canny logic.

She rested her hands on her hips. "Why do ye think he saved me, lad? Out o' Christian charity? Pity for a homely clubfoot lass? Out o' the goodness of his wee black heart? Ha!" Eve grabbed him by the front of his plaid. "He saved me because I was carryin' in me belly the future chieftain o' Clan MacDonnell."

Sabrina bit back a gasp. Her heart ached for Morgan. She had never seen him so vulnerable, his face a raw palate of doubts and contradictions. "But you were only . . ."

"Twelve years old," she finished for him, her words steely with remembered pain.

Sabrina swallowed a knot of sickened pity. A pity

she knew Eve would disdain. Morgan's head dropped. "If you hated him so, why did you stay all those years?"

"Don't ye know, lad?" Eve whispered. "I stayed to be near ye. I knew he'd never let ye go. He'd hunt me to the ends of the earth if I dared take ye. He hid me away till ye were born. He dinna want anyone to know I was yer mother. A pathetic, twisted creature such as I?" Sabrina flinched to hear her own fears echoed so bluntly. "He feared the clan would say yer blood was tainted. That they'd demand one of Angus's cousins or brothers for chieftain. He wouldna let me tell ye, and by the time he was gone, 'twas too late. Ye were already wed to the Cameron wench."

Sabrina could not help but feel Eve's pain, realizing that the woman's own scheming had thwarted her at every turn. By murdering Angus, she had unwittingly forced Morgan into a Cameron's bed. By causing Sabrina's accident, she had earned her son's undying hatred.

Morgan still stood with head bowed as if trying to absorb a flurry of blows. Sabrina held her breath as in a gesture of foreign tenderness, Eve reached up to brush the hair from his eyes. But her patience was her undoing. The faint sounds of panicked shouts and the hungry crackling of flames finally reached the hall.

Sabrina began to fight her way to her feet, clawing her way up the balusters of the gallery railing with the raw fingers of one hand. Splinters tore at her flesh.

Morgan lifted his head, his dazed eyes slowly clearing. "Dear God, woman. What have you done now?"

He started for the door. In a motion that reminded Sabrina eerily of Morgan, Eve stepped into his path and drew a pistol from her plaid. She leveled it at his chest.

The note of steel was back in her voice. "Don't. I'll see ye dead before I'll see ye owned by them. Everythin' I did, all the years I held me silence, were all for Clan MacDonnell. The Camerons'll die screamin' and beggin' for mercy like the cowards they are. I'll let no one interfere. Not even ye."

Morgan warily raised his hands, inching the right one toward the gap in his plaid. Sabrina knew what he kept there over his heart. She also knew that heart well enough to be certain he would waver before shooting the mother he'd never known he had. And to know that that instant of hesitation would cost him his life.

She caught the railing and dragged herself the rest of the way to her feet. From somewhere outside came the sound of glass shattering and she drew strength from fresh hope. "How did you get back to Cameron so quickly?" Morgan asked, obviously trying to distract Eve.

Sabrina released the railing and stepped away from it, knees locked to keep her from swaying.

"I left London hours before ye. I saw the lass come to yer street. When she saw her father had purchased yer favors, I knew she'd run here to hide behind her mother's skirts."

With agonizing effort Sabrina lifted the massive blade of the claymore off the floor an inch at a time, her muscles strained to the snapping point.

Eve's laugh was ugly. "A spineless chit like her ain't got the guts to fight for a man like ye."

Sabrina threw back her head, tossing her tangled hair out of her eyes. "You've made many a mistake, Eve MacDonnell," she called out from the top of the stairs. "But that may have been your costliest one yet."

Chapter Thirty-three

Morgan stared at the ghost at the top of the stairs, wondering if he was going mad. He blinked, but she was still there: Sabrina, her white nightdress spattered with blood, her dark hair tumbling down her back in shimmering disarray. Sabrina standing straight and tall, gripping the hilt of the massive claymore like a glorious angel of vengeance.

A pang of sweet longing pierced him, and he was not surprised to learn her blade had never truly left him, not since that moonlit night in the solar when she had laid his heart bare with no more than a kiss.

Eve turned, crying out at the apparition. It was all the distraction Morgan needed. Catching Eve's forearm, he swung her back around. He cupped her cheek in his palm, shaking his head with regret as a misty joy claimed her eyes at his tender gesture.

"Forgive me, Mother," he muttered. His fist connected sharply with her jaw. She slumped in his arms.

Dougal, Elizabeth, their sons, and a handful of servants burst through the splintered remains of the main door, their garments singed and their faces black with soot. Elizabeth cried out and clapped a hand over her mouth at the sight of her daughter standing at the top of the stairs. Brian rushed forward, but Dougal threw out an arm to stop him.

The tip of the claymore clanked to the gallery. Sabrina leaned on its hilt for support. "What will you do with her?" she asked.

Morgan searched the familiar, rawboned planes of his mother's face. Angus had driven her half mad with his twisted ambitions, but all Morgan could think of were the years they'd been robbed of each other's comfort. All the years he'd yearned for the tenderness of a mother's touch while Eve, held in thrall by Angus's selfish will, went childless and unloved.

He lowered her gently to the floor. "I'll take care of her." He moved to stand at the foot of the stairs. A clear message flickered in his eyes as he looked up at Sabrina. "We MacDonnells always take care of our own."

Sabrina felt all the burdens of the past hanging in the air between them—his stubbornness, her fear, his pride, her pride. Gazing deep into his eyes, she recognized the worth of what he was offering her if she only had the courage to take it. His heart, through good times and bad, tears and laughter, sunshine and rain.

Sabrina dropped the claymore and stood swaying on the top step. Brian clutched Alex's shoulder without realizing it. Dougal sucked in a shuddering breath. Tears streaked through the soot on Elizabeth's cheeks. Morgan raced halfway up the steps, then stopped. He nodded, favoring Sabrina with one of those rare and fierce smiles.

In that smile she saw all of his cruelties in London for what they had truly been—kindnesses. The same kindness her mother had shown when she'd denied her her selfish way as a child. A kindness that had refused to bend to a will that had been twisted and reforged by her terrible fall.

"Come, lass," he whispered. "I'm right here. I won't let you fall."

Drawing in a deep breath, she lowered her foot, carefully feeling for the stair beneath her. She shifted her weight, took one step toward Morgan, then another, her brimming eyes locked on his face. Risking her shaky balance, risking everything, she slowly stretched out her arms toward him.

This time Morgan caught her, wrapping her trembling body in his loving embrace. His strong arms enfolded her, drawing her so close that she could hear the thundering of his mighty heart beneath his plaid. She had finally cracked the giant's stony façade. Something salty and wet struck her cheek and ran into her mouth.

"Aye, lass," he whispered against her hair. "I give you my word. I'll never let you fall again."

"Don't make promises you can't keep, Morgan MacDonnell," she scolded through a veil of joyful tears. "I don't mind falling as long as you're there to catch me."

He smoothed her hair back and stared deep into her eyes. "I always will be, lass. That's one promise I can keep."

Sunlight poured into the ceilingless kirk. The charred stones of three walls jutted stark against the azure sky, but the interior of the kirk had been swept clean of soot by a bevy of joyful servants. Clouds drifted overhead like fat, fluffy sheep content to graze on the sunlight of a perfect summer morning.

The small kirk was packed to overflowing with both Camerons and MacDonnells. The collapsed western wall afforded the villagers thronging the hillside a fine view. They'd been robbed of witnessing their laird's daughter's first nuptials, and they had no intention of being excluded again.

An old man squatted in a circle of children. "Aye,

some say there's only one thing can tame a beastie as wild and fierce as a MacDonnell."

"Oh, what is it? Do tell!" begged a freckled little girl.

"A kiss from a bonny lassie!"

Cackling with glee, the old man screwed his eyes shut and puckered his withered lips. All he got for his trouble were trills of giggles from the girls and moans of disgust from the boys. When he opened his eyes, the freckled lass was gone. He saw her a few feet away, smiling shyly up at a barefoot blond boy who had appeared at dawn with the other MacDonnells.

Inside the kirk, Dougal escorted William Belmont to his seat. He clapped his brother-in-law on the shoulder. "Aye, I thought she was going to let us burn to death before breaking one of those damnable German windows. We were all done for until Pugsley started to wheeze. Then she picked up one of her precious candlesticks and tossed it through the window like a caber!"

Uncle Willie brayed with laughter. "You should have seen her when she was ten years old and I accidentally sat on her . . ."

Honora and Stefan huddled together, both politely trying not to stare at the MacDonnell scratching his crotch on the pew beside them.

Brian and Alex rushed to what had formerly been the back wall of the kirk to break up another fracas between the Camerons and the MacDonnells, who had been sizing each other up since early that morning. Their shoving match was punctuated by petulant cries of "The savage pushed me first!" and "But he trod upon me bloody toe!"

The combatants stopped shoving as the minister appeared to usher the two grooms to their respective places at the charred altar.

Ranald beamed beneath his luxuriant bagwig as Enid appeared at the back of the kirk. The women aahed with delight as she traversed the scarlet runner to the altar. They took great pains to avoid staring at her enormous belly. Elizabeth reached behind her and gave Honora's hand a comforting squeeze.

"Take off yer bonnet," Fergus MacDonnell bellowed, slapping one of his clansman. "Ain't ye got no respect for a lady?" Alwyn cuddled beneath his arm, soothing his temper with a kiss.

An awed hush fell over Cameron and MacDonnell alike as Sabrina appeared, garbed like an angel in white, her arms draped with a profusion of wild roses cut fresh from the meadows. If anyone noticed her pronounced limp as she marched down the aisle, they did not dare to comment upon it. Not with a towering giant of a MacDonnell scowling fiercely at them from the altar.

Sabrina concentrated on each step as if it would be her last, determined not to stumble. Each time she faltered, she simply lifted her head and searched the face of the man who awaited her at the end of her long trek.

The fierce pride in his eyes infused her with strength. Her heart swelled with love until she thought it would surely burst from her chest.

As she stepped up to face him, clutching the roses for courage, she stumbled over a bump in the runner. A single thorn pricked her thumb and a small cry escaped her. A drop of blood spattered on her gown.

Morgan steadied her, then brought her thumb to his mouth and gently sucked away another welling drop.

"Oh, no," she wailed softly, rubbing the stain on her bodice. "I wanted everything to be perfect this time."

He chucked her chin up with one of his big, warm fingers and winked at her. "Nonsense, lass. Remember the MacDonnell motto. You've got to shed a little blood in any fight worth winning."

Sabrina's lips twitched, then broke into a smile. Her smile spread to an impish grin. Ignoring the reproving gaze of the minister, Morgan threw back his head and roared with laughter.

Their lips met in sweet and tender accord as they

fell together, crushing the roses between them, releasing their fragrance in a whisper, a shout, and a joyous song as sweet and eternal as their love.

Taking the MacDonnell motto to heart, Fergus threw the first punch.

New York Times *bestselling author TERESA MEDEIROS* *was recently chosen one of the Top Ten Favorite Romance Authors by* Affaire de Coeur *magazine and won the* Romantic Times *Reviewer's Choice Award for Best Historical Love and Laughter. A former Army brat and registered nurse, she wrote her first novel at the age of twenty-one and has since gone on to win the hearts of critics and readers alike. The author of thirteen novels, Teresa makes her home in Kentucky with her husband and two cats. Readers can visit her website at www.teresamedeiros.com.*

WHITE DOVE

SUSAN EDWARDS

White Dove was raised to know that she must marry a powerful warrior. The daughter of the great Golden Eagle is required to wed one of her own kind, a man who will bring honor to her people and strength to her tribe. But the young Irishman who returns to seek her hand makes her question herself, and makes her question what makes a man.

Jeremy Jones returns to be trained as a warrior, to take the tests of manhood and prove himself in battle. Watching him, White Dove sees a bravery she's never known, and suddenly she realizes her young suitor is not just a man, he is the only one she'll ever love.

___4890-6 $5.99 US/$6.99 CAN

WHITE DREAMS
SUSAN EDWARDS

Why has the Great Spirit given Star Dreamer the sight, an ability to see things that can't be changed? She has no answer. Then one night she is filled with visions of a different sort: pale hands caressing her flesh, soft lips touching her soul. She sees the flash of a uniform, and the handsome soldier who wears it. The man makes her ache in a way that she has forgotten, in a way that she has repressed. And when Colonel Grady O'Brien at last rides into her camp, she learns that the virile officer is everything she's dreamed of and more. Suddenly, Star Dreamer sees the reason for her gift. In her visions lie the key to this man's happiness—and in this man's arms lie the key to her own.

Also includes the twelfth installment of Lair of the Wolf, a serialized romance set in medieval Wales. Be sure to look for other chapters of this exciting story featured in Leisure books and written by the industry's top authors.

WHITE WOLF

SUSAN EDWARDS

Jessica Jones knows that the trip to Oregon will be hard, but she will not let her brothers leave her behind. Dressed as a boy to carry on a ruse that fools no one, Jessie cannot disguise her attraction to the handsome half-breed wagon master. For when she looks into Wolf's eyes and entwines her fingers in his hair, Jessie glimpses the very depths of passion.

___4471-4 $5.50 US/$6.50 CAN

Searching for her missing father, the determined Emma
O'Brien sets out for Fort Pierre on the Missouri River, but
when the steamboat upon which she is traveling runs aground,
she is forced to travel on foot. Braving the wilderness, the
feisty beauty is soon seized by Indians. Surrounded by
enemies, Emma learns that only Striking Thunder can grant
her release. The handsome Sioux chieftain offers her freedom
but enslaves her with a kiss. He takes her to his village, and
there, underneath the prairie's starry skies, Emma learns the
truth. The danger Striking Thunder represents is greater than
the pre-war bonfires of the entire Sioux nation—and the
passion he offers burns a whole lot hotter.

___4613-X $4.99 US/$5.99 CAN

White Nights

Susan Edwards

Eirica Macauley sees the road to better days: the remainder of the Oregon Trail. The trail is hard, even for experienced cattle hands like James Jones, but the man's will and determination lend Eirica strength. Yet, Eirica knows she can never accept the cowboy's love; the shadows that darken her past will hardly disappear in the light of day. But as each night passes and their wagon train draws nearer its destination, James's intentions grow clearer—and Eirica aches for his warm embrace. And when darkness falls and James stays beside her, the beautiful widow knows that when dawn comes, she'll no longer be alone.

Lair of the Wolf

Also includes the fifth installment of *Lair of the Wolf*, a serialized romance set in medieval Wales. Be sure to look for future chapters of this exciting story featured in Leisure books and written by the industry's top authors.

___4703-9 $5.50 US/$6.50 CAN
Dorchester Publishing Co., Inc.
P.O. Box 6640
Wayne, PA 19087-8640

DON'T MISS THESE HEART-STOPPING HISTORICAL ROMANCES BY LEISURE'S LEADING LADIES OF LOVE!

Lakota Renegade by Madeline Baker. Alone on the Colorado frontier, Jassy can either work as a fancy lady or find a husband. But what is she to do when the only man she hopes to marry is a wanted renegade? For Jassy, the decision is simple: She'll take Creed Maddigan for better or worse, even if she has to spend the rest of her days dodging bounty hunters and bullets.

_3832-3 $5.99 US/$7.99 CAN

White Wind by Susan Edwards. Searching the Old West for her father, lovely young Sarah Cartier doesn't make it far before she crosses paths with Golden Eagle, the brave who rescued her years before. Golden Eagle has already pledged to marry another when Sarah comes back into his life. But with Sarah provoking him like no other, he vows no obstacle will stop him from tasting her sweet lips, from sharing with her an unforgettable ecstasy as he forever claims her as his own.

_3933-8 $5.50 US/$7.50 CAN

Dorchester Publishing Co., Inc.
P.O. Box 6640
Wayne, PA 19087-8640

Please add $1.75 for shipping and handling for the first book and $.50 for each book thereafter. NY, NYC, and PA residents, please add appropriate sales tax. No cash, stamps, or C.O.D.s. All orders shipped within 6 weeks via postal service book rate. Canadian orders require $2.00 extra postage and must be paid in U.S. dollars through a U.S. banking facility.

Name_____
Address_____
City_____ State_____ Zip_____
I have enclosed $_____ in payment for the checked book(s).
Payment <u>must</u> accompany all orders. ❏ Please send a free catalog

FREE BOOK GIVEAWAY!

As a special thank you from Dorchester Publishing Co., Inc., for purchasing *White Dawn*, we'd like to give you a free copy of *White Nights* by Susan Edwards.

An experienced cattle hand and a young widow find the comforts of each other's arms soften the hardships of the Oregon Trail. Also includes the fifth installment of *Lair of the Wolf*, a serialized romance set in medieval Wales.

PLEASE NOTE

You must submit proof of purchase for *White Dawn*.
U.S. residents: Please include $2.50 for shipping and handling. All non-U.S. residents: Please include $5.00 USD for shipping and handling.

MAIL ALL MATERIALS TO:

Dorchester Publishing Co., Inc.
Department SE
276 5th Avenue, Suite 1008
NY, NY 10001

NAME: _____

ADDRESS: _____

_____

PHONE: _____

E-MAIL: _____

Offer good while supplies last.